Dear Parent:
Your child's love of reading starts here!

Every child learns to read in a different way and at his or her own speed. Some go back and forth between reading levels and read favorite books again and again. Others read through each level in order. You can help your young reader improve and become more confident by encouraging his or her own interests and abilities. From books your child reads with you to the first books he or she reads alone, there are I Can Read Books for every stage of reading:

SHARED READING
Basic language, word repetition, and whimsical illustrations, ideal for sharing with your emergent reader

BEGINNING READING
Short sentences, familiar words, and simple concepts for children eager to read on their own

READING WITH HELP
Engaging stories, longer sentences, and language play for developing readers

READING ALONE
Complex plots, challenging vocabulary, and high-interest topics for the independent reader

ADVANCED READING
Short paragraphs, chapters, and exciting themes for the perfect bridge to chapter books

I Can Read Books have introduced children to the joy of reading since 1957. Featuring award-winning authors and illustrators and a fabulous cast of beloved characters, I Can Read Books set the standard for beginning readers.

A lifetime of discovery begins with the magical words **"I Can Read!"**

Visit www.icanread.com for information
on enriching your child's reading experience.

For Laura Parish Lake
and Herman Stanley Parish IV,
with love

Color markers and a black pen were used for the full-color art.

HarperCollins®, ☎®, and I Can Read Book® are trademarks of HarperCollins Publishers.

Merry Christmas, Amelia Bedelia Text copyright © 1986 by Margaret Parish Illustrations copyright © 1986 by Lynn Sweat All rights reserved. No part of this book may be used or reproduced in any manner whatsoever without written permission except in the case of brief quotations embodied in critical articles and reviews. Printed in the United States of America. For information address HarperCollins Children's Books, a division of HarperCollins Publishers, 195 Broadway, New York, NY 10007. www.harpercollinschildrens.com

Library of Congress Cataloging-in-Publication Data

Parish, Peggy.
   Merry Christmas, Amelia Bedelia / by Peggy Parish ; pictures by Lynn Sweat.
       p.   cm. — (An I can read book)
   "Greenwillow Books."
   Summary: As Amelia Bedelia helps Mrs. Rogers prepare for Christmas, she bakes a date cake with a calendar in it and stuffs the children's stockings with turkey stuffing.
   ISBN-10: 0-688-06102-8 (lib. bdg.) — ISBN-13: 978-0-688-06102-9 (lib. bdg.)
   ISBN-10: 0-06-009945-3 (pbk.) — ISBN-13: 978-0-06-009945-9 (pbk.)
   [1. Christmas—Fiction. 2. Humorous stories.] I. Sweat, Lynn, ill. II. Title.
PZ7.P219Me 1986   85-24919
[E]   CIP
                                                                                                                                  AC

❖ Originally published by Greenwillow Books, an imprint of HarperCollins Publishers, in 1986.
15 PC/WOR 20 19 18 17 16

I Can Read!™

READING
2
WITH HELP

Merry Christmas, Amelia Bedelia

story by Peggy Parish
pictures by Lynn Sweat

HarperCollins*Publishers*

"Amelia Bedelia," said Mrs. Rogers,

"Christmas is just around the corner."

"It is?" said Amelia Bedelia.

"Which corner?"

Mrs. Rogers laughed and said,

"I mean tomorrow is Christmas Day."

"I know that," said Amelia Bedelia.

"There's still so much to do,"

said Mrs. Rogers.

"We'll never finish!"

"We'll make it," said Amelia Bedelia.

"Just tell me what to do."

"First," said Mrs. Rogers,
"make a date cake.
Put lots of dates in it."
"All right," said Amelia Bedelia.
She started to the kitchen.

"Wait," said Mrs. Rogers.

"Put these nuts in the cake, too."

She gave Amelia Bedelia

a bag of nuts.

"Anything else?" said Amelia Bedelia.

"Do pop some corn," said Mrs. Rogers.

"I want to make popcorn balls."

"How much should I pop?"

said Amelia Bedelia.

"I'll need six cups," said Mrs. Rogers.

Amelia Bedelia went to the kitchen.
"I have never heard of date cake,"
she said.
"But I'll try my hand at it."

Amelia Bedelia put some of this
and a little of that into a bowl.
She mixed and she mixed.
Soon her batter was ready.

11

"Now," she said,

"I need lots of dates."

Amelia Bedelia thought about this.

"A calendar!" she said.

"That has lots of dates."

Amelia Bedelia got a calendar.

She cut off all of the dates.

She dumped them into the cake.

14

"Now for the nuts,"

said Amelia Bedelia.

She opened the bag of nuts.

She dumped them into the cake.

Amelia Bedelia mixed some more.

Then she put the cake

in the oven.

"I'll make a spice cake, too,"

she said.

"I do love spice cake."

So Amelia Bedelia

made a spice cake.

"Now for the popcorn," she said.

Amelia Bedelia measured
six cups of corn.
Then she popped and she popped
and she popped.
"Mrs. Rogers must love
popcorn balls,"
said Amelia Bedelia.

Amy came to the back door.

"Amelia Bedelia," she called.

"Santa Claus is coming tonight."

"He's coming here?"

said Amelia Bedelia.

"Yes," said Amy.

"Thank you for telling me,"

said Amelia Bedelia.

"I'll tell Mrs. Rogers."

Amy went on her way.

"That cake smells good,"

said Mrs. Rogers.

She came into the kitchen.

She stopped.

"Amelia Bedelia!" she said.

"Why did you pop so much corn?

I only need six cups."

"And I popped six cups,"

said Amelia Bedelia.

"I meant six cups of popped corn,"

said Mrs. Rogers.

"Then you should have said so,"
said Amelia Bedelia.

"I know," said Mrs. Rogers.

"Amy said Santa Claus

is coming tonight,"

said Amelia Bedelia.

"Did you know that?"

"Oh yes!" said Mrs. Rogers.

"He comes every year.

Don't you remember him?"

"You mean the man
in the red suit?"
said Amelia Bedelia.
"The one who
comes down chimneys?"

"That's right," said Mrs. Rogers.

"Oh my," said Amelia Bedelia.

"That chimney is a sight.

I'll have to clean it."

Mrs. Rogers laughed and said,

"Don't bother. Santa Claus

will manage."

The telephone rang.

"I'll get it," said Mrs. Rogers.

"I'll see to my cakes,"
said Amelia Bedelia.

She opened the oven.

"Just right," she said.

"I'll set them out to cool."

"Oh, Amelia Bedelia,"

called Mrs. Rogers.

"This is dreadful."

Amelia Bedelia ran to Mrs. Rogers.

"What is it?" she said.

"We forgot

about Aunt Myra.

We must go

and get her,"

said Mrs. Rogers.

"Can you finish everything?"

said Mrs. Rogers.

"Of course I can,"

said Amelia Bedelia.

"I made a list," said Mrs. Rogers.

"I hope you will understand it."

"Don't you worry,"

said Amelia Bedelia.

"We will be back about eight o'clock,"
said Mrs. Rogers.
"Aunt Myra loves Christmas carols.
Could you greet her with some?"
"I'll do my best," said Amelia Bedelia.

A car horn blew.

"That's Mr. Rogers,"
said Mrs. Rogers.

She went out to the car.

"I better get busy,"

said Amelia Bedelia.

"What must I do first?"

She looked at the list and read,

"Stuff six stockings

for the neighbors' children."

Amelia Bedelia shook her head.

"Now that beats all,"

she said.

"I've stuffed turkeys.

But I've never

stuffed stockings."

Amelia Bedelia went to the kitchen.

"That will take lots of stuffing,"
she said.

So she made pans and pans of it.

"That should do it,"
said Amelia Bedelia.

She found six stockings.

And Amelia Bedelia stuffed them.

She looked at her list.

"Hang the stockings on the mantel."

Amelia Bedelia got some rope.

She hung those stockings
on the mantel.

"Stuffed and hung," she said.

"What's next? Trim the tree."

Amelia Bedelia looked

at the tree.

"It looks fine to me," she said.

"But if she wants it trimmed,

I'll trim it."

So Amelia Bedelia

trimmed the tree.

"Maybe it was too fat," she said.

Amelia Bedelia looked at the list.

"Oh, oh," she said.

"I have to go to the store."

In a bit Amelia Bedelia was back.
"The list says to put on
colored balls," she said.
"I hope I bought enough."

Amelia Bedelia put colored balls

on the tree.

But the balls rolled right off.

"Shoot!" she said.

"I'm going to tie you on."

And she did.

"String on lots of lights,"

read Amelia Bedelia.

She found lots of lights.

She found some string.

And she strung on those lights.

"What a fancy tree,"

said Amelia Bedelia.

"I wonder what's next?"

She looked at the list.

"My word," she said.

"Put a big star on top of the tree.

What kind of star does she want?

A movie star? A rock star?

A baseball star?"

Amelia Bedelia sat down to think.

"I would like to be a star,"
she said.

"I guess everybody would."
Suddenly Amelia Bedelia
had an idea.

"That's it," she said.

"Everybody can be a star

on this tree."

Amelia Bedelia made a sign.

It said,

She put it on the tree.

She got a mirror.

She tied it on the top

of the tree.

Amelia Bedelia looked

in the mirror.

"Hurray!" she said. "I'm a star."

Amelia Bedelia looked at the list.

"That's it," she said.

"I'll make those popcorn balls.

Mrs. Rogers won't have time."

Amelia Bedelia made dozens

of popcorn balls.

"Maybe Mrs. Rogers wanted these
for the tree," she said.
"I'll put them on."
Amelia Bedelia wrapped the balls.
She tied them on the tree.
"That does look nice," she said.
"Now I must make
some telephone calls."

Amelia Bedelia made her calls.

She looked at the clock.

"My, it's getting late," she said.

"I need some supper."

Amelia Bedelia made her supper.

She ate it.

Then she cleaned up the kitchen.

"The folks will be here soon,"

she said.

"I'll wait up front for them."

A little later the doorbell rang.

Amelia Bedelia opened the door.

"Come in," she said.

Three children came in.

They sat and talked

with Amelia Bedelia.

A car turned into the drive.

"Here they are," said Amelia Bedelia.

"You know what to do."

The door opened.

"We're here," said Mrs. Rogers.

Aunt Myra came in.

"Now!" said Amelia Bedelia.

"Greetings, greetings, greetings,"
said the three children.
"What's this about?"
said Mrs. Rogers.
"You said to greet Aunt Myra
with Carols," said Amelia Bedelia.
"Here's Carol Lee,
Carol Green,
and Carol Lake."

"What lovely Carols,"
said Aunt Myra.
"Thank you."
The children left.

Mrs. Rogers saw the tree.

"Amelia Bedelia!" she shouted.

"What did you do to that tree?"

"Popcorn balls!" shouted Aunt Myra.

"I love popcorn balls."

She ran to the tree.

"Look!" shouted Aunt Myra.

"I'm a star!"

Mrs. Rogers began to splutter.

"Don't be angry, dear,"

said Mr. Rogers. "It's Christmas.

And Aunt Myra is happy.

Be thankful for that!"

"Oh, all right," said Mrs. Rogers.

"Let's have some cake."

"Just what I wanted," said Mr. Rogers.

They all went to the kitchen.

"Amelia Bedelia," said Mrs. Rogers,

"where is my cake?"

Amelia Bedelia put the cake

on the table.

Mr. Rogers sliced it.

"What kind of cake is this?" he said.

"It's full of paper and rocks."

"Let me see the paper,"
said Aunt Myra.

She looked at it.

"I know!" she said.

"It's a date cake."

"And your rocks are nuts,"

said Amelia Bedelia.

"So they are," said Mr. Rogers.

"I was all set for some good cake."

"Here you are," said Amelia Bedelia.

She gave him her cake.

"Spice cake!" said Aunt Myra.

"Amelia Bedelia, you're my kind

of person."

"Delicious," said Mr. Rogers.

"I'll have another piece,"
said Mrs. Rogers.

"So will I," said Aunt Myra.

They ate until most of the cake
was gone.

"It's past my bedtime," said Aunt Myra.

"We should all go to sleep,"
said Mrs. Rogers.

"You, too, Amelia Bedelia,"
said Mr. Rogers. "Santa Claus
won't come if you're awake."

"He can wait a bit," said Amelia Bedelia.

"I have work to do."

Amelia Bedelia washed the dishes.

She heard something outside.

"What is that?" she said.

Amelia Bedelia opened the door.

"Santa Claus!" she said.

"Wait till I tell the folks!"

"Shhhh," said Santa Claus.

"You should be asleep.

You shouldn't see me."

Amelia Bedelia closed her eyes.

"Now I can't see you," she said.

"Please go to bed," said Santa Claus.

"I have work to do."

"I'm on my way," said Amelia Bedelia.

"Good night, Santa Claus,"
called Amelia Bedelia.

"Good night," called Santa Claus.

"And Merry Christmas,
Amelia Bedelia."

MECHANICS·
MERCANTILE
LIBRARY.

Recent Titles in
Moving through History: Transportation and Society
Guillaume de Syon, Series Editor

Engines of Change: The Railroads That Made India
Ian J. Kerr

CLIPPING THE CLOUDS

HOW AIR TRAVEL CHANGED THE WORLD

Marc Dierikx

Moving through History: Transportation and Society
Guillaume de Syon, Series Editor

Westport, Connecticut
London

Library of Congress Cataloging-in-Publication Data

Dierikx, M. L. J.
    Clipping the clouds : how air travel changed the world / Marc Dierikx.
        p.   cm. — (Moving through history : Transportation and society, ISSN 1932-4766)
    Includes bibliographical references and index.
    ISBN 978–0–275–98910—1 (alk. paper)
    1. Air travel—History.   I. Title.
    HE9787.D54   2008
    387.7—dc22   2008008894

British Library Cataloguing in Publication Data is available.

Library of Congress Catalog Card Number: 2008008894
ISBN: 978–0–275–98910–1
ISSN: 1932–4766

First published in 2008

Praeger Publishers, 88 Post Road West, Westport, CT 06881
An imprint of Greenwood Publishing Group, Inc.
www.praeger.com

Printed in the United States of America

The paper used in this book complies with the
Permanent Paper Standard issued by the National
Information Standards Organization (Z39.48–1984).

10 9 8 7 6 5 4 3 2 1

Contents

Introduction

One day, something fell from the sky. Xi had never seen anything like it in his life. He wondered why the gods had sent this *thing* down to the Earth. "Film images depict the gentle, almost utopian world of the Kalahari Bushmen, untouched by the rigors of modern society. Oblivious of life beyond the horizon, the Bushmen are portrayed as close to the traditions of their forebears. Yet even in this remote corner of the world the twentieth century intrudes. Sometimes thunderous, rumbling sounds pervade from a cloudless sky. High above, strange new things can be heard:" Noisy birds that flew without clapping their wings.[1]

Filmmaker Jamie Uys took this seemingly insignificant incident to set the story in motion of his film *The Gods Must Be Crazy* (1980). The *thing* that fell from the sky was an empty coke bottle, thrown out by a carefree pilot of a passing plane. The unexpected arrival of this singular *thing* changed life in the small tribal community in the middle of the Kalahari that straddles the border between Namibia, Botswana, and South Africa.

In a wider meaning, the arrival of the airplane itself, over three quarters of a century earlier, also produced changes that sent ripples through society. Like the bottle in the movie—a versatile *thing* that everybody wanted for different reasons—the airplane too was a new *thing* that mesmerized people, and found many uses. At the beginning of the 21st century it is difficult to even imagine our world without aircraft. Airplanes are everywhere, and rapid air transport has become one of the necessities of our time. Yet one of the peculiarities of powered flight is that it has stayed in the public focus for over a century. From its early days, everything to do with aviation has been immediately reported by newspapers the world over. Even from the dawn

of aviation, a flood of photographs and film images have survived—proof of the media genius of airplanes and their daring pilots.

The first time that "strange new things appeared in the sky, noisy birds that flew without clapping their wings," was in the decade following the well-known experiments of Orville and Wilbur Wright at Kill Devil Hills, Kitty Hawk, North Carolina. From that first decade, aviation, and thereafter air transport, went on to touch upon the lives of just about everyone on the planet, no matter how remote from the urban centers with which we associate air transport generally. Flying machines have left deep impressions on contemporaries, right from the times of early aviation. Finnish sculptor Adolf Aarno went as far as to buy a Demoiselle airplane in France in April 1911 to put on display in Tampere, Finland, simply to have people experience the strange new machine shape. The aircraft never flew.[2]

Powered flight has always been spectacular. Even in its first decade, *air meets* brought out hundreds of thousands of spectators. And although we now live more than a century later and over 1.7 billion people have flown on aircraft as passengers, the spectacle of flight has maintained its forceful effects. Air shows mean excitement. They still bring out crowds by the hundreds of thousands. Even if we can sense only a trifle of the exhilaration that spectators must have felt 100 years ago, present-day low-level aerobatic spectacles like the Red Bull Air Races bring out people in daunting numbers. On June 12, 2005, for example, over 700,000 spectators watched the "races" in Rotterdam, Holland, cheering the participating pilots, although they were well encased and hardly visible inside their aircraft. People stood on their toes as pilots raced under a bridge at speeds of around 200 miles per hour and rounded inflatable pylons less than 60 feet above the ground.

But what do we know about the development of world air transport— and about the way it influenced, and was in turn influenced by, society? Well, perhaps, not as much as one might think looking at the many library stacks that have been filled with books on the various aspects of the history of flight. Traditional literature predominantly deals with the technological aspects of aviation: aircraft and their environment. Typing the keyword "aircraft" in the search engine of a big online shopping company will result in over 100,000 titles—and that is just for books in the English language. Yet aviation is much more than aircraft, or airports. It touches on geography, domestic and international politics, war, economic trends, industry and trade, social developments, culture, arts, literature, music, environment and health, and above all people. The present book represents an attempt to connect these very diverse aspects of flight and the way aviation has interacted with society. This means the book aims to look at the history of aviation in a challenging new way. Not very many books have done so to this extent, and the reader is wise to treat this result of several years' work as an experiment. While maintaining many standard elements of the history

of world air transport in the present overview, it is hoped that the reader will find the perspective offered here interestingly *different* from established knowledge. It would be nice if it could provide food for thought for new research on the way air transport intersected with the history of the 20th century.

It should, however, be noted at this point that one of the basic ideas behind this book was that it should be written from a non-American viewpoint. Because a companion volume dealing with the development of air transportation in the United States was envisaged at the time the work on this book started, it was agreed beforehand to focus the present story on "the rest of the world." Yet no book on aviation can be written without referring to the leading role of the United States, or to the effect that developments in America had worldwide. It was like the British novelist James Graham Ballard, rekindling adolescent memories of plane spotting at airports in the 1940s, noted in his essay *The Ultimate Departure Lounge*, "Airports were then places where America traveled to greet us, where the world of tomorrow touched down in Europe."[3] Although Eurocentric to a degree—the geographical location of the author, Holland, the accessibility of sources, and the command of languages have all left their mark on these pages—this book offers a history of air transport that has more on developments beyond the North American and European continents than textbooks generally offer. The history of aviation, after all, is more than the sum of developments in the old world and the new.

That does not mean that *Clipping the Clouds* covers, or even aspires to cover, "everything" that took place in commercial aviation over the past century. The approximate size of the book was determined beforehand, which necessitated numerous choices, especially given the global reach of the story. Some of these choices are bound to appear more logical to the reader than others. The specialist will have no problems indicating blank spots. They are the inevitable result of processes of selection—and narrative demands as the author saw them.

The text of this book is divided into four chapters, arranged chronologically. Each has its own characteristics. Like this introduction, each chapter opens and closes with an excerpt from a movie that depicts elements of air transport that illustrate the theme of the chapter. After all, air transport has always maintained a highly visible profile in society and has often featured in, or been a background for, movies. Before the general public started using air transport, it familiarized itself with the world of flight through books and pictures. To a considerable extent, these defined what the public expected to find at airports and on board aircraft.

Chapter one (1919–1945) takes "heroics" as its point of departure. The early years of aviation brought forward a good number of names—pilots' names mostly—that acquired lasting fame. Heroic exploits defined much of the public image of aviation and gave it its special position in society, apart

from other new areas of technological or business development. The chapter traces how and why aviation came to play an important role in international, colonial, and domestic politics and how it influenced existing concepts of distance. Chapter two (1945–1961) is more technology-orientated and analyzes how the rapidly changing technology of air transport in the 1940s and 1950s was heavily influenced by decolonization and the Cold War yet created new travel patterns that contributed to the emergence of an increasingly global society. Chapter three (1961–1977) deals primarily with the usage of airlines as a worldwide mass transport system and focuses on such things as the changing social stratification of air passengers and the rise of air tourism. It also looks at the use of aircraft to carry cargo, both for commercial purposes and as a vehicle for relief in crisis areas. The chapter details how the ascent of commercial aviation affected its position as an icon of Western society and why that society became increasingly critical of the consequences of mass air transport. Chapter four (1977 onwards) then primarily looks at the effects of air transport as a mature, increasingly "normal" transport mode and analyzes how it was detached from the national interests and state controls that influenced so much of its development. It also traces the role of air transport in the creation of a global society but regards the downsides of this development as well.

This book could hardly have been written 10 years ago. While much of it is based on literature, and on primary archival sources, the research has relied to a considerable extent on modern digital storage of information and on the Internet. New search technologies made it feasible to pose questions, and retrieve and arrange information, in a way that was not previously possible. The amount of information available out there is absolutely amazing. Even after decades of research on various aspects of the history of international air transport, the work for this book brought its author something new to think about almost every day. Particularly helpful to this particular project were the digitized online collection of prewar newspapers made available on the Internet by the Koninklijke Bibliotheek (Royal Library) in Holland[4] and the digital version of the monthly journal *Keesings Historisch Archief* (*Keesing's Record of World Events*)[5] that allowed search with various keywords, producing an array of information on past events that could hardly have been gathered using traditional paper-based research methods. The reader will find references to these and other digital sources in the footnotes.

Several people helped me along in my preparations for this book. The initial request to think about "a book on the history of non-American air transportation" came in August 2004 from Guillaume de Syon of Albright College (Reading, Pennsylvania) and Franklin & Marshall College (Lancaster, Pennsylvania), series editor of Praeger's *Moving through History: Transportation and Society* project. Guillaume not only stimulated me to come up with the outline for this book but also provided much-appreciated encouragement along the way. I would like to thank him for his outspoken

support. One of the things I felt I needed for this book was a time series of statistical data on the development of world air transport. Collecting such data proved more complicated than I had imagined. While such data are readily available for those who can and wish to pay extraordinary amounts of money to retrieve them from online databases geared towards air transport professionals and airline consultants, such data are way beyond the financial scope of the ordinary historian. I was therefore fortunate that my friend Dick Jansen, senior archivist of Air France-KLM, was able to provide me with access to printed and digital statistical overviews of the International Civil Aviation Organization (ICAO). Through his help I was able to compile much of the statistical annex at the back of this book which, I hope, will be of value to readers seeking information on long-term developments in world air transport.

Because this book tries to bring together such varied types of information, it was a good thing that some colleagues allowed me to take a peek at some of their work in progress. Gordon Pirie of the University of Western Cape, South Africa, was kind enough to let me read what he had about prewar tourism on the African air routes. Javier Vidal Olivares of the University of Alicante in Spain, shared some of his writings with me to enlighten me on developments in the Spanish-speaking world. Chandra Bhimull of the University of Michigan was kind enough to let me in on her ongoing research on air transport in the West Indies. Hussein Kassim of the London School of Economics helped me come to grips with recent regulatory events on the European level. Roger Bilstein, formerly of the University of Clear Lake, Houston, and now *éminence grise* among aviation historians, encouraged me to persevere on the chosen path. My very dear friend Joanna Hawlena of the Academy of Economics in Katowice, Poland, was so kind as to advise me on recent economic trends and on the impact of low-cost airlines. Nonetheless, the mistakes and misinterpretations that remain are the author's. After all, aviation presented, and continues to present, a fast-moving and confusing spectacle. Just how captivating that spectacle of the world of air travel is, is displayed in the popularity of *Airline*—a "docusoap" television series that depicts the stressful life in front and behind the check-in counters at the world's airports. From the comfort of an easy chair, any viewer who has ever been at an airport can easily identify with the human drama that appears to unfold daily in expectation of the next takeoff. For those who are interested in the background to it, is this book.

Heroics: Flying as an Icon of the Modern Age, 1919–1945

Pitch dark skies above the coastal region of Patagonia, Argentina. Lightning flashes and violent storm clouds all around, a single engine monoplane is fighting the elements. Inside its dimly lit cockpit, we see the pilot, Fabien, crouched over his controls. His figure emanates strength and competence. Yet the aircraft's altimeter indicates rapid descent. Seeing this, he pulls the stick towards him to gain height as he peers out into the dark void, calculating his chances to get his plane safely to the small airportat Trelew— before his fuel runs out.[1]

Pilots were revered idols of the early decades of the twentieth century. Their lives and exploits were sources for heroic legends that inspired novelists and filmmakers, even if the realities of flight could be grim and dangerous. A pilot himself, French novelist Antoine de Saint-Exupéry combined his personal reminiscences of piloting with an effort to spread the magic of the flying experience as such. It was his firm belief that air travel, partaking in the enchantment of flight, would create bonds of friendship between all humans inhabiting the Earth, and thus contribute to a new and better society, a true *Terre des Hommes* (Planet of Man).[2]

When the first commercial airplane flights took off in the spring of 1919, they were commonly greeted as the heralds of a new age in which air travel would "shorten" distances and contribute to a better and more integrated world. Scheduled passenger flights had been a long time coming. In the first decade after the invention of powered flight by Wilbur and Orville Wright in December 1903, aviators would, on occasion, move over on top of their flying contraptions to allow space for a passenger willing to risk an early

death in order to sample the new technology, the arrival of which had been anticipated for centuries.

Such anticipations had become more precise in the course of the nineteenth century, as technological developments made it easier to imagine how air travel might become possible. In 1850, for example, German pharmacist and balloon enthusiast Heinrich Zeise put forward his vision of dirigible hydrogen "balloons" outcompeting steamboat shipping between Europe and America in his booklet *Die Aeronautik früher und jetzt* (Aeronautics then and now).[3] Some of those who read his predictions may have witnessed the first attempts to use balloons for air transport during the siege of Paris by the German army in the war of 1870–1871. In January 1871, would-be passengers queued up in front of the Paris city hall for an aerial escape from the besieged city, taking letters with them in the first ever "airlift." In a period of 4 months, over sixty balloons went up, carrying eighty-eight people and some 4 million letters to the outside world.[4] In the prevailing winds, three of these balloons drifted as far north as the Netherlands. One balloon, *La poste de Paris*, went aloft on January 18, 1871 hoping to reach Bordeaux, 100 miles southwest of Paris. Instead, a change of wind direction blew its three passengers some 350 miles north before touching down in Dutch wetlands 11 hours later. The air travelers were met by farmers bewildered at the sight of people descending from the sky. Ballooning, flying as such, inspired people's fancy. Those who conquered the air, whether in real life or in imagination, would henceforth be depicted as daring superheroes, decidedly larger than life.

The Heroic Airmen

Just such a character was the protagonist of Jules Verne's 1886 novel *Robur le Conquérant* (Robur the Conqueror), who "circled the world" in his electrically driven, giant flying machine, *Albatross*. Aviation, from the very first, was associated with technological prowess, superiority, and territorial conquest. Passing over Dahomey (Benin) in Africa, Verne's imaginary *Albatross* carried out something of a violent civilizing mission, firing its guns at native people on the ground in an attempt to stop a fight. On the other hand, Verne also showed that flying machines might be used for peaceful purposes, such as rescuing shipwrecked sailors off the coast of Chile.[5] The former, however, caught on quicker than the latter. Within years of its invention, powered flight was embraced by the military. Airplanes and airships were evaluated as a possible new weapon. In November 1906 the British newspaper magnate Lord Northcliffe (Alfred Harmsworth) was one of those to take stock of the consequences in his famous quote, "England is no longer an island," and henceforth at risk from military attack from the air.[6] Ideas like these were also proposed by the British science fiction author Herbert

George Wells in his famous 1908 book *The War in the Air*. Wells predicted a world that would be terrorized by the all-powerful airships harboring military *Drachenflieger* (dragonflyers: box kites, large enough to carry a man and armaments). It was evident that aviation would revolutionize war. Primarily inspired by fear of its potentially destructive power, the first decade of the new century saw an upsurge of ideas about how aviation might affect the world. Fright would remain a byword that accompanied aeronautical developments—and for good reason. No one could be expected to remain safe from an aerial attack. On the other hand there were those who aired that aviation might contribute to *end* violent conflict and unite humanity across the globe, bringing profound changes for the better in life. Few went as far as envisaging an "alti-man," a new and better kind of humans, whose superior state would depend on dwellings in the sky.[7] One inspired pioneer, the eccentric Brazilian aviator Alberto Santos-Dumont who in November 1906 set the first official world record for powered takeoff and sustained flight—220 meters in just under 22 seconds—even hand crafted special 6-foot high furniture so that he could host "aerial dinner parties" in his chic Paris apartment that would entice his guests to "imagine what life was like in a flying machine."[8] His fame was such that the Brazilian city of Palmyra, where he was born in 1873, decided to change its name into Santos-Dumont on July 31, 1932, a week after the (suicidal) death of its native celebrity.

Something of the high expectations of the meaning of flight for modern society transpired in the social backgrounds of early participants in flying. An expensive hobby, aeronautics was the domain of the affluent few, and membership of aeronautical societies was in effect limited to the upper classes. In Europe such societies customarily enjoyed royal patronage. The social elevation of its participants helped foster hopes of flight as a positive force to modernize society.

Ordinary men and women who flocked to early air shows entertained rather different perspectives. They did so primarily in anticipation of thrill and the distinct possibility of watching a young pilot's life come to a sudden end. In the words of H.G. Wells in 1908, "They flew—that was all right; they flew in machines heavier than air. But they smashed. Sometimes they smashed the engine, sometimes they smashed the aeronaut, usually they smashed both."[9] Mortal danger was one of the prime attractions of aviation, the magnet that brought out the masses. It is difficult now to fathom the ring that the term *aviator* had in the minds of those who had never before seen human-made objects in the sky, very visibly commanded by daring men, and equally daring women, who strapped themselves atop their feeble constructions of wood, linen, and wire to brave perhaps the most dangerous and unforgiving of elements: the air. Something of the depth of the excitement can be deduced from the distance people traveled to witness such events and the physical and manmade obstacles (like border crossings) they had to overcome—and the time, effort, and cost it took to get there.

Air meets, sometimes lasting a whole week, like the *Grande Semaine d'Aviation* at Reims, the capital of France's Champagne region, in August 1909, attracted hundreds of thousands of spectators from halfway across the continent of Europe. Ambrosius Hubrecht, an anatomist in the medical faculty of the University of Utrecht, came all the way from Holland, convinced that the Reims air meet represented a significant event in modern cultural history.[10] Czech novelist Franz Kafka traveled over 500 miles from Prague with his friends to see the air meet in Brescia, in northern Italy, in September 1909. Seeing the Frenchman Louis Blériot's lengthy preparations for takeoff, he noted in disbelief, "And on this trifle he wants to fly?"[11] The public cheered and wept with the achievements of the heralds of the air age. Thrill seekers were served at their beckoning call in December 1910 when eight airplane crashes cost the lives of ten men in a single month—a sad record but one that added to the excitement of aviation.[12] In the following year ninety-six aviators lost their lives in accidents worldwide.[13]

Air meets established aviation as a heroic activity and pilots as a breed onto themselves, especially when *international* flights added a chauvinistic tinge to the thrill of flying as such. After Frenchman Louis Blériot was the first to fly across the English Channel on July 25, 1909, over 100,000 people flocked to Paris' Gare du Nord train station to give him an exhilirated hero's welcome in the nation's capital. For weeks newspapers expanded on Blériot's flight, heralding it as a great French victory.[14] His aircraft became the centerpiece in the world's first aeronautical exhibition, held at the Grand Palais in Paris in October 1909 to boast France's achievements in aeronautics before awed spectators. Air races between European capitals fed such nationalist sentiments. In May 1911 Frenchman Jules Védrines became a national celebrity winning the Madrid to Paris air race. Not 2 weeks later, in early June, his countrymen Jean Conneau and Roland Garros came in first and second in a race from Paris to Rome. Another few weeks later Conneau also won the Circuit d'Europe, flying from Paris to Brussels, Holland, London, and back to Paris—a race that left thirty-two out of forty competitors stranded.

But the real challenge to aeronautical technology came with the outbreak of war in August 1914, as a new phenomenon, aircraft, appeared over the battlefield for reconnaissance. Precise aerial observation of enemy positions took away much of the surprise element in attacks and helped bring about the stalemate in the war, with the opposing armies digging themselves in in trenches all the way from the North Sea coast to the Swiss border. These "scouts" had to be combated and kept from crossing enemy trenches. That autumn war added an extra dimension to the heroics of flying, as the popular press zoomed in on "aces"—pilots who managed to shoot down several adversaries. They became the epitomic heroes of modern warfare, although most aerial casualties over the front did not result from aerial "dogfights" but occurred in accidents caused by inexperience and mechanical breakdowns.[15]

Védrines and Garros went on to become such aces. Neither lived long enough to cash in on their fame. After spending 3 years in a prisoner of war camp, Garros escaped in 1918 to die an airman's death in the final month of the war when his plane exploded in a dogfight; Védrines crashed in April 1919 in a new Paris to Rome contest.

While aces were the "heroes" who deployed their chauvinistic bravery in the actual war theater, more ominous of the changes aviation brought to warfare were those pilots who were *not* depicted in the popular press. These were airmen who carried fear and destruction without actually firing a gun. Aerial bombing was invented by the Italians in November 1911 over their north African colony Libya.[16] Even before 1914 the French, as well as the Germans, Russians, and Austro-Hungarians, had begun developing aircraft specifically designed to carry and drop bombs. In Europe, wartime bombing raids made aircraft into fearsome tools of mechanical warfare for a much wider section of society than those involved in the fighting. In 1914 German bombs fell on Liège and Antwerp (Belgium), Paris, but also on Minsk (Belarus) and Warsaw (Poland). Six months later, in January 1915, German army and navy Zeppelin airships began strategic raids on Britain. On May 31, 1915, the first bombs hit London. Many more would follow. And although aerial bombing was ineffective in terms of property damage— according to some sources, less than 1 percent of the damage caused by rats—the psychological harm was substantial. It literally brought the war home.[17] Even so, not everyone was equally affected: there were those in London for whom the Zeppelin attacks meant a relief from the boredom of everyday life, a source for excitement that was sadly missed if one heard of an attack elsewhere. Feminist, poet, and novelist Vera Brittain noted in her diary, "I quite hoped a raid would come while I was there, as I have always since the war began been anxious to see a Zeppelin, and I knew I should not be afraid."[18] In later bombardments aircraft were also used. Raids against civilian targets were flown by both sides in the war, with Allied bombing runs on coastal cities in German-occupied Belgium in the spring of 1917, and on industrial cites in Germany, like Cologne and Saarbrücken, later on.

Nor did the effects of air warfare remain limited to those nations that took an active part in the fighting. Aircraft would stray occasionally, as a result of navigational errors or carelessness, and bomb towns in neutral countries like Holland. In the night of April 29, 1917, a British bomber strayed some 50 miles North from a raid on the German-held port of Zeebrugge in Belgium and hit the Dutch town of Zierikzee instead. Around 2:30 A.M. eight bombs made a good part of a street disappear. They left a family of three—father, mother, and their 3-year-old adopted son—dead and rendered their neighbors homeless.[19] Between 1914 and 1918 a total of forty-five attacks on neutral soil took place, leaving deep impressions of unsafety and vulnerability.[20]

More than the physical damage inflicted, the psychological effects of aerial bombing nurtured ideas on the use of airpower after the war. The British became the front-runners in pioneering air power as a new means to control their vast empire. Following successes of the Royal Flying Corps against the Ottoman Turks in the Middle East during the First World War, aircraft were widely used throughout the 1920s as a cost-effective way to exert power. In Somaliland (Somalia), Sudan, Iraq, and Afghanistan the newly established Royal Air Force (RAF) bombed villages suspected of supporting or harboring insurrectionist elements. In the 1930s airpower even partially replaced ground troops in British East Africa.[21] The heroics of serving in the RAF was appealing even to such weathered war veterans as Thomas E. Lawrence (Lawrence of Arabia), whose posthumously published novel *The Mint* details Lawrence's attempt to join the ranks of a new kind of soldiers, aircraftmen: "The sight of flying would hearten us, as a reminder of our profession—to help conquer the air."[22] To achieve this, airfields and landing strips were built throughout the British Empire in Africa and Asia to enable aerial operations supporting the colonial status quo. The French and the Spaniards did the same in north Africa, establishing a chain of airstrips at military forts that subsequently doubled as staging posts for long-range civilian air services. At one such base, Cape Juby, in the Spanish colony Rio de Oro, south of Morocco, Antoine de Saint-Exupéry was based from 1928 to 1929. It was while stationed there that he wrote *Vol de Nuit*, overlooking the shore of the Atlantic.[23]

The first to make a nonstop crossing of the Atlantic, British airmen John Alcock and Arthur Whitten Brown came to celebrity status in June 1919, flying from Newfoundland (Canada) to Ireland. They were unlikely pilots for the feat, and this added to the spectacle of their success. Both Alcock and Brown had spent the last years of the war in a German prison camp and had only limited flying experience. On June 14 they took off from St. Johns, Newfoundland. Sixteen hours later, on the morning of June 15, their aircraft crash-landed in a bog near Clifden, Ireland. When local people asked Alcock where he had come from, his reply that they had flown across the Atlantic brought on roaring laughter. Nonetheless, England soon erupted in celebrations. Alcock and Brown were knighted by King George V and received the Daily Mail Prize for the first to fly the Atlantic from the secretary of state for War and Air, Winston Churchill. The two gallant airmen toured England and were praised from banquet to banquet until tragedy struck. In December 1919 Alcock was killed in a plane crash. Brown never flew again.[24]

Of other record-breaking aviators there were similar stories to tell. Between November 12 and December 10, 1919 the Australian brothers Ross and Keith Smith, and their mechanics Wally Shiers and Jim Bennett, were the first to fly from Britain all the way to Australia and win £10,000 (the equivalent of nearly half a million dollars today) in prize money, a knighthood, and

eternal fame. Two-and-a-half years later Australia was in mourning when Ross Smith died in a plane crash on April 14, 1922 while preparing for a round-the-world flight.

Personal tragedy added to the heroics of airmen, strengthening their image as icons of a new age. On December 15, 1922 Portugal's number one airman, Sacadura Cabral, went missing on a flight over water in dense fog, never to be seen again, not 6 months after he and Gago Coutinho had been the first to fly across the South Atlantic. Their flight had begun in Lisbon on March 30, 1922 and ended, after replacing their Fairey hydroplane twice as a result of accidents en route, in Rio de Janeiro on June 17. It put them, and their aircraft, for all of posterity right next to the monument commemorating Henry the Sailor's vision of Portugal's naval empire on Lisbon's Belém waterfront, from where the Portuguese explorers started their sea voyages five centuries before.

Alcock, Smith, Cabral—the list of record-breaking flyers that had their names added to a growing roll of aviation casualties increased with every year. It added to the lure of aviation as a "live fast, die young" activity and furthered the identification of pilots as a breed onto their own, role models for the daring youth. It seemed in the 1920s as if every self-respecting country had to have its own international record-breaking flights. Pilots and their feats made headline news, and successful flyers became household names. The phenomenon was omnipresent, even in the otherwise nonindividualistic Soviet Union. The new hero of the early decades of the twentieth century was the lone male who risked his life to overcome seemingly insuperable obstacles through the use of the spectacular technology of aviation. When Charles Nungesser and François Coli, two former wartime aces, disappeared in May 1927 in an attempted Atlantic crossing, less than 2 weeks before Charles Lindbergh's epic nonstop flight, French newspapers depicted it as a national tragedy. And if the French were still in doubt whether to see Saint-Exupéry as a pilot or as a writer, such uncertainty did not exist towards his contemporaries Jean Mermoz and Henri Guillaumet, famous for their long-distance flights in the service of the mail-carrying airline Latécoère. Guillaumet especially lived up to his hero status, battling through a mountainous snow blizzard on foot for 5 days to be reunited with his wife, Noëlle, after crashing his Potez-25 in the Andes Mountains on Friday, June 13, 1930. Guillaumet's odyssey went right into the French collective memory, along with the feats of wartime aces.[25] The same year he and Mermoz were among the crack pilots selected to fly the experimental French transatlantic mail route to Brazil.

Aircraft constructors like Dutch-American Anthony Fokker deliberately tapped into this trend by sponsoring daring record flights and marketed their products in the wake of pilots' fame. The risks taken in order to qualify for immortality were considerable, even when the biggest rush for record flights was already past. In July 1929 Australian pilot Charles Kingsford Smith

arrived with his crew in Amsterdam, on a flight that had started over a year before May 31, 1928 in Oakland, California, in a quest to be the first to complete a round-the-world flight in a westward direction. Fokker offered them a free overhaul of their aircraft in his Amsterdam factory—and not a moment too soon, as it turned out. It was discovered that the crew had "repaired" major structural damage to the (wooden) main wing spar of their Fokker F-VII trimotor aircraft by simply nailing a few planks to it.[26] After the overhaul, Kingsford Smith safely made it back to Oakland, where he landed on July 4, 1930.

At any rate, flying remained a risky business, and in Holland, the national airline, KLM (Koninklijke Luchtvaart Maatschappij), only hired pilots who had previously proven themselves coolheaded and capable of making and surviving several emergency landings.[27] Nonetheless, there were limits to the heroics performed, dictated by the natural desire of the early airlines not to estrange themselves from their potential clientele by allowing hair-raising stories to get out. When one of KLM's pilots, former Russian fighter ace Iwan Smirnoff, made a forced landing on October 19, 1923, with his Fokker F.III, and put himself and his three passengers down on a sand bank in the English Channel off the coast of Deal, his bosses decided this was bad publicity and kept the story out of the papers. After spending several increasingly anxious hours vainly trying to attract attention from passing ships, Smirnoff's party was rescued by a coal freighter only shortly before the sand bank (and the airplane on it) disappeared beneath the waves.[28] Nonetheless the need for national heroes of the air manifested itself in Holland too. After the first trial flight from Amsterdam to the capital of the Dutch East Indies, Batavia (Jakarta), the nation welcomed Abraham Thomassen à Thuessinck van der Hoop and his crew as national heroes upon their return. In The Hague, an afternoon-long spectacle was put on, on April 25, 1925, culminating in royal decorations for the three daring airmen on the grandstand of the sports grounds before thousands of spectators. The festivities comprised of horse shows, musical bands, parades of sportsmen, acrobats, motorcars, farmers, and fishermen and were specifically designed to link modern day achievements with tradition and Dutch folklore.[29] A week later, similar festivities were put on in Rotterdam. Soon after, and somewhat uncharacteristically for a venerated airman, the pilot, Thomassen à Thuessinck van der Hoop, decided he had received enough cheers to last him a lifetime and retired from aviation to become the secretary of the Royal Society for Arts and Sciences in the Dutch East Indies.

The heroes were not all men. In the late 1920s and 1930s a number of women carved a niche for themselves in aviation's hall of fame, despite the considerable problems they faced, on grounds of gender, to obtain a professional pilot's license. These were mostly affluent ladies, like Germany's Marga von Etzdorf and Britain's Sophie Heath and Mary Bailey, the last two of whom made return flights from London to Cape Town, South Africa,

in 1928. They challenged the odds by undertaking such flights in private aircraft. One of the internationally best-known female pilots of the time was record-setting aviatrix Amy Johnson, who in May 1930 became the first woman to fly from England to Australia. Determined to become an equally dextrous aviator, New Zealand's Jean Batten was inspired by her achievements. In 1934 she established her own solo flight record, flying from England to Australia in 14 days, 22 hours, 30 minutes, beating Amy Johnson's time by 6 days. The range of her De Havilland Gipsy Moth was insufficient to fly across the Tasman Sea to New Zealand, but the welcome she received from cheering crowds in Auckland was none the less spectacular for it. For 6 weeks she toured her native country, giving speeches. After that, she flew all the way back to her starting point, London, the first woman to do so. Known as the "Garbo of the Skies," Batten stood for adventure, daring, exploration, and glamour—she even packed evening dresses on her 1935 solo flight across the South Atlantic to Brazil—and is still counted among New Zealand's national heroes.[30]

Aerial celebrity status, whether male or female, not only featured on the high plane of national consciousness but was also identified as a potential moneymaker in commerce. The instant success of Saint-Exupéry's *Night Flight* not only led to a Hollywood movie that appealed to masculine perseverance but also provided inspiration for a special *Vol de Nuit* perfume for women. Perhaps the most important rallying point was the October 1934 MacRobertson Air Race from England to Melbourne, Australia. In this big international event, for which $75,000 in prize money was put up by Sir Macpherson Robertson, a wealthy Australian confectionery manufacturer, an international field of twenty competitors took part. Before, during, and after the race, the participants and their endeavors were closely followed in newspapers and cinema newsreels the world over. The race formed the backdrop for novels and films and was an incentive to float various new products, ranging from pilots' attire clothing for adults to board games and "aviation chocolate bars" for children.

Serving the Nation-State

The return to peacetime conditions at the end of 1918 brought several unanswered questions about aviation to the fore, including how to provide safety standards to protect aircraft passengers and people on the ground and how to ensure that foreign aircraft would not present a detriment to the territorial integrity of the state. The first question was one to be answered in national legislation and (government) control of aircraft operating under national laws: most nations set about developing national aviation legislation in the years following 1918. The second question was to be addressed in the international arena.

In 1919 these issues were the focus of the international conference in Paris on the law of the air, which took place in the shadow of the Versailles Peace Treaty negotiations that formally ended the First World War. The spirit of the times was reflected in the discussions and in their outcome. After 4 years of war, aviation—particularly German aviation—was considered a threat. Reducing, possibly eliminating, the perceived dangers of foreign aircraft was paramount to the delegates of the thirteen countries participating in the conference. Representatives of the defeated Central Powers were not invited, nor were those countries that had remained neutral during the war. On October 13, 1919, negotiations resulted in the signing of the Paris Convention relating to the Regulation of Aerial Navigation.

Three basic concepts shaped this treaty—and international air transport as such. The first was the French desire to safeguard Paris from future surprise air attacks, reflected in the demand for absolute national sovereignty in the air. The second idea was to oblige the British demand for the right of innocent passage for civil air transportation, which London considered a vital future instrument to strengthen the bonds with its vast overseas possessions. And thirdly, the victorious powers wished to block the development of German aviation by reserving international air transport for the Allied and Associated Powers only. German aviation was curtailed, and Germany was effectively banned from joining the Paris Convention, while aircraft from nonsignatory states were denied access to the airspace of the countries that signed the treaty. The mutually exclusive French and British interests resulted in an internally contradictory regime that sought to combine absolute sovereignty with a provision for permitting specific air services between the Allied signatory states.[31]

The terms of the treaty opened the door to prestige-dictated political and diplomatic skirmishes regarding aviation, and this was indeed what happened. The convention officially established the rule that aircraft from other countries were forbidden to cross borders, unless explicit prior consent had been given to do so. This provision was also a stab at the interests of the neutral countries to participate in the new mode of transport. Aircraft registered in these countries needed a special and temporary permit to fly into the airspace of the states adhering to the treaty. The establishment of international civil and commercial air services thus had to be arranged through international diplomacy and soon took the form of bilateral exchanges of notes between governments.

Yet the provision of air services was related to the state in more ways than one. As highly visible signs of national pride pilots and their aircraft set standards for the public perception of just how "modern" a nation was. This became especially evident in the European context in the early 1920s. The end of the First World War had created a number of new countries in Europe, while redrawing the borders of others. Such newly defined nations needed new symbols contributing to a sense of national identity, and

having prominent pilots and a national airline provided just that. In such a setting, it was inevitable that governments should support airline ventures that sprung up within their borders. Moreover, aeronautics represented one of the prime technologies through which nation-states expressed power and prestige.[32] Air transport companies needed little encouragement to use such chauvinistic sentiments to wrest subsidies from their governments in order to keep their ventures afloat until such a time when there would be enough passengers and goods to be transported by air that civil aviation might "fly by itself," as British Air Minister Winston Churchill quipped in March 1920.[33] Airline pilots landing at a foreign airport were instructed to proudly hoist the national flag from their cockpit window and show passengers, spectators, and foreign airport officials that yet another envoy of their great nation had arrived. Such blatant displays of the flag could not remain unanswered and called for counterrepresentations in foreign ports of call. It put air transport at the high end of the negotiating table where bilateral issues between countries were discussed. A new practice emerged in which nations exchanged "landing rights" for their national flag-carrying airlines, balancing such rights on an equal footing. Bilateral relations and state interests would dominate international air transport from 1919 onwards with serious consequences for the development of civil and commercial flying

In a number of countries air services, and aviation in general, performed a specific task in the service of the state—and received support for that reason. This was especially so in countries where aviation was considered vital to the functioning of the state itself, as was the case in the Soviet Union. Indeed, in the early 1920s the Communist Party leadership embarked on a specific campaign to portray aviation as "the great instrument of the future" that would liberate Russia from the shackles of its past. Aviation was promoted as one of the key instruments that would help build the new, modern state that the revolutionaries of 1917 said they wished to establish, in both a political and cultural sense. In more ways than one the airplane was perceived as a tool to foster a new national solidarity—and pride in the new society. One of its roles was to bridge the divides between the new communist structures in the cities and the disconnected rural peasant communities.[34] Special demonstration squadrons toured the country to familiarize villagers with aviation through "agit-flights" that not only promoted airmindedness but also served to prove to uninformed peasants the atheist and antireligious convictions of the communists that the heavens held neither God nor angels. Many thousands of rural inhabitants were taken up among the clouds to see for themselves. The effort was supported by a mobilization of the press, the cinema, and the publishing industry.[35] The enormous size of the country, its relatively poor surface infrastructure, and the drive that emanated from the Central Committee of the Communist Party to bring all fifteen republics that made up the Union of Socialist Soviet Republics under the effective control of

the Kremlin in Moscow were also strong incentives to establish a nationwide air transport system. It served in a dual role as a tool to forge the nation *and* as an instrument that (literally) transported repression and control of dissent.[36] In February 1923 the Kremlin issued a resolution empowering the Central Air Fleet Administration to supervise air services. Five months later scheduled flights were initiated, with German Junkers aircraft, on a route between Moscow and Nizhny Novgorod, and gradually expanded to cover most of the outlying regions of the Soviet Union. Passengers were few: 1,433 in 1923 and a modest 8,653 in 1928.[37] In February 1932 the various operations were amalgamated as Aeroflot, which not only carried out the transportation of passengers and goods but also provided for crop dusting in agriculture and other aviation-related services.

Another big incentive to support air transport companies in the interest of the state was present in those European countries that held overseas colonial territories. This was the case in Belgium, Britain, France, Holland, Italy, Spain, and Portugal. In Belgium, the first survey on the possible use of airplanes in its vast African colony Congo dated back to 1911. In 1919 two "study companies" were founded: SNETA (Société Nationale pour l'Étude des Transports Aériens), which focused on international air transport from Belgium, and CENAC (Comité d'Études pour la Navigation Aérienne au Congo) focusing on air transportation in the colony itself. With royal support, the latter started services in April 1920 under the name Ligne Aérienne Roi Albert (LARA), on a route following the Congo River from Léopoldville (Kinshasa) to Stanleyville (Kisangani). The aim of LARA was to improve the effectiveness of the Belgian colonial administration by offering rapid transportation of mail, goods, and passengers. It was the first (more or less scheduled) air service operating in Africa, and it reduced travel time between the two cities from 18 days by river on a boat to some 15 hours of flying time—a huge improvement in communications for the colonial administrators.[38] The next phase in Belgian air transport planning came late in 1924, when preparations went under way in Brussels to organize a trial flight to Léopoldville. Taking off from Brussels on February 12, 1925, pilot Edmond Thieffry, a former wartime ace, and his crew needed 51 days to cover the 5,000-mile distance, which was rather more than the 18 days it took to cover the distance by ship.

But the *real* challenge lay in the organization of a scheduled service to follow the trial flight. Negotiating agreements on passage and traffic rights for a Ligne Belge-Congo (LBC) with the big colonial powers Britain and France was one of the key factors that held up the opening of a scheduled service. After initial diplomatic skirmishes with the British over a route following the river Nile, the Belgians settled on negotiations with France, hoping they could build on the pioneering work of the French carrier Latécoère. The talks took years to progress, as the French were in no hurry to allow a foreign airline's presence in their colonies before French services were firmly

established there. A tentative agreement on a joint Franco-Belgian service was only reached in January 1929. However, Paris revoked its promises soon afterwards, when the French government decided that the "integrity of the French colonial airspace" was more important than the maintenance of good aeronautical relations with its smaller neighbor in Europe. Nonetheless, a revised agreement was signed in May 1930, under which the Belgians were granted rights for a route to the Congo, to be operated jointly with the French. In exchange Brussels promised cooperation in Belgian Congo for the establishment of a service between France and Madagascar, the French-held island off the East African coast. Nothing came of it. In Belgium the economic crisis of the 1930s meant that government money for unremunerative airline adventures—however prestigious—was scarce. In France lingering doubts about the joint service were heightened in 1931 by a sudden collapse of Aéropostale, the guise under which Latécoère operated mail services to French colonial Africa and to Brazil, Argentina, and Chile. Aéropostale had been designated to fly under the agreement with Brussels but was forced to cease all operations by the end of March 1931 as the result of a political scandal over subsidies. After that, there could be no question of allowing the Belgians to operate before French aeronautical interests in Africa had been restructured. The Belgians felt humiliated. The eight Fokker aircraft that they had bought in 1930 to operate the route remained in their hangar at Brussels' airport, collecting dust. It was February 23, 1935 before LBC could finally initiate its service to the Congo.[39]

The Belgian example was typical of the way in which colonial prestige and aviation diplomacy intersected. The idea that colonial rule necessitated a *national* air service to the possessions overseas was held in common by all colonial powers. Operating such an air service added to the national prestige to the point that *not* having one was almost unthinkable. This element of chauvinism dictated perceptions, meaning that colonial air services were considered in comparison with those of other colonial powers in speed and standards of service. And these were precisely the elements that added weight to the political controversies over operating rights. Air services infringed on an imperial prestige that was there to be protected.

The British acted in much the same fashion as the French. In April 1924 the four airlines operating in Britain were merged to form Imperial Airways. As its name suggested Imperial Airways was founded with the specific intention of opening up air services between England and the British Empire. However it was not before the Imperial Conference of 1926 that a coherent strategy was conceived in this respect. It was decided to establish a network of air services that would knit the British Empire closer together. Short-term and long-term aims were agreed upon, the former being that Imperial Airways was to develop plans for an airplane service to India, which would act as a sort of stop-gap until the long-term aim of using large, luxuriously fitted airships would become a reality on the route from Britain to India, Ceylon,

and Australia.[40] In 1927 Imperial Airways took the first step to establish the air route by taking over the RAF service across British-mandated territory in the Middle East. Scheduled flights were initiated between Cairo (Egypt) and Basra (Iraq). Indeed, the company was so focused on its prestigious imperial goals that it lost interest in European operations. By the mid-1930s it had just two services in Europe: London–Paris–Zurich (Switzerland) and London–Brussels–Cologne (Germany).

At the same time, the Dutch were planning an air service of their own to connect Amsterdam with Batavia (Jakarta), the capital of the Dutch East Indies (Indonesia). It was evident that such a service would depend on British cooperation, as it had to cross the vast expanse of the British Empire that stretched from the Middle East through India all the way to Malaysia. In The Hague a Dutch service was considered of prime importance to colonial interests. Indeed, the very reason the government subsidized its national air carrier Koninklijke Luchtvaart Maatschappij (KLM) was to develop this service.[41]

In the mid-1920s preparations went under way in London and in Amsterdam to connect with their respective empires. Yet Imperial Airways' colonial plans were hampered by a lack of suitable aircraft and by the Air Ministry's long-term plans to use airships. Because of this, the British plans did not move forward with the same speed as the Dutch, and it was not long before they encountered British opposition. Conscious of imperial prestige, Britain embarked upon a policy of obstructionism in the air, granting permission only for a series of trial flights, referring to insufficient ground organization as the reason for this attitude.[42] That, of course was a scam. A Foreign Office confidential note read, "The real reason for our refusal to allow further Dutch flights (. . .) is *not* the state of the ground organisation in India, but the desire of the Government of India that a regular British or Indian service should precede the Dutch."[43]

KLM had to desist until "improvements" could be effected at several airfields along the route, notably at Baghdad in British-held Iraq. These improvements were scheduled to be completed by the end of April 1929,[44] which also happened to be the date on which an Imperial Airways service to Karachi was supposed to begin. Nonetheless, the British dragged their heels until May 1930, when the Dutch threatened to administer the same restrictionism regarding the passage of British airplanes across the Dutch East Indies to Australia.[45] In exchange for the KLM permit, London demanded that reciprocal rights be issued for a future British service between Singapore and Australia. These were granted in an exchange of notes in the spring of 1930. Thereafter Britain and Australia successfully used the conditions laid down in the exchange of notes to block Dutch attempts to gain landing rights in Australia, which developed into a major strain on Anglo-Dutch aviation relations. Indeed, despite Australian doubts, the British and Dominion governments reached an agreement in May 1932 to create a

joint Anglo-Australian air service, Qantas Empire Airways (QEA), between Singapore and Brisbane in 1934. The Australian Prime Minister, Joseph Lyons—incidentally the first Australian Prime Minister to use air travel to meet people across the country—assured the Dominion Office in London "... that consideration will not be given to any suggestion for inclusion of foreign interests until the possibility of a co-operative British-Australian service shall be fully exhausted."[46]

And so the matter dragged on until, in 1937, Britain and Australia reached an agreement to reequip their joint air service with (British-built) flying boats. The idea was to use the cargo capacity of the flying boats to combine the carriage of passengers with the transportation by air of *all* first class mail between Britain and Australia. The plan hinged on imperial prestige. Unable to compete in speed and efficiency with Dutch and French air services to the Far East, the Air Ministry in London decided to go for volume and comfort instead. Poorly conceived and regarded with suspicion by the Australians from the very start, the flying boat service combined disastrous economics— operating costs were almost six times higher than expected—with a poor record for reliability.[47] Because mail received priority over passengers, no more than five people traveled as passengers each week on Imperial's India route in 1937 (against an average of seventy-five passengers per week for Imperial's competitor KLM).[48] Yet on the section between Singapore and Australia the flying boats needed a whole new ground organization of their own for moorings, fuel depots, and passenger accommodations. The Dutch made the construction of the necessary facilities in the Netherlands East Indies conditional to the British and Australian consent for a Dutch air service that would connect Batavia and Sydney. Indeed, such operating rights were granted, not to Imperial's major competitor KLM as the Dutch had hoped, but to the Dutch colonial airline KNILM (Koninklijke Nederlandsch-Indische Luchtvaart Maatschappij). Thus a situation was avoided in which a single Dutch airline would compete with the services offered by Imperial Airlines and Qantas Empire Airways between London and Australia. But although the flying boats soon proved unable even to transport the bulk of first class mail—at Christmas time in 1938 mail bags literally piled up in "dumping stations" along the route for lack of transportation capacity— Dutch offers of assistance were vehemently rejected, even after war broke out in the Pacific and the three countries became allies in the fight against Japan.

The list of diplomatic incidents was much longer than that. Indeed, with such strong nationalist feelings—and ample legal and diplomatic means to block foreign services—it was almost miraculous that the 1920s and 1930s saw the development of an extensive international network of air services. More often than not the political obstacles that were encountered at the negotiating table were even bigger than the actual problems to be overcome en route.

The issues were not limited to the European arena, or the colonial routes for that matter. In Asia, Japan was, in October 1928, the first nation to follow the European custom of establishing a subsidized flag-carrying national airline: Nihon Koku Yuso Kabushiki Kaisha (NKYKK) or Japan Air Transport Corporation. It operated services to territories in the Japanese sphere of influence: Korea and Taiwan. From the start of Japan's military campaign in Manchuria in 1931, Japan's civilian air transport capacity was, however, largely taken up by the armed forces. Thereafter, political and military circumstances—like the Japanese advance in China—precluded the development of regular international air services in Asia. Allowing foreign air services into Japan was out of the question entirely.[49]

The same protectionist spirit ruled aviation politics in the Western hemisphere, where the British actually blocked the emergence of an indigenous Caribbean Airways in the British West Indies in 1932 to protect the long-term interests of Imperial Airways as a global carrier.[50] The United States also pursued such restrictionist policies. Between 1925 and 1929 the Colombian carrier SCADTA fruitlessly negotiated to acquire landing rights in Florida for an airmail service to the United States.[51] Despite the American-inspired liberal aviation treaty for the Western hemisphere signed in Havana on February 20, 1928, Washington categorically denied landing rights for the Colombian service. The reason was not just that SCADTA, short for Sociedad Colombo Alemana de Transporte Aéreo, was foreign, but particularly that it was a joint venture that combined Colombian and German money, operating German-built Junkers and Dornier aircraft. Through SCADTA German interests were perceived to threaten the protected position of Pan American Airways, Washington's "chosen instrument" to monopolize international air transportation to and from the United States. Successive American governments were adamant that this should not happen.

Because Germany was excluded from the mainstream of aeronautical development under the terms of the Paris Convention, German aviation was inherently political. Despite the fact that some airlines, like the Deutsche Aero-Lloyd, had financial ties to merchant banks and shipping lines, as did other European airlines, early German airlines were typically sponsored by local or regional authorities. Municipal and regional subsidies enabled the development of a domestic air network that boasted reliability under all weather conditions. Fostering its growth was an act of defiance of the Allied terms of the Versailles Peace Accords and the Paris Convention.[52]

Although the initial focus was on establishing a domestic network, air transport did not remain confined within the national borders. Since German airlines could not be prevented from flying to states that did not sign the Paris Convention, German air carriers were able to operate international routes to the surrounding neutral countries like the Netherlands, Denmark, Sweden, and Switzerland. Long-range services were also contemplated, particularly to the Soviet Union. Pariahs of the international community of

the early 1920s and excluded from membership of the League of Nations, Germany and the Soviet Union engaged in a series of secret negotiations that aimed to bring the two countries closer together. One of the fruits of German-Soviet cooperation was a joint air service. Via the German eastern provinces along the Baltic Sea, a long-distance route from Berlin via Königsberg (Kaliningrad) in East Prussia to Moscow was initiated on April 30, 1922. The service—operated daily from 1924—was a huge improvement on train travel: traveling time was reduced to a day's flight, versus 5 days by train. Between Königsberg and Moscow the route was maintained by a joint company, Deutsch-Russische Luftverkehrs Gesellschaft—Deruluft for short. Deruluft, operating suitably neutral Dutch-built Fokker aircraft, was also highly political. It fitted the semisecret structures that connected Germany and the Soviet Union, along with production facilities for Junkers aircraft in Moscow's Fili suburb and Germany's secret army and air force bases near the Russian city of Lipetsk, some 300 miles south of the Soviet capital.[53]

In Germany itself governmental involvement from Berlin culminated, in 1926, in the founding of a national airline, Deutsche Luft Hansa. It would subsequently develop into the largest airline in Europe, after the Nazi regime came to power in 1933. Although most traffic was carried within Germany, German aviation already had a history of services beyond the limits of the Reich by that time, even apart from Deruluft. Indeed, German aviation interests came to span much of the globe before the 1920s were out. This remarkable development was brought about by the peculiar combination of aeronautical research and government capital surrounding the Junkers Werke in Dessau. Utilizing its worldwide sales network for Junkers gas appliances, the company developed a sizable export market for Junkers' innovative all-metal airliners. Apart from eastern Europe and Russia, Latin America in particular saw a proliferation of Junkers aircraft—and of airline ventures using these aircraft. They were sponsored by start-up capital provided by the Junkers company with support from the government. Junkers would give up to 33 percent discounts to new airlines buying its aircraft, in exchange for a lasting allegiance to the manufacturer. Two special holding companies for such investments, aimed at the creation of a network of Junkers-controlled air services, were set up in 1923 with financial support from the German government.[54] Using Spain, where German capital made up approximately 66 percent of the means of the Spanish carrier Iberia, as a stepping-stone to expand and consolidate German interests in Latin America over the course of a decade, the Germans built a string of affiliated companies in Latin America. The spread of these interests followed the pattern of sizable German migrations to South America—predominantly Brazil and Argentina—in the previous six decades.[55] The airlines were tied together by the purpose-founded Condor Syndicate that held offices in Hamburg and Rio de Janeiro. In January 1927 the Condor Syndicate began operating a

scheduled air service along the Brazilian coast from Rio de Janeiro southwards to Porto Alegre and northwards to Natal in September of the same year.[56] Airlines belonging to the Condor Syndicate also contributed to the development of air transport in Colombia, Peru, Ecuador, and Argentina, where Condor provided important air links for the transportation of passengers and goods, thus contributing to the economic development of these Latin American countries.

Likewise, the Germans entered into a 10-year agreement with the Chinese Transport Ministry in February 1930 for the operation by Luft Hansa of a joint airline called Eurasia. From June 1931 it started operations on a route between Berlin, Shanghai, Che'ng-tu, and Hong Kong. Here too geopolitics ruled: neither aerial maps of China nor radio stations, repair shops, and airports in China existed—only the most basic landing strips. Several pilots got lost along the way because of navigational errors or were stranded for weeks after breakdowns, waiting for spare parts. By 1939, the Sino-European service extended over nearly 5,000 miles; Junkers aircraft had carried over 50,000 passengers and 1,000 tons of cargo.[57]

The political perspective also showed in the demonstration tour of the giant Dornier Do-X flying boat. This airplane that was the largest in the world at the time flew from Lake Constance, Germany, via Amsterdam and Lisbon to Bathurst (Banjul) in the British West African colony Gambia and then across the Atlantic to moor in Rio de Janeiro, Miami, and New York—a trip that took almost 10 months from November 5, 1930 to August 27, 1931.[58] The flight was intended to be a display of German aeronautical prowess, not unlike the scheduled summer flights to Brazil with the airship *Graf Zeppelin* from 1929, while the British still labored on the construction of their own passenger airships R-100 and R-101. What these flights had in common was that they were undertaken, with government subsidy, to counter growing American, British, and French influence in South America. Aviation was one of the high-profile manifestations of Germany's intentions to hold on to its considerable trading interests that followed from German emigrations in the latter part of the nineteenth century.[59] The political perspective also applied to the visit of the *Graf Zeppelin* to the Chicago World's Fair in 1933 and the (disastrous) flight of the *Hindenburg* to Lakehurst in 1937. After the Nazis effected a full nationalization of Luft Hansa in 1937, other highly publicized aeronautical ventures had similar goals, consistent with the general political plan of the Nazi government. German airmail operations across the North Atlantic in 1938 and 1939 were a case in point.[60] And while the British and the Americans were experimenting with transatlantic air services that used flying boats, Germany pointed the way ahead with the Focke Wulf Condor landplane that carried its highly visible swastika emblem nonstop from Berlin to New York.

Apart from prestige, such flights had covert military objectives too. In the late 1930s Germany used the Deutsche Luft Hansa to familiarize

military pilots with foreign air routes, airports, and navigational procedures. Their European colleagues remarked that familiar faces disappeared
from the crews of Luft Hansa aircraft landing at various ports of call.[61] In
the Far East, the Japanese did the same.

But aviation also served politics and prestige in a different fashion. As
airplanes became safer, royals and political leaders dared to risk using them
to enhance their profile. In May 1926 Britain's Prince of Wales, later King
Edward VIII, was perhaps the first royal to fly abroad (from Paris to London
in a Handley-Page W.10 airliner). Before long, flying became less unusual for
government officials and cabinet members. Yet the rising dictators in Italy
and Germany were, in the 1920s and 1930s, the first to use aircraft with
the specific intention to show how well in tune they were with the modern
world—as did the Communist Party in the Soviet Union. Indeed, aeronautics resided at the heart of Italy's fascist movement. In Benito Mussolini's
conception, aviation expressed the unique spirit of the 20th century, and
aviators represented the new, vigorous, vital, and adventurous Italy that he
wished to build. To acquire first-hand experience, Mussolini even took flying
lessons. After he came to power in 1922, he readily expanded the budget for
aeronautics. Expenses and public perception of the place of aviation within
fascism culminated in the spectacular, if risky, transatlantic flights undertaken by the Italian Minister for Aviation, Italo Balbo. In 1930 Balbo took
a whole squadron of Savoia Marchetti S55 flying boats to Rio de Janeiro;
in July 1933 he flew with another twenty-five planes to the Chicago World
Fair, returning to Rome via New York. Hundreds of thousands of people
flocked to watch these demonstrations of Italy's aeronautical prowess.[62] It
was no coincidence that Mussolini's two sons both became pilots and helped
promote their father's politics through displays of flying. Mussolini himself
traveled the country aboard aircraft whenever he made public appearances
and used the same mode of transportation for foreign visits.

A little more reluctant, Adolf Hitler followed this pattern. In 1932 he bid
for the German presidency, touring ninety-six cities in two fortnightly tours.
To do so, he had to overcome his fear of flying. Although he lost the election,
the new president, Paul von Hindenburg, appointed him chancellor a year
later, effectively setting the wheels in motion for the Nazis to take control of
the nation. Aviation was of crucial importance to the Nazis as a symbol of
Germany's technological prowess. To demonstrate this they chose Berlin's
Tempelhof Airport as the location for their first mass rally 3 months after
they had come to power. On Labor Day, May 1, 1933, an estimated 1.5
million people converged on Tempelhof to take part, making the airport and
all it stood for into a manifestation of Germany's new national ambitions.
The year after, the Nazi party organized their famous week-long Nuremberg
Rally from September 4 to 10, intended to celebrate Hitler's first year in office
and present the symbols of his "new Germany," the embodiment of Hitler's
message that a powerful nation was in the making. Something of the vigor

that the use of aircraft had on the crowds gathered at Nuremberg showed in the opening sequence of Leni Riefenstahl's illustrious propaganda film of the event, *Triumph des Willens* (Triumph of the Will). It showed Hitler flying over Nuremberg with his airplane casting a giant, symbolic, and imperious shadow over the land and over his marching troops. The next film shots provided forceful images of thousands of followers welcoming him at the airport, shouting rhythmically, "Sieg Heil."[63]

The Nazis used the same aeronautical symbols before a worldwide audience on the occasion of the 1936 Olympics in Berlin. Visitors were treated to a giant air show designed to impress foreign spectators with Germany's reborn aerial proficiency. Hitler himself continued to use airplanes on highly visible political and diplomatic missions, such as the September 1938 conference on the future of Czechoslovakia in Munich. It was the world's first top conference to which statesmen traveled by air and as such the start of a new trend in international diplomacy. No longer were important conferences the prerogative of professional diplomats "on the ground" but directly influenced and decided by the heads of their governments, flown in especially for the occasion. In Munich Hitler and Mussolini were joined by the French Prime Minister, Edouard Daladier, and the British Prime Minister, Neville Chamberlain, both arriving by air. In fact Chamberlain, already over seventy, made his very first airplane flight on September 23 to confer with the dictators. Six days later, on the evening of September 29, he and Hitler signed the agreement that Chamberlain described as "symbolic of the desire of our two peoples never to go to war with one another again." He returned to London for a hero's welcome after he and the German Fuhrer had had a further meeting on the morning of September 30 in which they agreed "that the question of Anglo-German relations is of the first importance for our two countries and for Europe." As he stepped off the plane at London's Heston Airport to deliver his famous "Peace for Our Time" speech later that day, he waved the "peace accord" they signed the evening before to a jubilant crowd.[64]

The Munich crisis demonstrated that by the end of the 1930s air travel had become a normal means of transportation for those dealing with international politics—not just to keep the peace but also to prepare for war. Direct contact between world leaders offered a chance for face-to-face conversations intended as shortcuts for diplomacy. It also enhanced the element of unpredictability in international politics. Pressures were brought to bear on those present at the negotiating table to reach immediate decisions. This was demonstrated when on the evening of August 22, 1939 the German Foreign Minister, Joachim von Ribbentrop, flew to Moscow where the Soviets were, at that time, involved in negotiations with the British and the French on a military pact. Von Ribbentrop carried with him Hitler's specific instructions to strike a nonaggression deal with Joseph Stalin. Von Ribbentrop had made it clear to the Soviets beforehand that time was of the essence

and that he would not be able to spend more than 24 hours. The two air-craft of the German party—with thirty in all, including advisers and official photographers, a group too large to fit into Von Ribbentrop's Focke Wulf FW200—arrived in Moscow on the 23rd. In Germany covert preparations for an imminent invasion of Poland on September 1 were already under way. The following day Von Ribbentrop and Soviet Foreign Minister Vyacheslav Molotov signed the bilateral nonaggression pact that Hitler wanted, which gave Germany a free hand to invade Poland the next week.[65]

After that the pace of world events dictated the use of air travel for political leaders. During the war, British Prime Minister Winston Churchill made extensive use of air transport, as did American President Franklin D. Roosevelt, who was probably the first statesman to have his personal plane, a Douglas VC-54C nicknamed *Sacred Cow* in which he flew to the Yalta conference to meet Churchill and Stalin in February 1945 and set the stage for the postwar world.

Business Versus Adventure

The fact that air transport became a factor in national prestige and interna-tional relations was something of a blessing in disguise for the air transport companies that sprung up in the aftermath of World War I. The earliest efforts in air transportation did not generally start out in the service of the nation. On the contrary, shared expectations of profits from the transporta-tion of mail, passengers, and cargo defined the venture capitalists who were present at the birth of this new transport mode. The rapid development of aviation technology and aeronautical industries during the war fostered prospects of an enormous technological potential under postwar conditions. At the same time the return to peace gave rise to the expectation of an upsurge of trade and travel. Aircraft had proved themselves during the war, grow-ing in reliability, effectiveness, and size. Now with unused aircraft around in abundance, the chances of developing a network of international air services looked promising. In several European countries corporate interests with an international angle to their businesses, like shipping lines, merchant banks, and oil and trading companies joined efforts to found airlines that would connect their various centers of business.

That Britain would be at the forefront of developments was hardly sur-prising. Peacetime conditions gave the Entente Cordiale between London and Paris a new dimension, and aerial crossings of the English Channel provided important gains in traveling time: it transformed a 12-hour land and sea journey into a 2½- to 3-hour flight. The peace negotiations in Paris, demobilization of troops, and a rekindling of old commercial ties brought a surge in demand for transportation and communication between the two capitals, both in the shape of telegrams and of letters and printed matter

such as newspapers and commercial printing. In the wake of these developments, entrepreneurs recognized a nascent demand for the transportation of people in the air. Venture capital joined forces with the larger British aviation firms, who were seeking out new markets for their products. Hence aircraft constructor and newspaper proprietor George Holt Thomas, who had founded the Aircraft Manufacturing Company (Airco) in 1914, with Geoffrey de Havilland as its principal designer, hastened to be the first to start an airline. Air Transport & Travel Limited (AT&T) started operating in August 1919 between London and Paris with the de Havilland aircraft that Airco built. AT&T was well ahead of a provisionary agreement between the two countries that was only signed 3 months later, on November 6. Its first flight carried a single passenger, a consignment of leather, a few grouse in baskets, and jars of Devonshire cream. A week later, aircraft constructor Sir Frederick Handley Page founded his own airline that would use machines designed in *his* factory: Handley Page Transport. In early 1920 Samuel Instone's shipping line followed and also began an air service to the European continent. Inevitably, given the prestige attached to aviation, the British operators were soon joined on the route by French companies, notably the Lignes Aériennes Farman, powered by the aircraft constructor of the same name and the Compagnie des Messageries Aériennes (Air Courier Service), which was backed by a conglomerate of French aviation firms that had struck it rich as a result of the war and included Blériot, Breguet, Caudron, Morane, Renault, and Saulnier. They were joined, on the cross-Channel route to London in May 1920, by the Dutch carrier KLM, which found its backing in commercial banks and trading firms.

Financial results, however, proved disastrous right from the start. Ruinous finances were a thing all pioneers of the airline industry shared. Before the Second World War, hardly any airline came anywhere near a financial breakeven point. Part of the reason for this was that most airlines had to operate in the area of tension between politics and commerce and were thus not always free to concentrate on flying the more profitable routes or operate the most cost-effective aircraft. Those airlines wishing to operate that most cost-effective equipment found they had to depreciate and replace their aircraft every 3 years.[66] Successes, such as there were, depended on the willingness of national governments to invest annually growing sums of money. In the late 1930s subsidies in Europe still ranged from around 10 percent for the most business conscious airlines, such as KLM and the Swedish ABA, to over 60 percent for those airlines that were closely linked to their respective governments' political objectives, such as Deutsche Luft Hansa, Air France, and the Italian national air carrier Ala Littoria.[67]

Even so, there were simply not enough passengers and goods to go by. As a consequence, daily services were offered only on the busiest routes. Despite the fact that the early airlines focused on the most interesting markets

and concentrated their efforts on offering rapid cross-Channel services to compete with the much slower ferry steamers, it proved impossible to keep all operators aloft. Traffic statistics for the cross-Channel route were only kept from 1923, when a modest 2,303 passengers were transported. The year 1929 was the first in which the number of passengers passed the 10,000 mark.[68] Worldwide, the airline industry transported just 639,000 people that year, plus 12.9 million tons of cargo. The average airline flight had but two passengers on board.[69] Such figures were sources of constant anxiety for airline managers. As early as September 1919 the executives of the early airlines flocked to The Hague to confer on how to minimize losses and avoid competition. They decided to found an International Air Traffic Association (IATA) to watch over their joint interests and contribute to an even distribution of passenger revenue on routes operated by more than one carrier. Passenger revenue had been negligible up to that point. Income of the early airlines depended almost exclusively on the carriage of goods and mail. Here the continental airlines were in a much more favorable position than their British competitors: all of them secured lucrative contracts from their respective postal authorities for the transportation of airmail, which gave them some sort of basic income. The British companies, by contrast, ran into serious financial difficulties before the year was out, as London kept its distance from the new mode of transport. All the same, by the end of 1920, companies were clamoring for financial support from their governments. In December of that year AT&T was the first to fold. After that, the government owned and paid up. Handley Page and Instone were saved in March 1921 through a provisional subsidy arrangement. KLM labored on, sponsored by the Dutch Post Office, burning corporate capital on every flight, until the government stepped in in 1923.

The French were in a rather better position to muster financial support. The government in Paris had been deeply involved in air transportation from the very start. Initial postwar efforts to get air transportation going depended on the specially created Service de la Navigation Aérienne (SNAé), a government organization that employed military personnel to undertake trial flights and develop new air routes. SNAé generally tested the waters with experimental services in 1918 and 1919. To do so, it was able to tap into the vast resource of some 10,000 aircraft the armed forces no longer needed since the signing of the Armistice Agreement in November 1918. Over 12,000 disbanded pilots were available to use them. The first SNAé services connected Paris with the northeastern cities in France that had been behind enemy lines in the past 4 years. But plans extended to a *much* grander scale. Even before 1918 was out, the first attempts were made to set up an air service between Toulouse and the Moroccan city of Rabat on the Atlantic shore, then under French suzerainty. Regular services, operated by Latécoère, started as early as September 1919. Military pilots and navigators reconnoitered the new routes over uncharted terrain.[70]

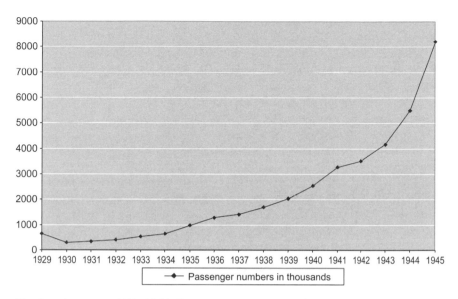

The Development of World Air Transport, 1929–1945. *Source:* ICAO figures.

If French national ambitions dictated the expansion of its air services in North Africa, the *real* combination of politics and adventure lay in the pursuit of aerial connections to the French sub-Saharan colonies, and across the South Atlantic to Brazil, Argentina, and Chile, where France wished to create a counterweight against the presence of the German Condor Syndicate. In May 1923 the first proving flight, operated by Latécoère, reached Dakar (Senegal). Despite astronomical costs, a prestigious transatlantic mail service (operating ex-navy destroyers while suitable aircraft were being developed in France) was initiated in 1928. It connected to the South American network of Aéropostale, the guise under which Latécoère operated from April 1927. In March of that year Aéropostale had begun flying in Brazil, expanding its airmail services to Argentina, Paraguay, Bolivia, Peru, Chile, and Venezuela in the following years.[71] The risks taken to operate these flights over the vast distances and rugged terrain of North Africa and South America were considerable, and reliability of services depended to a large extent upon the personal perseverance and endurance of Aéropostale's mail pilots. Pilots who came in late or damaged their equipment, were actually fined by their employers, according to Saint-Exupéry.[72] Their often highly adventurous exploits en route supplied material for three of Saint-Exupéry's famous aviation novels, heralding the idea that flying would contribute to a sense of global bonding between people scattered across the Earth.[73]

Politics and audacity also combined in Europe, where French carriers were particularly encouraged to establish international services that lent substance to the Parisian conviction that aviation would become an important part of postwar economic development and a means to extend French influence abroad. As early as 1920 aerial ties were established with Francophone and semi-Francophone countries, such as Belgium, Switzerland, and Romania. The latter was part of a Franco-Romanian joint venture agreed upon at the Trianon Peace Conference, where the Allies supervised the breakup of the Austrian-Hungarian empire in 1920. Under the leadership of the former chief of France's military aeronautics, Maurice Duval, the Compagnie Franco-Roumaine de Navigation Aérienne began its first, highly adventurous survey flights in April 1920. After the first aircraft touched down in Bucharest, the Romanian king, Ferdinand, held a royal reception in honor of the pilots.[74] Following the pattern of international train services, western and southern Europe were served as well.

The British, by contrast, were less interested in Europe and set out to connect the United Kingdom with its overseas territories. Accordingly, proving and survey flights aimed at establishing an aerial link between London and the *Jewel in the Crown*, British India, which was reached by Imperial Airways in 1929. Apart from that much effort was poured into an aerial connection to the British-held territories in Africa. In December 1919 the Air Ministry announced that the Royal Air Force had completed preliminary surveys and that a string of provisional airfields had been established along a projected East African route from Cairo (Egypt) to Cape Town (South Africa). Sponsored by the their government, two South African military pilots, Pierre van Ryneveld and Christopher Quintin-Brand, set out in February 1920 in a converted Vickers Vimy bomber and headed for Cape Town. After losing two aircraft in crashes along the way, they were knighted upon completion of their flight on March 20.

Bravery and panache again combined in November 1925 when Alan Cobham, Britain's most famous aviator of the era, made a survey flight to Cape Town and back in a single engine De Havilland DH-50 airplane, for which he was awarded the Air Force Cross upon his return in March 1926. Just over 3 months later, Cobham was off again, this time for a return flight all the way to Melbourne, Australia. Tens of thousands of people crowded the embankment of the Thames and cheered upon his return to London on October 1, 1926. It earned him a knighthood. Another year, and several more survey flights, went by before he set off again for Africa— this time in a flying boat with his wife, a cameraman, and a crew of three. His mission was to reconnoiter a possible water-based route for air services to Britain's African colonies and shore up support from colonial authorities for such a service.[75] Indeed, the first British scheduled air services to Africa would all use flying boats, as water based aircraft did not require the

expensive construction of a system of airfields. In February 1931 a regular airmail and passenger service was initiated from Cairo to Mwanza on the southern shore of Lake Victoria in Tanganyika (Tanzania), and on to Cape Town, South Africa, in 1932.[76] Landplanes came later, after the colonial governments in Uganda, Kenya, Tanganyika, and Southern Rhodesia (Zimbabwe) had completed the necessary ground infrastructure. But on a continent where intercolonial trade was scant and only the colonial upper classes had money for travel there was only limited local demand for scheduled air services. As far as demand existed, it was primarily geared towards freight and mail, although Imperial Airways probably carried some 15,000 to 16,000 passengers on its African services.[77] Nonetheless, Africa had "few roads, yet plenty of space to accomodate aircraft wheels, and lots of sky for wings," as Kenyan-born author and aviatrix Beryl Markham wrote in her famous memoir *West with the Night* (1942).[78] According to one source roughly 2 percent of Imperial's African passengers were going on safari, mostly to Kenya and Uganda, the more daring of them with flying adventurers such as the hunter Denys Finch Hatton.[79] For those traveling to remote destinations where aircraft could land, Wilson Airways of Nairobi (Kenya), East Africa's first indigenous airline, operated aerial taxi services. On the Imperial route between London and South Africa, traffic between intermediary points on the African continent remained limited. By the end of the 1930s, it accounted for no more than some 1,300 passengers per year. Most flew to, or out of, Lorenço Marques (Maputo) in the Portuguese colony Mozambique.[80]

Pampering the Rich, or Flying the Mail?

The state of aviation technology in the 1920s meant that discomfort ruled in air transport. Although advertisements and publicity photos often depicted accommodations on board as the flying equivalent of a luxury railway carriage, early passengers entered a stark environment. Passenger aircraft cabins were austere: in most aircraft seating consisted of lightweight wicker chairs instead of the advertised leather cushioned upholstery. Aircraft had insufficient heating, poor ventilation, and nothing for the passengers to eat or drink. Besides, during the flight the noise was deafening. Passengers were presented with earplugs to reduce headaches, but conversation on board was near impossible. Because aircraft usually cruised at an altitude of about 1,500 feet to enable pilots to compare aeronautical charts with landmarks on the ground, flights were bumpy, and many passengers suffered from airsickness. Most were relieved to disembark after landing. Six to seven hours on board was about the longest anyone could be expected to endure on a single day, and flights were seldom longer than that. In these pioneering air services crews and passengers shared, in one form or another, a sense of adventure. Early passengers could ask the pilot of their flight for an

official, signed certificate to prove to disbelievers they had actually flown. What worried airline executives and pilots alike was that aircraft had a hard time competing in speed with express trains, and flight crews were instructed to be careful so that passengers could not see railway lines for fear that they might watch an express train overtaking them. In 1921 the city-to-city time between Amsterdam and Paris was 6 hours 45 minutes by air, compared to 9 hours 30 minutes by train.[81] The journey by air was 30 percent faster than the one by rail but nonetheless took up most of a working day. If the flight arrived at all, that is, for in the early 1920s airlines had a hard time coping with navigational errors and mechanical breakdowns. No more than 50 percent of the flights arrived on time. In the first years of air transportation, winter conditions grounded the airlines altogether between November and March. In 1923 as many as one in three of KLM's flights had to be canceled, or discontinued because of the weather or mechanical problems en route. Air transport competed with difficulty against overnight rail services, and aircraft load factors were well below 50 percent on average. Some early business travelers remarked that the only advantage flying offered was that of a hotel bed over a bed in a railway carriage. An adage of the day ran, "If you have time to spare, go by air." As a result, annual passenger figures were disappointing, and although the airlines were already losing money on each flight, they saw themselves forced to reduce fares to attract customers. Between 1920 and 1923 the ticket price between Amsterdam and London dropped by more than half.[82]

Airports were as sober as the aircraft that served them. In the early 1920s most European airports looked like large pastures with a white circle in the middle and chalked arrows indicating the usual takeoff and landing directions. To the side of the landing ground one would find wooden sheds that served as hangars for overnight shelter of aircraft. More often than not commercial air transport depended on the use of military airfields. This posed serious limitations as military funding dried up after 1918. In Copenhagen, Denmark, for example, the military aerodrome of Christianshavns Fælled served civil aviation until 1925, when it was replaced by the purpose-constructed airport Kastrup. It had no meteorological service, no lighting, no radio, and did not even provide for a windsock.[83] Despite such minimal conditions, DDL, KLM, and the Deutsche Luft Reederei used it for their joint Copenhagen-Hamburg-Amsterdam service.[84] The next stop, Hamburg's Fuhlsbüttel Airport was similarly unequipped. In Amsterdam, services were not much better. Schiphol, Holland's airport, had been constructed in 1916 by the military as a reserve airstrip, which meant that facilities were minimal. A provisional log cabin served as passenger terminal, and baggage handling was done in a corner of the airport's only real hangar. Until the late 1920s the single road leading to Schiphol was unpaved. Such conditions were not uncommon. Airports were often difficult to get to for lack of public transportation and poor road accessibility. The idea of offering public

transport between the city and the airport was undeveloped, and bus services were limited to those maintained by the airlines themselves. Before 1940, Gatwick near London was the only airport that had a railway connection.

Terminal buildings of a more permanent nature and paved aprons only began to appear in the second half of the 1920s. Such facilities were constructed at London's Croydon, Berlin's Tempelhof, and Amsterdam's Schiphol. Other airports followed at a distance. Prague, situated near the geographical center of Europe and hence a logical hub for international flights, was a latecomer in this respect. In 1929, the Czechoslovakian Ministry of Public Works bought 108 hectares of land near Ruzyně, some 6 miles west of Prague, to replace the earlier use of rather basic facilities at the military aerodrome Kbely. To the side of the grass-covered trapezoid-shaped airfield, Ruzyně featured a paved platform with a modest passenger terminal.[85] Despite its geographic centrality in Europe, flights were few. Ruzyně was a typical European airport: it served less than ten aircraft a day.

In the early years of air transport Europe's only major airport was Le Bourget, Paris. Until 1934, when its position was overtaken by Berlin-Tempelhof, it was the busiest airport on the continent. It had been constructed in 1914 as a military airbase to serve in the aerial defense of Paris, but civil aviation was admitted there from February 1919. Its new function necessitated the aerodrome to be split into civil and military sections, with a more or less triangular landing field in between. For France, the Parisian airport signified much more than the capital's landing ground. Le Bourget was both an airport and a showcase of French aeronautical pride. From early on the government vigorously took charge of its development. In 1922 a monumental terminal building was opened that combined architectural reminiscences of an 18th century country estate with elements of 19th century railway station designs. The building was not just meant to meet the emerging demands in air transport but also to appeal to the spirit of the new age that aviation represented. In Paris, as elsewhere, the airport became a rallying spot to celebrate national—and international—achievements in aeronautics. Next to the terminal building five large hangars were erected with further edifices for the various branches of the airport's administration and structures for workshops and aircraft maintenance. But despite their monumental qualities, Le Bourget's buildings were short-lived. In 1936 a new terminal was constructed, built to the latest conceptions in modern architecture and design, incorporating a lot of concrete and glass. It linked avant-garde forms with functionality while appealing to the grand future of French aviation. An official brochure explained why neither costs nor labour had been spared in the construction:

> For the good name of France, the prestige of its aviation and of its administration, it is pleasing to give the air passenger, upon his first contact with our country, an impression of ability and of harmony. The architecture of the *aérogare* aims to achieve this end.[86]

The only structure to surpass this grandeur was that of Germany's Tempelhof Airport in Berlin, expanded by Hitler's Nazi regime in the second half of the 1930s with the singular intention to impress. A whole city quarter was demolished to enlarge the landing ground. Towards the end of 1935 a colossal terminal complex came under construction, the total costs of which amounted to 100 million marks (then US $40.3 million). It comprised of a curved terminal building, with an immense departure hall and adjacent aircraft hangars, extending to a total length of over half a mile and literally embracing the northwestern tip of the airfield. At the time of its completion, Tempelhof's size was unrivaled anywhere in the world. It served to express the function of aviation within the National Socialist society and embodied the desire to make Berlin the world's number one aeronautical center.[87]

But if passengers shunned away from the new means of transportation, despite investments in airport facilities and progressively more comfortable aircraft, how then did it achieve its growth? The answer to that question was, apart from government subsidies, freight and mail. Goods were obviously indifferent to the noisy environment in which they were transported. In the 1920s freight and mail carriage did much more for the growth of the European airline industry than passenger transportation. At Le Bourget, western Europe's main traffic hub, the volume of goods transported through the air increased seventeen times to 1.9 million kilos in 1929. More tellingly, the total value of goods moved through the airport went up 2,000-fold from 24 million in 1921 to over half a billion French francs in 1929 (then about $19.7 million).[88] Within a decade air transportation had taken its place as mover of high-value merchandise, such as electrical equipment, jewelry, and international gold shipments between central banks. Because of the low temperatures in the air, aircraft were also discovered as ideal vehicles for long-distance transportation of perishable goods, such as fresh flowers, fruits, and various delicacies like gourmet cheeses and ice cream. By the end of the 1920s specialized shops in Europe's capital cities were able to offer a far wider range of such foreign products than had hitherto been possible, although these goods were obviously expensive. Importers in foreign foodstuffs catered to the tastes of the affluent few. Nonetheless, for those who could afford to cast their glance beyond the immediate horizon, life acquired a more cosmopolitan touch. National postal authorities were quick to provide new services that fostered such changes. Recognizing the possibilities for speeding up international mail deliveries, they established a new category of international express mail: airmail. Holland, where the founding of KLM in October 1919 was linked to verbal and written assurances from the postmaster general to deliver mail contracts, was a case in point. The postal authorities subsidized KLM through excess payments for mail carriage on its routes to London, Scandinavia, and Paris, with the long-term goal of establishing a national airmail service to the Dutch East Indies (Indonesia).

Surcharges were levied from the public to send letters by air through the sale of special airmail stamps. Nonetheless, the actual time gained by using airmail was limited. The reach of the air transportation network was such that only a limited number of destinations could be served rapidly. Connections between the individual air services by various national airlines left much to be desired and letters and parcels spent valuable time stacked in transit at airports. A 1930 report drawn up under the auspices of the League of Nations complained about the lack of international coordination of flight schedules.[89] Only on shorter airmail routes, such as Paris–London, where international coordination was not an issue because each aircraft operated the complete route, mail services flourished. Their volume expanded by some 500 percent between 1923 and 1929.[90]

The growth of passenger traffic was rather slower than that. Here the big increases only came about in the 1930s, when aircraft had become more comfortable and dependable to travel in. On Europe's main routes, luxury aircraft such as Imperial Airway's Handley Page HP-42 and its French adversaries came into service in 1931. These offered more spacious cabins, better soundproofing, improved heating and ventilation, and seating arrangements that came a lot closer to railway comforts that airline advertisements had been promising for over a decade. Although tickets were still well above the price range for anyone but the very well-to-do, the improved conditions in the air, and on the ground at airports, plus a higher frequency of services began to draw a wider range of customers, including leisure travelers. By the mid 1930s air transport had made it possible for the happy few to spend a long weekend sightseeing in, say, Prague, and be back for work the next week.

Those who ventured furthest afield, were treated best, but then again they paid the most. In 1931 a one way ticket on Imperial Airways from London to Karachi cost as much as £162 (about $810 then), and although prices dropped to £81 in 1933 ($324 according to contemporary exchange rates), they were still equivalent of nearly half the annual salary of the average British craftsman, who brought home about two-thirds of a pound a day.[91] Therefore, customers were pampered. At the ticket office, special lightweight suitcases were provided by the airline. Airlines operating smaller aircraft, such as KLM and the French company Air Orient, both operating Fokker trimotors on the route to the Far East, used a weight limit of 20 kilos (42 lb.) per passenger. Bags were stowed under each passenger's seat. Excess baggage was liable to a surcharge of about $3 per kilo. At the airport airline officials personally welcomed intercontinental passengers. Passports, visas, and health certificates—on the Amsterdam–Batavia route passengers were required to have visas and health certificates valid for each of the seventeen countries over which their aircraft passed—were checked. Each departing flight was waved off by family and airline officials. On board intercontinental airliners the operators introduced such luxuries as adjustable,

reclining seats, headrests and footrests, and tray tables. Aircraft on these long-distance routes also incorporated a kitchenette, where crew members could prepare simple refreshments for their prized customers. Most often the flight engineer or the radio operator doubled as steward, serving coffee, tea, and sandwiches. Only the large flying boats of the second half of the 1930s offered additional, shiplike comforts like a bar, dining tables, and an observation deck. But for the *real* treats passengers had to wait until the end of the flying day when they were taken on guided sightseeing tours by the airline's local agent if they so desired and could be wined and dined at choice restaurants—if these were available of course, for refueling and refreshment stops could be in quite remote places. In the early 1930s Imperial Airways made approximately thirty stops on the London to Cape Town journey, a number that had been reduced to twenty-two by 1936. Outside Europe night flying was impracticable in the absence of navigational aids, and aircraft would therefore land well before darkness to spend the night on the ground. Notably, many Imperial Airways stops were off the beaten track. Although airlines took care to arrange flight schedules in such a way that their passengers could spend the night in places that offered some "suitable" (i.e., urban colonial) entourage for their affluent clientele, they sometimes had to resort to creating their own little "home away from home" in the shape of purpose-built guesthouses at isolated, inland colonial outposts, creating "little Englands" for its passengers and flying crew.[92]

A typical passenger was the Dutchman Joop Hardeman, a colonial administrator who flew from Amsterdam to Batavia from 3 to 10 May 1934 in a KLM Fokker F.XII trimotor. He kept a diary of his experience, which offers some idea of how passengers fared on the colonial routes. The first night stop, after some 8 hours of flying, was Budapest in Hungary. Here crew and passengers were lodged at the luxury art deco Hotel Gellért, famous for its stunning hot water baths. At sunset, KLM arranged for a sightseeing tour by taxi, after which the crew and passengers had a sumptuous dinner at a good restaurant. The next morning, the journey went on to Cairo (Egypt). By that time Hardeman, tired of the long hours of noise and of the turbulence, was already losing interest in the exotic surroundings that Egypt's capital offered. He declined the sightseeing tour and went to bed early to be well rested for next day's flight to Basra (Iraq), where the night was spent at the purpose-built Imperial Airways' hostel at the airport. From there, the journey led to Jodhpur, India, where the weary traveler again went to bed early. By 1934, KLM boarded its passengers at the brand-new Jodhpur State Hotel, built, with no expenses spared, like an exotic palace by the Maharajah Umaid Singh Bahadur. Before passengers were carried on the route, KLM's mail pilots were occasionally wined and dined by the Maharajah—himself a pilot and aviation enthusiast—at his palace. Yet to Hardeman the main attraction of the Jodhpur State Hotel was that it served European-style meals. Travelers who were not so particular about

their food and drink were prone to suffer from intestinal problems, which were treated with medicine from the onboard cabinet. Only by the time that the aircraft reached its next night stop, Calcutta, had Hardeman adjusted to the noisy and turbulence-prone conditions on board, and actually enjoyed the 62°F (18°C) cabin temperature brought about by cruising at an altitude of about 11,000 feet. He was happy to be treated on another sightseeing tour by KLM's local representative, who served as his guide. Nonetheless, the long traveling hours—waking up around 4 A.M. when the aircraft took off at first light, only to stop between 5 and 6 P.M. when the light faded—took their toll on the next leg to Bangkok (Thailand), where Hardeman again went to bed as soon as he arrived. Next day's flight ended at Singapore, the last night stop before the final destination, Batavia, and the location of another sumptuous dinner. On the final leg of the flight, the pilot made a special detour because Hardeman wanted to see the Krakatau Volcano off the coast of Java. After all, instructions were to please the passenger, if at all possible.[93] For flying, especially on these intercontinental routes, was not all about travel; it was also a tourist experience. The aerial panoramas were a part of the imperial geography which no traveler could escape. From 1935 on, KLM distributed an illustrated guidebook for its international passengers on the Amsterdam–Batavia route. It held descriptions of the tourist highlights along the route, gave an impression of local cultures and habits, and offered photographs, city maps for late-afternoon sightseeing, and route maps to track the aircraft's progress during the flight.[94]

But who were these passengers, flying across the globe? In the 1930s, when intercontinental passenger air transport first became possible, most were senior civil servants and business executives. Together they made up over 70 percent of all European airline passengers. Some 20 percent may have been traveling for pleasure, whereas urgent private journeys and unknown travel motives accounted for 5 percent each.[95] Civil servants traveled in the process of increasing control from the motherland over the colonial administration. In the past senior officials had also traveled, but as the sea voyage took about 2 to 3 weeks between Europe and southern Africa, 3 to 4 weeks to India, and over a month to reach southeast Asia and Australia, it was inefficient to send out personnel to assist in solving problems at hand. Now people could travel the distance in a week or less. This option did not only extend the span of control of the colonial administrators, but it also increased the span of control of the executive within large international corporations, such as the oil industry, the rubber business, coffee and tea traders, etc. Such businesses had hitherto known two separate management levels: one at the (European) headquarters and another at a relatively autonomous local management at the production spot. Although the local managements had already been losing influence after the introduction of the telegraph and the telephone, air travel brought an even more serious inroad into their

authority: managers and specialist engineers could now be "flown in" rapidly to assist in dealing with crises or general organizational matters. Face-to-face meetings could be held where written exchanges failed to produce results. At the highest corporate levels the preception of distance began to change.

A smaller, nonetheless distinctive category of travelers, who were very much on the backs of colonial authorities' heads when supporting airline ventures, was made up of military personnel. In fact, one of the main reasons why Dutch interests founded a separate, colonial airline in the Netherlands East Indies, the Koninklijke Nederlandsch-Indische Luchtvaart Maatschappij (KNILM) in 1927, was to have a troop carrying possibility in the case of anticolonial uprisings, such as those that had taken place in several areas of Java and Sumatra late in 1926. British and French thinking operated along the same lines. Not just to the tropics but in the tropics too, flying was a "white man's business." KNILM kept figures on the ethnic background of its passengers. On average, 90–95 percent of its passengers were Europeans; 5–7 percent people of Chinese extraction, and only about 1 percent Indonesians.[96] The latter appeared sensitive to the Indonesian explanation of the acronym KNILM: "Kalo Naik Ini Lekas Mati" ("enter into one of these, and you will soon be dead."). Although the Dutch tried to compensate for this by organizing traditional ceremonial baptisms for the KNILM aircraft, the division of passenger numbers remained what it was. Not just in Indonesia but throughout Asia and Africa the airplane was the colonizer's new travel instrument, an agent of European vigor and power. It offered important time savings too compared to surface transport modes and carried people away from tropical heat and dust. By the 1930s aircraft operated at an altitude between 10,000 and 13,000 feet. Passengers, in their customary light colonial wear, were even cold on board and needed coats and blankets to keep warm (or had the heater turned on), perhaps partly due to the reduced oxygen levels that made them feel light in their heads.[97]

Nonetheless, fostered by its predominantly white affluent clientele the airplane became accepted globally as a travel mode—harbinger of both good and evil, as in the all-time classic movie *Casablanca*. The story was set in December 1941 in Casablanca, French Morocco, where the (Nazi-friendly) Vichy government maintained an uneven balance with German occupational authorities. It centered on refugees whose only option to reach the neutral Portugal and board Pan American's transatlantic *Clipper* service to the safety of the United States was to get a passage on a flight to Lisbon. On the other hand the airplane also brought members of the German secret police into the plot. The film forcefully portrayed the airplane as a recurrent symbol of hope for refugees to escape the horrors of war and persecution. As if to prove just how much air transport had become embedded in modern society—recognizable even for a wide cinema audience—the final scene of the movie

was set at the airport. On the apron the male and female protagonists, Rick Blaine (Humprey Bogart) and Ilsa Lund (Ingrid Bergman) parted as Lund's Lockheed Electra readied itself for takeoff, forever separating the two loved ones—a theme that would become recurrent in postwar films when the aircraft gradually became an accepted mode for long-distance travel.

Technology: Air Transport around the World, 1945–1961

In the cockpit the flight crew refuses to believe the eccentric scientist Theodore Honey. Yet he insists that the aircraft with which they have just crossed the North Atlantic to Gander, Newfoundland, is absolutely unsafe to fly any further and must be grounded immediately because of critical metal fatigue in the tail. Honey knows all about it; he has been working on the phenomenon in his laboratory for many months. In despair he takes a step towards the pilot's seat and pulls the undercarriage lever to the *up* position, crying, "If you won't ground this aircraft, I will."[1]

Four years after the release of the film *No Highway in the Sky* in 1951, the premonitions of aeronautical engineer-turned-novelist Nevil Shute Norway about the possibility of metallurgical problems wreaking havoc in modern airliners became headline news. The year before a de Havilland Comet, the world's first operational jet airliner and the pride of the British aircraft industry, crashed into the Mediterranean near the Island of Elba en route to London on January 10, 1954. It was already the sixth Comet to go down since its introduction into airline service in May 1952. The aircraft's experimental cockpit voice recorder revealed that the accident happened without warning. It silenced the pilots in mid-sentence. There were no survivors among the crew of six and twenty-nine passengers. In response, the opera-
, British Overseas Airways Corporation (BOAC), decided to ground its
et fleet temporarily, pending inquiries and possible modifications. On
h 23, the Comets returned to airline service. Sixteen days later, on April
e was another crash, under similar conditions to the Elba disaster. It
avoidable that the Comet's certificate of airworthiness had to be
vn. To help determine the causes of the accidents, the decision was

taken to test the cabin of a sister aircraft to destruction and try and make a complete reconstruction from the debris of the aircraft that crashed at Elba, dredged up from the bottom of the sea. From this it became evident in 1955 that the fatal accidents were due to metal fatigue. The frequent pressurization of the aircraft's cabin combined with the very high altitude at which the Comets flew to enable their jet engines to operate efficiently—over 35,000 feet, about twice the cruising altitude for piston airliners—caused small cracks around the rivet holes on the edge of the cabin windows that went undetected until it was too late and caused a fatal explosive decompression.[2] The accident revealed the hitherto incomplete understanding of the effects of cyclical stress loads on aluminum alloys used in aircraft construction and triggered a flood of new research aimed at preventing accidents like these from happening.[3] Clearly, the introduction of new technologies in commercial aircraft was not without its hazards, and it was probably a good thing that the forecast vented by the International Civil Aviation Organization (ICAO) in its 1956 outlook—to expect nuclear powered aircraft in 20 years' time—never materialized.[4] Indeed, despite gruesome accidents from which few airlines were spared in the 1940s and 1950s, flying was on its way to become the safest travel mode.

Technological Leaps

Between 1939 and 1945 the technological development in aeronautical engineering had been tremendous. The aircraft of 1945 flew faster, higher, and further and carried more payload doing so. Such developments could primarily be traced back to improvements in engine technology. Over the 6 years of the world conflict, average airplane engine horsepower doubled. Besides, new, revolutionary types of engines that had hardly progressed beyond the test bed phase in the last years of peace became operational in the course of the war: turbine jets that generated much more power than the more traditional engines that used pistons and propellers to transform explosive combustion into movement. Of all the warring nations, the Germans progressed most rapidly, combining these new types of engines with fighter and bomber aircraft of revolutionary designs that were years ahead of their nearest technological competitors, the British. Other major technological innovations were less visible but just as important. They included the development of new lightweight and fiber-reinforced plastic aircraft material synthetic glues for metal bonding, flush riveting, radio detection and raing (radar) for tracking aircraft in flight, improved radio-based navigati equipment, landing aids for operations under darkness or in bad we and pressurized cabins for aircraft operating at high altitudes.

The large-scale use of aircraft in the war meant that aviation specific setting of airfields and faraway places known only by nan

general public. Now aircraft were "everywhere," bringing developments in technology home even to ordinary men, women, and children on the ground—and with unprecedented violence. Long before August 6, 1945, when three American B-29 bombers appeared in the morning skies over Hiroshima, aviation lost its innocence. At 8:16 that morning one of the aircraft released its load that would in the next minute destroy the Japanese city—and change the world. But the signs of cataclysm had already been "in the air" for over a decade. In the 1930s military dogma accepted that the devastation from aircraft could hardly be prevented in a war. An adage of the day went, "The bomber will always get through."[5] And through they did get. Even before the big onslaught of global war began with the German air attacks on Warsaw, Poland, in September 1939, cities across the world collapsed into rubble because of aerial bombardment, from Guernica in Spain to Nanking in China. After that the technology of aviation was unleashed on an hitherto unimaginable scale in efforts primarily aimed to destroy morale. This worked against the Dutch when the city center of Rotterdam was laid to waste on May 14, 1940: the nation surrendered to Hitler's armies the next day to prevent further civilian bloodshed. It worked much less against the British in Coventry, Birmingham, and London in the latter months of 1940 and in 1941 and equally less against the Germans and the Japanese, despite monstrous atrocities from the large-scale use of incendiary bombs that burned complete cities, and their inhabitants, while suffocating survivors in their air raid shelters.[6]

When the war ended in 1945 aviation faced new challenges. The material consequences of the global conflict were immense. In those regions touched by the fighting and military occupation, the surviving population was impoverished. Houses and towns had been damaged or destroyed, agricultural areas devastated, and livestock decimated. In Europe industry was virtually paralyzed as a result of the destruction of prime installations and looting. The transport infrastructure lay in ruins. Governments the world over realized that they needed aircraft to create something of a provisionary means of transportation at a time when roads, bridges, railway depots, and canals still had to be rebuilt. International trade was considered an important contributor to reconstruction, and it depended on infrastructure. Therefore air transport received attention at an early stage. Suddenly reliable transport aircraft were very much in demand. For immediate use hundreds of military cargo aircraft were converted for civil service. Where there was a lack of these, or the means to acquire them for scarcity of dollar-convertible currency, bomber aircraft were converted as well. Early British, French, and Italian intercontinental air services operated civil versions of the Lancaster and Halifax bombers and Sunderland anti-submarine flying boats. In 1948 the number of aircraft in airline use was up 83 percent over that of the last year of peace, 1938. By the end of that year world airline inventory consisted of 3,646 aircraft, of which some 840 were four engine types, most of

them converted American transports (390 in all). The majority of these large aircraft found their home base in the United States (444 of them) and in Europe (270). Only a mere forty-seven were on African, Asian, or Australian registries. But the most numerous types in airline service were two engine planes (2,459), primarily the ubiquitous Douglas Dakota (1,653 units).[7]

The largest aircraft, such as the Lockheed Constellation, carried the most visible signs of the various technological leaps of the past war years. Building on Allied wartime experiences with long distance flying and transoceanic aerial navigation, the new generation of aircraft was put to use to create a worldwide network of air services. To demonstrate the enormous potential of aircraft, an American Boeing B-50 bomber flew nonstop around the world in 94 hours and 1 minute in February 1949. To facilitate scheduled intercontinental services nine countries, among them the United States, Britain, France, Belgium, and the Netherlands, signed an international agreement in London in 1946 to operate a series of weather stations to set up a new civilian air route across the North Atlantic—a route that was understood as vital to postwar economic development.

The new political, economic, and technological conditions that came into existence from 1945 brought profound changes to air transport. For the purpose of reconstruction the countries liberated by the Western Allies looked towards the United States for goods and guidance. The attention was most welcome, particularly to the American aviation industry, where manufacturers lost money in 1946 as sales dropped a precipitous 91.5 percent from the 1944 wartime peak.[8] Even before America's Marshall Plan for the economic reconstruction of Europe came into effect in 1948, the market for air transport to and from the United States showed very rapid growth. In 1946, a total of 104,980 people flew across the Atlantic; 253,000 in 1948. Over the same period the total world passenger number increased by 35 percent.[9]

In western Europe the economy picked up after 1948. Agriculture and industry set new production records year after year, and international trade prospered. Through the 1950s average disposable incomes increased, and consumer spending grew with it. Modern luxury commodities such as refrigerators, washing machines, and televisions entered European households. The number of cars went up, with the ensuing increase in people's mobility. World trade as such expanded in the 1950s. The total value more than doubled.[10] Economic growth manifested itself in a growing demand for transportation, air transportation included. World passenger numbers went up by one-third from 15.5 million in 1946 to 20.9 million in 1948, and then climbed steeply to 97 million in 1959 and 111 million in 1961. Growth figures averaged 15 percent annually.[11] As a consequence, aircraft sizes needed to grow, emphasizing the need to incorporate the latest technological innovations. While the average size of short-range aircraft doubled between 1945 and 1955, the size of long-range types nearly tripled. However, on the technological level, developments in the United States and in

Europe were markedly different. If American constructors went for increased economy through size, western European firms went for economy through innovations in engine technology. Both Britain and France had their own jet airliner projects, competing against indigenous designs for innovative turbine-driven propeller aircraft.

The European aviation industry relied on exports for its survival against American competition. Hence policymakers valued commercial opportunities. For Britain, its lead in jet technology offered a logical contribution to foreign earnings of hard currency, much needed for reconstruction. Export opportunities were in abundance, since even major American firms had been competing for years for the use of British research on jet engines. Faced with serious financial shortages, Clement Attlee's Labour government liberalized aviation exports in November 1945. The government authorized the sale of manufacturing licenses as well, so that Britain's trading partners could pay for the right to produce British aircraft and engines in their own factories. Suddenly highly sophisticated jet engines could be sold abroad with only minimal government supervision, the assumption being that they would soon be rendered obsolete by imminent new inventions. By the spring of 1946, London's jet manufacturers had signed contracts with the United States, France, (Nationalist) China, Canada, Switzerland, and other nations. The licenses for the Armstrong-Siddeley Sapphire and Bristol Olympus jet engines were sold to Curtiss-Wright in the United States, the rights to the de Havilland Goblin to General Electric.[12]

Then, in May 1946, the Soviets made Rolls Royce an offer for several of the company's best jet engines, including the Nene and the Derwent, and for a manufacturing license to mass-produce these engines in the U.S.S.R. The request came as a complete surprise in London, where security issues of such a sale were discussed, but in the end the cabinet decided in favor of the remuneration of the sale and the possibility for Britain to obtain the status of preferred supplier of engines to the Soviets. The government regarded permission for the sale as a demonstration of trust between West and East, and Attlee personally brokered a compromise within his government. In an astounding act of political naïveté, it was decided to allow the export of complete engines to Moscow, although London denied the sale of a manufacturing license. Attlee questioned the ability of Soviet designers to "reverse-engineer" the jet engine technology as long as the design specifications remained in Britain. Much to the dismay of the Americans Rolls Royce exported ten each of the Nene and Derwent engines to the Soviet Union in October 1946. A second shipment followed in the spring of 1947, bringing the total number of Rolls Royce jet engines exported to the Soviet Union to fifty-five before Britain's export policy was revoked in the fall of 1947 as a result of rising Cold War tensions.[13]

These sales had repercussions in the field of jet technology that became apparent when the Soviets launched their MiG-15 jet fighter in 1948, the

engine of which was based on reverse-engineered Rolls Royce Nene technology. Thus warned, sales of the Rolls Royce Avon powered Comet-II airliner were hampered by security restrictions. These regarded the technology of its axial flow jet engines, a field in which Britain was years ahead of the rest of the world. For fear of espionage—as the Avon engine was also used in the Hawker Hunter fighter then under development for the RAF—and possible Soviet copying of the technology involved, foreign operators were forbidden to fly over Soviet-held territory and required to have all maintenance done by British engineers, at British facilities. Fearful lest British exports would contribute to bring the United States within reach of Soviet jet bombers, American officials even moved to thwart De Havilland's sales. In August 1953, less than a year before the first Avon-powered Comet IIs were scheduled for export, American diplomats demanded the right to approve or veto their sale. By way of justification, the U.S. State Department claimed that the axial-flow technology was a joint Anglo-American invention and insisted that such combined-field products could only be exported with both countries' consent. References were made to Britain's dependence on America for the funding of its reconstruction efforts. This was, of course, not acceptable in London, but serious consequences for Anglo-American relations did not follow, as the repeated Comet crashes put the British jetliner program on hold. By the time the problems with the Comet design had been straightened out, the axial-flow engine technology had already proliferated and found use in Soviet military and civil aircraft.[14] To the surprise of many in the West, and even in the U.S.S.R. itself, the Soviets won the race for the reintroduction of jet aircraft in airline service. Their Tupolev Tu-104 jet had been so deeply shrouded in secrecy that even the Kharkov State Aircraft Manufacturing Company in the Ukraine that was designated for series production in 1954 had no prior knowledge of its existence.[15] Aeroflot put the Tu-104 into scheduled service in September 1956, 2 years ahead of the redesigned British Comet.

Of course not all problems in air transport technology had a link to East-West relations. More than a few were lodged in normal practices of industrial competition and government efforts to protect domestic economic interests. An example was the British Vickers Viscount airliner. After the introduction of turbine-driven propeller engines in the Viscount in 1950, it took London years to breach American protectionism and obtain import licenses for these aircraft in the United States.[16] By that time the Europeans were losing their lead in technology to the Americans.

The prime example of this was the combination of jet engines and a jump in aircraft size by the end of the 1950s. In October 1958 Pan American was the first airline to operate the Boeing 707, a commercial jet derived from a flying kerosene tanker developed under the umbrella of America's strategic deterrent programs. The Boeing was followed a year later by the competing Douglas DC-8. These aircraft offered a very much larger

seating capacity than anything before—in fact twice the size of their piston engine predecessors—and a much longer range. After a decade of high
traffic growth and forecasts of continuation of this trend, airlines the world
over scrambled to acquire these new machines. The World Bank played a
significant role in this process, assisting both industrialized nations, such
as Australia, and developing nations, like India, in financing the expensive
jets. Air India determined that three Boeing 707s would have the same service capacity as ten Super Constellations. A loan from the World Bank for
$5.6 million enabled the airline to buy three Boeings in March 1957. The
first was received in February 1960. They enabled Air India to extend its
Bombay to London service to New York, which represented a major step in
the airline's expansion into new markets and confirmed India's place on the
world stage.[17] The economy and carrying capacity of jet aircraft, and their
technological attraction to the traveling public, made them the precursors
of a revolutionary development in transportation that was to have a lasting
effect on the world: mass air travel.

The Right to Fly

The construction and the use of tens of thousands of airplanes during the
war brought unprecedented growth to the aviation industry, especially in
the United States. Between 1939 and 1945 the aeronautics industry came to
belong to the core of the core of America's economic activity. This reflected
in government policy towards postwar commercial aviation, particularly in
diplomatic initiatives towards a new, decidedly liberal regime for international air transport. There was some urgency to this, as events in 1919 had
brought to light that negotiations concerning "the right to fly" could easily
produce results that ran counter to the interests of an unimpeded development of air transportation. Thus far, the United States had remained aloof
from the legal structures of the Paris Convention that governed international air transport, but with transatlantic air services on the horizon a new,
a worldwide treaty was called for.

In 1944 American foreign policy identified the importance of establishing
such a treaty as it would serve the interests of American airline companies
seeking to open international routes. This would also boost the sales potential for the American aircraft industry, which had expanded dramatically
during the war. With this in mind, Washington invited the governments involved in the process of forming the United Nations to convene in Chicago
that November. Thus, for the second time around, the wheels were set in motion to develop a legal framework ahead of international air transportation
itself.[18]

The British, traditionally the protagonists of liberalism even though this
did not always show in actual conduct of policy, were skeptical. London

wished to avoid American dominance in postwar international aviation. Hence it was not surprising that Britain now cloaked itself as a supporter of regulation, pointing to Washington's long-standing support of its *chosen instrument* of international air policy, Pan American Airways, as evidence of American intent to dominate among the clouds.[19] To counter this, London suggested the creation of a supranational agency that would oversee the operation of vital air routes around the world and make sure that all nations were allotted their fair share of the traffic.[20] Liberalism thus stood against supranationality. What united these extremes was a departure from the principle of absolute sovereignty that had hitherto ruled international aviation. Refusing to consider such a departure, the Soviet Union withdrew from the conference before it had even begun.

As expected, the two contradictory approaches collided in Chicago, where the Americans held the strongest position because they contributed most to the Allied war effort. Nonetheless the British delegates did manage to keep the dreaded freedom of air transport out of the treaty that was signed, after a month of negotiations, as the Chicago Convention on International Civil Aviation on December 7, 1944. It established a set of basic principles underlying international air transport worldwide. Somewhat surprisingly, given the American and British opening gambits, the treaty reaffirmed the full and exclusive national sovereignty in the air for the member states. International scheduled air services remained subject to the express previous consent of the state operated into. Only aircraft which were operated outside the scope of international scheduled services, such as charter flights, would be admissible without prior bilateral settlement of landing rights, on an ad hoc basis. The conference did, however, also yield the International Air Transit Agreement, which acknowledged the rights of innocent passage and of technical stops (for refueling purposes and the like) for aircraft engaged in scheduled international services. American emphasis on liberalism also produced a second settlement: the International Air Transport Agreement. It provided for the exchange of commercial freedom to operate scheduled international air services between signatory states. Yet this agreement was only signed by the United States and a handful of other countries. The International Air Transport Agreement defined five so-called Freedoms of the Air. The "First Freedom" held the privilege to fly over a state without landing. The "Second Freedom" allowed for technical stops. The "Third Freedom" and "Fourth Freedom" recognized the privilege to transport passengers, mail, and cargo from the home country to another country, and vice versa. The principal interests of airlines to pick up traffic en route to a final destination (the "Fifth Freedom") were also defined.[21] To supervise these rules and set common technical standards for international air transportation in the interest of safety and efficient operation, the Chicago Convention installed an intergovernmental organization, under the umbrella of the United Nations: the International Civil Aviation

Organization (ICAO). Twenty-six nations ratified the treaty that installed ICAO in 1947.

As the treaty solidified the links between national states and air transportation, international diplomatic problems were not long in coming. To most governments the political and economic value of air services was self-evident, as was the need to secure operating rights for their national airlines. Before 1945 was out, the leading aviation countries expanded their diplomatic corps with the new figure of the air attaché—a civil servant specifically appointed to negotiate and safeguard air transport rights. Theirs was not an easy task, for international tensions and restrictionism were on the rise. The United States set the tone when Washington abandoned liberalism and returned to the prewar custom of bilateral negotiations over the exchange of landing rights. In February 1946 Washington and London reached an accord on a standard formula for such bilateral exchanges: the Bermuda Agreement.[22] It devised to balance capacity offered by their respective airlines on the contracted routes. But what was paramount to Britain, which at that time faced a commercial backlog compared to its American competitors, was that the Bermuda Agreement provided for ticket prices to be determined between the two governments concerned. With this "Bermuda Formula" as the basis for future policy, the United States announced to withdraw from the International Air Transport Agreement in July 1946—thus effectively ending the brief spell of liberalism in air transportation.

The result of these developments was a restrictive international regime under which everything was forbidden, unless express previous agreement had been reached between governments. In many cases, national politics and commerce were mutually exclusive, and airlines were only able to operate those international routes that their national government had been willing and able to negotiate for them in bilateral civil air transport agreements. From the late 1940s it became increasingly difficult to arrive at such agreements. Small countries especially ran into serious diplomatic skirmishes in attempts to secure foreign traffic rights.[23] Despite such problems, the airline business developed from a predominantly short-haul industry, focusing on services of up to 500 miles or so, to a global industry that concentrated on long-haul routes. In fact, the 1940s and 1950s saw a race between the world's leading air carriers to be the first to offer, and then to have the best, round-the-world service. Supported by a combination of U.S. aviation policy and superior aircraft technology, Pan American, and to a lesser extent TWA (Trans World Airlines), came out as winners of this global contest. Their international route patterns followed the spread of America's increasingly global political and strategic military influence and presence, yet also aimed to develop new markets. Small wonder then that the American empire after 1945 has been charcterised as an air empire.[24]

Problems over landing rights developed everywhere, but particularly so in Europe, where the postwar reality of the newly established Soviet sphere of

influence posed severe limitations on aviation. With the descent of the Iron Curtain air services between western and eastern Europe became embroiled in political controversies. Although services did not cease to exist—in the summer of 1945 Pan American even hoped that Prague could feature as a staging point on its projected round-the-world route—they were very few in number. In 1946 the countries in the Soviet sphere began to withdraw from negotiations on air transport services with Western nations. In October of that year Pan Am was forced to abandon its services to Prague and elsewhere in eastern Europe on express instructions from Washington.[25] Nonetheless, aviation discussions were kept going until 1948, when the Soviet blockade of Berlin caused a crisis in East-West relations. The Western response was an airlift on an unprecedented scale. For the first time in history, air transportation became a crucial factor in global power play. Until May 12, 1949, Allied aircraft transported over 2.3 million tons of supplies to the besieged city.[26] Berlin was secured to the western alliance, but political relations across the Iron Curtain declined to freezing point. The arrival of Marshall Aid for America's western European allies later in that year solidified the division of Europe and made all prospects of an air transport agreement with the Soviets evaporate.

In keeping with President Truman's Containment Policy to isolate the Soviet Union and its satellite states, America actively discouraged its European allies from providing air services to the East. As if to confirm American warnings, Soviet fighter aircraft actually shot down several commercial airliners. On April 29, 1952, an Air France DC-4 received no less than eighty-nine hits from bullets fired by a Soviet MiG-15 when the airliner allegedly deviated from its course to Berlin-Tempelhof. Two passengers were injured. Two months later a Swedish Dakota disappeared over the Baltic Sea with eight people on board; even the search plane was shot down by Soviet fighter aircraft. In June 1954 Soviet fighters stationed in Hungary killed two people on board a Sabena DC-3 near the Austrian-Yugoslav border (in present-day Slovenia), and a year later an Israeli Constellation en route from Vienna to Tel Aviv was shot down by Bulgarian jets after it strayed off course. All fifty-eight occupants on board were killed.[27] The tragic incident led to a UN resolution, adopted by the General Assembly, that called upon nations not to resort to immediate military action if civil aircraft accidentally strayed off course.[28]

Against this background Western governments were advised to reject overtures from Soviet bloc nations in aviation. The Americans particularly feared that the Czechoslovak airline CSA could serve as a vehicle to gather intelligence, facilitate the placement of agents in the West, and provide communist parties in western Europe with a rapid link to Moscow.[29] In 1950 and 1951 Allied obstructions grounded Czech air services to Western capitals to a halt. Not before de-Stalinization in the second half of the 1950s did services between West and East again become politically viable. KLM, Sabena, Swissair,

and SAS were the only airlines to defy American pressures.[30] Their flights to Czechoslovakia meant that Prague stood as practically the sole gateway for air travelers between West and East. Western passengers traveling to destinations behind the Iron Curtain were required to change planes there as the Soviets did not allow Western airlines to operate flights beyond Prague. Changing planes there was a grim experience as armed soldiers stood guard over aircraft and passengers from the West. Even so, the situation was a precarious one—and easily disrupted. When the American propaganda station Radio Free Europe, located in Munich, Germany, started floating balloons with Western agitprop across the Czech border, the Czechs temporarily curtailed Western air services in January 1956.[31] Politics and market combined in the separate development of air services on both sides of the Iron Curtain, with close government involvement as the common denominator.

Both in the East and in the West aviation featured as one of the spearheads in economic and political cooperation. In eastern Europe airlines were essentially considered as service branches of the government, providing transport for officials and generally speeding up governance as such. Hence the role of airlines in building the structures of economic and political cooperation between the nations of the socialist bloc came as natural.[32] From January 1949 the development of routes between member states of the Council for Mutual Economic Assistance (Comecon) gave evidence of political, rather than economic incentives for air services. Contrary to western Europe, where commerce demanded daily flights, two to three services a week sufficed to connect the capitals of eastern Europe.

In the Soviet Union itself domestic services took centerstage. The air transport network was expanded annually, with emphasis on connections between Moscow and eastern Siberia and the central Asian republics.[33] In 1951 Soviet authorities claimed that the internal air network surpassed that of the United States in length. Soviet airline services beyond the Iron Curtain only came about in the second half of the 1950s, when party leader Nikita Khrushchev's policy of de-Stalinization allowed for increased contacts with the West. Agreements were reached with France and the Scandinavian countries on the exchange of landing rights. In 1957 Aeroflot jets started flying to Paris via Prague and to Copenhagen (Denmark) via Helsinki (Finland). As a result of treaties on economic cooperation with India, Burma, and Afghanistan drawn up in December 1955, Aeroflot also initated a service to Kabul (Afghanistan) and New Delhi (India) and on to Australia. At the end of the decade, Aeroflot had by some counts even become the world's largest airline, its seat mileage (though not its number of passengers) surpassing that of the second largest carrier, America's United Airlines, by about 25 percent.

In western Europe too, air transport featured big on the agenda for closer political and economic cooperation. Initially, the reinstatement of international air services preceded this process. The second half of the 1940s saw

a rapid expansion on the number of air services in Europe—and from Europe across the globe. In 1945 and 1946, connections with London, still the center of the Allied decision-making process, were of vital importance for politicians and ministers returning to their native countries from wartime exile in Britain. From the release of the British airports for civil transport in February 1946 London was the most frequented destination in the European air network. All the same, even the densest air route—that between London and Paris—carried only 10 percent of the surface traffic between the two capitals.[34]

By 1950 air transport even became part of a wider process towards western European integration. France and Italy signed a customs union agreement to this effect in March. Under the auspices of the Council of Europe, discussions on several plans for European cooperation to integrate and facilitate air transport and travel, including the formation of a joint European airspace under supranational authority, also got under way that year.[35] Parallel to these discussions, six European airlines—Air France, BEA (British European Airways), KLM, Sabena, SAS, and Swissair—installed a joint Air Research Bureau in October 1952 to study possibilities for various forms of cooperation. Somewhat surprisingly the conclusions, drawn after a year of study, were in favor of competition, rather than regulated cooperation.[36] On the political level, talks on "air integration" resulted in an intergovernmental conference on coordination of air transport in Europe in April and May 1954. It led to a decision to relinquish visa duties for air travelers, abolish sanitary checks on departing passengers, and preflight customs inspections of luggage. In December 1955 the process of "normalization" of air travel resulted in the foundation of a permanent structure for consultation on air transport matters, the European Civil Aviation Conference (ECAC), in which nineteen countries participated, both from western and eastern Europe. They agreed on a single European structure of air corridors for commercial aviation, something copied from the American practice and under discussion since the introduction of designated air corridors in 1952. Civil aviation also starred as a distinctive topic to be addressed after the formation of the European Economic Community (EEC) in 1957. The EEC Treaty identified air transportation as one of the areas which would, in principle, be suited for a liberal approach to international services.[37]

In the late 1940s something resembling a global air network emerged that extended beyond the prewar colonial context in Asia and Africa, which connected even to South America (by way of Dakar, Senegal) now that aircraft had the range and payload to operate profitably across the South Atlantic. This fitted the high hopes of politicians and economists alike that air transport would not only contribute to the economic development of South America, but also to that of the newly independent nations in Asia and Africa. In fact, these countries found themselves with a choice of air links,

in which the lure of New York competed with the old luster of London and Paris.

In the decolonization of the 1940s and 1950s aviation also played a role and formed a part in the process of nation building that followed independence. India founded its own international carrier, Air India International, in March 1948 as a venture that combined private and public capital (51 and 49 percent respectively). The landing of Air India's first Lockheed Constellation at London's Heathrow Airport, on June 9, 1948, was celebrated as a special occasion: it was a symbol of the fact that India as a nation had, in more sense than one, arrived in the modern world.[38] In neighboring Pakistan, the relationship between the government and civil air transport was even clearer: in 1951 Pakistan International Airways was founded as a department within the Ministry of Defense. The very names of these two carriers already indicated the desire to connect the new nations to the international arena. Yet early international routes were to London only, the gravitational center of the new Commonwealth of Nations. Other new nations were also quick to found their own airline ventures, however great the burden on the national finances. In the second half of the 1950s an emerging globalization (expressed in schemes for economic and political cooperation), trade links, United Nations development programs, and military partnerships contributed to the expansion of the market for air travel between the industrialized countries to the north and developing countries south of the equator. The first multilateral development schemes for sub-Saharan Africa provided for the construction of air transport infrastructures, as transport was considered vital for development. The spreading network was considered a stimulant for economic and social growth. It was a factor in political developments too, as air travel enabled the political elites of the new nations to meet and exchange ideas at international venues such as the Asian-African Conference that convened at Bandung in Indonesia in April 1955. Bandung was attended by political leaders from twenty-nine countries and gave rise to the movement of Non-Aligned States—a new force in international politics. At the same time air transportation also catered to an emerging internationalization of (Western) lifestyle and culture. Finely tuned into this development, TWA's slogan read, "Where the World is One."[39] In Holland, KLM's Albert Plesman maintained, "The air united all peoples." Politics aside, there was considerable pressure on airlines worldwide to develop new route patterns in correspondence with the increase in trade.

Those Western airlines that were finely tuned to the changing political circumstances in Asia and Africa hurried to acquire landing rights from newly independent governments, even if they did not always have direct plans to operate services. There was a sense of urgency about this just in case a market *would* develop. In return European airlines entered into partnerships with newly founded national airline ventures in these new countries. The latter served the dual purposes of all national airlines: to show the flag at

foreign ports of call, and earn foreign currency—particularly U.S. dollars. These formed the international trading currency of the postwar world and were extra important for nations that were otherwise mainly dependent on the relatively unremunerative export of raw materials.

The start of this process was when BOAC aided the foundation of Hong Kong Airways in 1947, hoping it would bring extra traffic from China. In Malaya (Malaysia) BOAC acquired a shareholding in Malayan Airlines in 1948. Air France participated in Air Vietnam in 1951. And despite diplomatic squabbles between the Netherlands and Indonesia, KLM was deeply involved in Garuda Indonesian Airlines from its foundation in 1950—so deep indeed that some interpreted Garuda was an acronym for "Going All Right Under Dutch Administration." KLM built up similarly intimate relations with Air Ceylon from 1955, fearing that new controversies with Indonesia over the continued Dutch presence in New Guinea (Irian Jaya) could otherwise endanger its presence in Asia.

In Africa, BOAC was financially involved in, and leased aircraft to, the East African Airways Corporation (EAAC), the carrier jointly founded by British governors of Kenya, Uganda, Tanganyika, and Zanzibar (Tanzania) in 1945. It also provided capital and technical assistance to West African Airways Corporation, owned by the (colonial) governments of Nigeria, the Gold Coast, Sierra Leone, and Gambia. When Ghana became independent in 1957, the joint carrier was split up, although BOAC continued as a partner in Ghana Airways which emerged as the national airline in July 1958. It did the same in Nigerian Airways that was founded the same year. In the former French territories, new national flag carriers like Air Mali, Air Ivoire, and Air Cameroun all started with aid from Air France.[40]

In the Western hemisphere aviation also featured as one of the fields identified to further international cooperation. In the Caribbean, Britain, France, the Netherlands, and the United States signed an agreement in March 1950 on a program aimed at raising the standard of living. A crucial part of the plan was the development of tourism through aviation. Peru and Brazil signed a similar agreement in 1953 facilitating air transport as one of the means to stimulate bilateral cooperation and economic growth. More than in Asia, economic, political, and technological developments in Latin America created a basis for the emergence of national flag-carrying airlines on the South American continent to reciprocate the services offered by U.S. and European airlines. By the late 1940s the first Latin American airlines— Avianca (Colombia) and Panair do Brasil—inaugurated flights to the United States and to western Europe, having divested themselves of European and American majority ownership and political involvements.[41] Something of the trust that the Brazilians had in the power of flight for the development of the country transpired even in the shape of the new capital city that came under construction from 1956, Brasilia. Located in the geographical center of the country, Brasilia depended entirely on air transport to get connected

to the distant traditional urban centers Sao Paulo and Rio de Janeiro on the Atlantic shore. Indeed, one observer was quoted to have said there were only three good things about Brasilia: "the skyline, the clean air, and the plane to Rio."[42] This dependency on air transport was even reflected in the layout of the city center that was based on aeronautical themes, resembling a bird in flight.

Politics Paramount

Even before the outbreak of war in September 1939 commercial aviation in Europe virtually ceased to exist. As international tension mounted, the countries most directly affected closed their airspace to all foreign air traffic. From the end of 1939 to the outbreak of war in western Europe in May 1940, only a rudimentary network of air services across the North Sea remained. The gravitational center of the development of air transportation thus shifted to the United States and to a lesser extent Canada, where commercial aviation came into its own while it temporarily went out of existence in Europe and Asia. The return of peace did not immediately change this. Berlin, Europe's most important air transport center in the 1930s, no longer featured on the European map. In 1945 the city was divided into American, British, French, and Russian sectors, and air transport to the three Western zones was ruled to be the express prerogative of Pan American, British European Airways, and Air France. On Moscow's instructions, the Polish carrier LOT serviced East Berlin, connecting with Aeroflot in Warsaw.

Across the North Sea Britain found itself in a predicament as far as commercial air transport was concerned. Restrictive civil aviation agreements were needed to ensure that Britain had a breathing space during which foreign competitors in air transport could be kept at bay. In view of a shortage of suitable aircraft London favored maintaining a military type of air transport regime for as long as possible. Britain lacked aircraft to operate civil services on the one hand and faced a shortage of dollars to obtain such machines on the other.[43] Against this background London refused to release British airports for commercial flights until 1946. The only exceptions were those made to Pan Am and American Overseas Airways, which were allowed to carry out passenger operations at RAF Hurn air base, 90 miles southwest of London on the English coast. To reestablish a British presence across the globe was considered important. Although air transport did not feature prominently in the policy outlook of Atlee's Labour government, London reaffirmed the need for considerable subsidies to BOAC in 1946. Imperial possessions were to serve as staging posts for various world routes.[44]

French policy followed along similar lines. Full military control over the two Parisian airports—and civil aviation as such–was only abolished a year after the end of hostilities in Europe. That same year, 1946, Henri

Desbruères, Air France's managing director, voiced the commonly held opinion in Paris that "the radiance of a country can be measured through the importance of its civil air transport."[45] This showed in state influence in Air France, which was 70 percent government owned, with virtually all of the remaining shares of the formally private company in the possession of public institutions. Private interests represented a mere 2 percent of the share capital.[46]

In a geographic sense, the Soviet occupation of middle and eastern Europe resulted in an essentially banana-shaped air transport network in western Europe, with the North Sea region as its center. From there air services thinned out to Scandinavia, Italy, and Greece.[47] The network showed the continued centralistic approach to international air transport that most governments adhered to. Virtually all air services focused on national capitals and governments allowed little room for the development of international services from regional airports, despite their autonomous economic potential. The notable exception was West Germany, where the federal structure of the country and denied air sovereignty combined with a ban on German civil aviation until 1955 precluded the emergence of strong centralistic tendencies. This enabled regional centers like Hamburg, Cologne/Bonn, Frankfurt, Stuttgart, and Munich to claim their positions in international air transport. As a suitably neutral carrier, KLM profited from this. The Dutch airline grew by developing the so-called Sixth Freedom traffic: scheduled transport of passengers and cargo from other European countries to intercontinental destinations through a transfer at KLM's home base in Amsterdam, and vice versa. With the absence of Lufthansa, Germany was an important and lucrative market. KLM offered more services to cities in Germany than to any other country.[48]

Nonetheless, with the return of peace in 1945 the environment for air transport changed dramatically. Independent of the release of actual operating permits airline planners started developing ideas on a global scale. New military, political, economic, cultural, and technological ties emerged between the United States, Canada, and western Europe that created a new setting for air transportation. The effect was a change in perception of what air transportation was about: offering politically important connections to foreign capitals and colonial possessions or providing an economically viable form of rapid transport, especially in the area of the North Atlantic, where high demand and expectations of high returns went hand in hand.

Regular air transport across the North Atlantic actually preceded the return to civilian conditions. In June 1945 the United States evacuated more than 5,000 wounded and sick soldiers by air. A month later U.S. Air Transport Command deployed 150 Douglas C-54 Skymaster aircraft to ferry 20,000 soldiers home from Europe and 30,000 monthly thereafter.[49] Although civilian transatlantic air transportation in 1945 was limited to priority passengers that had been approved by their respective governments

(as had been the case during the war) the return to normal commercial operations and procedures from 1946 onward brought a sharp increase in passenger numbers. Already in 1947 an astounding 194,000 people traveled the Atlantic air route, 85 percent more than the previous year. In 1948 American Marshall Aid to western Europe accounted for a yet another 30 percent rise. The growth of European air transport to the Middle East, Asia, and Africa, did not keep pace.

Such developments shielded that air transport as an economic activity remained firmly embedded in the political entourage. Even within the group of Western nations, liberalist and protectionist approaches collided constantly. The new, lucrative routes to the United States were a case in point. Early in 1946 America decided to limit the number of entry points for international air services to a single gateway, New York. The idea was to protect America's domestic carriers from foreign competition while increasing the likelihood that American air passengers would seek their transatlantic journey on board American airline companies offering such services. Only the Swiss were exempt from this rule, receiving landing rights in Chicago in May 1949, in exchange for permission for TWA to operate a service between New York and Geneva, the location of the European headquarters of the United Nations.[50]

Although this restrictive approach was challenged by the Europeans, changes were slow in coming and hinged on increasing American concerns over Soviet military objectives in the Cold War. In 1952 the perceived Soviet threat necessitated the installation of a series of American radar stations in Greenland (Denmark) and arctic Norway. In return for permission to build and operate these installations, the Danish, Norwegian, and Swedish governments demanded that rights be allocated to their joint carrier Scandinavian Airline System (SAS), to run scheduled commercial air services across the North Pole to Los Angeles. The State Department took a year to consider this but then went along with the request in November 1953 in the interest of NATO cooperation.[51] In 1954 airlines from Australia and Japan, America's main allies in the Pacific, were also granted rights to fly to the American West Coast. Just how much politics mattered showed in June 1955 when Washington granted the resurrected German Lufthansa landing rights at no less than seven points in the United States.[52] These rights were part of a package with which Washington welcomed the new Federal Republic of Germany to the NATO alliance.

This turn of events brought an upsurge of commercially motivated requests for more liberal operating rights to the United States from other European countries, pushing transatlantic aviation up the international political agenda. In 1957 Britain's BOAC was the first of the traditional European airlines to receive an operating permit to fly to Los Angeles. It was part of a deal aimed at restoring the Anglo-American *special relationship* from the damage it had suffered when the United States had forced Britain and

France to withdraw their troops from the Suez Canal Zone after Egypt's nationalization of the strategic waterway in 1956.[53] At the same time the permit went some way to appease British concerns that the United States had "as a primary objective, the attainment of complete world domination in air transport, regardless of cost."[54] Two years, and repeated threats to "re-evaluate France's contribution to NATO" later, Paris wrangled similar operating rights from Washington in 1959.[55] Smaller countries, like Belgium and the Netherlands, carried less political weight and continued to face American obstruction to their desires to expand their air transport to the United States. Washington remained unimpressed when the Dutch threatened not to ratify the Treaty of Friendship, Commerce and Navigation between the United States and the Netherlands. Not even a public plea from Queen Juliana to President Dwight Eisenhower could change this.[56]

Services across the South Atlantic were developed simultaneously, now that aircraft had the range to cross the great divide. European airlines competed for traffic rights in Brazil, Argentina, and Latin America generally. Though apparently commercial, not all of these services were without political sidelines. KLM, which got about one-third of its passengers from Germany, established services to Rio de Janeiro (Brazil) in October 1946, and extended these to Montevideo (Uruguay) 2 months later. Thus the Dutch cashed in on the German prewar efforts to tighten the bonds with the German immigrant communities on the South American continent. For more than a few Germans disillusioned by the outcome of the war, KLM provided fast and comfortable emigrations. Passengers and earnings expanded more than tenfold between 1946 and 1949.[57] From mid-1946 other airlines—Iberia, SAS, the Argentinean carrier FAMA, and Alitalia—joined in to get a share of this lucrative market. Estimates about German postwar emigration to South America vary widely, from 10,000 to 350,000. Airline figures indicate that numbers ran into the tens of thousands, but as a rule migrants arrived by ship. Statistics digressed widely because a numerous emigrants dodged statistics and buried their past before taking flight. Escape routes for war-incriminated persons ran via Geneva and Zurich (where the Swiss turned a blind eye), Rome (Italy), and the Iberian Peninsula.[58] In Spain, the fascist regime of Generalissimo Francisco Franco deliberately set out to tap into this market—and acquire influence in the Spanish speaking regions of Latin America at the same time. As a vehicle for this policy, Franco used the national airline, Iberia. It was a matter of high-priority that an air link between Madrid and Buenos Aires (Argentina) was established in the summer of 1946. This was after Juan Perón, who combined socialist principles with fascist ideas borrowed from Mussolini and Franco, won the Argentinean general elections in February of that year. Perón welcomed European refugees with a tainted past and encouraged their migration to Argentina. Spanish air services across the South Atlantic were duplicated by FAMA in May 1947. Under encouragement from Madrid, Iberia's Latin American

network extended to Brazil and Uruguay. At the end of 1949 Iberia opened routes to Caracas (Venezuela), San Juan (Puerto Rico), and Havana (Cuba) and in 1950 to Mexico.[59] Other airlines followed in its tracks.

In the opposite direction, airlines were experimenting with transpolar routes that would connect Europe with its new political and economic ally in the Pacific region, Japan. The polar route was pioneered as early as 1946, when an American B-29 bomber flew nonstop from Honolulu, Hawaii, via Alaska and the North Pole to Cairo (Egypt), a distance of about 9,300 miles. Yet in the adverse political climate of the 1940s and 1950s, agreement with the Soviet Union on permission to operate routes across the North Pole could not be reached. Likewise, European airlines found it difficult to obtain permission from the United States to allow their aircraft to fly across Alaska and refuel in Anchorage en route to Tokyo. Not before the end of the 1950s did Washington release the route to its western European allies.

But although the emphasis, in terms of marketing and the numbers of passengers and goods, was on the transatlantic routes, air transport's main weight in political terms was connected to the decolonization of overseas possessions. From a European perspective, the emerging independence movements in Asia and Africa put the reinstatement and continuation of national air services near the top of political agendas. Right after the return of peace in Europe, the resumption air services to what was left of the colonial empires had been high on the list of government priorities anyhow.

In Holland, for example, services to the Dutch East Indies (Indonesia) started in November 1945, as soon as The Hague possessed aircraft capable of operating the route. This was even before a return to normal civilian rule allowed for scheduled intercontinental airline operations, and the flights were therefore disguised as a military Netherlands Government Air Transport service (NGAT). Operations were undertaken with aircraft obtained from the United States under military priority contracts. After several months of operations, the Dutch let it be known in London that they wished to change the service back to its prewar civilian guise and have KLM operate the route as soon as the airline would take delivery of new Lockheed Constellation aircraft from the United States in August 1947. However, a scheduled service required permission not only from London but also from the governments of India and Pakistan that were about to gain independence on August 15, 1947. Anxious that India and Pakistan, once independent, might link the issue of the air service to political disapproval of Dutch presence and military action in Indonesia to repress an increasingly strong Indonesian movement for independence, The Hague brought pressure on London to sign a long-term agreement that would overlap the approaching transfer of sovereignty. This came about on May 31, 1947.

Five months prior, Dutch armed forces had imposed a full naval and air blockade of Java, aimed at quenching republican forces into surrender. To circumvent this blockade the Indonesian nationalists resorted to the charter

of civil aircraft from sympathetic Asian countries to act as blockade-runners. Two companies were particularly active in this field: Kalinga Airlines from India and Pacific Overseas Airways from Siam (Thailand). Under the cover of darkness they operated flights to ferry supplies and people to the Indonesian-held territory on Java. On their part, the Dutch tried to intercept such flights, especially after The Hague issued orders in July for a large scale military "policing action" against the Indonesian nationalists.[60] The cat and mouse game lasted till July 29, when a Dutch Mustang fighter shot down one of Kalinga Airlines' blockade-running Dakotas. Before the day was done, the government of India retaliated and revoked KLM's operating rights, condemning the hardhanded manifestation of Dutch colonialism in no uncertain terms. Dutch aircraft operating under the new agreement signed in London were held up en route: an eastbound machine at Karachi and a westbound plane at Calcutta. The next westbound aircraft thereafter stopped at Bangkok, where the captain had extra fuel tanks fitted and then went on to fly directly to Ceylon (Sri Lanka), asking—and receiving—permission to land at RAF's Negombo air base near the Ceylonese capital Colombo while on approach and low on fuel.[61] Luckily for the Dutch, to whom the air service to Jakarta was absolutely vital, London agreed to an emergency route that would bypass India and Pakistan. Henceforth, KLM would fly directly from the RAF base in Sharjah (United Arab Emirates, on the southern shore of the Persian Gulf) to Colombo in Ceylon, which was still under British rule.[62] The measures were temporary and an indication of further trouble in the air should the Dutch persist in their Indonesia policy.

On December 19, 1948 Dutch armed forces began what was called a second "policing action" against the Indonesian nationalists but in effect amounted to a full-scale military offensive. Three days later, India stopped a KLM Constellation in Calcutta and searched it under the suspicion of carrying military equipment. This time India revoked KLM's operating permit for an indefinite period. As a consequence, a second Constellation was stranded in Basra (Iraq) and forced to return to Amsterdam a week later. By that time, Ceylon, Pakistan, and Burma had also closed their airspace to Dutch flights. Politics grounded the air service to a halt.[63] Yet KLM had just prepared for such an eventuality. Secret contingency plans lay ready for an emergency route via Khartoum (Sudan) and the island of Mauritius in the middle of the Indian Ocean. Operating specially stripped Constellations fitted with extra fuel tanks and accepting greatly reduced payloads, the aircraft could just cover the distance between Mauritius and Java.[64] Permission for a technical stopover in Mauritius was applied for in London, under the International Air Services Transit Agreement, as Britain controlled the air rights over Sudan and Mauritius.

Pending this, KLM secretly mounted eight Constellation flights across Pakistan and India between January 4 and February 6, 1949. These were clear violations of the closure of the air space of the two countries, and

the flights were therefore shrouded in deep secrecy and carried out at night. Pilots were instructed to switch off their navigation lights and maintain strict radio silence. If questioned crews were to provide false navigational data. Doing so, the Dutch counted on the fact that their high-flying aircraft would remain undetected as neither India nor Pakistan possessed radar installations.[65] However, some of the activity transpired nonetheless. The KLM aircraft were spotted on intermediate stops on both sides of the Indian subcontinent, and the Netherlands ambassador in New Delhi had a very embarrassing morning when questioned by Indian authorities about the flights, on which The Hague had kept him in the dark. The British permission for the alternative route via Mauritius, issued on January 22, 1949, was therefore welcomed with immense relief in The Hague. Four days later the first machine on the emergency route departed from Amsterdam, after which the ambassador was instructed to state to the Indian government that the Dutch would no longer violate their airspace.[66] Five months later, the last of the Mauritius flights touched down on the runway of Amsterdam's Schiphol Airport on July 20, 1949, after American and international pressure through the United Nations had put an end to the military conflict in Indonesia and secured the country's imminent independence on December 27 of that year.

The rapidly changing political situation in Asia brought out more connections between politics and aviation. In 1946, General Claire L. Chennault, famous for his wartime Flying Tigers volunteer squadron that operated against the Japanese, set up a cargo airline in China, Civil Air Transport (CAT). He hoped the airline's fortunes would rise with China's economic development. However, Chennault's friendship with China's Nationalist leader Chiang Kai-shek and his Kuomintang movement soon drew the airline deep into the Chinese Civil War with Mao Zedong's Communist forces. At great personal risk, CAT's American pilots ferried Nationalist troops, delivered supplies to besieged cities, and even bombed Communist positions to aid the Nationalist forces in their struggle against Mao's Communists. Against the backdrop of these developments Chennault approached the State Department early in 1949, seeking American aid for his airline in the course of Washington's support for Chiang Kai-shek. Although the State Department did not see much in this, the CIA did and the airline became one of the instruments of America's containment policy in Asia, aimed to stop the spread of communism. Nevertheless, CAT's efforts could not prevent the collapse of the Nationalists on the Chinese mainland in October 1949. With aid from the CIA, CAT was relocated to Taiwan. From there it flew increasingly dangerous missions into China. Up to 1954 CAT evacuated isolated Nationalist troop detachments to Taiwan, along with their dependents. During the Korean War CAT also provided "civil" air transport for American troops on missions behind enemy lines.[67]

Such examples indicated that air transport mattered a great deal in the politically complex world of the 1940s and 1950s. In the first 75 days of the

fighting in Korea, American civil air carriers supplied most of the transpacific airlift. In the course of the conflict airlines under contract from the Pentagon flew over 100,000 military personnel and a substantial part of army supplies and equipment to Korea.

Whom to Cater to?

As had been the case before the war, postwar air transport essentially catered to government officials and business travelers. Supported by their governments, the various European airlines operated in an environment that was largely untrammeled by competition. Within Europe fares and conditions for contest were set in bilateral negotiations; worldwide the periodical IATA tariff conferences ensured that competition between the airlines—mostly semistate enterprises—was kept in check.

Nonetheless air transport did begin to show the first signs of a change in character after 1950—a trend that coincided with the shift from colonial to commercial interests. The latter was expressed most clearly in the marketing of the airlines. Here emphasis gradually shifted from stressing the combination of technology and luxury to emphasizing sightseeing characteristics of the various destinations served. So far air travel had been the privilege of the *happy few*. For the average European citizen sitting on an aircraft seat was something one could only dream about. The magical aura of aviation endured, despite the increased value the airlines attached to commercial interests. Flying, with its ingredients of unattainable luxury and exotic locations fascinated the public—something noted not only by airline marketeers but also by the film industry. Airport scenes became a customary ingredient of stories depicting the life of the affluent. The closest ordinary people could get to this magical world was to visit an airport as a family outing. And to the airports spectators flocked. In the first decade after the war Amsterdam's Schiphol Airport drew no less than 7.7 million tourist visitors (against 4.2 million actual passengers) and became Holland's biggest tourist attraction.[68]

For the airports, the start and finish of such luxury travel, it was of importance to keep up with passenger expectancies. In the second half of the 1950s most large airports embarked on plans for prestigious terminal buildings that would pair ultimate modernity to a high quality—functional environment which also left room for further growth of traffic. *The* yardstick of this approach was, beyond doubt, the Trans World Airline terminal under construction at New York's Idlewild (John F. Kennedy) Airport. Designed by Finnish architect Eero Saarinen, the futuristic building, opened in 1962, was shaped as a gull spreading its wings.[69] Next to it, PanAm built its terminal shaped like a giant flying saucer. European airports followed the trend to providing a luxurious environment for waiting passengers, even though in

most plans functionality far exceeded form. Such functionality illustrated that air travel had begun to lose some of its magical aura.

A category of passengers that cared little for that aura were emigrants. Most European countries faced an imminent population surplus that was considered an impediment to economic growth at a time in which traditionally large employment sectors, such as agriculture, were shrinking. International discussions between governments resulted in policies to stimulate emigration to countries that had a shortage of laborers. About 1.5 percent of the population of western Europe departed between 1946 and 1965. Both the emigrant countries and the Intergovernmental Commission for European Migration provided financial incentives for this. The main recipient nations, Canada, the United States, Australia, New Zealand, and South Africa also contributed to the costs. Between 1946 and 1961 they welcomed well over 3.5 million new inhabitants from war-torn Europe. Over a million Britons left the United Kingdom; nearly 800,000 people departed Germany.[70] The other European nations made up the remainder of emigrants. Although most of them left by ship, some 20–30 percent—between 300,000 and 400,000 people—went by air, typically on special emigrant charter flights. The number of air passengers rose as time went by and flying became less expensive. By the mid-1950s the various assisted passage schemes that were in force to help emigrants make their way to a new life overseas provided for a choice between sea and air passage. In a typical recipient country like New Zealand, about one-third of new arrivals came by air in 1950, rising to 55 percent in 1960.[71] In the United States too, immigration by air became more common as the 1950s progressed. Although the number of new arrivals was smaller than in Canada and Australia, New York's Idlewild Airport still came to be known as "the modern-day Ellis Island."[72] Records of immigrants arriving by air in New York from the mid-1950s show they did not only come from Europe but also from Brazil, on Varig flights.[73]

Such flows of people had a considerable impact on recipient countries, more so if the latter were sparsely populated. Yet there was one case where the arrival of immigrants by air made all the difference right from the start: Israel. Israeli immigration by air started out on a small scale with charter flights from Europe in the postwar years. A special case was provided by immigrants from other Middle Eastern countries, particularly Iraq, which had a sizable Jewish community. After 1945 Jewish citizens in Iraq were under increasing pressure as a result of nationalist policies. In 1947 freight aircraft chartered by the Israeli secret service, Mossad, began to smuggle people wishing to flee the difficulties of daily life in an increasingly Islamic country. In British-occupied Palestine, where the state of Israel was starting to emerge, improvised camps were set up to house them. As a result of the outcome of the 1948 War of Independence, which put Israel on the map, pressures on Jewish inhabitants of Arab countries increased. At the same time the new state was desperately short of people needed to build a viable

Jewish nation. Considerable means were therefore diverted to initiatives that assisted in populating Israel. Iraq was a case in point. In 1948 increasing numbers of Jews were brought across the Euphrates River into Iran, and hence flown to Israel by Iranian Airways. Later flights were carried out from Baghdad, contracted to American charter operators such as Trans Ocean Airways and Near East Air Transport, allegedly flying to the island of Cyprus in the Mediterranean, but in fact delivering their passengers in Tel Aviv. Between 1948 and February 1952, 121,512 Jewish Iraqi citizens left the country. In all Israel secretly airlifted close to a million Jews from the Arab countries in the Middle East between 1947 and 1951.[74]

In Europe airline passengers predominantly traveled for business, but in the United States the situation was different. American air travelers also flew for private reasons or simply because they were in a hurry. In the late 1940s the air transport industry first began to realize that, next to the combination of speed and luxury, air transportation might also attract passengers that would settle for speed as such. In 1948 Capital Airlines was the first to introduce *coach class* on the busy air route between New York and Chicago. Traveling *coach*—i.e., in DC-4 aircraft fitted with sixty instead of the customary forty-odd seats—represented a rebate of 25–40 percent from the standard airfare, and Capital hoped this would enable the airline to compete against the railways.[75] International discounts were Pan Am's territory. At the end of the war, Pan Am's chief executive officer Juan Trippe, as well as officials at TWA and Northwest, realized that it might be possible to develop a market for international air tourism. Large numbers of decommissioned soldiers had experience of airplane travel and an increased familiarity with foreign destinations. As early as 1946 Pan Am had already been pressing the British to allow fares as low as $275 on its route across the Atlantic and had experimented with 20 percent rebates on flights to Latin America.[76] However, for the European airlines the time was not yet ripe to consider such low prices. Despite repeated threats by Pan Am to reduce prices on its own accord, the IATA cartel managed to oppose Pan Am's quest for fare reductions until May 1, 1952. That day the first *tourist-class* flight left New York, a reconfigured Pan Am DC-6. It had thirty more seats than usual, and passengers were only served sandwiches. Later passengers fared better. Return tickets between New York and London went from $711 to $486.[77] In general, tourist-class fares were 32 percent below *standard*. It turned out to be a golden idea: in 1953, the first full year that tourist-class tickets were sold, the IATA airlines already had 53 percent (equal to 178,000) more passengers on board than in 1951, the last full year before the rebates. But even at reduced fares, tourists essentially meant *American* tourists. With very high exchange rates for the dollar and currency restrictions in force in a number of European countries, few Europeans were able to afford even such reduced tickets. Nonetheless, the tourist class gave rise to a new phenomenon: the holiday break, in which those who

could afford the price could go on a vacation that took no more than a week or two. An actual travel boom developed. American trips across the Atlantic to Europe went up from 376,000 in 1953 to double that number in 1959 (750,000).[78] Before transatlantic air travel, such trips had been true voyages, as ships took 5 to 7 days to cross the vast expanse of the ocean.

But in the uncertain world of the late 1940s and early 1950s, even tourism had its political angle. In 1948 the United States created a separate travel development section within the Economic Cooperation Administration (ECA) of the Marshall Plan. The idea was to enable average Americans to participate in transatlantic group tours utilizing reduced fares. Coordinated efforts were made to promote tourism to Europe as a contribution to the fight against communism. The idea was that exposure to American tourists, and through them with the *American Way of Life*, would help secure a lasting allegiance to the United States. Besides, American tourists would contribute to the costs of European reconstruction by visiting (or revisiting) interesting sites. By one estimate, American tourists provided one-fourth of all dollars earned by western Europe in 1949.[79] In the United Nations, America called for the "immediate symplification" of visa and border crossing procedures and restrictions.[80] Paris, or France in general, was a preferred choice for such travels. Given tourism's economic impact, it was not surprising that ECA planners actually hoped to discourage *domestic* French tourism. This way more hotel accommodation would be available to American guests, bringing in much-needed dollars. By mid-1949 American official circles had expanded the Marshall Plan concept of tourism's functions to a general Cold War contributor—bolstering a sense of a unified transatlantic culture, embedded in the Marshall Plan and in the newly founded NATO alliance.[81] To at least *some* U.S. officials in the early 1950s, American tourists in Europe were "America's most democratic weapon against communism."[82]

With verbal support from Washington, Pan Am successfully plea-bargained the case for lowering fares even further. Technology was also a factor in widening the market. Aircraft factories were turning out substantially larger aircraft every few years—sooner than airlines could recoup their investments. If the DC-4 of the postwar years seated between forty and sixty people, planes like the Super Constellation and the DC-7, which appeared not 10 years later, nearly doubled that number. By that time larger, jet-propelled aircraft were already in their test phase. These again doubled seat capacity—to the extent that capacity increases actually began to worry airline executives. Because jets offered much higher speed, the prime attraction of air travel, the airlines wondered how to fill these large aircraft and find use for their relatively new propeller aircraft that were still pressing on the balance sheets. The answer, it became clear, hinged on a further reduction of ticket prices in an attempt to open up air travel to a much wider section of society. Again Pan Am was the first to embrace this notion.

After years of discussion, IATA agreed to the introduction of *economy class* as a new, cheaper way to fly in 1958. Tickets were again 20 percent below tourist class.[83] To fill the jets the creation of traffic became more important than fostering the image of luxury. To stress this point economy-class services were initially operated with propeller aircraft, reserving the novelty of the jets to the full fare clientele. Not before the general changeover to jets was completed did the multiclass aircraft cabin become fashionable. Arrangements in economy class were stark, a reminder of the first tourist class flight in 1952. With the back of the seats pitched 86 centimeters (34 inches) apart and a menu that only mentioned cold sandwiches, intercontinental travel held few comforts. Perhaps that explained why colorful depictions of the destinations served were much emphasized in airline advertising, offering even the economy-class passenger something to look forward to during the flight. To give a clear signal that economy-class travel had little to do with "normal" air travel, IATA members agreed that *economy* passengers would only be served a basic sandwich on their 20-odd-hour trip across the Atlantic. As a consequence, IATA adopted resolution JT12(16)100a later that month, paragraph nine of which categorically stated, "Only meals consisting of sandwiches may be provided to passengers travelling in economy service (it being understood that the sandwiches shall be simple, cold and inexpensive)."[84]

Nonetheless, a transatlantic economy ticket still cost as much as $534 in Holland, which was quite a hefty amount for prospective passengers, about half the price of a small car in local currency.[85] In view of these prices, several European airlines soon developed second thoughts about the relationship between ticket price and the level of service on board, rightly worrying that the traveling public might expect more than a cold sandwich at the prices charged. Their decision to offer the customer a bit more, led to complaints from Pan Am and TWA against KLM, Air France, Swissair, and SAS that they treated their economy-class customers too generously, because the four companies served sandwiches "which were neither simple nor inexpensive and [were] presented so as to give the appearance of a cold plate."[86] But despite all that, the tickets were an instant success. Even in 1958 some 60 percent of European travelers to the United States flew on economy-class tickets. For the airlines, the lower fares were the final breakthrough in their long competition against the transatlantic shipping companies, and 1958 became the first year in which more people flew between the Old World and the New than traveled by ship. Forty years after the inception of commercial aviation, scheduled air transport was now on the brink of mass transportation.

Airlines that were not allowed to offer scheduled services by their governments could not cater to individual passengers. They depended on charter contracts. In the first postwar years the going was tough, but in Europe prospects suddenly brightened with the Berlin Blockade of 1948. To

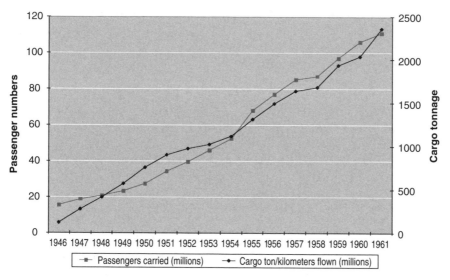

The Development of World Air Transport, 1946–1961. *Source:* ICAO figures.

provide for the city, practically all aircraft tonnage that was available in western Europe was called upon. But with the blockade ending in the late spring of 1949, demand lapsed, and companies reverted to subsistence. Nonetheless, by the end of the year small start-up companies like Horizon Holidays in Britain came up with something new: foreign holidays by air. They did so in the wake of the lifting of the postwar ban on foreign travel in the United Kingdom, imposed in 1948 to save valuable currency. After initial opposition from the established corporations and the Ministry of Civil Aviation had been overcome, Horizon received permission in March 1950 to charter aircraft for holiday flights to the Mediterranean island of Corsica, catering specifically to students and teachers seeking a sojourn in the sun. On Sunday, May 21, 1950, a single chartered DC-3 took off from Gatwick Airport, London, carrying ten paying passengers, and relatives and friends of the organizers, to start a new megatrend in European travel: the package holiday in the Mediterranean sun.[87] From the mid-1950s the example was followed elsewhere and spread through Scandinavia and West Germany. In March 1956 Lufttransport-Union (LTU) started as a second German airline next to Lufthansa. It depended entirely on inclusive tour charters flying passengers from Frankfurt to Catania, on the Italian island of Sicily, in its single Vickers Viking. Beginnings were modest indeed; no more than a few hundred passengers were carried annually before the decade was out. Slightly bigger was Condor, founded in December 1955 as Deutsche Flugdienst GmbH by the Norddeutsche Lloyd and Hamburg-Amerika shipping lines, in collaboration with Lufthansa and the German railways. It

too started flying in March 1956 with a small fleet of three Viking aircraft and offering flights to the Spanish Mediterranean island Mallorca and to Tenerife (Canary Islands).[88]

As the beginnings of this new phenomenon were so modest, independent airlines often depended on military contracts to carry troops. In Britain "trooping," or the carriage of military personnel and their dependents to bases in Europe and overseas, was a mainstay for the independent airlines throughout the 1950s. For the government, this was a way to build up a substantial air transport reserve that was considered vital in the event of war. Most of the chartered flights went to those colonial regions where the British maintained substantial garrisons, as was the case in Gibraltar, Cyprus, Aden, Singapore, Hong Kong, and Kenya. Apart from troops independents such as Airwork and British Eagle also began exploring the possibilities of cheap air travel over long distances, known as *colonial coach* services—no-frills flights to central and east Africa via Malta or Cyprus and Cairo (Egypt). The first of these services were initiated in 1952.[89] The independent carriers also played a role in moving troops to the Suez Canal Zone in 1956. On August 12 an airbridge was begun to ferry troops to the British military bases in Cyprus. In December, civil aircraft were again used in connection to the Suez Crisis—this time to end it, as Swissair transported the first United Nations Peacekeeping troops of the Canal Zone on thirty-seven flights from Naples (Italy).[90]

Away from the North Atlantic and European areas, air transport developed at a much slower pace. The international air traffic of the newly independent nations in Asia continued to be geared at the former colonizer. Much of the gap in development resulted from the backlog in economic development. Despite its vast surface area, a population of over 367 million, and considerable trading links with other Asian economies, air transport in India—Asia's largest air market by far—was until the early 1960s no bigger than that that of Switzerland (population about 5 million). In 1953, Asian air transport stood at over 1.6 million passenger-kilometers, which was a mere 20 percent of that in Europe.[91] Nonetheless, similar developmental patterns were discernible as had guided the development of air transport in Europe in the decades before the war. Geographical obstacles, as well as politics, played a major role in furthering air transport. It was no wonder then that air transport in Pakistan showed the biggest growth. Split in a western and an eastern part separated by the landmass of India from the time of independence in 1947, Pakistan needed the development of air services across neighboring India to connect the two parts of the nation. Indeed, maintaining air services was vital to the functioning of Pakistan as such. Hence the government's direct involvement in the Pakistani airline industry. Between 1953 and 1961 Pakistan's air transport, measured in passenger-kilometers, grew by a spectacular 1195 percent, which was the largest increase anywhere in the world. Such figures surpassed the development of air transport

in India, which increased over threefold in the same period. For Asian air transport to develop, geographical separation was vital. This particularly showed in the cases of Indonesia and the Philippines. With a population a quarter of India's and a landmass only half, Indonesian air transport was still 50 percent of India's.[92] But then again, Indonesia had the benefit—in terms of circumstances furthering the development of air transport—of being an archipelago. The fact that islands mattered also showed in transport figures for the Philippines, which were on par with those of Indonesia, although the size of the population was again only a quarter of Indonesia's. Standards of living were more or less comparable between the two island economies.

Such figures were still double those in African air transportation. Here traffic concentrated in those regions that were of prime strategic interest to the Western powers. As had been the case before the war, French and British airlines operated to their colonial possessions. Air France and Union Aéromaritime de Transport linked Paris with the African colonies and French-speaking regions, providing them with rapid connections to the motherland. Belgium's Sabena operated a service between Brussels and Leopoldville in Congo, while Portugal's TAP provided scheduled flights to Portuguese Guinea, Angola, and Mozambique. In the north of the continent, BOAC provided scheduled flights through Egypt to East Africa. Cairo, Africa's largest city, continued to serve as the main center for air transportation on the continent. Ethiopia also generated considerable air transport, because the nation maintained close ties with the West. Traditionally pro-Western, Emperor Haile Selassie secured a relatively high level of development aid in the first decades after the war, which proved beneficial for the development of air transport operations in this semiarid region. Ethiopia's share in African air travel was as big as Egypt's. In sub-Saharan Africa, air transport was slower to develop and hardly came into its own until after the African "decolonisation year" 1960, when sixteen African nations achieved independence. Before that time, air transportation was concentrated in those areas that had a substantial population of European settlers, particularly South Africa and Rhodesia (Zimbabwe).[93] Together they provided four times the traffic volume of Egypt and Ethiopia combined and likely dominated African air transport as such. From South Africa, BOAC and South African Airways (SAA) jointly maintained the prewar East African route through Kenya and Uganda to Cairo and on to Europe. To accommodate BOAC's Comet jet service to Johannesburg, facilities at Uganda's Entebbe Airport were specially updated in the early 1950s. In the late 1950s a new west African route with one stop at Kano in Nigeria was introduced, cutting flight time to London to around 22 hours. Athens and Amsterdam were also added to the network. Routes to the Middle East and Australia were also developed, the latter stopping at Mauritius and the Cocos Islands before terminating in Perth.

Developments in Latin America were rather different. For starters, South America provided three times the traffic volume of the African continent. And besides, air transport was different both in the shape of the air services network and in its use. Contrary to the situation in Africa and, to a lesser extent, in Asia, services were not primarily geared towards intercontinental flights but were essentially continental by nature. Brazil, by far Latin America's largest and most populous country, generated most of the air transport. Argentina, roughly a third of the size of Brazil in surface area as well as population, nonetheless provided only a modest 21 percent of the air transport. What also set apart the situation in Latin America was that air services were not quite so concentrated on the transportation of passengers but left more room for the transportation of goods—ten times more than was the case in Asia, a reflection of international trading patterns on a continent with a relatively undeveloped road infrastructure. Airfreight was a negligible quantity in African air transport in this period.[94]

Passengers First and Foremost

From its inception, air transport and nationalism had gone hand in hand. If early airline pilots hoisted the national flag upon arrival at a foreign landing ground, the increasing technological complexity of passenger aircraft, the expanding size of airplanes and airports, and the increasing bustle of air transport as such rendered this practice obsolescent in the years following 1945. But if literally brandishing the flag became less practical, this did not remove national symbols from air transportation. On the contrary, in foreign cities airlines occupied booking offices in the most expensive and fashionable shopping streets, proudly displaying the typical touristic stereotypes of their nation to entice affluent potential travelers. In the postwar years a practice developed of airliner tailplanes donning the national colors. Rising high up in the air for maximum visibility, symbols like the Union Jack, the Swiss flag with its white cross against a bright red background, or various representations of the color bands of national flags quickly became commonplace. Not even Lufthansa, whose nationality was seriously blemished by wartime national socialist aggression and which downplayed its past by striking the adjective "Deutsche" from the name of the company, escaped the showing of the new, West German colors. Those airlines that did not emphasize their nationality on the tailplane of their aircraft had the national carrier's name painted in large letters on the fuselage for all to see. This was not just the case in Europe but a worldwide phenomenon at a time when all major air transport companies had their national governments as owners or majority stakeholders and airlines as such were extensions of the national pride. National political dignitaries—and if it was felt that the

stakes were high enough then even royalty—went on the first flight to a new foreign destination.

The leading airlines bought new, faster, and more comfortable aircraft almost as soon as they came off the drawing board. New aircraft like the Constellation, the DC-6, and the Stratocruiser incorporated such improvements as pressurized passenger cabins. These allowed aircraft to operate at considerably higher altitudes, assuring a more tranquil voyage and less stress on passengers' stomachs and organs of balance. Travel times were further reduced after the discovery of the jet stream phenomenon in the stratosphere. Utilizing a powerful jet stream tailwind a Boeing Stratocruiser booked a time gain of no less than 3 hours on its eastbound crossing of the Atlantic in October 1952. Subsequent calculations showed that deliberate use of jet stream winds also saved time and 10 to 15 percent in fuel costs.[95]

For those enticed to fly these flag carriers the aircraft cabin was an equally important measure of national aspirations. Because areas of real competition between airlines were few, much effort was spent in creating an atmosphere of comfort and luxury on board, particularly in aircraft used for long-distance flights. On such flights, luxury was not superfluous. Crossing the North Atlantic to New York took 20 to 24 hours, including refueling stops in Shannon (Ireland) or Prestwick (Scotland) and Goose Bay or Gander (in Labrador, Canada).[96] Flights from western Europe to Japan took considerably longer—31 to 34 hours until the introduction of jet aircraft, including refueling stops in Stavanger (Norway) and Anchorage (Alaska). During those long hours, it was necessary to keep the passenger entertained and happy. Cabin arrangements reflected this. Boeing spent nearly $250,000 designing seats for its Stratocruiser.[97] Reclining, adjustable seats were often boxed in pairs of two, facing each other in the fashion of a railway compartment, so that passengers could enjoy polite conversation with those sitting opposite them. If the aircraft was not fully booked, passengers could even lie down for the night. In between the pairs of seats a table could be folded down to change each compartment into a sleeping berth for two. In some aircraft, like the Douglas DC-7, overhead bins could also be pulled down, creating further sleeping arrangements. Once at cruising altitude, passengers were free to leave their seats and have a smoke and a drink in the fashionable, cosmopolitan atmosphere of the aircraft's bar. The leading airlines spent much energy—and money—on cabin decoration and architecture. International top designers and architects were contracted to come up with cabin styles that would emphasize the general impression under which the national airline was marketing its product. Air France's high-water mark was the cabin of its Lockheed Constellations of the 1950s, custom designed by Raymond Loewy, America's "pope of industrial design."[98] The harmonious interior made for a cabin clad with beige gabardine fabric and windows framed with golden yellow curtains embroidered with the Air France logo.

Amenities included individual reading lights, a mirror, a plug for an electric razor, and an adjustable vent.

Much effort also went into the reduction of cabin noise levels through padding the fuselage with new, rubberized materials, additional acoustical blankets for soundproofing, and double-glazed windowpanes. Exhaust mufflers of special design constituted further noise control measures. Improvements followed each other quickly. The Lockheed L-1049G Super Constellation—in 1954 already the seventh variant of the stretched Constellation design—had 107 design improvements over the L-1049E, including better cabin soundproofing with blankets of fiberglass attached to the inner surface of the cabin skin, cabin divisions constructed of sound-reducing plyboard, and new rubber shock pads on the engine mounts to reduce vibration and noise.

Services on board changed quickly too. In the immediate postwar years of sobriety most European airlines did not expand beyond drinks and cold sandwiches. Even so, they carried a lot of them for their esteemed clientele: on a typical flight from Amsterdam to New York, KLM's DC-4s took on 300 kilograms (662 lbs.) of food for forty-three passengers and ten crew members at 5.66 kilograms (12.5 lbs.) per person, that was more than the average passenger could muster.[99] Air France was, in 1948, among the first airlines to introduce warm meals. These were prepared at the company's specialized kitchens at Paris' Orly Airport, preheated on the ground and then carried on board in insulated containers for distribution soon after takeoff. Airlines learned to experiment with foods on board, served under artificial atmospheres. Nonetheless, conditions inside the aircraft cabin did have their effects on taste and the appreciation of foods and drinks. Wines had to be specially selected with the atmosphere under which they were served very much in mind. With the arrival of the Super Constellation in 1953, a new level of service became possible, offering luxury foods, as these aircraft were equipped with an onboard electrically operated kitchen stove that allowed post-preparation of meals. Air France in particular employed recognized chefs and advertised French culinary tradition on the long flights to New York to lure national and foreign customers on board.[100] As a pleasant distraction for the traveler the major airlines served exquisite "seven course champagne-dinners" and other goodies.[101] This contributed to the oft-repeated image of luxury travel, with the friendly and servile stewardess offering a tray of refreshments and beverages to passengers traveling in the comfort of first class seating. The picture was so successful that it achieved an almost automatic association between airplane travel and onboard comforts. Nonetheless, the long duration of intercontinental flights, the ceaseless drone of the engines, and the constant vibrations took their toll of the passenger's endurance. Most were relieved to disembark at the end of their long journey.

Once off the tarmac, arriving passengers were welcomed under the high ceilings of airport buildings that were specifically designed to allow a lot of

light to penetrate, emphasizing spaciousness and modernity. Nonetheless, airports had a hard time keeping up with the growth of aircraft and passenger numbers. The time frame for airport planning and expansion was quite a different one than for aircraft development. Nonetheless, the 1940s and 1950s saw an enormous boost in airport construction. If in early 1946 passengers at London's new Heathrow Airport met the most spartan conditions in a reception center housed in a series of tents on Heathrow's northern perimeter, a permanent building was opened—for intercontinental passengers only—before the year was out. A European terminal took longer to find funding and was not opened until 1955, as government priorities in the reconstruction era lay elsewhere.[102] After that, planning and building efforts got into high gear as London readied itself for the arrival of larger numbers of jet aircraft by the end of the decade.

Like the aircraft they served, airport buildings were designed as expressions of national approaches towards air transportation. In Europe, France provided the showcase. In 1945 General Charles de Gaulle created a new civil organization, Aéroports de Paris (ADP), which received as its task the management of all airports within a 50-kilometer radius around Paris. The underlying thought was the aspiration to make Paris Europe's air capital and thus add luster to France's reclaimed status of great power.[103] The attention soon focused on the development of Orly, a former airship ground located just south of the city. Like Le Bourget before the war, Orly was to become something truly special: the new airport was planned in the dual capacity of aerial port and aerial city and was therefore to combine its function as an air terminal with the offering of residential areas and shopping facilities.[104] As a first step a new, centrally located terminal was finished in 1954. This was a semipermanent structure. A large-scale expansion plan came under construction in the second half of the 1950s. Between 1957 and 1960 some 300 million francs (approximately $61 million then) were invested into the construction of a new terminal building, with which ADP planned to stay ahead of the expected dramatic increase in passenger air transport.[105] A spectacular design was laid out for the new facilities: the *aérogare* was an enormous, hypermodern construction in steel and glass built across a wide access road. It paid architectural tribute to the Bauhaus designs of Mies van der Rohe that were fashionable in European reconstruction and was intended as a prestigious showcase of France's postwar recovery. President De Gaulle opened the building on February 24, 1961, with the full cabinet in attendance.

No other European airport could boast of quite such spectacular architecture, but construction of facilities that aimed to get the message of efficiency and modernity across was the norm around the world as air services acquired a global reach. A host of airport construction projects in Asia, Africa, Australia, and the Americas reflected the need to cope with the increased size and weight of aircraft and the growth of passenger and cargo transport. In

Brazil, first stop of the new air services across the South Atlantic, the existing landplane facilities at Rio de Janeiro's Aeroporto Santos-Dumont soon proved inadequate for the new generation of postwar airliners. It was therefore decided to open up the Galeão military air base for commercial services and construct longer runways and terminal facilities there.[106] In Argentina, then South America's fastest growing economy, President Juan Perón issued a special decree in December 1945 for a new airport to be built near Buenos Aires, Aeropuerto Internacional de Ezeiza. It was opened April 30, 1949, in anticipation of the expected rapid growth of worldwide air services, as one of the largest airports in the world, comparable in size to Chicago O'Hare. Ezeiza's layout, with its tangential runway system emanating from a central terminal area, counted as a prime example of modern airport construction for airport planners in Europe and elsewhere.[107] In Uruguay too, the arrival of new transatlantic air services from Europe also gave rise to changes in infrastructure. Montevideo's Aeropuerto Internacional de Carrasco was inaugurated in 1947.

In the late 1940s airport terminals everywhere emerged as buildings in their own right, adorned with artful motives that sought to appeal to their affluent clientele. Singapore's Paya Lebar Airport, which opened in 1955 after a construction cost of $37.5 million, was a case in point.[108] Traffic was booming. Within a decade Paya Lebar was struggling to keep up, and plans got under way to eventually replace it with a completely new airport, built at the former RAF base Changi. Further "down south" developments went even faster. In 1952 Sydney's Charles Kingsford Smith Airport needed a $10 million expansion program. In the early 1950s Sydney's was the busiest airport in the world outside the United States, as Australia's domestic and international air services showed double digit growth figures. In Africa, King Farouk Airport in Cairo (Egypt) was the busiest, already coping with 200,000 passengers in 1946, which was double the number of passengers who passed through the two Paris airports that year.[109] Second was Johannesburg (South Africa) where a new airport was opened in 1952 to cope with the increased number of flights and passengers from Europe. Elsewhere in Africa the building spree was more modest. In Nairobi (Kenya) for example the British built the rather austere Embakasi Airport to replace earlier facilities at the RAF base Eastleigh in the decade before the country's independence in 1963. In opened in May 1958. Although growth was modest compared to other parts of the world, passenger facilities were expanded and updated everywhere as the 1950s progressed.[110]

The construction of new airports and new terminals indicated that the emphasis in air transportation was on passengers and their special requirements. But aircraft were increasingly used to carry freight as well. The growing size and carrying capacity of the aircraft made it into an ideal vehicle for long-distance transportation of valuable goods and luxury items. In the first 5 years after the war, the transportation of cargo by air was only

of limited importance, but when European economic growth kicked in after the introduction of the Marshall Plan in 1948, air cargo shipments began to show considerable increase year after year.[111] Contrary to the prewar era, when freight had been limited to small shipments befitting the average size of airliners and manual loading procedures, air transportation of freight was slowly being integrated into the normal options for shipping cargo. In the 1950s airports everywhere began to open their own specialized cargo facilities where the use of forklift trucks and mechanized conveyor belts facilitated transloading between ground and air transportation. Air transport companies, for the most part small independent airlines operating on a charter basis, had a hard time to keep abreast of technical developments. Freight transportation had its own specific requirements that differed from passenger carriage. Before each flight, special weight calculations had to be made to establish which goods could be taken on board. The order of shipment was furthermore influenced by the size and weight of the goods themselves and the possibilities to offload shipments en route. Like loading, unloading cargo en route had its consequences, as it required adjusting the balance of the aircraft. Drafting a *booking survey* and a *load sheet* for each individual flight was specialized work and required the exchange of numerous telegrams.

Not all commercial aircraft were suitable for the transportation of increased quantities of freight. Commercial aircraft were, on the whole, not designed with cargo carriage very much in mind and often needed special adaptations (such as special cargo doors) to be able to accommodate larger size goods. Lockheed actually developed a special *speed pack* in the shape of an aerodynamically curved external cargo hold to be hoisted underneath their Constellation type aircraft and attached to the bottom of the fuselage. Douglas aircraft were more versatile, but even so, airlines had to divert to the use of specialized cargo aircraft to accommodate "special cargo" loads such as thoroughbred cows and other livestock, which were increasingly shipped across the globe by air to contribute to crossbreeding programs. Indeed, to fly cargo at all, airlines needed to remove passenger accommodation and strip the cabin of their aircraft. Following the example of such American airlines as Slick Brothers and Seaboard & Western, KLM was one of the first European carriers to start its own dedicated cargo services in 1952.

Freight transport was not only important in a European context; it was also of particular importance in Africa as well. In a continent where the surface infrastructure was extremely limited, the transportation of mined gold bullion and diamonds depended on aircraft right from the start. In the 1950s the range of products transported by air diversified, with luxury fruits and vegetables coming into the picture, to be sold in Europe and the oil countries along the Persian Gulf. By the end of the decade, air transport of luxury products from Africa had already outgrown sea transport.[112]

But apart from providing transport, aircraft also began to play a different role in the economic development of nations. All over the world, aerial photography and cartography proved to be a valuable by-product of aviation, especially in developing countries. From 1949 the United Nations embarked on the Extended Program of Technical Assistance (EPTA) to boost the development of newly independent countries with Western know-how, technology, and aid. One of the prime technologies that were proposed was the use of aerial photography and cartography in the search for mineral reserves, land reclamation, irrigation, and flood control measures. Although most of the actual flying and photography was done by American and European companies, the United Nations and various Western countries offered special courses to civil engineers from developing nations in Asia and Africa to interpret the photographs taken as a form of development aid. The Food and Agricultural Organization (FAO) especially made extensive use of aircraft to determine possibilities for agricultural projects. The oil exploration industry was another big customer. Aerial surveying in Iran produced likely new locations for oil drilling in 1953. In Afghanistan, the technique was used to chart mining opportunities.[113] In Gujarat, India, aerial photography was also used in preparation of the Saurashtra Project for the desalination of swamps and their conversion to dry arable land.[114]

In the 1950s, about 35 percent of Africa's vast continent still remained at best only partly mapped or was without the kind of detailed surveying needed to track potential for economic uses such as mining. From 1953 onwards, a deliberate policy of aerial mapping was started in the British African territories. In Sierra Leone's Marampa area for example, it took only 6 days of photography to select a new possible site for iron ore mining, instead of many months of surveying on the ground. Likewise, a mere 132 hours of aerial photography, instead of 2 years of ground surveying, was sufficient to plan the location for the Kariba hydroelectric dam in the Zambesi River between Zambia and northwestern Rhodesia (Zimbabwe) that was constructed between 1955 and 1959. Aviation was also used for crop-dusting, seeding, top-dressing, and forestry supervision, but perhaps one of the more spectacular uses was as a cost-effective way to combat locust plagues. In 1954 aircraft were used to spray insecticides to fight a locust invasion in Kenya and Tanganyika (Tanzania). Certainly in those days, expectations of widespread use of aircraft to combat insects and diseases were high.[115] Similar projects were carried out in Indonesia and Latin America. In Surinam extensive aerial surveys were made in 1947 in connection with the discovery of bauxite in the Nassau Mountains. As a result, plans were drawn up for a hydroelectric dam in the Surinam River. The dam's electrical power was necessary for the extraction of alumina from the mineral and its purification into aluminum, to be used in the American aircraft industry.

By the end of the 1950s, that American aircraft industry had become dominant in commercial aviation. Between 1958 and 1961 the number of

jet aircraft operating in commercial services went up rapidly. The size, shape, and speed of jet aircraft flying across the globe captivated the imagination of many a would-be passenger hoping to one day join the new and pleasingly highlighted class of travelers that became commonly known as the *jet set*. They formed the material for the emergence of a new, glamorous, and cosmopolitan role model of Western lifestyle, advertised across the globe through films that showed bright young people speeding across the continents in search of adventure, fortune, and fame. Protagonists such as Ian Fleming's James Bond captivated the imagination of millions and enticed a longing for remote exotic destinations. In October 1962 the first Bond movie, *Dr. No*, showed the promise of air transport's new jets. In the early scenes of the film actor Sean Connery, who played British secret agent 007, was summoned to leave his luxury playboy life in London on 4 hours' notice to fly to Kingston, Jamaica, so that he might save the planet from evil schemes of world domination. The "shortening of distance" and the rapidity of the trip were translated visually into a Pan Am Boeing 707 touching down on the Jamaican tarmac. Unintentionally, the film also showed the commonality that air transport had achieved in the preceding decade. Upon arrival in the newly independent island nation, Bond was received in a spotless, ultramodern steel and glass airport building, easily recognizable as such by cinema audiences irrespective of their nationality. Such an airport, it was clear, could have been situated almost anywhere in the world.

Usage: The Rise and Fall of the Jet Set, 1961–1977

"Global two: 25 miles out of eastern marker. Turn right heading 2-6-0. Begin descent at your discretion to two thousand." The calm with which the air traffic controller instructs the flight crew of the crippled jet in its emergency landing procedure is almost unreal. Minutes before, a bomb has gone off on board and has blown a hole in the fuselage, damaging the aircraft's control surfaces. Despite heroic efforts from the stewardesses to ensure their safety, passengers are panicking. On the ground, frantic preparations are in progress to clear the runway of the airport as a winter blizzard continues, while demonstrators in front of the crowded terminal building call for immediate action against noise nuisance and threaten the overburdened airport management with a lawsuit.[1]

The film *Airport* (1970) condensed how the circumstances under which commercial aviation functioned altered dramatically in the 1960s, when a veritable revolution in air transportation took place. Aircraft changed in appearance, size, and operating characteristics. The high speed of jet aircraft dictated that pilots became subject to precise radio instructions from air traffic controllers on the ground, who continuously monitored each and every plane on radar to ensure flight safety. Except in first class, cabin crews were less able to take care of the personal needs of the rapidly growing numbers of passengers the way they had done when aircraft were smaller and slower. Despite the fact that flying continued to be an expensive way to travel, the "lucky few" who had hitherto enjoyed the comforts of flight were overrun by middle-class travelers who flew simply because they needed or wanted to go places and could pay the price. The latter had to content themselves with the cramped environment of coach- or economy-class seating in the rear of

the aircraft. From their vantage point an aircraft cabin looked rather like an elongated bus with an extra seat on both sides of the isle and undersized windows. Only those sitting immediately next to the small panes were able to take in the cloudscape—one of the customary attractions of air travel. Outside, the high squeak of turbine jets pushed away the lower tones of piston engines and propellers. Because of jet noise as well as safety, airports needed to separate aircraft and people, meaning that passengers were confined to the indoor environment of terminal buildings and enclosed jetways, while ground crews were mechanized to cope with aircraft maintenance requirements and transportation logistics such as fuel, luggage, and freight. Jet engines, described by one observer as producing "the maximum amount of environmental injury and social disruption,"[2] also brought air transport at loggerheads with a considerable section of society. Demonstrations against the effects that noise and pollution had on those living in the vicinity of the airport became an almost universal phenomenon as time progressed. For airport and airline operators alike it was henceforth necessary to take the external effects of air transportation into serious consideration. Nonetheless, jet aircraft lent a new meaning to the old adage that the air unites all people: for those who traveled on them, the world was shrinking.

Travel and Technology

While the external effects of air transport were many, perhaps the most far-reaching of them was the emerging link between aviation and tourism. This was a phenomenon that found its roots in the continuing process of economic growth in the Western world. The upward trend of the 1950s continued through the next decade. Between 1960 and 1970 the volume of world trade doubled—and would have doubled again between 1970 and 1975 had it not been for the 1973 Oil Crisis.[3] Agriculture and industry increased their productivity almost every year, feeding optimistic expectations of continuous prosperity. As the economy expanded, business activity became much more international, necessitating more frequent and more rapid movement of people. In the western European countries the booming economy yielded much improved living conditions for the population at large. After a series of wage increases that pushed up disposable incomes, material existence looked brighter than ever before. This newfound wealth translated into a sharp rise in consumer spending. Improved education and a much wider distribution of printed news broadened the horizon for many. Car ownership proliferated. The consequence of the emergence of the consumer society was a dramatic rise in mobility. Leisure travel grew like never before. Figures indicate that Western Europeans spent no more than 1.2 percent of their annual income on holidays in 1958. By 1967 this percentage had more than doubled to 2.5 and continued to rise to 4.4 percent in 1978.[4]

The increased willingness, and ability, to spend money on holidays manifested itself in a rapid increase in foreign travel. A vacation abroad, which had been the exception for most of Europeans in the 1950s, now came within the financial reach of a much larger section of society. A complete international travel industry developed, catering to tourist budgets—large and small. The wider outlook and reach into the world was further enhanced by the spread of television. If only one in every five European households possessed a television set in 1960, that ratio had become almost one to one by 1970. What the decade also saw was an expansion of the reach of television beyond the Western world. More than any other form of "static" media that used written words and still images to convey news and notions, television spread vivid, immediate, and moving pictures, with sound. It also spread conceptions of foreign lands and places. In a geographic sense, television encouraged travel, as it created a very direct image of what foreign places looked like. At the same time, it created something of a common understanding of what "Western life" was all about and what tourists might expect to find on their holiday destination. The combined result of these developments was little short of revolutionary. By the early 1970s, tourism had grown into the world's biggest foreign currency earner. Aviation played a significant role in this. The combination of fast, large aircraft and a reduction of fares made air travel into a mass travel phenomenon. This spread of air travel put new demands on the aviation infrastructure everywhere.

Such demands were fed by forecasts of continued high growth. Even for a small country like Holland, then logging about 13 million inhabitants, air transport forecasts ran over 100 million air passengers annually by the year 2000.[5] At the end of the 1950s it appeared obvious that the air transport business would continue to boom. These ideas were fed by the popularity that jet aircraft enjoyed with passengers right from their introduction. When Pan Am began nonstop jet services to Europe in 1959, initial demand for tickets was such that there were simply not enough seats available, and passengers had to be bumped off to propeller airplanes.[6] This appeared to be an indication that capacity was of overriding importance in air transportation. Through the 1950s it had not been clear whether the general development of aviation technology would be towards speed or capacity. In fact, these two goals had thus far combined in new aircraft designs. Yet with the introduction of jet propulsion, the engineers had arrived at an obstacle that could only be overcome with great difficulty: the sound barrier.

Speed had been a major factor in the technological development air transport from its inception. With the introduction of jet engines, civil airliners had achieved cruising speeds of around 600 mph. This meant that the new passenger aircraft were operating fairly close to the speed of sound (around 660 mph, depending on the altitude). In the late 1950s and early 1960s much effort was put into the development of supersonic commercial airliners as the

logical next step in the quest for ever faster flight. The technological chal-lenges were enormous, just as the investments necessary for research and development of such aircraft. Yet on the horizon shimmered the prospect of a world market for supersonic air transportation. For that reason Britain and France linked their aeronautical industries in 1959 in a joint effort to recapture the position on the world market for commercial aircraft that they had lost to American producers. A bilateral agreement between the two governments was signed on November 29, 1962, which resulted in the first flight of the Sud-Aviation/British Aircraft Corporation Concorde on March 2, 1969. Concorde presented not only a technological breakthrough, but also a leap forward in air travel as such. In little over a decade the flight time between Europe and the United States had been reduced by 80 percent. Flying at twice the speed of sound—about 1450 mph (2330 kilometers)—Concorde covered the distance Paris/London to New York within 4 hours. For the passenger this promised an enormous advantage over the regular subsonic jets, because it did away with the disturbing effects of *jet lag*, the luxury affliction of the biorhythm of long-range aircraft passengers.

Supersonic flight thus held specific attractions. Once it became clear that the British and the French were serious about the Concorde project, neither the United States nor the Soviet Union wanted to stay behind for reasons of prestige. In June 1963 President John F. Kennedy announced a federal program for the construction of an American Super Sonic Transport (SST). Three years later Boeing received a contract to develop advanced studies for a prototype of the SST. In the Soviet Union a design team from Tupolev worked on the Tu-144, which had a concept similar to the Anglo-French Concorde. The prototype of the Tu-144 was the first to fly, on December 31, 1968, 2 months ahead of the French-built Concorde 001.

To the casual observer it looked as if commercial aviation was heading towards supersonic flight. On January 1, 1968 the Anglo-French consortium building the Concorde proudly announced to have received preliminary or-ders for seventy-six aircraft, while more possible purchases were pending. It was a development welcomed by the luxury travelers but watched with concern by airport managers and politicians alike. Both were increasingly confronted with the effects of noise nuisance that subjected airport expan-sion programs to negative reactions from people living in the vicinity, re-actions that appeared to gain in strength with each new jet that went into service. It was evident early on that the use of supersonic aircraft would considerably increase annoyance, not only because supersonic flight caused shockwaves each time the sound barrier was broken but also because the very powerful engines of the supersonic airliners would vastly increase the already considerable noise problems around airports.[7] At the 1963 confer-ence of the European airport authorities in Geneva, Switzerland, a resolution was passed which laid down a package of noise requirements that a super-sonic airliner would have to match to be admissible. In March 1964 the

American Airport Operators Council gave out similar soundings. In a statement on the impact of the possible operation of supersonic transport aircraft the organization stated that unless a radical reduction of engine noise could be effected, the aircraft could "only be operated at the expense of land acquisition around airports," which would "add immeasurably to the overall costs of the SST program."[8]

Even before a single supersonic airliner had flown, these aircraft were heavily debated. In March 1971 the U.S. Senate called a halt to the allocation of further funds for the development of the American SST by the smallest of majorities: 51 against 49 votes. By then more than $1 billion had been spent on the project since 1963. But despite the small voting margin the decision was generally welcomed. In the years leading up the Senate's cancellation international attention had been called to the harmful effects that high altitude supersonic flight would have on the protective ozone layer in the Earth's atmosphere, which shields all living beings from ultraviolet radiation from the Sun. Originating in circles of environmentalists, the concern that the operation of large numbers of supersonic airliners in the upper layers of the atmosphere would lead to ozone depletion, and indirectly to a spread of skin cancer and other cosmic radiation-related diseases, was growing rapidly. Compared to these effects, noise nuisance was but a minor consequence.[9] At any rate, it became evident that widespread supersonic transport would be inadmissible given the technology of the day. That the Anglo-French Concorde could, nevertheless, be put into scheduled service in 1976 was the result of political choices in Britain and France, huge amounts of taxpayers' money, and long diplomatic skirmishes with the United States over landing rights for these noisy aircraft in New York and Washington, D.C.[10] By that time the development of the Concorde's Soviet counterpart, the Tupolev Tu-144, had been stagnant for years. After a problematic development that resulted in major structural changes in the aircraft and a spectacular crash at the Paris Air Show of 1973 that was witnessed by thousands of spectators, the operational use of the Tu-144 remained limited to experiments with supersonic transport of mail and cargo between 1975 and 1978.

But if the quest for speed ran aground in the limitations of technology, it opened up the airways to its competing phenomenon: the quest for size and economy. At Boeing, the contractor for the American SST project, the sights had long been adjusted in this direction. From 1967 the company's main efforts had been concentrated on the development of its model 747. This project represented the other end of the spectrum in aeronautical development and had very different roots. In December 1964 the U.S. Air Force had issued a design competition for a very large transport aircraft to be used as a troop and heavy equipment carrier. And though Boeing's design lost out to Lockheed's C-5 Galaxy in September 1965, Boeing did save the government-paid preliminary design studies. It was decided to use these as a basis for the development of a replacement aircraft to the successful

Boeing 707 series. The very wide fuselage (*wide body*) of the model 747 was designed to seat some 350 to 400 passengers, double the number of seats provided in the existing jets. Its scale surpassed anything that had been tried before in commercial aviation. In December 1965 Pan American agreed to become the aircraft's launching customer, a move that fitted Pan American's long dedication to lowering ticket prices in air transport. A contract for twenty-five *jumbo jets* was signed 4 months later in Seattle. With the development of the 747 Boeing took an enormous risk—the biggest in the history of the aircraft industry, according to some observers—and chanced the future of the company on this single project.[11] The gamble paid off. Profitability per capacity ton-kilometer, the customary unit of measurement in the air transport industry, was much increased over the first generation jets. The Boeing 747 achieved an enormous success in sales, over 1,400 units to date, and the wide body concept found many followers in the international aircraft industry. Both Douglas and Lockheed came up with wide body designs of their own: the DC-10 and the L-1011 Tristar. In Europe the Airbus project, which started as an intergovernmental endeavor in 1967, also concentrated on the development of an aircraft in the same category, the A-300.[12] All this had a considerable impact on the development of aviation in the 1970s. On board and on the ground the big numbers took over. Airports and their functioning had to be redesigned because of it. Air travel finally came within reach of the increasingly affluent masses of the Western world. In the first few years of the new decade world passenger figures went up by 30 percent.[13]

These developments were disrupted by the consequences of the Oil Crisis of 1973. Oil prices quadrupled—an immediate prelude to a period of international economic stagnation that would come to overshadow the image of the 1970s and 1980s. For the fuel-guzzling air transport industry the short-term consequences of the recession were enormous. They made a reorientation on future developments inevitable. Costs and economics acquired overall dominance in airline thinking and planning. Automation, a process that had begun in the second half of the 1950s, took on a whole new meaning as a way to cut costs.

The increased size and use of aircraft also had important consequences in the area of safety. Aircraft accidents were, of course, as old as powered flight itself, but decades passed before crashes claimed large numbers of victims. Nonetheless, aircraft accidents had always made news headlines. Yet, from the 1950s flying had steadily become safer. The annual increase in passenger numbers far exceeded the growth in the annual number of airline victims. After the introduction of jet airliners the number of victims had even stabilized. Compared to the increase of mileage in commercial aviation, the number of deaths per million miles was reduced by half.[14]

In contrast, the public's sensitivity to aircraft crashes increased, rather than diminished. This not only reflected the growth of first-hand experience

of flying that resulted from the steady drop in ticket prices but was also connected to an increasingly critical assessment of technology in the public eye so typical of the 1960s and 1970s when technological artefacts invaded every Western household. Besides, with the increasing size of aircraft there were more victims to be mourned per accident. The press paid much attention to these, as the depiction of disaster and human failure appealed to latent feelings of fear present in almost all airline passengers. Moreover, the inescapable death in a flying accident evoked a morbid fascination with crashes in the media. Whereas no one in Europe or in the United States would know if a local bus in Indonesia disappeared into a ravine, an accident involving even a small airliner would be sure to receive worldwide press coverage. Typically, the crash on the Indonesian island of Sumatra of a Garuda Fokker F-28 at Palembang's Talang Betutu Airport in September 1975 was reported in American and European newspapers alike, although the number of casualties to be mourned (twenty-five) was well below the number of victims that would be involved in a bus accident.[15] The disaster theme not only appealed to the press but was also evident in popular fiction novels and in film. In this respect *Airport* was a trendsetter. It had three sequels, all attracting millions of viewers worldwide.

The most important difference between fiction and fact was the prior determination of the plot's happy ending. In the real world this was, of course, not so. In March of 1974 a brand-new Douglas DC-10 belonging to Turkish Airlines went down near Ermenonville, north of Paris, with 346 passengers on board—the biggest crash in the history of aviation thus far. The cause, as was discovered later, was a design error in one of the rear doors of the aircraft. The DC-10 was grounded three times before the decade was out. The last time was in June 1979, 2 weeks after an American Airlines machine had lost its port engine after takeoff from Chicago O'Hare Airport as a result of faulty maintenance. In the crash that followed, 259 passengers, thirteen crew members, and two people on the ground perished. Investigations underlined that the human element remained the weakest link in the chain of events preceding such calamities. Two years before that, on March 27, 1977, the same weak human link had devastating consequences at the airport of Tenerife, on the Spanish Canary Islands. Confusing radio communication resulted in the world's worst airline disaster, when a KLM Boeing 747 on its takeoff run collided in dense fog with a Pan American jumbo crossing the runway. Of the 637 people on board the two aircraft 575 died in flames—a sad, lasting record in the history of air transport.

Air Transport in International Politics

In the early 1960s international tension between East and West again peaked with the construction of the Berlin Wall that began in August 1961. At first

it appeared that another airlift operation to West Berlin might be necessary. In Washington it was recognized that air access was the most precious of the various means of transport to the city, because it was the only method that defied Soviet monitoring of what was being moved. As a show of America's continuing resolve to defend Berlin, President Kennedy had Vice President Lyndon Johnson flown in especially.[16] After Moscow had claimed that West German "anti-Soviet extremists" were deliberately offered free air passages to Berlin, the United States, Britain, and France warned the Soviet Union on August 26, that any interference with Western air traffic to and from Berlin would have "grave consequences." The Soviets, however, were undeterred and in February 1962 even temporarily "closed" one of the air corridors to the city in use by Western aircraft. To test Soviet tenacity, the United States considered flying commercial airplanes with military crews, although without passengers. In Washington, voices called for armed fighter escorts if the Soviets continued their restrictions.[17] Further escalation was near when a plane carrying the British ambassador to West Germany, Sir Christopher Steel, was intercepted by Soviet fighter aircraft although not fired upon. Retaliation plans included proposals for Western air forces to intercept and escort all flights of Soviet bloc airlines above western Europe. In response to further diplomatic skirmishes, Moscow issued a statement that the civil air corridors to Berlin had never been formally established under international agreement and that air services to West Berlin needed to be settled in negotiations with the sovereign government of the German Democratic Republic (GDR) or East Germany, well knowing this would be a major diplomatic problem since none of the Western nations recognized the GDR.[18]

The involvement of aviation in the Berlin Crisis did not stand on its own. While tensions between East and West continued to run high air connections remained precarious, and in October 1962 the Cuban Missile Crisis heightened anxiety. But after that relations stabilized at a more sedate level. International aviation profited from this. Unforeseen political disruptions such as the crisis over the Soviet invasion of Czechoslovakia in August 1968 apart, aviation relations became less turbulent. Negotiations on landing and traffic rights gradually shifted from the region of "high politics" to "low politics" in the sense of bilateral economic and trade relations. In 1963 the United States even dared turn away from a policy of strict containment of communism in air transport. Nonetheless, aviation remained a touchy subject. British intentions to export a series of Vickers Viscount airliners to Communist China—a sales order vital to the ailing British aircraft industry—caused a severe strain on Anglo-American relations, when Washington refused to allow American-made electronics and radar equipment to be used in the aircraft on security grounds. In effect this blocked not only the sales of British commercial airliners but also the long-term prospects of Britain's commercial aircraft industry. It was a policy that fitted the U.S.

Department of Commerce's interests in furthering American aeronautical exports.[19]

But the worst conflicts where politics and air transport intersected happened elsewhere, particularly in Africa. They were the by-products of fierce nationalism that followed in the wake of political independence. Initial efforts to weave air transport agreements into new regional schemes for political and economic cooperation met with little success. Early in 1960 Egypt and Syria decided to add aerial prestige to their 1958 political union of the United Arab Republic by merging Egypt's Misrair and Syrian Airways into United Arab Airlines. This was despite the reluctance of the Syrian Airways' shareholders to accept the merger terms. Marred by politics, split over operating bases in two countries 500 miles apart, and divided by different corporate cultures, the airline was a quick failure. In October 1961 Syria pulled out and created a new government-owned Syrian Arab Airline, leaving United Arab Airlines in disarray.[20] Similarly, Central African Airways (CAA), which had come into being as a joint venture of Southern Rhodesia (Zimbabwe), Northern Rhodesia (Zambia), and Nyasaland (Malawi) in June 1946, did not survive the postindependence desire of the three new governments to have their own flag carriers. In December 1963 CAA was split into separate subsidiaries—Air Malawi, Zambia Airways, and Air Rhodesia—to operate in each country. The Southern Rhodesian government's unilateral declaration of independence on November 11, 1965, however, upset the precarious balance, and CAA was dissolved in 1967.[21] East African Airlines, also founded under British colonial rule in 1946, lasted longer. In it Kenya, Tanzania, and Uganda cooperated until 1977, when Uganda's dictator Idi Amin withdrew support because of protracted conflicts with Tanzania. In former French Africa, Ivory Coast-based Air Afrique, founded in March 1961 as a collaborative venture of eleven countries, was the only multilateral airline to last.

The multilateral failures indicated that more than a few newly independent nations on the African continent regarded air transport—and the prestige involved in it—in a particularly bright and blinding nationalistic light. Trouble began in 1960, the year in which sixteen African nations became independent. In July, not 2 weeks after the independence of (formerly Belgian) Congo (Zaire), separatists in the Katanga province declared their own independence. Years of intense turmoil, violence, and civil war followed. From the start, the Belgians, who maintained something of a military power base in postindependent Congo, called upon their national airline, Sabena, to play a role in the conflict. The airline was used to fly military personnel and equipment to Leopoldville (Kinshasa), and evacuate Belgians and other Westerners on the way back in what soon amounted to a major international airbridge. Between 9 and 28 July, Sabena evacuated over 25,000 people. Something of the urgency of the air bridge transpired from the figures: on flights to Brussels, Sabena's brand-new Boeing 707s, designed to

seat 174 passengers, carried up to 303 people.[22] In an effort to stop the fighting, the United Nations sent troops, and UN Secretary-General Dag Hammarskjöld personally tried to mediate. To his misfortune, at a quarter past ten in the evening of September 17, 1961, while flying from N'Djili Airport near Leopoldville to Ndola in Northern Rhodesia, his Swedish DC-6B crashed under suspicious circumstances just before landing.[23] Although Katanga was reunited with Congo proper in 1963, a smoldering rebellion continued, and in September 1966 Congo's new president, Joseph-Désiré Mobutu, closed all air services with neighboring Angola for fear that his political rival Moïse Tshombe, former leader of the Katanga uprising, might use scheduled airliners to transport mercenaries into his unstable country.

Despite the dangers of flying in a country engulfed by civil war, Sabena continued to provide air transport within Congo. After the transfer of power its aircraft operated under the new guise of Air Congo, hoping the Congolese identity would stop them being fired upon. Theirs was an important task in the vast underdeveloped country but an expensive one. Sabena, minority shareholder but major banker to Air Congo, annually lost between 700 and 900 million Belgian francs ($14 to 18 million) on its operations between 1960 and 1967, when Mobutu revoked Sabena's landing rights to punish Belgium for its continued involvement in Congolese affairs. To Sabena, the Congolese affairs of which were wholly political and under the strictest scrutiny from the Belgian government, this was a heavy blow: the airline garnered as much as one-third of its total revenue from the service between Brussels and Kinshasa. Had it not been for government intervention, Congo would have bankrupted the Belgian flag carrier in 1967. Mobutu, who on his part depended on Belgian economic and financial aid, repeatedly played the "airline card" in his relations with Brussels, giving and taking landing rights on the basis of short-term policy goals.[24] And playing the "airline card," Mobutu finally caught up with his rival Tshombe, who had come to settle in Spain. On June 30, 1967, the plane on which Tshombe traveled to the Spanish Mediterranean holiday island Mallorca was hijacked by a Frenchman, acting on instructions from Kinshasa, and forced to land in Algeria, where Tshombe was forced to remain under house arrest until his death in 1969.[25]

Political and military interference in African air transport was unparalleled and revealed just how prominent air transport was in the affairs between the new nations. The storming, on October 29, 1966, by Ghanaian troops of a Pan Am plane provided an extreme example. The Pan Am flight had on board a delegation of diplomats and politicians from Guinea traveling to the annual conference of the Organisation of African Unity in Addis Ababa, Ethiopia. At an intermediate stop in Ghana's capital Accra, the nineteen-strong delegation from Guinea, among whom Guinean Foreign Minister Louis Lansana Beavogui, was forcibly taken from board and incarcerated in Accra. Ghanaian authorities announced that they would only let

the delegates go if and when Guinea would stop its public campaign against Ghana's incumbent new ruler, Lieutenant General Joseph Ankrah, and "allow" Ghanaian citizens who had followed Ghana's ousted first president, Kwame Nkruma, into exile in Guinea to "return home." That was after Nkruma, one of the leaders of the Pan-African Movement, had conferred with the heads of state of Guinea and Mali to establish ways and means to get him back into power in Ghana, and an armed column of Guinean forces to bring this about had been stopped at the border of Ivory Coast (situated between Guinea and Ghana). The storming of the Pan Am plane brought further repercussions the next day, when Guinea's (anti-Western) President Ahmed Sékou Touré gave out a public statement holding the United States responsible for the kidnapping and placed the American ambassador to his country under house arrest. Violent protests against American interests in Guinea followed. In retaliation, the United States froze all American aid to the country on November 2. It took a full week to resolve the hostage crisis. On November 5 the Ethiopian emperor Haile Selassie, Egypt's President Gamal Abdel Nasser and President William Tubman of Liberia, managed to secure release of the hostages. Nonetheless, anti-American sentiments in Guinea continued to run high. President Sékou Touré revoked Pan Am's landing rights, closed the airline's offices in the capital Conakry, and expelled all American citizens, including Peace Corps volunteer aid workers.[26]

The seizure of civil aircraft almost appeared to become an accepted form of "hard diplomacy" in west Africa when just half a year later, in June 1967, Ivory Coast grounded a KLM flight that had diverted to the Ivorian capital Abijan because of bad weather. The aircraft had been scheduled to land at the airport of Conakry, Guinea. For the second time within a year Guinea's foreign minister, Beavogui, found himself, and his diplomatic entourage, marched from a plane at gunpoint, this time to force his government to release the crew of an Ivorian fishing boat and an Ivorian official from Guinean imprisonment. The Guinean government, on its part, did not hesitate for a moment to retaliate and the following day arrested the KLM representative in Conakry (who doubled as the Dutch consul in the country), asserting that the Netherlands government had colluded with the Ivorians to capture the Guinean delegation. As a further measure, all exit visas for Dutch citizens living or working in Guinea were annulled. The diplomatic scope of the incident thus widened—and widened even further when the Netherlands approached UN Secretary-General U Thant a week later to intervene and secure the release of its citizens. Mediation was, however, to no avail, and it was October before Guinea and Ivory Coast reached an agreement on the exchange of prisoners and the release of the Dutch hostages in Conakry.[27]

By that time a new crisis in civil air transport in Africa was developing. On May 30, 1967, months of mounting tribal tensions and political unrest in Nigeria over the control of the oil-rich eastern Nigerian region of Biafra

escalated when Biafra declared its independence. Both the (military) federal government in Lagos and the Biafran separatists hastened to bolster their positions with weapons bought in Europe, shipping them by air. The gambit were the oil fields of eastern Nigeria—the reason why the government in Lagos could count on Western support for its efforts to restore control over the territory. Preparing for war, the Nigerian government chartered British and French aircraft to deliver guns and ammunitions, while Soviet cargo aircraft flew in a number of MiG-15 jets and Czech L-29 training and ground attack aircraft. Despite a ban on all civil flights over eastern Nigeria, the Biafran rebels also used air transport to build up their position. Across Europe cargo planes were chartered to fetch guns, ammunition, and even old military aircraft from private sellers. This dropped air transport into the cauldron of the unfolding Biafran war. In August the military leadership in Lagos declared "total war" on Biafra. Nigerian forces closed all borders and soon enforced a naval blockade of Biafra's only seaport, Port Harcourt. In the spring of 1968, Nigerian troops managed to surround the insurrectionist forces, cutting all surface supply lines. This had disastrous effects on the food situation of millions of people living in the area. Famine broke out and began to attract attention from Western media. By the end of May television broadcasts all over Europe and North America aired disconcerting images of people suffering from war, air attacks, and widespread starvation. Suddenly, the dramatic events in Africa were unfolding in the living room of television audiences the world over—and with considerable consequence. In Geneva, the International Red Cross declared an emergency and demanded that the naval blockade be lifted to allow food aid to reach the 600,000 refugees that the war left stranded in camps. The Nigerian authorities, however, refused to cooperate, fearing that fresh food supplies would end up feeding the very troops they were fighting. Lagos only agreed to open specific Nigerian airports that were under their control to relief flights. Supplies would have to be transported by road from there. But with the gravity of the situation deepening every day and approximately 12 million Biafrans virtually without food, such a roundabout delivery route was not a realistic option for the crisis at hand. Besides, Biafran leaders on their part refused to consider the option for fear of Nigerian involvement in the transports.

While Western and African governments were conferring how to bring an end to the conflict, private aid agencies decided to act on their own accord, propelled by the drama that occupied news broadcasts and newspaper front pages daily as the war and famine intensified. They chartered cargo aircraft and crews willing to risk the threat that any aircraft entering Nigerian airspace without prior consent from the authorities in Lagos would be shot down. On the Spanish island Fernando Póo and the Portuguese island São Tomé off the Nigerian coast in the Atlantic, organizations such as Joint Church Aid, Caritas International, and Oxfam established makeshift warehouses and temporary operating bases for cargo flights delivering food

to Biafra. In the summer of 1968 an international air bridge run by Christian aid organizations, nicknamed Jesus Christ Airlines after the abbreviation JCA for Joint Church Aid, came into effect. It operated under the cover of darkness on improvised landing strips in Biafran territory to supply the starving population. Despite the risks—such as the loss of a Red Cross Super Constellation on approach to a jungle airstrip on July 6, 1968—the operations went on for 18 months. In this first big international aerial relief operation a total of 5,314 illegal food flights saved the lives of over a million people before the conflict finally ended with the military collapse of Biafra in January 1970. Despite the relief efforts, another million people did not live to see the end of the conflict and died of starvation.[28]

The direct involvement of worldwide nongovernmental organizations in the Biafran conflict evidenced how the combination of modern communication technology and air transport could bring a global reach to a regional conflict. Biafra was by no means the only illustration of this. The prime example of how commercial aviation provided such a link was the invention of the political hijack of airliners. Although the phenomenon of aircraft hijacking was much older—the first hijack took place over Peru in 1930—such incidents had, thus far, been rooted in personal circumstances of the hijackers, although political convictions often played a role as well. Over the years more than a hundred airliners were hijacked in the United States to fly to Fidel Castro's Cuba. From the summer of 1967, however, the dramatic escalation of the Israeli-Arab conflict introduced to the world an entirely different category of unlawful seizures of airliners, detached from the personal circumstances of the hijackers, and rooted entirely in hard-line political strife. Considering hijacks to be a legitimate weapon in their fight against Israel and its Western allies, Palestinian resistance movements targeted commercial aviation as a vehicle to get media attention for their cause. In the wake of the Six-Day War in the Middle East (June 1967), the international airline industry was hit by a wave of terrorist attacks.

The first such action took place on July 22, 1968, when an El Al Boeing 707 flying from Rome, Italy, to Tel Aviv, Israel, was hijacked by three armed Palestinians of the Popular Front for the Liberation of Palestine (PFLP) and forced to land in Algiers. There the hijackers received a warm welcome from the Algerian government, which was sympathetic to their cause. Of the thirty-eight passengers on board, the nineteen who carried non-Israeli passports were released by Algeria later that day, while four Israeli women and three children were also allowed to leave on the 23rd, along with three stewardesses. The remaining people on board were subsequently held hostage in collaboration with Algeria. Throughout the Western world there was a resounding outrage. The International Federation of Air Line Pilots' Associations (IFALPA) called for a complete stop of all air traffic to Algeria and a worldwide boycott of Air Algérie flights, a proposal that received

considerable support in airline circles. Meanwhile solutions were hammered out on the diplomatic front through the efforts of the Italian government and the International Red Cross. Nonetheless, the situation was not resolved until August 31, when Algeria finally released the remaining hostages in return for Israel's agreement to free sixteen Palestinians held for anti-Israeli actions.[29]

In the years that followed, hijacks and attacks against commercial aviation became recurrent events that made headline news around the globe. In 1969 there were no less than seventy successful hijacks, while twelve more attempts failed. Terrorist actions against aviation targets, initially mainly aimed at the Israeli airline El Al but soon expanded to include all airlines from Western countries that supported Israel, turned out to be highly successful media weapons to bring the Palestinian cause into the spotlight of world opinion. The aura of aviation guaranteed widespread press coverage. Aircraft were at once the symbol *and* the Achilles' heel of the Western technology and support that enabled Israel to gain military victory on the battlefield. In principle, a group of terrorists needed but a single bullet to hit that Achilles' heel with the destructive power of an aircraft cabin's sudden decompression at high altitude.[30] Aggression was not limited to acts committed on board but also took the shape of attacks with firearms against aircraft on the ground. In December 1968 two members of the PFLP attacked another El Al Boeing as it was about to depart from Athens, Greece, to New York, while a similar incident happened in Zurich, Switzerland, 2 months later. Because of the success of the method used, other political "resistance groups" copied the Palestinian example. What subsequently united terrorist groups such as the Japanese Red Army and Germany's Red Army Fraction was a rejection of Western, capitalist society as expressed through aviation technology.

Existing and new countermeasures proved ineffective at first. In September 1963 most ICAO member states had signed the Convention on Offenses and Certain Other Acts Committed on Board Aircraft in Tokyo. The treaty's aim was to declare actions which endangered the safety of civil aircraft unlawful and internationally punishable. But this could only work as a deterrent if and when all signatory governments were prepared to uphold the treaty. Events in the late 1960s showed that if shared political ideas underpinned a hijack, this was not always the case. In aviation circles and international politics this caused great concern. On its annual meeting of March 1969, IFALPA, representing 44,000 airline pilots in over fifty countries, tried to pressure the international community into action. Anxiety spurred the ICAO nations to agree on a second, more sharply formulated antihijack treaty in The Hague in December 1970. It was a sign of the size and severity of the attacks against commercial aviation that ICAO met for a third time on the issue before the next year was out, setting up a wide-ranging international system of measures to combat the terrorist threats.[31] Yet despite the introduction

of precautionary checks on airports, hijacks and attacks could not be stopped before technological and security developments had had the time to evolve.

This showed particularly forcefully on September 6, 1970. On this *Hijack Sunday* no less than three aircraft were taken in a violent demonstration that hijacking had become a general anti-Western weapon. That afternoon a TWA Boeing 707 that had taken off from Frankfurt (Germany), a Swissair DC-8 from Zurich, and a brand-new Pan Am Boeing 747 from Amsterdam, all bound for New York, were hijacked in support of the Palestinian cause. The hijack of a fourth aircraft, an El Al Boeing 707, went awry when Israeli "sky marshals" shot one of the hijackers, a Nicaraguan traveling on a forged Honduran passport, and overpowered his accomplice. The next day, Pan Am's 747 was blown up with dynamite on Cairo Airport after the passengers and crew had been allowed to leave the aircraft. While the ensuing crisis was still evolving, a BOAC Vickers VC-10 was hijacked on a flight from Bahrain to London 2 days later. At the end of a chaotic week, the Swissair, TWA, and BOAC machines were blown up simultaneously on the abandoned airstrip of Zerqa, north of the Jordanian capital, Amman, after stops in Beirut (Lebanon) and Damascus (Syria), hotbeds of anti-Israeli sentiments. The fireball of the explosion left fifty-five passengers stranded in the Jordanian desert amid chaos and a civil war that followed when King Hussein of Jordan had his army clamp down on the Palestinian movement in his country. It would be several weeks later before the passengers were released and able to return home.[32]

These actions resulted in a further tightening of security measures at airports, precautions that had a degree of success. The number of aircraft hijacks dropped, although aircraft remained vulnerable to in-flight attacks with explosives. After simultaneous bomb attacks on a Swiss and an Austrian airliner on February 21, 1970, ten European airlines temporarily stopped the transportation of mail and parcels to Israel until new security measures could be enforced. Improvements took time, more than airline pilots cared to accept. By mid-1972 aircraft from fifty-two nations, with a grand total of 15,000 passengers on board, had fallen victim to hijacks. On June 19 of that year IFALPA issued a 24-hour pilots' strike, grounding air traffic worldwide, and demanded that the United Nations take action against air piracy forthwith. Yet countermeasures were always one step behind. The start of hijacks and hostage dramas began to shift to locations away from aircraft and airports, with the primary role of aircraft redrawn as escape vehicles. This was prominently so when Palestinians raided the Israeli sports team at the Munich Olympics on September 5, 1972. A hostage crisis ensued, leading up to a negotiated "getaway" by helicopter and a Lufthansa Boeing 727 passenger jet, which ended in a dramatic nightly shootout at the nearby Fürstenfeldbruck Air Base that left all hostages dead. Seven weeks later, on October 29, another Lufthansa jet,

flying from Beirut to Munich was hijacked to effect the release of the three surviving terrorists who were being held in Germany for trial. These were indeed released and eventually boarded the hijacked airliner at Zagreb (Yugoslavia) to be treated to a hero's welcome when they touched down at Tripoli, Libya.[33]

Away from the Middle East, such dramas were answered with new levels of precautions and international agreements on counterterrorism as governments realized their common interest in stability. Airports worldwide installed metal detectors to curb hijack attempts. In many countries airports came to be heavily guarded fortresses, surrounded by high fences and supervised by cameras and armed guards. After a prolonged hijack of a Southern Airways DC-7 in November 1972, which made stops in eight cities in the United States and Canada before its captors disembarked in Havana, even the United States and Cuba agreed that something had to be done to stop the armed takeovers in the sky. An accord to try or extradite hijackers was signed on February 15, 1973.[34] Yet it was not before the second half of the 1970s that preventive measures finally began to take effect the world over. Attacks on aviation targets shifted even further away from airports to the less risky practice of placing bombs at airline offices, a development which left few Western airlines unaffected.[35]

Meanwhile air transport demonstrated its vital capacity in yet another round of the Arab-Israeli conflict: the Yom Kippur War of 1973. American chartered civil aircraft flew ammunitions and military equipment to be picked up by El Al on airfields in the Azores. Israeli cargo planes were also observed loading military supplies in Amsterdam and elsewhere in Europe.[36] From October 13, an all-out American military airlift took supplies directly to Tel Aviv, which helped tilt the balance of the war in Israel's favor. On the other side, the Soviets masterminded an air bridge of their own to resupply the forces of their allies in the war.[37] In such circumstances any air traffic to the belligerent states became highly political. Because of its perceived support of Israel, the Dutch carrier KLM was boycotted in Arab countries and saw its landing rights revoked in Syria and Jordan after the Dutch shipped considerable quantities of munitions and reserve parts for Centurion tanks to Israel.[38]

To restore the peace once the guns fell silent, U.S. Secretary of State Henry Kissinger collected air miles shuttling his former *Air Force Two* between Egypt, Israel, and Syria in January and February 1974. Brimming with communications equipment, his Boeing 707 acted as a flying office and conference locale for his staff in frantic preparations en route to the next negotiation meeting. "Without it shuttle diplomacy would have been impossible," Kissinger later noted in his memoirs.[39] Pressures to achieve a successful outcome mounted with each flight. Yet aviation-based diplomacy had its downside too. The speed of air travel put a severe strain on the diplomats. Kissinger's aides later confided they preferred the earlier stages

of the American mission. The flying time to meet Egypt's president, Anwar el-Sadat, in Aswan allowed them 75 more minutes to prepare compared to the later shuttle between Israel and Syria.[40]

A Protected Business

After more than a decade of continuous high growth, the introduction of jets in the late 1950s appeared to be the logical next step to accommodate future passenger numbers. But what no one, not even airline executives, had foreseen at the time was that they would plunge the international airline industry into deep deficits. Between 1960 and 1964 losses in the airline industry ran over $1 billion—$417 million in 1961 alone at the deepest point in the crisis.[41] The industry went through the worst period in its history thus far. The problem was that proliferation of the new aircraft doubled world air transport capacity within a few years. In 1960, no less than 258 new jets left their factories, pushing capacity up by 16 percent.[42] That was well over and above the already considerable growth of 9.3 percent in passenger numbers.[43] In 1962 ICAO registered 572 jet aircraft in airline operation; in 1964 their number passed 1100. Load factors dropped to around 49 percent.[44] Against this background the IATA annual conference agreed in October 1962 to a 5 percent raise in economy-class fares to combat the worst effects of the alarming airline deficits. U.S. authorities, however, declared such a raise in fares "not in the public interest"—an attitude that was hardly surprising since American passengers accounted for approximately 60 percent of all ticket sales on routes across the North Atlantic. Washington refused to allow American carriers to charge the new rates of the IATA cartel. Canada took a similar view. Consequently, the airlines from the Western Hemisphere maintained their (lower) old fares. Several European countries, Britain and France at the vanguard, thereafter threatened to revoke the landing rights for American and Canadian airlines, forcing them to charge the new IATA ticket prices. With difficulty, a compromise was hammered out in Montreal in May 1963. It was a victory for U.S. diplomacy and resulted in an annulment of much of the fare raise.[45] In 1964 and again in 1966, ticket prices for transatlantic flights were lowered. These rate cuts contributed to a considerable jump in passenger numbers, amounting to 35 percent.

While economic circumstances changed, scheduled air transport as such remained trapped between bilateral politics and trading interests. In a business where national governments were either in full control or majority shareholders, dealing with the much-increased financial risks inevitably had political repercussions. Competition, such as there was, was limited by government-approved landing rights and ticket prices, and commercial disturbances therefore gave rise to diplomatic controversies. In the lawyers'

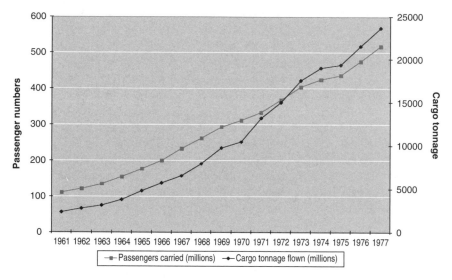

The Development of World Air Transport, 1961–1977. *Source:* ICAO figures.

game of bilateral negotiations, financial and economic arguments now became pivotal. The first major step in this direction dated back to 1954, when the United States had made the granting of commercial rights to foreign carriers dependent on "an equitable exchange of economic benefits."[46] It set the stage for a general trend much to the sorrow of smaller countries, for whom an evenhanded trade-off was always problematic. Such negotiations assumed that national traffic markets existed, markets that were "owned" by the government whose territory defined them. Yet, by its very nature, international air transport defied such definitions. After all, airlines could pick up passengers or cargo in any country they had rights in to do so. They could also transfer such passengers or cargo at their home airport and fly them on to a final destination in yet another country. The custom became known as "sixth freedom traffic" in the lawyers' jargon of international air transportation. It was most consciously carried out by those airlines that had outgrown the (limited) home markets that they supposedly served. The practice presented political difficulties on the hitherto lucrative North Atlantic routes, where the capacity offered had outgrown demand. The Icelandic carrier Loftleidir was such a carrier that had developed beyond its home market. It transported many times the number of passengers the thinly populated island republic had—and did so well below IATA rates too. Few countries accepted such "predatory" approaches to international air transport. Loftleidir was practically banned from most major airports in Europe and found itself forced to offer its low-cost transatlantic services from the Grand Duchy of Luxembourg. The reason it was able to defy

restrictive politics was that its American landing rights were rooted in the strategic position of Iceland, where the U.S. Air Force maintained one of its operating bases at Keflavik.[47]

In Holland, KLM's prominent position among the world's ten largest international airlines was also based on carriage of sixth freedom traffic. To effect an expansion of its market for traffic to the United States, KLM had floated a substantial percentage of its shares on the New York Stock Exchange in May 1957. It was hoped that American shareholding would reduce opposition to sixth freedom carriage. A bilateral agreement with the United States extending KLM's American landing rights was indeed signed later that year, but throughout the 1960s and 1970s federal authorities remained concerned about the origin of "Dutch" passengers and repeatedly moved to curb the Dutch flag carrier on the basis of the uneven distribution of market shares between New York and Amsterdam. KLM, on its part, refused to disclose from where its passengers originated.[48]

On the whole, negotiations over scheduled air services became ever more complex in character. The emphasis on economic and financial issues made sure that air transportation became linked to detailed systems of remunerations between airlines to ensure equity of the exchanged benefits. Often, such agreements also touched upon other areas of bilateral trade. In a good many countries securing the right of foreign airlines to operate scheduled air services came to depend on (usually confidential) agreements on scheduled payments, preferably in hard currency. From the end of the 1950s the access to each other's bilateral market suffered from a mushrooming of restrictive conditions.[49]

All in all, transatlantic relations in air transport remained edgy, particularly because Washington was not forthcoming to accommodate European desires for additional landing rights. One way around this was tried by the Spanish national carrier, Iberia, which used funds provided by Franco in an attempt to strengthen its position in Latin America by investing in airlines in Panama and in the Dominican Republic. For this very purpose a joint Spanish-Panamanian holding company was set up, with a dual seat in the Bahamas and in Panama. The idea was not only to boost transatlantic air travel between Spain and Latin America but also to build up a position in north-south air transport in the Western Hemisphere that would then feed Iberia's transatlantic services. This way the Spaniards hoped to circumvent American restrictionism and open up a back door into the United States. This was to little effect, as Pan Am (and subsequently Braniff) got the Torrijos government, which came into power in Panama after a military coup at the end of 1968, to favor American business interests and even adopt a closed skies policy towards Iberia. Between 1965 and 1978 Iberia lost $24 million in Air Panamá Internacional. Of Iberia's investment into the Dominican Compañía Dominicana de Aviación a similar story could be told.[50]

American protectionism was extremely problematic for those European carriers, such as Air France and BOAC, that suffered from a dramatic loss of traffic on their African routes around this time, resulting from the end of the French and British empires in Africa.[51] While the British had to agree to further reductions of fares across the North Atlantic in 1965 and 1966 to boost passenger demand, they put up hurdles for American carriers wishing to extend their services eastward beyond London. For years it was an obsession of American negotiators to get permission for TWA for a link from London through southern Europe, the Mediterranean, the Middle East, and on to Bombay (Mumbai), India. This seemed likely to damage both BEA and BOAC by almost doubling the impact of American competition east of London. It would also open the way for a second American "round the world service" next to Pan Am's. Hence Britain refused to budge to American demands. The final move was in 1964 when the United Kingdom indicated willingness to let TWA fly on to Cairo to connect there with its southern route terminating in Bombay but only in return for a considerable extension of British operating rights in the United States. That, of course, went counter to the American interests in the transatlantic market, and the response was a sudden drop of interest in the issue of the TWA routes.[52]

If the political environment in which the international flag carriers operated put serious constraints on their growth potential, the evolution of nonscheduled air transport added yet another problem. To the national airlines, charter flights were potentially disruptive. Operating outside the restrictive settings of bilateral agreements between governments, nonscheduled operators needed only simple permissions to fly and were thus able to fine-tune their operations to the needs of the moment. According to the time of the year, this could mean flying Western tourists to holiday resorts that began to spring up in geographic regions blessed with sought-after diversions from everyday city life, such as the Mediterranean coast, or—in the American context—the Caribbean islands. But it could also mean flying deeply religious Muslims from Indonesia to Mecca, Saudi Arabia, for the annual Hadj Pilgrimage. In effect, tickets for such nonscheduled operations were sold at prices well below those for scheduled flights. They could be cheaper because the charter airlines sold their entire seating capacity up front to a tour operator that organized each flight, instead of having to sell individual tickets directly to the general public. Because of the substantially lower fares and the less restrictive environment, it was not surprising that the charter concept met with growing success. If total world air transport tripled between 1963 and 1973, the share of charter airlines went from 2 to 20 percent.[53] The number of people using air transport increased rapidly, while the geographic spread of air travelers also widened.

The charter phenomenon transpired most prominently in those markets, and on those routes, that had the strictest regulation—i.e., western Europe and on the transatlantic routes to the United States. In Europe the start-up

charter airlines of the 1950s were able to profit from the rise in disposable incomes that followed economic development. It brought a rising demand for
holidays that combined the blessings of sun, sea, and sand. Within Europe
travel on charter flights grew at an average of 2.5 percent per year between
1965 and 1973—twice the growth rate of scheduled air transport.[54] To protect their business, national airlines followed several lines of defense. First of
all, the flag carriers of the leading nations of the European Economic Community investigated the possibilities to form an Air Union that would unite
their respective competitive strengths, distribute European air traffic among
them, and present a unified front against American competition. Such multi-
lateralism of European air transport would have provided a radical departure
from established custom. Discussions started in 1957, but the project only
gained real momentum in 1961 as a result of the airline crisis. With active
support from their governments, the Belgian, French, German, Italian, and
Dutch flag carriers negotiated on the formation of an Air Union but failed to
reach a satisfactory conclusion. The inroads into national sovereignty that
such a joint carrier represented, and the division of traffic shares among its
participants, presented just insuperable odds. Half-hearted discussions were
continued intermittently until the final collapse of the project in 1967.[55]
Secondly, a variety of legal obstacles were put up through which national
operating permits for the nonscheduled airlines could be denied. Such was
the case in Britain, where the Air Transport Licensing Board bent its ear to
complaints from BOAC and British European Airways (BEA) about unfairly
liberal permits for independent and charter airlines. In 1961–1962 charter
carrier Cunard Eagle was denied permission to start its own transatlantic
passenger and cargo services to the United States because it would lead to
"a material diversion of traffic from BOAC." In the process a variety of
routes all over Europe were also considered, on the basis of applications
for individual flights. But BEA—Britain's designated scheduled airline for
Europe—raised objections.[56] Besides, the Air Transport Licensing Board
ruled that the total price of a ticket that combined travel and (holiday)
accommodation in a single arrangement, the inclusive tour, must not be
less than the corresponding scheduled return fare to the same destination.[57]
Thirdly, national airlines, profiting from the financial strength emanating
from government ownership or large government shareholding, bought into
nonscheduled carriers and effectively made them into semi-independent, but
noncompetitive, endeavors contributing to their own earnings. Following
the German example where Lufthansa held a 26 percent share in the charter
carrier Condor right from the start, this happened in Belgium, when Sabena
gobbled up Sobelair in 1960, and in Holland, where KLM acquired a 25
percent shareholding in Martinair Charter in 1964. A fourth strategy was
the introduction of tickets specifically developed to fend off the charter carriers and offering special discount rates that were more or less competitive

with those of the nonscheduled airlines. To compete against charter traffic with its package deals through travel agencies, the concept of the inclusive tour was embraced by the scheduled airlines as well.

Competition from the charter carriers was considered especially problematic on the transatlantic routes. Here various companies operating outside the ownership structures of the national airlines pruned profits away from the latter. Initially aircraft could be chartered only by travel agents or groups of people who showed a distinctive common "affinity" because of which they wished to travel together. Throughout the 1960s a gradual relaxation of the rules for "affinity" groups vastly increased to popularity of this travel mode. "Affinity" could mean anything, the extreme example being the American "Left Hand Club." It attracted its members on the basis of cheap air tickets until the club was exposed as fraudulent and saw its travelers taken off a transatlantic flight in 1971.[58] Besides, the charter airlines profited from the sale of young, relatively inexpensive propeller aircraft by the national flag carriers. Around 1970 the charter carriers again benefited from the changing technology in commercial aviation. When the scheduled airlines replaced their first generation jets with the newly available jumbos, they purchased the secondhand aircraft. With them the share of the charter traffic between the United States and Europe rose from 8.6 to 26.3 percent, i.e. 3,691,000 passengers, between 1968 and 1973.[59] The responses of the IATA airlines to these developments were erratic. Market fluctuations and anticipated investments in wide-body jets necessitated fare raises of 5 percent between 1969 and 1971. As a result competition from charter airlines grew even stronger.[60] The pressures on the scheduled carriers became such that in July 1973 the U.S. Civil Aeronautics Board agreed to allow American and foreign scheduled airlines to take passengers traveling on inclusive tour tickets. On the other hand, the introduction of an Advanced Booking Charter was also agreed upon. This was an extra low-priced charter ticket that could be bought individually from a travel agent, provided the passenger booked well in advance of the flight. As ever more people were flying, scheduled and charter traffic became increasingly alike.[61]

The economic stagnation after 1973 added a special dimension to the issues at hand. Expensive new equipment in the shape of wide-body jets like the Boeing 747 and the Douglas DC-10, increased competition, monetary instability (after the collapse of the dollar in 1971), and security precautions made for an explosive brew in commercial aviation. The Oil Crisis, which quadrupled fuel prices, further sharpened the issues at stake. By necessity, ticket prices had to be increased—35 percent on intercontinental services—which resulted in a drop in passengers. Between the United States and Europe the slump totaled 1.2 million in 1974, and the numbers decreased further in 1975. In these 2 years the accumulated deficits of the international airline industry again ran into hundreds of millions of dollars.[62] In the same time

period, the United States instigated a renegotiation of the existing air transport agreements with the smaller European countries, notably the Netherlands, Belgium, and the Scandinavian nations, Denmark, Norway, and Sweden, in order to redraw the balance between American and European operators across the North Atlantic. It was part of a larger protectionist strategy on the part of the Civil Aeronautics Board to readjust the "balance of benefits" of operations of foreign airlines to the United States in favor of America's own loss-making international carriers. In South America, Aero Peru was one of the airlines to undergo a similar treatment when it had to agree to have Pan Am and Braniff increase their market shares between the Peruvian capital Lima and the United States. On October 2, 1974, the U.S. Department of Transportation even issued a federal action plan for improved profitability of America's international air carriers. This plan was built around a "Fly US Flag" program, encouraging Americans to travel on U.S. airlines and requiring that any travel associated with government contracts be solely on American carriers.[63]

The net result of the mix of increased competition, fuel prices, protectionism, and reduced passenger numbers was an enormous pressure on the air transport market in the mid-1970s. Those airlines that readjusted their positions by focusing on efficiency were able to keep up with market forces; others had to turn to their governments for additional support.[64]

Consequently, the scheduled airlines, especially those which received a relatively small part of their revenues from cargo, were intent on bringing the charter carriers under the controls of the bilateral system. This way the respective governments would be better able to watch over the interests of their national airlines and safeguard their position. Even a proclaimed protagonist of liberalism in the air like the Netherlands let the interests of KLM prevail over those of its charter airlines. Within the European Civil Aviation Conference (ECAC) Holland led the field in attempts to bring charter traffic under the control of the bilateral treaty regime.[65] Internationally, the process resulted in a growth of protectionism and a further tightening of bilateral regulations.[66]

Such protectionism and regulation created their own counterforces—in the form of voices that pointed out the negative effects of too much regulation for the consumer. These opinions were especially strong in circles of aviation lawyers and transport economists and could be heard in America and Europe alike.[67] In 1975 it led to an air transport policy review by the Department of Transportation in Washington, the outcome of which was a major change in policy announced in February 1977 under the authority of the newly elected president Jimmy Carter. Carter presented a bill that aimed to increase competition in the domestic air transport market. This Airline Deregulation Act took effect as of October 24, 1978, but even before that it had become evident that deregulation in the United States was likely to get an international sequel.

Reaching for the Masses

Throughout the 1960s airline advertisements the world over were happy to linger in the realm of the rich and famous, promoting the business with photographs showing celebrities as satisfied customers. Regardless of their national origins, movie stars and popular musicians—the generally accepted icons of youth and success—were filmed and photographed in the doorways of shiny passenger jets or underneath their mighty wings. Nationality did not matter much: American movie stars such as Katherine Hepburn, Kirk Douglas, and Orson Welles were just as soon put on proud display by Air France as their French counterparts like Anouk Aimée, Brigitte Bardot, and Yves Montand.[68] Likewise, Alitalia ostentatiously recorded its famous passengers such as opera star Maria Callas, jazz musician Louis Armstrong, and of course the Pope, along with national film icons Sophia Loren, Marcello Mastroianni, and Sergio Leone.[69] Extending this image of luxury, flight attendants, especially female, were adorned with designer uniforms as if the cabin aisle doubled as a catwalk in the sky. A combination of both national and airline prestige dictated that uniforms, formerly sober and businesslike, were now contracted out to internationally famous fashion designers such as Christian Dior, Pierre Cardin, Ralph Lauren, Mary Quant, Anne Klein, and Nina Ricci.[70] Airports too claimed their share in this glamour. Within 12 months after it opened its new terminal, Orly Airport registered as one of Paris' biggest attractions, receiving over 3 million visitors per year who came to gorge on its combination of modernity and richness.[71] The spread of automotive mobility made airport terminals into places where crowds gathered to cheer the demigods of the modern age as they descended from the clouds.

In a league of their own were pop stars. In the 1960s thousands of fans flocked to welcome them wherever they went. The Beatles were the ultimate example. Airplane travel added a crucial element of tangibility to their worldwide popularity. Whether they landed at New York's Kennedy Airport or Tokyo's Haneda, cheering fans came out in daunting numbers. On the occasion of their first visit to the United States (February 7, 1964) some 3,000 people, screaming girls mostly, gathered at Kennedy Airport's International Arrivals Building just to see them. Pan Am cleverly used the "Fab Four" as live ads, generously supplying them with carry-on bags donning its corporate logo before the 200 reporters and photographers who turned up. The stars almost had to fight their way to the airport press lounge, where they had the biggest press conference they had given thus far. An airport official was quoted in *The New York Times* as saying, "We've never seen anything like this before. Never. Not even for kings and queens."[72] Not a week later, on February 13, The Beatles' arrival at Miami International Airport caused a 4-mile long traffic jam, as teenage fans tried to get close and catch a glimpse of their idols. The pattern was repeated everywhere,

but no reception was as big as the one in Adelaide, Australia. On June 12 of that year, the city turned on the band's biggest welcome ever: an estimated 350,000 people crowded the 9 miles from the airport to the Southern Australia Hotel.[73]

Such a public focus on the rich and famous masked the fact that air travel was in the process of being "democratized," even though tickets were still relatively expensive. To join the *jet set* of airplane travelers meant to taste something of the modern life as displayed in films, cinema, commercials, and in popular novels, where airports and aircraft featured as symbols of a lifestyle that came with success. For many people the experience of "riding on a jet plane" became a goal in itself. Over the course of the 1960s developments in air transport brought air travel within reach of middle-class wage earners. It meant that the world of flight became attractive as a setting in advertising to broad audiences. Besides publicizing travel destinations as such, air transport imagery, particularly the sleek and streamlined shape of the jet airliner, was used to sell goods—particularly modern luxury goods such as cars and also perfumes, tobacco, drinks, and even clothing. In 1968 Dutch newspapers carried advertisements of one of Europe's major clothing stores depicting a good-looking young man against a background of jet airliners, wearing a well-cut business suit. The quote underneath read, "A suit with confidence." For women, such professional confidence was expressed through the "stewardess look."[74] Airline gadgets such as imitation carry-on bags donning an airline logo, but otherwise wholly unconnected to air transport, became coveted items with which to flaunt a connection to the world of flight, whether real or imaginary. The jet magic even featured in pop songs, such as John Denver's "Leaving on a Jet Plane" (1967) where the jet plane stressed the rapid increase of distance between the two loved ones in the song and the British band Magna Carta's melancholic "Airport Song" (1970) on the sense of loneliness that may descend on a traveler stranded in an airport lounge, waiting for the fog to lift and board a flight to meet "a face in a photograph."

Once the effects of the changeover to jets had been overcome, airlines annually reported new record traffic figures. World trade doubled in the 1960s, and air transport expanded with it. In its 10-year survey, ICAO noted that "'air transport for yet another decade" had "maintained its position as one of the most expansive sectors of national economies."[75] Embarkations went up very rapidly indeed: in 1960 the world's scheduled airlines carried 106 million passengers; in 1966 their number reached 200 million, 311 million by 1970, and 404 million in 1973. Despite the temporary downturn caused by the Oil Crisis the 500 million mark was passed in 1977 (517 million).[76] Revenues climbed even steeper, despite the pressure on prices. In 1960 the world's scheduled airlines earned $5,370 million—a figure that grew to $18,015 million in 1970 and then to $54,062 in 1978. Indeed, the mid-1960s was the first period ever in which the air transport

industry achieved a normal rate of business profitability. This hid the fact that the yield per passenger-kilometer in scheduled air transport had actually decreased.[77] If passenger numbers were built on economy-class passenger traffic, profits came from the business traveler sitting up front in the new multiclass jets. Despite the cramped accommodation in economy, the coach traveler took over on board. It prompted the airlines to consider ways to keep their passengers occupied during the flight. In 1967 Pan Am came up with something new. From July it advertised its "Theatre in the Air" on board flights across the Atlantic: an entertainment system offering a film, plus nine channels of music programs to choose from, to which passengers could listen on individual hollow tube ear pieces.[78] With the introduction of the wide body jet, such entertainment became standard in air travel. It was considered important to keep passengers seated in the middle of the cabin occupied, as they could no longer see outside.

Never before in history had so many people been able to travel such long distances, whether for business or for pleasure. Something of a universal travel familiarity was maturing which presented passengers—or at least those who could afford it—a "seamless travel experience" that included not just air travel itself but also a sojourn in a subsidiary hotel chain run by the airline and a possibility to hire a car from an affiliated rental company.[79] Although designed for the business environment, these amenities were, at least in principle, also available for tourists. Indeed, tourists were the great expectation of the airline and travel businesses combined. Tourism even appeared to hold a promise for developing nations. The first United Nations Conference on Trade and Development (UNCTAD), held in Geneva, Switzerland, in 1964, agreed that air tourism should be used to boost economic development in Asia and Africa by cutting fares on intercontinental routes. Tourist visits were seen as a likely way to increase foreign earnings of Third World countries.[80] Although nothing came of it, the recommendation was repeated at the following UNCTAD meetings in 1968 and 1972.

Yet tourists could be a liability too. In 1965, and again in 1968, U.S. president, Lyndon Johnson, actually tried to curb foreign tourist travel, as it had become an economic liability. Johnson called upon Americans to refrain from flying abroad. On January 1, 1968 he proposed a 2-year restraint program on all "nonessential" foreign travel to help cope with the American balance of payments deficit that had been running up since the late 1950s. However, the legislation that accompanied the plea—a 5 percent tax on international air travel and a levy on each day spent abroad—failed to make it through Congress. American airline companies were dead set against the measures from the start and their lukewarm cooperation, in the national interest, did not extend beyond emphasizing the desirability to travel on American carriers. Figures suggest that about 50 percent of

Americans traveling abroad departed on foreign carriers, scheduled airlines mostly.[81]

Yet the growth in airline passenger numbers did not result solely from the development of the scheduled carriers. Especially in western Europe much of it came from a true explosion of cheap travel on charter airlines, flying tourists to their holiday destinations. A booming economy, an expansion in the number of days of leave, and the introduction of financial holiday bonuses in labor relations meant that consumers were now able to spend more on their annual holidays. In cooperation with tour operators charter airlines managed to develop an enormous growth market for low-priced tourist air travel. A reflection of the disparate economic development of northwestern Europe as compared to southern Europe, a growing stream of tourists boarded relatively cheap charter flights to spend their annual holidays on Mediterranean beaches. In the first half of the 1960s the number of Europeans who went on holiday by air doubled (to around 6 percent of all holiday makers).[82] But although the share of air travelers in European tourism was moderate in the 1960s, the impact it had on chartered air transport was tremendous: passenger embarkations increased twelvefold before the decade was out.[83] By 1965 charter airlines had already captured some 40 percent of the total European air passenger market. Ten years later, 60 percent of all miles flown within Europe were on charter flights.[84] A linear-shaped seasonal network of air services emerged, of which Spain was the main recipient. If air tourists were counted in the thousands in 1960, their number shot up to 1.9 million by 1965, and figures continued to climb to 13.4 million by 1975.[85] In the United Kingdom, as much as 30 percent of all air travelers (both scheduled and nonscheduled) went to Spain.[86] Germany held second place. The rapid growth in air transport of sun-seeking tourists being flown to the fishing communities along the Mediterranean coastline led to dramatic changes there, evidenced in concrete and glass through the ever-rising numbers of hotels and tourist facilities. In many places the coastal landscape was altered beyond recognition. Within a decade the aircraft transformed the Spanish Mediterranean island of Mallorca into a major international tourist resort. In terms of geography, the charter network had another distinctive feature. It did not connect national capitals, like the scheduled airlines did, but dropped tourists at (initially) small airstrips in the Mediterranean coastal region.[87] Growth was stimulated by expanding the existing airports (like Barcelona, Malaga, and Valencia) and through the construction of new ones, such as Palma de Mallorca and Alicante. The latter opened in April 1967, and its subsequent growth was such that the first of a big two-phase expansion project had to be initiated within 3 years. The new facilities were unlocked in 1975.[88]

In 1965 Spain's tourist receipts already accounted for 47.7 percent of the nation's export earnings, making it the country's largest export sector.[89] By the mid-1970s, when about a quarter of all arrivals came by air, tourism

contributed around 7 percent of the total Spanish national income.[90] Secondary destinations for charter flights from northern Europe were Greece, Italy, and Portugal, jointly welcoming just under one-third of the annual visitors who were flying to Spain by the late 1970s. For the first time in history air transport became visible as an autonomous force in economic growth.[91]

These developments took place on the macro level. But within air transport itself the changes were also profound. Jet aircraft necessitated numerous technical and operational changes. To meet the increasing demand and at the same time recoup investments in these expensive aircraft, airlines opened more routes and pushed up the frequency of services. The biggest surge occurred in the second half of the 1960s. In 1970 the average number of scheduled services per week in Europe was 76 percent higher than it had been in 1960 and grew another 14 percent through the new decade.[92] In the same era, the average number of seats per aircraft also went up by 28 percent—from around 105 to around 135 seats.[93] There was no way that airport infrastructure could keep up. The number of passengers at Europe's larger airports doubled in the 1970s.[94] The growth in aircraft sizes and numbers, as well as in passengers and cargo, required a rapid expansion of existing facilities. Those new expansions that were planned and built proved too small almost as soon as they were opened. The *jumbo jets*, discharging between 300 and 400 passengers each time they landed, especially necessitated major investments. The *jumbo* demanded wider runways, stronger and wider taxiways, and a complete redivision of available space on the platform. Airport terminals had to undergo major expansions, while the *jumbo* also required new handling equipment. The costs of such adaptations were recouped by changing the managerial basics of airport operations. The emphasis began to shift from providing infrastructure and facilities for air transport to an approach that increasingly hinged on the provision of shopping facilities and real estate development. Airports, although in general closely linked to governments, began to acquire more businesslike characteristics.[95] In Europe, where air transport was geared towards international services, shopping meant tax-free shopping. The concept dated to the second half of the 1950s, when it was tried out as an attraction at Ireland's Shannon Airport. It was copied—and vastly expanded—in the new terminal facilities of Paris-Orly, Amsterdam, and Copenhagen. Before the decade of the 1960s was out, tax-free airport shopping had not only become commonplace but also a big business and was on its way to replacing landing fees as an airport's prime source of income.

Throughout western Europe, or indeed throughout the Western world, a veritable airport building frenzy developed in the 1960s. For example, at Heathrow, Europe's busiest airport by any standard of measurement, extension plans focused on providing additional terminal capacity. Between 1957 and 1961 a second terminal, capable of receiving jets, was erected. As

it was still not enough to cope with traffic, construction of a third terminal had to be initiated almost as soon as the second was ready. To create room for this, drastic steps had to be taken. One of the airport's runways was demolished, and with it the overall airport concept was drawn up in 1945.[96] Yet no amount of building was sufficient to keep up with the growth in transport figures. The annual number of passengers through Heathrow expanded from just over 6 million in 1961 to almost 24 million in 1977.[97] Before the end of the decade it necessitated the construction of yet another, fourth terminal.

In Paris, the challenges of traffic growth and changes in aircraft technology were approached in a more radical fashion. In January 1964 the French cabinet decided to build a completely new airport that would replace the existing infrastructure. Roissy, North of Paris, was indicated as the location where the new airport was to be built. Roissy (Aéroport Roissy-Charles-de-Gaulle) was unique in Europe in being the only airport that was completely new. The expense involved—over 3 billion francs (some $700 million), including motorway access and an underground rail terminal (initially intended for airport personnel only)—served as an indication of just how pressing the issue of future airport capacity was.[98] Roissy-Charles-de-Gaulle opened for business in 1974, but its landmark terminal—of an innovative circular design—turned out to be ill fitted for the expansions that the growth of air traffic demanded, and new facilities had to come under construction before the decade was out.[99] As in London, it appeared that no amount of building was sufficient to keep up with the ever-increasing mobility and the use of air transport as such.

Although economic growth was much lower than in the Western world, the trend in eastern Europe, where air transport was built on a markedly different conception of routes, primarily dictated by politics rather than commerce, was not altogether different. Air travel was a privilege of the nomenklatura, of state representatives on official business. In the 1960s Sofia, Warsaw, Budapest, and Bucharest even demonstrated a higher rate of traffic increase than that of most airports in western Europe. Such growth was, however, relative, because the actual passenger numbers were small compared to western European figures. Nonetheless, on the most important routes between the Comecon countries traffic developed quickly. The largest increases were recorded in the mid-1960s when economic reforms within the socialist system, increasing trade and more stable east-west relations, contributed to a growing demand for air transport between the Eastern Bloc countries, and between East and West.[100] In the following years flying became accessible to a somewhat wider public. The more prosperous Comecon nations even saw a modest beginning of air tourism to foreign countries, especially to Black Sea destinations. A sense of competition developed in attracting international air traffic. Hungary actively pursued opening connections with India and Brazil.[101] In Prague, traffic at Ruzyně Airport

more than doubled (to 1.75 million, which was comparable to the level of traffic in London and Paris in 1954). To meet capacity demands, a new terminal was opened in 1968.[102] Air services to western Europe flourished: if in 1963 47,000 people from Czechoslovakia traveled to the west, their number grew to 258,000 in 1967.[103] Nonetheless, political developments played a much more prominent role than in the west. After 1968 air traffic in Prague languished and actually declined as a result of the Warsaw Pact invasion of Czechoslovakia in August of that year, which brought renewed isolation. Passenger numbers stabilized at around 1.5 million in the early 1980s.[104]

Not all airports in eastern Europe had such high numbers of passengers, although demands on the infrastructure were common in all countries behind the Iron Curtain. As in the west, airport planning could not keep up with the development of air traffic, and the political environment in which expansions had to fit socialist planning structures increased the problems at hand. When Warsaw's Okęcie Airport (rechristened Frédéric Chopin Airport in March 2001 to give Poland's national airport a name with a worldwide appeal) opened a new terminal in 1969, it was already too small. Designed for 700,000 passengers per year, actual numbers already stood at over 850,000.[105] In 1972 passenger numbers on the international air services between the seven Comecon states totaled 4.8 million, which equaled the number of passengers passing through London's secondary airport, Gatwick, the year before.[106]

Of all the Comecon capitals, air traffic in Moscow showed the fastest growth, which was not altogether surprising given Moscow's dominant position within the Eastern Bloc. By 1971 Aeroflot alone transported nearly 100 million passengers, 98 percent of whom traveled on domestic routes.[107] But although Aeroflot was a self-regulating body and in charge of both infrastructure and air transportation itself, its planning seemed to have trouble to keep up with developments. Part of the reason for that was the desire to keep domestic traffic separated from foreign traffic, especially from traffic to the West. This transpired in Moscow's airport situation. Air passenger movements were divided over three locations. Until 8 years after the opening of the new purpose-built Sheremetyevo Airport in August 1959, all international passenger traffic was handled at Vnukovo Airport, which had been constructed in the late 1930s. The situation changed only gradually, awaiting the completion of new passenger facilities at Sheremetyevo in September 1964; Vnukovo even received a second terminal in April 1963. Still, scheduled international flights were only initiated from there 3 years later in September 1967. By that time a third airport had come into use, Domodedovo. It handled long-distance domestic traffic within the U.S.S.R., opening in May 1965.[108]

Both in the Soviet Union and in the West only a modest part of traffic was airfreight. All the same the share of cargo carried rose from 16.5 percent

in 1960 to 21.9 percent in 1970.[109] While air transport maintained its position as one of the most expansive sectors of national economies air cargo was both expensive to ship and unattractive to carry for the average airline. Less remunerative than passenger transport, it required considerable investments in storage and handling facilities and was at the same time a logistic and operational puzzle in loading and carriage due to the limited freight capacities of the aircraft used. This situation changed at the end of the 1960s with the introduction of the Boeing 747 and other high capacity jets. Between 1960 and 1976 world trade in merchandise grew at an average of 7.4 percent per year, but air shipment of these goods went up at double that rate.[110]

The fastest growth occurred in the 1970s in Asia, where international airfreight expanded sixfold. The growth of cargo from the Middle East came second, followed by Africa and Latin America, while the lowest increases were reported from the developed air transport markets in North America and Europe (increases of 1.7 and 2.7 times respectively). The geographic division of growth figures indicated that more and more merchandise was shipped by air from developing countries, a process through which air transportation began to contribute to their economic development.[111]

The global structure of the air transport network as such, however, showed no major shifts and remained concentrated in the Western world. The North Atlantic route between Europe and the United States continued as the most important market for intercontinental traffic, representing about one quarter of all international passenger movements, and one third of all air cargo.[112] Although aviation was potentially important in the developing world to overcome absent surface infrastructure, the share of developing countries in international air transport remained small, despite the growth of air cargo shipments from Third World countries. In Africa the eleven (from 1968, when Togo joined the group, twelve) nations that constituted the joint carrier Air Afrique together represented no more than 0.7 percent of world air transport in 1970—a percentage on the level of that of Iceland.[113] Nonetheless, the number of passengers doubled in the 1960s, although the real increase was in the 1970s when passenger carriage more than tripled.[114] Due to poor demand, African air transport was generally based on smaller aircraft, like the ubiquitous DC-3. Airfreight formed a comparatively important element because of poor road and rail infrastructure and the high value of the commodities carried, like precious metals and diamonds.

Political insecurity added an extra element to this mix. When Rhodesia declared its independence in 1965, Zambia closed its border to isolate the white minority regime there. It became impossible to use the railroad through Salisbury (Harare) to export Zambia's copper. It had to be air freighted. Zambia Airways' Hercules transport aircraft took 20 tons of copper on each flight to Dar es Salaam, Tanzania, loading oil and mining equipment on the return leg.[115] While surface links in Africa deteriorated from the late 1960s,

because of regional and ethnic conflict, bad financial and economic policies, and failing maintenance, air transportation became relatively important. As one account put it, "More and more of the observable life in Africa takes place within twenty miles of its three dozen international airports."[116] Small wonder then that the construction of airports and landing strips featured among infrastructural projects in development aid to Africa.

Asia and Latin America always had a higher presence in air transport. Apart from industrialized Japan which, as a by-product of its amazing economic growth, went from being the fifteenth largest contributor to world air transport in 1960 to occupy fifth place in 1970, India ranked big.[117] The biggest increase happened in the 1970s, when the share of Asia in world air transport doubled, and Asian passenger numbers more than tripled.[118] In Latin America Brazil and Argentina both represented large markets. Brazil showed especially rapid growth. The number of ton-kilometers performed increased over 500 per cent between 1960 and 1970, surpassing even the growth rate of air transport in the United States.[119] Here too passenger figures tripled in the next decade.[120]

By that time the global carrying capacity had become big enough to make an immediate and real difference on the international scene. More than anything, this showed in reactions to natural and manmade disasters. When a cyclone hit East Pakistan (Bangladesh) in November 1970 and caused severe flooding in much of the country, aircraft turned out to be the only practical means to get aid to the surviving, waterlocked victims. The International Red Cross set up a relief airbridge to the capital Dacca and organized food droppings from aircraft and helicopter rescue flights to isolated communities. Six months later, in June 1971, aircraft were again needed, this time to evacuate refugees from the civil war that followed in the wake of the flooding and ensuing political chaos. In 8 weeks' time Russian and American aircraft flew over 700 people a day to refugee camps in India. A similar pattern evolved in the Sahel droughts and famines of 1973–1974 in Africa. Within a decade, air transport had become the vital carrier of humanitarian relief aid to disaster areas the world over. Aircraft were also the preferred mode of travel to carry refugees to safety in cases of political crises. After the 1973 military coup in Chile the UN High Commissioner for Refugees provided air transport to various Western countries for several thousand opponents of the new regime. But the role of air transport was never bigger than in efforts to resolve the refugee crisis that developed after the collapse of South Vietnam in 1973. In the subsequent decade nearly a half-million Vietnamese were transported by air to resettle in the United States and western Europe.[121]

By the end of the 1970s there was no denying that air transport had become an important vehicle for mass transportation the world over. With more than 500 million passengers fastening their seat belts annually, the imagery of romance and thrill, still dominating air transport in the first

years after the introduction of the big jets, was fading. In its place had come an emphasis on more average comforts on board, the ease of the journey, and destinations to go to. Whether for business, pleasure, or sheer necessity, flying had become everyone's favored means of long-distance travel.

The Noise Barrier

These developments had important consequences for air transport itself and also effected important changes in the relationship between aviation and society at large. The changes manifested themselves in external effects of air transportation. Beyond the airport perimeter air transport hit the limits of its hitherto unparalleled growth. Between 1958 and 1970 the world's airlines took a delivery of no less than 3,757 commercial jet aircraft.[122] Jets meant not just noise, but ear shattering noise, and this brought the consequences of the growth of air transport into focus everywhere. As a result, airport planning became a difficult, political process that needed to take ever more wide-ranging spatial aspects into consideration, with noise nuisance as the central point of departure.

Noise was a problem that had first surfaced in the early 1950s, when increasing engine power of propeller airliners and the arrival of the first jet aircraft prompted awareness that commercial aviation could become a source of noise nuisance. Until then complaints about aircraft flying over-head remained relatively rare and isolated, with the exception of those air-ports that were located amid heavily built-up areas, such as New York's La Guardia and Newark, where the hitherto fairly harmonious coexistence between airports and their neighbors began to show signs of wear and tear. Both in Europe and in the United States airport authorities commissioned extensive studies to collect data on noise conditions. The first had been conducted at Heathrow Airport in 1951 and 1952 to establish the sound characteristics of the de Havilland Comet-I airliner. New York had followed with tests on aircraft noise in 1952. The problem, however, was how to in-terpret the data. Initial measurements were taken exclusively at the airports themselves, because authorities were primarily concerned with the effects that jet operations would have on embarking and disembarking passengers. Solutions were sought in the area of soundproofing airport buildings. Yet on the basis of the noise characteristics of military jet aircraft, airport author-ities became more anxious as the decade progressed. Seriously concerned the Port of New York Authority (PONYA) even refused to grant permis-sion for flight tests with the prototype of the Boeing 707 at Idlewild (John F. Kennedy International Airport) in 1955.[123] To nonetheless prepare for the inevitable arrival of jet aircraft PONYA began collecting noise emission data from both sides of the Atlantic. Somewhat surprisingly, these showed that the latest version of the British Comet jetliner, the Comet-IV, which

was equipped with mufflers, produced 4 decibels (i.e., about 40 percent) *less* noise than the latest versions of the propeller-driven Lockheed Super Constellation and the Douglas DC-7. On the other hand, it was also put on record that the Comet was audible up to 60 percent longer than the propeller aircraft. Even so, test results appeared to indicate that the noise characteristics of the Comet were roughly comparable to those of the four-engine propeller airliners that were already in use.[124] But in September 1958 tests at Paris' Le Bourget Airport with one of Pan Am's brand-new Boeing 707s provided disconcerting results. The group of volunteers who had been assembled on the platform to establish human reactions to the 707's engines, returned from their task numbed and sound shocked.[125] And another negative phenomenon of the jet engine was also discovered: test persons complained of nausea as a result of the kerosene fumes the jet engines discharged. It appeared that jet aircraft would have to be parked at remote stands, away from the airport buildings if nauseating fumes were to be kept out.[126] Yet noise remained the number one priority. In New York a series of flight tests with the Boeing 707 led to unheard of protests. The mayor of the Village of Woodsburgh on Long Island even wrote a special address to President Dwight D. Eisenhower demanding guarantees that the Port Authority's earlier restrictions on the operation of jet aircraft would not be encroached upon through government lenience towards airlines in the future.[127] Measurements done with the same aircraft revealed that the unmuffled engines of the 707 produced between 103 and 130 decibels of noise on the airport apron—which registered to the human ear as up to six times as much as what had been noted in earlier tests. Even inside the terminal building, the noise level still reached between 83 and 112 decibels—too loud even for normal conversation.[128] At airports the world over, the concern over noise and exhaust smells began to influence planning concepts: either aircraft were kept away from the terminal and passengers were transported in buses or other specialized vehicles, or finger piers with covered boarding ramps were constructed to prevent passenger exposure to the new outdoor airport environment.

If measures to reduce annoyance were relatively successful from a passenger's point of view, preventing the rise of adverse social effects from the growth of air travel, and from the technological changes in aviation, proved much more difficult and on occasions even created political problems. In April 1958 the French aviation authorities tried to refuse permission for Czech carrier CSA to operate the Tupolev Tu-104 jet airliner on their Prague–Paris service.[129] The problems with the Tu-104 were multiple. Apart from producing a terrifying noise, especially on takeoff, the aircraft was unable to make the steep climb necessary to reduce noise effects. Confidential information, leaked to the French by CSA, mentioned that the Tupolev's engines were not allowed to operate at full thrust for more than 80 seconds. Apart from that, the aircraft had a very high landing speed (and indeed

could only be stopped with the aid of a braking parachute). It was, however, impossible for political reasons to refuse the Tu-104 access to the Parisian airports, since the Soviet carrier Aeroflot planned to operate the same aircraft type on its service between Moscow and Paris.[130] Authorities in London were likewise concerned and in August 1958 demanded that Aeroflot make a proving flight with the new jet to ascertain the acceptability of the noise impact of the Russian plane before taking a decision about a permit to use the aircraft in scheduled service.[131]

But apart from banning operations with jet aircraft between certain hours there was not a whole lot that airport authorities could do, as the noise produced by each aircraft was a product of the engine technology that was available at the time. All the same the airport environs became a factor to be taken into account by aeronautical engineers and airport planners. If the latter had hitherto looked at airport planning concepts from an aeronautical point of view—with the desirability that aircraft should have headwind for takeoff and landing—the introduction of jets required new thinking. By the early 1960s it was evident that runway orientation was an important factor in the relationship between airports and neighboring communities. Yet runways required a lot of land, which was not always available. Lacking such space, conflicts over aircraft noise were inevitable. Even in cases where empty space was abundant problems loomed. International norms for noise nuisance, set by ICAO, turned out to be poor, theoretical constructions that did not reflect people's personal experiences with noise over extended periods of time. In Amsterdam, plans for new runways at Schiphol Airport were developed without recourse to the effects on nearby residential areas, as they appeared to remain (just) outside the zone that would be affected by noise according to the ICAO norms of the day. Within years the untenability of the existing theoretical norms became evident in emerging protests against noise nuisance. Outcries against aviation were heard everywhere. At airports where existing runways were used, problems could hardly be avoided.

As the impact of jet operations became evident, exceptionally noisy aircraft were the first to encounter problems. In 1964 the Swiss refused to issue a permit to BOAC to use its deafening Vickers VC-10 at Zurich's Kloten Airport.[132] In Europe and elsewhere the social basis for large-scale commercial aviation began to erode. In Frankfurt, Germany, one of Europe's fastest growing airports, annoyance complaints from neighboring communities increased to such an extent that the airport authorities decided in 1964 to invest 200,000 marks into the installation of a purpose-developed sound monitoring system in an effort to keep tabs on the spread of jet noise. As a first result of these measurements, recommendations on changes in approach and takeoff procedures to reduce the noise effects went out to the federal air traffic control authorities in 1965.[133] Such efforts to appease residents could not prevent the plans for the expansion of the airport from running aground in 1968, when a court order revoked an earlier permission

on environmental grounds. After prolonged legal battles that lasted some 10 years, the airport authorities finally received authorization to move forward with their extension plans in 1978—only to become bogged down by full-scale battles with thousands of environmental activists dead set against the encroachment of aviation upon the surrounding woodlands.[134] Growing pressure from neighborhood communities and special interest groups that focused on jet noise forced changes at other airports too. Within a few years nuisance had become the yardstick for the further development possibilities of airports and air transport everywhere.

Throughout the Western world protests were becoming an obstacle to airport planning. But protests were, perhaps, nowhere as intense as in Japan. In 1966 the Japanese government passed a law to construct a new airport to relieve the overcrowded Haneda. The sights were set on flat farmland about 35 miles east of Tokyo. Yet the Japanese government failed to take account of the strong emotional attachment of local farmers to their land and their willingness to resist the encroachment of air transport upon their personal sphere. Initial attempts to persuade landowners to sell failed, after which the government resorted to forced expropriation to build the first runway for the new airport. The controversy over Narita Airport led to a series of increasingly violent clashes between riot police and farmers and left-wing student symphathizers of the local population that saw about a 1,000 police officers and villagers injured and even left thirteen people dead. The airport, planned in 1966 to be completed in 1971, did not open before May 1978. During that time the dedication ceremony had to be postponed eleven times. When Narita finally opened for business, it was under a level of security that was unprecedented. To ensure that protesters would remain at bay an opaque metal fence was constructed that went around the complete airport. It was overlooked by guard towers staffed by riot police. Passengers arriving at Narita were subjected to baggage and travel document searches before even entering the terminal in an attempt to keep antiairport activists out.[135] The separation that had taken place between the aeronautical world and its surroundings could hardly have been clearer. At a time when over 500 million people were flying annually and air transport was losing its exclusive appeal, protests against the inroads that aviation made on life on the ground had become an almost universal phenomenon.

Just how much of that exclusiveness had been lost was, in a sense, condensed into the 1980 slapstick comedy *Airplane!*, a parody based on the 1957 film *Zero Hour!* The original script revolved around the crew and passengers of an airline flight suffering from food poisoning, who were saved by a reluctant and traumatized ex-war pilot. In *Airplane!* this chilling drama of the 1950s was wrought into a storyline that borrowed heavily from the absurd. Made by Jim Abrahams, David Zucker, and Jerry Zucker, who had "done every airplane joke (. . .) [they] could think of," the ostensibly funny film evidenced the enormous mental changes behind the air transportation

revolution of the 1960s and 1970s. It mocked the high-tech environment of air travel and turned it into a setting for common fun. With the magic and the luxury of air travel taken away, flying had become unexciting, boring almost, and the professional pilot almost a laughing matter. Cinema audiences the world over needed but a vague idea of airline operations to tune into the yarn.[136]

Effects: Global Travel for All, 1977–present

"This is the international transit lounge. You are free to wait here. You are not to leave this building. America is closed. (. . .) There's only one thing you can do here, Mr. Navorski: Shop!" While the location is indefinite, the setting bears reference to the International Arrivals Building of New York's John F. Kennedy Airport. Here a disconcerting story unfolds that addresses every international air traveler's silent fear: to have one's passport refused. Denied entrance into the United States, Viktor Navorski is released into the "twilight zone" of a modern air terminal. Alone, and with no more than a few words of English at his disposal, he is at a loss in a world utterly foreign. The audience watches him as he undergoes a sudden immersion into present-day air travel culture as put on display in the self-contained world of *The Terminal*.[1]

Inspired by the story of Merhan Karimi "Alfred" Nasseri, an exiled Iranian who curiously remained in limbo for no less than 18 years (August 1988 to August 2006) in Terminal 1 of Paris' Charles-de-Gaulle airport after he lost his passport,[2] *The Terminal* not just depicted a story of human drama amid bureaucracy but also offered familiar scenes of modern air travel. Indeed, the backdrop for the movie shifted, imperceptibly, between JFK, the terminal of Mirabel Airport, Montreal, Los Angeles International Airport, and Palmdale (California). Here a disused Boeing 747 maintenance hanger was used to construct an imaginary but archetypical airport terminal as the film's setting, abounding in modernistic architecture, roomy spaces, and lots of "natural" light. Research for the movie was done in Denver, Tokyo, and Frankfurt, so the story could be imagined to take place "anywhere."

To the average cinema audience, the scenes of the movie were immediately recognizable as vistas reminiscent of air terminals they might have been to. After all, airports had become increasingly alike in appearance in the closing decades of the 20th century. In part to recoup the large investments necessary to cope with ever growing numbers of passengers and streams of goods being shipped by air and as a self-generating process of business management, airports the world over had become self-contained aerial cities. In doing so, they embraced all kinds of commerce, whether aviation related or not, and developed into centers for much more than their original function as transport intersections. Indeed, by the end of the century major airports had become economic motors in their own right, places of employment for tens of thousands of people, the contribution of which to the regional and even national income could be measured as a distinctive percentage. For the average passenger the most visible of these changes was the transformation of airports into giant shopping malls, whether with tax-imposed or tax-free goods. For the business traveler, developments went even further: airports no longer were places to go to and leave from but places to convene at. The area around their perimeters became a sought-after location to establish commercial ventures for manufacture and logistics. What had happened?

Air Travel for All

Despite several temporary economic setbacks, the final decades of the 20th century brought unprecedented wealth to the nations of the Northern Hemisphere. Economic growth meant that business became increasingly international. Western life, both professional and private, followed along the same path and took on ever more international, or even global dimensions. Growing prosperity—with an increase of 21 percent in average disposable incomes between 1980 and the year 2000 in the United States alone[3] —was visible in patterns of increasingly conspicuous consumption that included travel by air. The declining price for air transportation was certainly a factor contributing to this trend.

Following the American initiatives in 1977 to deregulate air transport—first for the domestic market in the United States and subsequently on the international plain—politicians and lawmakers pushed air transport towards increased competition and normal business practices. The American example exerted considerable influence. Within a decade national governments the world over adopted processes of withdrawal from the regulatory structures that had characterized air transport since its earliest beginnings in favor of competition that would bring lower prices in the interest of the consumer. In several respects these policies were highly successful. Market forces had the effect of bringing down prices. Between 1977 and the turn

of the millennium the cheapest transatlantic return ticket from most western European capitals, in economy class, went from $500 to around $250, despite inflation and tripled fuel prices.[4] Since the 1970s air travel, both for business and for personal motivations, became a normal mode of travel—a necessity of life even, as one observer put it.[5]

For the airlines the start of deregulation in October 1978 marked the beginning of the most uncertain period in their existence. The industry went through dramatic changes that took air travel away from the atmosphere of luxury it had so long, and so intimately, embraced. While continuing to market "service," controlling and then cutting costs came to be central to the functioning of an airline—and for its continued long term prospects. This emphasis on costs brought out distinctive new features in economies of scale—and economies of technology. To become more competitive and offer lower prices, the international airline industry had to shed its warm blanket of nationality, develop new standards of operating efficiency, push up load factors, and fully embrace computer technology to streamline every aspect of operation and administration. The results were astonishing. Not only did the numbers of airline passengers show another steep increase—with some 517 million people boarding in 1977 and four times that number in 2006—the social composition of the average airplane cabin occupancy also broadened considerably.

With "everybody" flying, air travel lost the special appeal it had celebrated for so long and which set aviation apart from other business environments. Buying an air ticket was not even necessary to take in the changes. Gone were the days of the relaxed family outing to the airport to enjoy the general atmosphere and watch planes take off and land. For starters, reaching airports became increasingly difficult. In most Western countries, the combination of economic growth, a larger propensity to travel, and broadening airport functions manifested themselves in road congestion. With every passing year, the time it took to reach an airport lengthened as traffic increased. At any major airport, parking (or afterwards retrieving) a car among tens of thousands vehicles became problematic. To reduce such problems ground transportation needed to be improved. It was not before the 1980s that measures took effect, as the costs of constructing additional and new infrastructure were very high and did not warrant expenditure before the problems of road congestion were really beginning get out of hand. Airport planners were late in shedding the traditional conception that identified airplane travelers as car owners. When Frankfurt Airport opened its railway station in 1972, it was Europe's frontrunner in offering transport modes. Not even the brand new Charles-de-Gaulle Airport in Paris had a passenger rail terminal when it was opened for business in 1974.[6] In most countries the planning process for new or additional (rail) infrastructure involved extensive regulatory proceedings that took years to be completed.

Once at the airport, the traveler of the new millennium could hardly feel special or privileged any more. Hidden behind impressive arrays of shops and eateries, terminals were not even immediately distinguishable as air transportation facilities. To reach the check-in, passengers, toting their luggage, had to negotiate a veritable mall offering a choice of goods similar to what high street city shops would stock (though generally not at the same price: dedicated airport shoppers needed affluence). In the air terminal itself, the lines of people waiting to check in appeared to grow longer every year. The busy period of the summer holiday especially gave rise to discontent. Few airports had facilities spacious enough to deal with the tens of thousands of prospective travelers who assembled in front of the check-in counters at any one time. At peak days, traversing the check-in area became a major problem, more so when pushing a cartload of luggage. And while security precautions tightened further as aviation continued to be targeted by politically inspired terrorist activity, the time needed to obtain a boarding card lengthened. As passenger numbers went up (and ticket prices went down), taking a plane anywhere became a time consuming activity. The prospective traveler had to appear early—at least an hour before each flight, and the longer the flight, the longer the preboarding period—reducing the time saving that air travel was all about, certainly on shorter flights. In western Europe, high-speed rail services therefore became a serious alternative to flying. By the turn of the millennium the problems had become so bad that airlines and airports were willing to invest in novel ways of ticketing and check-in. To reduce queues experiments were undertaken with electronic ticketing from home through the recent proliferation of the Internet, including the assignment of seats on board each flight. In the early years of the new century more and more airports introduced computerized facilities to issue boarding cards, reducing former check-in counters to baggage drop-off stations. While such measures contributed to keep the overcrowding in the check-in area more or less manageable, the large flocks of passengers led to further congestion at passport and security checks. Having passed those, the actual boarding itself gave rise to new delays, as the ever-larger aircraft required more time for embarkation. Even then, the agony of waiting was not over. From the second half of the 1990s an increasing number of airports suffered from a lack of runway and air traffic control capacity. By the turn of the millennium some 31 percent of all flights in Europe suffered delays, with no improvements in sight, as traffic kept growing. To keep passengers happy, airlines and airports began to think of ways of offering distraction from the negative experience of waiting: *delaytainment*, as researchers dubbed it.[7]

The conditions of travel on board also changed. By the mid-1970s, the major airlines were still trying to enhance the quality of their service and beef up economy class to distinguish themselves from charter flights, offering more comfort and legroom and superior staff friendliness. Such efforts were vastly reduced in the following decades as operating margins became

progressively narrower. First only on short flights but thereafter on longer flights within Europe also, the customary meal services were cut back to a single sandwich roll with coffee or tea, while the distribution of free newspapers and beverages became limited to those traveling in business class. "In the back" airlines also experimented with seat pitch, even if it meant squeezing in an extra row of seats in cabins really designed for fewer passengers. Installing more seats enabled prices to be lowered.[8] Cabin crews were so busy that the customary demonstrations of the safety features were replaced by prerecorded television programming. From the second half of the 1990s, the entry of yet another category of competitors on the market, in the shape of low-cost, no-frills carriers, further enhanced this trend. By the middle of the first decade of the new millennium cost had become the dominant yardstick for all nonbusiness travel. In economy class "free" food and beverages were disappearing.

After landing, disembarkation was equally tedious: long and awkward waiting periods inside the cabin for the doors to open all the way at the front of the aircraft, long queues for passport controls and customs, and indefinite time spent to retrieve checked luggage, some of it only transported at a special surcharge.

Yet from a distance, the intensifying use of air transportation served as proof that air travel had become part of the structures of modern everyday life. This could be witnessed in the attire of air travelers—upscale no longer—and in their behavior. Around the turn of the millennium behavioral patters on board more and more reflected life on the ground, even including such phenomena as fights on board and problems caused by heavy drinking. Unable to effect a solution, several aircraft were forced to make an intermediate stop to allow police to incarcerate unruly passengers.[9] Even the typical role models on board evolved. Whereas there had been a fairly rigid distinction between the male world of the flight deck and the predominantly female world of the passenger cabin, such patterns shifted from the 1970s. And although the numbers of female pilots remained small— women suffered from an unreceptive environment, having to prove themselves again and again on every flight—cabin crews witnessed a minor invasion of male staff. Stewardesses no longer, flight attendants moved away from the focus on servitude to stress professionalism as guardians of order and safety on board, a development that was also reflected in changing dress codes.[10] Designer clothing as a statement of mundane luxury was on the way out.

Nonetheless, safety was not something that primarily resided with cabin attendants. The larger safety issues played elsewhere, both in the cockpit and on the ground. Under the aegis of ICAO a lot of effort was invested in improving international safety standards and advertising them to the general public. Although the number of aircraft accidents declined continuously from the early 1960s—the annual number of passenger aircraft involved in crashes was halved to about fifteen around the turn of the millennium—the

number of fatalities declined much slower, from around 800 to around 700 per year over the same period, an indication that larger aircraft meant there were more passengers involved per accident.[11] Human error continued as the major cause, accountable for 90 percent of crashes in 1985—a peak year-against a mere 7 percent caused by technical problems. The remaining 3 percent were weather related.[12] Crashes, invariably tragic, made spectacular news, more often than not receiving worldwide coverage. Technological failures were less likely to be dramatically exploited. In April 1988 an old Boeing 737 of Aloha Airlines lost almost half of its cabin roof over Hawaii, while flying at an altitude of over 24,000 feet. While the pilot miraculously managed to land the heavily damaged aircraft, the accident alerted aviation authorities to the hidden dangers of airframe ageing.[13] After all, the average life span of commercial aircraft was around 30 years, meaning that account had to be taken of the effects of the accumulation of tens of thousands of flying hours on the structure. Despite strict maintenance procedures and periodical checks, modern commercial aircraft were recognized to have a finite lifespan, particularly with respect to their number of completed takeoff and landing cycles.

Aircraft that suffered accidents because of technical failures generally did so before reaching that critical age. Such was the case in the crash of an Air France Concorde on July 25, 2000. The aircraft, chartered to take a travel party of mixed nationalities to a specially arranged shipping cruise in New York, hit a sharp piece of metal that had fallen on the runway of Charles-de-Gaulle airport from a Continental Airlines' DC-10 that took off minutes earlier. The metal shredded a tire. Heavy pieces of reinforced rubber bursting from the tire thereupon severed electrical and hydraulic cords and penetrated the aircraft's fuel tank, leading to a fire that went out of control. A minute later all passengers on board perished, as well as nine crew members and four people on the ground.[14] Up to then this high-profile showcase of Anglo-French aviation technology had held an impeccable safety record. The crash near Paris not only destroyed that but also formed a prelude to the end of end of commercial supersonic aviation altogether. After the crash, Concorde remained grounded for a year, pending improved safety sheeting in its fuel tanks. In July 2001 it went back into service, only to fall victim to the crisis in commercial aviation that followed in the wake of the attacks on New York's World Trade Center (WTC) on September 11. Concorde made its last commercial flights in October 2003. Nearly a full century after the start of powered flight, the last airworthy Concorde touched down on November 26 of that year in Bristol, England, where it had been built in 1979. That year the retirement of the French and British Concordes provided evidence that aviation had definitively and finally turned away from the aura of exclusiveness that came along with the charm of speed, to trade in these defining factors for the emphasis on mass carriage and the corporate balance sheet. In short, aviation had come of age.

At the Outer Reaches of National Control

With the era of high politics in civil aviation passed and international relations between East and West stabilizing, the traditional relationships between air transport and nation-states were redefined. In general, the role played by political interests became less dominant. This was a gradual process that took place parallel to the general relaxation of the grip that national authorities held on market conditions in air transport, known as deregulation.

Nonetheless, just off the main theatres of global conflict high politics remained important and air transport continued to depend on the larger international political and military setting. In the early 1970s India and Pakistan had provided a case in point. On January 30, 1971 the hijack of an Indian Airlines Fokker F-27 by two Kashmiri militants had started a chain of events that escalated beyond the foreseeable. Forcing the small airliner to land in Lahore, (then) West Pakistan, the two men were welcomed as heroes and immediately granted political asylum. Indeed, Pakistan's president Zulfikar Ali Bhutto visited the hijackers and applauded their heroism, giving rise to Indian claims that they had acted upon instructions from Pakistan. Over the next days the passengers were released—the aircraft itself was blown up—but tensions between the two nations, already at loggerheads after fighting a war over Kashmir in 1965, heightened. In New Delhi over 10,000 protesters marched on the office of Pakistan's High Commissioner. It was not long before India demanded extradition of the hijackers and compensations for the loss of the plane. As Pakistan refused to comply, India banned all flights by Pakistani aircraft in its airspace. The latter measure disrupted air communications between the two parts of Pakistan at a time of political unrest in East Pakistan, soon after leading to civil war and secession (with India's support) of the new state of Bangladesh. A full-scale war between India and Pakistan followed. It was 1974 before talks about normalization of bilateral relations began. While both countries identified air services as a marker for progress in this field, the hardened positions on the banning of flights, and the claims for compensations, took a long time to be settled. Only in May 1976 did diplomats from both sides reach an agreement on restoration of the severed air connections. Two months later, the two newly appointed ambassadors arrived in each other's capital aboard the first official airline flights, celebrating the return of peace and normality between the two nations.[15]

Likewise, aviation continued to be an important topic in relations between African countries. Sudan and Libya closed their airspace to each other's flights in 1976, while Syria and Iraq also suspended bilateral air services because of political problems. In June 1977 differences between Kenya and Tanzania resulted in a suspension of air connections and the disbanding of the joint East African Airways Corporation. And as a result of

the power struggle between Vietnam and China all flights between the two Asian powers were prohibited from 1979 until 1992. Clearly, air transport still mattered in international politics.

Even on the fringes of Europe, the disruption of air services was considered a prime weapon in bilateral quarrels. Greece and Turkey had closed their airspaces over the Aegean Sea to all civil flights in 1974 when the two nations went to war over the Mediterranean island of Cyprus. Not before February 1980 did a gradual return to normalcy allow the respective governments to agree to reopen a civil air corridor between the two NATO members.

Such developments, indicating the high profile that air services held in bilateral relations, were not limited to regional differences between neighboring states and were even topical in American-Soviet relations. When Poland declared a Moscow-induced state of martial law in December 1981 to combat rising dissent against the Communist Party's regime, President Ronald Reagan decided on a display of American discontent by an immediate withdrawal of Aeroflot's landing rights in the United States. The ban on the twice weekly flights from Moscow to Washington's Dulles International Airport represented the high end of a string of American signals of anxiety. In their turn, the Soviets retaliated by suspending the rights of American carriers to land in the Soviet Union. The sanctions against each other's airlines remained in force for 2 years, and were actually reimposed after a disastrous lack of judgment on the part of the Soviets led to the downing of a Korean Airlines jumbo jet by Soviet fighter planes on August 31, 1983. En route from New York to Seoul, the Korean Boeing 747 had—either inadvertently or on purpose as a civilian decoy for a major U.S. intelligence operation, as has been convincingly asserted[16] —entered restricted Soviet airspace. In the area northeast of the Kamchatka Peninsula, the presence of a U.S. spy plane flying in close proximity to the Korean airliner led to the assumption by the Soviet air defense forces that the Korean Airlines flight was in fact an American RC-135 reconnaissance airplane. An order was issued to shoot down the aircraft. Contrary to ICAO standards and procedures for such intercepts, exhaustive efforts to identify the intruder were not made. All 269 people on board lost their lives when a Soviet fighter fired two air-to-air missiles at the Boeing, and the crippled aircraft crashed into the Sea of Okhotsk in the dark of night. An international incident of major proportions ensued, reverberating in news headlines across the globe for weeks. President Reagan gave out a statement on September 1 in which he stressed that "words can scarcely express our revulsion at this horrifying act of violence (. . .) inexplicable to civilized people everywhere."[17] In the following days and weeks the uproar about the tragedy heightened tension between the two superpowers. In a televised speech to the nation, Reagan called for the expulsion of the Soviets from international aviation and claimed: "This was the Soviet Union against the world and the moral precepts which guide human relations among people everywhere."[18] On September 9, twelve of

the sixteen NATO countries suspended Aeroflot's landing rights for a fort-night (although France, Greece, Spain and Turkey kept their distance). In Washington, Reagan halted negotiations with Moscow on bilateral issues and declared Sunday September 11 a national day of mourning. Five days later Washington even appeared to try and expel the Soviet Union from the international community of nations by denying landing rights to the Soviet Foreign Minister Andrei Gromyko at New York's Kennedy Airport and barring him from attending the opening session of the United Nations Annual General Assembly.[19] All Aeroflot offices in the United States were forcibly closed, and federal authorities prohibited U.S. airlines henceforth from accepting any tickets issued by Aeroflot for travel to, from, or within the United States. In the following years Washington used the negative exposure that the Soviets received as a result of the tragedy to achieve gains at the East-West negotiating table. Indeed, fruits were harvested there. Reagan and the new Soviet leader Michael Gorbachev met in person in Geneva and Reykjavik and came to an understanding on how to improve safety in the air, and perk up relations generally. Both sides lifted sanctions on April 29, 1986.[20] It was eventually established in an official ICAO investigation, completed only in 1993, that Korean Airlines Flight KE007, had deviated from its preset course due to the fact that the flight crew "did not implement the proper navigation procedures to ensure the aircraft remained on its assigned track throughout the flight, resulting in KE007 eventually penetrating prohibited areas of USSR sovereign airspace."[21] How and why this could happen, remained guesswork. Yet in the end some good came out of the drama: to prevent such extraordinary navigational errors in future, the White House decided to make the newly developed military satellite-based Global Positioning System (GPS) available for civil uses in air transport and beyond when it became fully operational in 1988.[22] Navigation and communication would never be the same again.

Such high profile incidents showed that air transport remained an important element in international and bilateral relations. This showed in the series of hijacks and attacks against air transport as such in the late 1970s and 1980s, which had distinct political backgrounds. The disconcerting phenomenon was by no means limited to the Palestinian cause. Voluntary and involuntary, commercial airlines carried politics across the world. Evidence of the internationalization of attacks on aviation could hardly be clearer than in the case of the hijack of Lufthansa Flight LH181 on October 13, 1977. En route from the Spanish holiday island Mallorca to Frankfurt, four Palestinians from Lebanon took control of the Boeing 737 *Landshut*, its the five-strong crew and the eighty-two passengers, returning tourists mostly, and forced the captain to change course to Rome. Here a bizarre sequence of events began to unfold. The aircraft was refueled and took off again for Cyprus. In the following days, the jet touched down in Bahrain and then in Dubai, where the Palestinian hijackers suddenly demanded that nine

German ultra left-wing terrorists be released from prison in Germany, plus two Palestinians locked up in Turkey for an attempted bombing of an El Al jet. Then, a second set of demands surfaced through a Swiss lawyer from Geneva, written by a second cell of terrorists, in Germany. They called for the release of eleven of their comrades from jail, over $15 million in ransom, and linked the hijacking to the life of Hanns-Martin Schleyer, the chairman of the German employers' union whom they had kidnapped almost 6 weeks earlier. Once released, their cronies were to be flown to freedom in Vietnam, Somalia, or Yemen—whichever country was prepared to welcome them—making a stop in Istanbul to pick up the two "Turkish" prisoners. But demands went further than that: in a separate statement read out in Geneva the terrorists called upon the West-German government to abandon its pro-American stance in international politics. When the government in Bonn refused to budge, the *Landshut* took off for the small island of Mazirak in the Indian Ocean, to end up, after a series of unsuccessful attempts to land in the Middle East, where authorities blocked their airport runways, in Aden, South Yemen. Here Captain Jürgen Schumann managed to evade the blockade and land his jet on a sandy strip next to the runway. However, the Yemenite authorities refused to have anything to do with the hijackers, who shot the captain in cold blood and then decided to fly to Mogadiscio, Somalia. By then the hijack was into its fourth day and without much prospect for a peaceful ending as the *Landshut* was shadowed by a second Lufthansa jet, carrying a specialist assault team sent by the government in Bonn. Meanwhile, the EEC and half the Western governments held intensive crisis conferences on how to approach and end the drama, exercising diplomatic pressure behind the screens not to accommodate the hijackers anywhere. The Soviets and the East Germans offered to mediate, and Pope Paul VI even offered to take the place of the hostages on board the *Landshut*. That was not a viable option. In the middle of the night an elite unit of West German commandos stormed the jet and liberated the hostages, shooting three of the hijackers. A fourth was badly injured. In Germany, several of the incarcerated terrorists whose release had been demanded committed suicide in their cells. The body of the unfortunate Schleyer was subsequently discovered in France. Undeterred, Germany continued its pro-American foreign policy.[23]

Yet, successful or not, attacks against air transport continued to be politically inspired. Despite the ongoing commercialization that was taking the air transport industry away from its traditional entourage of national interests, civil airliners were persistently made out as powerful symbols of Western, particularly American dominance on the world stage. It made aircraft the target for violent action underlining political objectives or anti-Western discord in general. This was blatantly evident in the bombing of a Pan Am jumbo on December 21, 1988, high in the sky above the Scottish village of

Lockerbie. The bomb, hidden inside a radio cassette recorder, had started its journey to the United States in a suitcase ostensibly shipped by a Libyan secret service officer from the island of Malta in the Mediterranean, routed via Frankfurt and London. Libya was quickly fingered to be behind the attack in which all 259 occupants of Flight PA103 and eleven people on the ground died. In the previous years a prolonged series of military confrontations between the United States and Libya had taken place in the Mediterranean and the bombing was perceived as an act of retribution for aircraft and vessels lost to the U.S. Navy. As this information began to come out, Libya was excluded from all international air transport in April 1992, including even the annual carriage of pilgrims to Mecca. Yet bringing the case to a court of law proved very difficult and involved years of diplomatic maneuvers. In 1992 and 1993 further U.N. sanctions against Libya came into force to pressure Libya's ruler, Colonel Muammar al-Gaddafi, to extradite the accused to stand trial. It took 6 more years, and international mediation, for a compromise to be hammered out over the issue. In 2000 a special exterritorial Scottish court of justice convened in the Netherlands and ruled on January 31, 2001 that only one of the two Libyans accused of the bombing was indeed responsible. Amid lingering doubts about the evidence and the legal procedures followed, he was sentenced to life imprisonment.[24]

But the most terrifying collision between international politics and commercial aviation was still to come: the attacks of al-Qaeda terrorists against America on September 11, 2001. At the basis lay decades of rising anti-American sentiment in the Middle East. Such feeling was fueled by Washington's continued support for Israel in the Israeli-Palestinian conflict and by the rise to power of political Islam. For this latter phenomenon, the arrival on board an Air France Boeing 747 of Ayatollah Ruhollah Khomeini in Teheran, Iran, on February 1, 1979, formed a decisive moment.[25] Planned and prepared since 1999 at locations across the world, a group of dedicated extremists had plotted the coordinated hijack of several airliners to fly them into symbolic targets that represented American power and influence in the world. The list comprised of the World Trade Center, which represented the U.S. economy; the Pentagon as the symbol of American military power, and the U.S. Capitol, the perceived source of American support of Israel.[26] And although it appeared a coincidence that their choice date for the attack would be 9-11, the date could also be construed to hold a symbolic meaning: the number most Americans would recognize as America's universal dialing code for alarm. The hijackers strategically targeted four flights, and had their own trained to pilot the envisaged suicide missions. All four hijacked aircraft were early morning departures of transcontinental flights from the East Coast, heavily laden with fuel. To effect their plans, the al-Qaeda operatives also relied on airline hijack practices, based on historical experience.

It was an established practice in such cases to get passengers, crew, and hi-jackers back on the ground, and delay any and all developments around the hijacking to gain time. Evidence suggested that hijacks were more likely to end peacefully as their duration lengthened. Crew training therefore offered little guidance for confronting a specific suicide plot.[27] American Airlines' Flight 11, scheduled to fly from Boston to Los Angeles, was the first to be taken over. At 8.46 A.M., three-quarters of an hour after taking off from Boston's Logan International Airport and 33 dramatic minutes into the hi-jack the Boeing 767 hit the north tower of New York's World Trade Center. If a disbelieving world public initially assumed this to be a freak accident when the first reports went out, the crash of the second Boeing 767, United Airlines' Flight 175, into the WTC's south tower 17 minutes later effaced any such notion. While Internet news sites collapsed worldwide as they were bombarded with people trying to get information, citizens the world over gathered in astonished disbelief around television sets and radios to witness the unfolding of events no one could quite understand. Across the globe, work grinded to a halt. Disbelief gave way to sheer horror when, just over half an hour later, a third aircraft, American Airlines' Flight 77 smashed into Washington's Pentagon building. Only the fourth hijacked plane, United Airlines' Flight 93, en route from Newark to San Francisco, did not reach its target and went down in a field near Shanksville, Pennsyl-vania, as passengers tried to regain control of the Boeing 757. In all, 2,974 people died as a result of the attacks, excluding the nineteen hijackers, while another twenty-four victims went missing and had to be presumed dead.[28]

The attack against the Twin Towers had a dramatic impact on America, its perception of international political and military conditions in the world, and finally on air transport itself. While Washington focused on possible military and political responses that addressed the need to show force and resolve, all air traffic to, from and over the United States was banned for 3 full days. When commercial aircraft were again allowed to fly, operational circumstances had changed, both in the air and on the ground. At airports, an extravaganza of precautions took preflight security beyond the edge of reason. New preventative measures made inroads into national legislation of America's partners in air transport, requiring a collection of passengers' personal data that entailed a violation of privacy laws. New arrivals in the United States were even fingerprinted as if a potential criminal were hiding in every airline passenger. More than once, aircraft bound for a destination on the North American continent were forced to turn back halfway across the Atlantic in flagrant breach of the right of innocent passage as laid down in the 1944 Convention on International Civil Aviation. In such cases suspicion was that they carried one or more passengers against whom American intelligence sources held objections.[29] In the course of a morning, al-Qaeda's four hijacked airliners struck and destroyed the optimistic image of a world knit ever closer by rapid air transport. Instead, perceived threats

appeared to lurk everywhere. Aviation ceased to be civil. For years to come, aircraft and passengers were approached with suspicion.

In Europe, intelligence on possible threats to commercial air transport was also responsible for the unprecedented closure of Heathrow and the cancellation of all flights to British airports on August 10, 2006, as a plot to blow up planes in flight from the United Kingdom to the United States was uncovered. Plans were to detonate explosive devices smuggled in hand luggage on to as many as ten aircraft. It demonstarted the enormity of the changes that followed 9-11. Now even the *threat* of an attack sufficed to stop the mobility that was one of the core characteristics of our postmodern society. The sudden airport closure completely disrupted flights and left many thousands of passengers stranded. One commentator lamented to the BBC: "The way we travel will never be the same again."[30]

Dramatic events like these, involving the realm of high politics, masked that a fundamental redefinition of the role of nation-states in air transport had taken place that touched the fundamentals upon which the industry had operated since the 1920s. As long as commerce was the only thing at stake, Western governments were willing to loosen the grip they had exercised on air transport from its earliest beginnings in favor of leeway to market forces.

The starting point for this development lay in the Airline Deregulation Act that took effect in October 1978. Deregulation removed part of the controls that the Civil Aeronautics Board (CAB) had exercised on domestic air transportation in the United States since 1938. Hitherto airlines needed a permit from the CAB in order to serve specific routes. Apart from routes, the CAB also controlled fares and schedules in the general interest of the traveling public. The new law did away with these controls and opened up the American domestic air network to operators on a competitive basis.

In the international arena Washington hoped to entice European and other governments to release their grip on commercial air transport as well. In August 1977, President Carter gave out a statement that the United States would henceforth conduct an international aviation policy that encouraged competition. Similar notions had underpinned the signing of the Treaty of Rome in 1957 that established the European Economic Community. Yet, substantial government shareholding and outright ownership of the struggling flag-carrying airlines had hitherto precluded any movement in this direction. On the contrary, problems of capitalization to pay for the rapid succession of investments in expensive new aircraft, and the consequences of the 1973 Oil Crisis, had drawn the airlines even closer to their governments.

In March of 1978 the Dutch, who had always been supporters of a liberal approach towards international air transportation, were the first to put the American thinking to the test. In a new bilateral air transport agreement with the United States, it was established that American carriers would get full access to all European destinations through Amsterdam. In return,

KLM received a considerable expansion of its landing rights in the United States—a long-standing Dutch desire. The guiding principle of the equitable exchange of benefits, which had dictated international policy in the air since the 1950s, was thus discarded.[31] The new objective was to create an international competitive environment favorable for an increase in market share of American carriers in air transport to and from the United States.[32] Similar agreements with Belgium and West Germany hinged on the willingness of governments to set aside narrow national goals and turn away from the idea of ownership of the their air transport market.

Seeking to promote such developments further and break away from the traditional national settings of air transport to create wider opportunities for air travel between member states, the European Commission came with a memorandum in July 1979 to generate a fundamental discussion between the governments of the countries of the European Community (EC) on the possibilities for deregulation and liberalization at the European level.[33] The next year things were taken one step further, and new opportunities were created for interregional air services.[34] While discussions about liberalizing air transport were continuing, the European Court of Justice in Luxembourg ruled, on April 30, 1986, that the field of aviation—including the freedom to compete—was indeed covered by the Treaty of Rome. Appropriately, the court's verdict came in a case brought forward by a French travel agency, operating under the name Nouvelles Frontières.[35]

The court's ruling provided legal grounds for the political process of deregulation. The European Commission now set its sights on the creation of an internal European market for air transport by the end of the year 1992. This market would be freely accessible to all airlines from the EC member states.[36] Reactions were mixed. While the Dutch welcomed this process, hoping to create an international environment that would be favorable to KLM, France and Germany continued to offer protection to their flag carriers.[37] Spain and Italy also conducted their aviation policies along such lines, providing intimate political and financial support for their respective national airlines.[38]

In December 1987 the European Commission proposed a liberalization package with more room for the differentiation of fares. It did away with the traditional role of national governments in intra-European air transport and gave airlines from the EC member states freedom to operate within the area of the EC. At the same time the European Commission took a first step towards a supranational role in aviation matters in developing a policy with regard to the external aviation relations of the EC member states. In such contacts, the national governments had hitherto enjoyed full sovereign powers. This favored airlines from the larger and more populous countries vis-à-vis those from smaller nations that carried less political clout. The aim of the new situation was to create a level playing field for all European air carriers to compete in the world market.[39] With it the European Commission

put the final axe to the 70-year-old system of bilateralism in air transport that went back to the Paris Convention of 1919.[40]

A further package of liberalization measures, effective from January 1, 1993, formed the climax of the process. It replaced the old concept of *national* airlines with the new one of the *community* air carrier: an airline of which the majority of shares were held by nationals of member states. This "package" gave community air carriers full freedom to operate services within the European Union. Proponents—Britain and the Netherlands—again found France, Germany, Greece, Italy, and Spain in opposition. Nevertheless, a compromise was hammered out in which the EC ministers agreed to allow protective restrictions on domestic routes until April 1, 1997. In this transitional period national governments were authorized to impose limitations in market access for foreign airlines, based on economic rationale, lack of airport or air traffic control capacity, or environmental arguments.[41] Yet the new measures were little less than revolutionary. After all, a complete liberalization might well lead to the collapse of national flag carriers, and this touched upon the sensitive nerve of national pride. Although it did not end state interference, the effect of liberalization was profound: by the turn of the millennium, only just over half of the airlines flying in 1993 still operated scheduled services.[42] The changes also affected established scheduled national carriers. On October 2, 2001 Swissair was the first of the European flag carriers to fold, when the financial burdens of a string of ill-fated investments and shareholdings in foreign airlines became too much to bear. It was followed over the next days by its (then) Belgian subsidiary, Sabena. Despite the changes in the relationship between flag carriers and their governments, Sabena's demise led to a full-fledged parliamentary inquiry that lasted over a year to establish why matters could have become so bad and why the Belgian government had, in the end, allowed the bankruptcy to become irreversible.[43]

Less dramatic, but just as far reaching, was the fundamental reorientation on the role that nation-states played in international air transport brought about by the political developments of the early 1990s. The collapse of the political, economic, and social system in eastern Europe in 1989 and 1990 created revolutionary new conditions that had profound effects on air transport. For the first time since 1945 bipolar world politics became redundant as a factor influencing developments. At a time in which the air transport industry in the West was going through the motions of liberalization, its network of services came under pressure. With the political geography changed new connections to the east were developed—not only in the sense of flights but also in the sense of various cooperative arrangements between "western" and "eastern" carriers. While the former were keen to expand their reach eastward now that there was opportunity to do so, the latter discovered themselves in urgent need of such cooperation. At the very moment in which they most dearly needed extra funds to invest in new equipment to

cope with the onslaught of foreign competition in preparation for an envisaged entry into the European Union, the governments of the east European countries were unable to continue their role as guardians and financiers of their national flag carriers. Although some nations continued to protect the interests of their flag carriers to ensure their survival—like the Polish government that refused permission in November 1993 to British Airways to double its services to Warsaw as it would have been detrimental to the interests of its own carrier, LOT—such an approach to international aviation politics was on the way out. The new priorities lay elsewhere as the Eastern European nations faced the immense task of transforming society to a non-socialist setting.

But there were important changes in western Europe too that were a direct result from the end of the Cold War. Over the course of the 1990s the military presence that had guarded the status quo in Europe was downsized. Particularly in Germany, but elsewhere too, military air bases were closed, as it was no longer necessary to maintain the same strength of air power. In 1993, for example, the U.S. Air Force closed its base in Hahn, some 60 miles west of Frankfurt, handing over the facilities to the German civil authorities, which then decided to set up an operating company to develop the former base into a commercial airport. By the end of the 1990s, passenger traffic already surpassed the 100,000 mark with the arrival of low-cost operator Ryanair in 1999, proving its claim that people would not mind flying there, instead of Frankfurt itself, as long as the price was low enough.[44] Ryanair was soon followed by other low-cost carriers. Developments went very fast from then on. In 2000 passenger traffic already stood at 380,281, growing almost tenfold to 3.7 million in 2006.[45] At other ex-military facilities in Germany, such as the former RAF base Laarbruch, similar developments took place, but the model also applied to military airfields in eastern European countries. In fact, the new European network of low-cost air transportation that made increasing inroads into the air transport services of the flag-carrying airlines was to a considerable extent built on civilian use of former military facilities.

European liberalization then marked the beginning of the end of the system of protected national *flag carriers* and nationality-based air transport as such. The process culminated in the transfer of negotiating authority for international air transport agreements from the national governments to the European Commission in 2003. On June 5, the European Council of Transport Ministers agreed to pass responsibility for conducting key air transport negotiations on to the European Commission. The decision granted the European Commission a mandate to begin negotiations on a new transatlantic air agreement with the United States. "This is an historic decision," said Loyola de Palacio, commissioner in charge of Transport and Energy: "Today we have reached a deal that will enable the European Union to assert itself at international level and to work for the benefit of its consumers and

its aviation industry."[46] Nonetheless, in typical European fashion, it was *also* agreed to reserve rights for member states to conduct their own bilateral negotiations but subject to a degree of Community control. With the ball park for international aviation agreements completely redefined by the Commission's new authority, the Dutch were the first to draw the conclusion that the interests of the formerly national carrier would be best served if hooked up with a really large airline from a country that carried political clout at the European level. In October 2003 the takeover of KLM by Air France presented the first major reshuffling of the liberalized industry and at one stroke created Europe's largest international airline group.

The next milestone in this ongoing process was reached in 2007. On March 22 the twenty-five EU transport ministers unanimously approved the air transport agreement between the European Union and the United States reached 3 weeks earlier. A month later, the Open Skies Agreement—to come to force on March 30, 2008—was signed in Washington by Jacques Barrot, Vice-President of the European Commission responsible for Transport, European Council President Wolfgang Tiefensee, and U.S. Secretary of State Condoleezza Rice and Transportation Secretary Mary Peter. Its aim was to create an "Open Aviation Area": a single air transport market between the EU and the United States in which investment could flow freely and in which European and American airlines would be able to provide services without any restriction, including access to the domestic markets of both parties.[47]

The agreement provided ultimate evidence that in the first decade of the aviation's second century the role of governments continued to decline. Open Skies agreements were not limited to the United States and Europe either. In 2004 Washington signed such an agreement with India as well, in anticipation of further growth of the Indian economy and bilateral air services. A trend emerged in countries with common interests in Latin America, Asia, and Africa to unilaterally declare themselves open skies territories and invite both domestic and foreign airlines to operate available routes without restrictions. Australia and New Zealand agreed on a "Trans Tasmanian Single Aviation Market," while the Latin American countries of Mercosur (Argentina, Brazil, Paraguay, Uruguay, and Chile) also made efforts to develop a single civil aviation market, in the framework of economic and political rapprochement. The same process could be witnessed between the Andean Pact countries (Bolivia, Colombia, Ecuador, Peru, and Venezuela) and with Central American States (Guatemala, Nicaragua, El Salvador, and Honduras), all of which also had Open Skies agreements with the United States. Starting in the year 2000, the Middle Eastern countries also moved in this direction, aiming for the establishment of a Common Arab Aviation Market before the end of the decade.[48] It was widely recognized that one of the main reasons behind government decisions to open up national skies and aviation markets was the need to cater to the growing demand for air transport generated by the worldwide increase in travel and tourism. Under

such new conditions, airlines had to adapt to a redefined regulatory environment with more options for new competitors to enter the market. As a result the air transport industry faced an onslaught of new competitors. From the late 1990s so-called low-cost carriers turned air transport upside down, shunning away from the traditional glamour of luxury and state-of-the-art airports and focusing on fringe benefits derived from secondary routes. Yet the new regulatory environment did result in more routes served and more people flying.

Business Only—Officially

Ticket prices had been important in competition between the scheduled carriers and charter airlines from the start of chartered air transport in the 1950s. Compared to air transport over similar stage lengths in the United States, prices for intra-European services had always been high—so high that by the 1980s more than 40 percent of all European aircraft passengers traveled on charter flights.[49] Transatlantic travel showed a similar trend, with the share of (lower priced) charter traffic going up each year, much to the concern of the scheduled flag carriers, who tried to stem this trend. For that reason ticket prices became the bone of contention in the controversy between scheduled and nonscheduled airlines. In the adverse economic conditions of the late 1970s, anxiety about price competition on the Atlantic routes—the main moneymaker for the airline industry—was heightened by the arrival of yet a new competitor, threatening to take up a considerable part of the market for scheduled traffic.

At the center of the controversy stood new marketing and operational techniques tried out by the self-styled British aviation pioneer Freddy Laker. Pushing aside generally accepted customs for running an airline, Laker pioneered the concept of "no-frills" services. His Skytrain was the first air service for which no advance reservations could be made—the thinking being that this would only push up overhead. Instead, Skytrain offered strictly "walk-on, walk-off" flights. It provided no free onboard amenities, and Laker allowed less passenger luggage to be taken on than his competitors. Such ideas went against the grain of the airline industry. But slashing costs, Laker was able to market his Skytrain tickets for as much as 60 percent below the going rates. Skytrain began flying in 1977 as a novel way to travel between Europe and the United States, much to the disgust of the older scheduled operators. The question was how to counter Laker's rising popularity among (predominantly young) travelers. With a few exceptions, most of the major national carriers had a tradition of resisting lower fares. Production-driven and with relatively high cost structures, they had little choice but to pursue such objectives.[50] The initial success of Skytrain was such that its competitors put pressure on their national governments to agree to a general

reduction of ticket prices (and compensate financial losses). A flood of new *stand-by* fares, and other discount tickets was put on the market. On top of that IATA came with a coordinated action in 1978 to introduce the Advance Purchase Excursion fare (APEX) as a weapon against Laker and the charter airlines.[51] Customers for these tickets had to be prepared to run some risk, as a change of reservations was not allowed. APEX marked the start of a price war between the IATA companies, supported by their governments, and Laker.[52] Overstretched by rapid expansion and under heavy pressure from competition, Skytrain suddenly folded in February 1982.

Lower fares for the traveling public were also central to airline deregulation in the United States. The abolition of fare controls and encouragement of competition forced the airlines to focus on cutting costs. This they did through optimizing aircraft use. It quickly became important to reorganize existing route structures to ensure that the optimum number of passengers would be on board each individual flight. To achieve this airlines adopted a new operational model that became known as "hub-and-spokes." A carrier would chose one or more strategically located airports as "hubs" to serve as transfer points for passengers traveling along the "spokes" from their point of origin to their final destination. At the hubs airlines herded passengers to redistribute them over different planes for the next leg of their journey. To do so effectively, the airlines proceeded to schedule departures and arrivals of planes in concentrated "waves" of flights timed throughout the day. This ensured an optimum number of connecting flights at a hub. Given the size of an airline's fleet, the hub-and-spokes system allowed more destinations to be served than earlier point-to-point operations. The airlines most successful at "hubbing" proudly reported more revenue. The inconvenience to the public for having to transfer to a new flight was offset by lower fares. Never very remunerative to begin with, the air transport market suffered from progressively lower yield margins.[53] An additional problem was that during the late 1970s and early 1980s, the new competitive practices were hampered by a sluggish economy and spiraling fuel costs. The result was a series of mergers and shakeouts that rippled through the American air transport industry, leaving only the strongest in place.

Economies of scale became of overriding importance in air transport— and not just in the United States. With deregulation in Europe under way as well, the flag carriers of the major European countries squared up domestic competition by taking over their main competitors, often with the support, or at least silent blessing, of their governments. Britain led the way under Margaret Thatcher. Bent on privatizing British Airways, but eager to effect the highest possible price for the Treasury, the government protected its flag carrier until privatization was completed in 1987.[54] The following year British Airways took over its remaining competitor British Caledonian. In May 1988 the two top men, Lord John King and Adam Thomson, agreed on the takeover.[55] Air France needed longer for a similar process. After 2 years

of negotiations it succeeded, in 1990, to take its competitor UTA under its wings. If this consolidated Air France's market position, it did not resolve the airline's high cost structure.[56] In the mid-1990s the French government had to carry out a multi billion dollar infusion of new state capital into Air France to keep the airline aloft—an act that spurred vehement protests from the other EC member states. One estimate put the total government aid to the European flag carriers between 1991 and 1997 at $12 billion.[57] In Germany Lufthansa, branched off into some 250 subventures, had it easier. In 1990–1991 it had to but sit and wait for the bankruptcy of its "new domestic competitor" Interflug from the defunct GDR to bolster its position in the German market. Nonetheless liberalization meant that Lufthansa had to tolerate the founding of a new subsidiary by British Airways, Deutsche BA, as a competitor on Germany's domestic routes. Even in a small country like Holland, KLM made sure it acquired a majority holding in the two other Dutch carriers, Transavia and Martinair. With such domestic processes completed the way forward lay in acquiring sizable global networks.

The North Atlantic, still the number one moneymaking market for international air transport, provided the first area for globalization. The origins of the new trend were unexpected. In July 1989 KLM surprised the aviation industry by suddenly participating in a leveraged buyout of the fourth largest American carrier, Northwest Airlines. Between July 1989 and March 1991 the Dutch invested some $400 million in Northwest, representing an economic interest of 20 percent.[58] Cooperation went beyond the usual items such as routes, scheduling, and maintenance and included the linkup of the two carriers' computer reservations systems and code sharing of flights—all sold at one coordinated price. Code sharing was of crucial importance. It meant that a computer reservations system would present prospective customers wishing to book a flight with either airline with many more destinations than actually served by each individual participant. Every Northwest flight would also appear as a KLM flight, and vice versa. Both on the American federal and on the European level, such agreements had to be specially exempted from cartel restrictions. Northwest and KLM fully profited from their arrangement when a new, liberal bilateral air transport agreement between the United States and the Netherlands cleared some of the American legal obstacles for transnational airline investment and cooperation in 1993.[59] In the following years the alliance between the KLM and Northwest served as an example to other so-called strategic alliances. The decade saw the start of a series of talks on various forms of cooperation. By force of circumstance, market enlargement through competition—the envisaged effect of deregulation—was exchanged for the principle of market expansion through collaboration. But although Washington agreed to allow two relatively minor players in the field to hook up in this fashion, allowing the same privileges to major players in the market was something entirely different. British Airways found that out in 1992 when it pursued an alliance with US Air.

Cargo tonnage

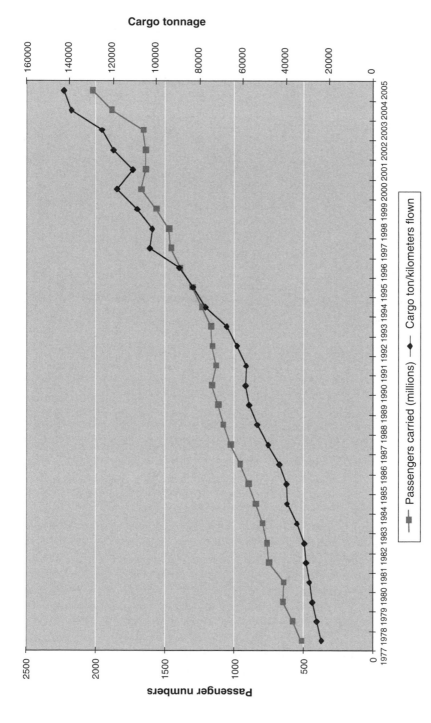

The Development of World Air Transport, 1977—2005. *Source:* ICAO figures.

—■— Passengers carried (millions)   —◆— Cargo ton/kilometers flown

While cash strapped US Air needed British Airways' deep pockets, the alliance theoretically opened up seamless air connections between 20,000 city pairs on the combined route networks of the two carriers—very nearly too much for the political sensitivities still connected with air transport, even in America. The deal almost stranded in American domestic law and politics, fearful of foreign influence in American air carriers. Yet a less obtrusive deal between the two airlines was approved in January 1993.[60] Three years later and to the surprise of many, British Airways gave up on US Air and signed an agreement with American Airlines instead. The background to this was that American had become its main transatlantic competitor, having taken over the landing rights of the ailing TWA at Heathrow. Appropriately the two mega carriers called their alliance OneWorld. After years of financial difficulties in the American airline business, it met with little protest. But then again, the two partners could point to the results of the GATT Uruguay Round, under which the General Agreement on Trade in Services had been signed in 1994 that provided for international collaboration in aircraft repair and maintenance, marketing of air transport services, and computer reservation services.[61] It was another sign that the traditional structures of air transport, built on foundations of nationalism, were changing. Air France and Alitalia subsequently hooked up with Delta, Lufthansa with United. By the turn of the century the latter's Star Alliance had expanded to include US Airways, Air Canada, Mexicana, All Nippon Airways, Air New Zealand, Thai Airways, Singapore Airlines, the Brazilian carrier Varig, Austrian Airways, and the Polish airline LOT. Other strategic alliances that came into existence aimed for a similar worldwide coverage, in effect forging global air transportation into three main competing conglomerates: Star, OneWorld, and Sky Team.

The circumstances under which such reshuffles came about were difficult and a reflection of the continued influence that the larger political, military, and economic developments in the world had on air transport. This was particularly so with regard to the effects of the Gulf War of 1990–1991, which gravely disrupted international air services. The Iraqi invasion of Kuwait on August 2, 1990 brought a 30 percent increase in fuel prices. Large areas in the Middle East and in the Persian Gulf became inaccessible to commercial overflight when the Allied offensive against Iraq got under way in January 1991, hampering services from Europe to Asia and Australia. Moreover the unstable international situation that resulted from the war caused a global economic downturn and a severe drop in passenger numbers. Although recovery commenced in North America in 1992, it was not until 1994 that it took hold in most of western Europe. Before that, the war plunged the air transport sector into yet another crisis. For the first time since 1930 worldwide passenger embarkations actually dropped in 1991. Airlines saw themselves forced to reduce frequencies and ground aircraft. Profits, already under pressure, evaporated. In the United States, airline companies

finished 1990 with a loss of more than $1 billion, which added acuteness to their already existing debt burden of $35 billion.[62] Old, established names in the business, such as Pan Am and TWA, found themselves in major financial difficulties. The problems were still aggravated by the impact of 12 years of deregulation. Moreover both Pan Am and TWA had a relatively old fleet and therefore faced higher fuel charges than their nearest competitors. Pan Am was the worse off. Since it did not have a domestic route network to speak of, it depended on transfers to its international flights from America's gateway airports. In January 1991, the formerly most prestigious airline company in the world sought protection under the umbrella of bankruptcy legislation. TWA did not fare any better. In December 1990 its CEO, Carl Icahn, indicated he wished to sell TWA's transatlantic routes to London to American Airlines, in order to relieve the airline's financial predicament. In December 1991 Pan Am went bust. TWA escaped bankruptcy in 1992, and again in 1995, and managed to stay aloft until April 2001, when it was absorbed by American Airlines.

Matters were not helped by the emergence of yet another threat to the surviving airlines. By the middle of the 1990s a new type of competitors was emerging: the "low-cost carrier." This was a new type of airline, built on the same principles as pioneered by Laker two decades before: high aircraft utilization and no-frills service. But by the middle of the 1990s important changes had taken place that enabled such airlines to grow. Culture played no small role in this. As more and more people had traveled by air, the exclusivity of the travel mode as such had eroded. Becoming a normal travel mode, the price tag of each air ticket was gaining importance as an element in modal choice. Added to this were the development of the Internet and the growth of its number of users. Low-cost airlines soon built their marketing on this. The Internet enabled suppliers of air transport to pitch their services directly to prospective consumers, dispensing with travel agents as relatively expensive middlemen in the sale of tickets that could now be bought directly online. After examples in the United States, such as Value Jet, low-cost services were also developed in Europe, where new entrants to the air transport market could now profit from the series of liberalization measures effected by the European Union. Here a 28-year-old Greek entrepreneur, Stelios Haji-Ioannou, founded EasyJet as a new type of airline in March 1995. In October of that year EasyJet started operations from London's secondary airport Luton with flights to Edinburgh and Glasgow, expanding to Amsterdam 6 months later. Despite political problems over landing rights and fare conditions in several European countries, EasyJet managed to achieve an unprecedented growth. In 2006, the airline possessed a fleet of 122 aircraft and carried 33 million passengers.[63]

The impact of the new style of air transportation was tremendous. In exchange for low fares passengers were prepared to accustom themselves to the absence of amenities: designated seating, food and drink on board, and

a varied service level all went. In the year 2000 EasyJet got the attention of many prospective travelers when it offered online discount tickets for as low as £2.50 ($3.80) for a single trip. Within years, all airlines developed their own Internet booking facilities, offering discounts over the traditional ticket sales through travel and airline agents. And whereas EasyJet operated to and from Europe's main destination cities, liberalization also made it possible to operate low-cost services outside the traditionally busy and expensive major airports.

One of the factors behind this development was a lack of airport capacity. By the 1990s traffic at major centers such as London and Frankfurt had become so heavy that capacity shortages occurred at peak hours. As a description of the possibility of the airport and air traffic control combination to provide capacity for an aircraft to land, receive ground and gate handling, and take off again, a new term came into use: the *slot*. These slots were given out on the basis of "grandfather rights." This meant that the airline with the oldest rights at a certain airport also held the best rights, limiting the options for new entrants to compete. For slots that remained open after the grandfather rights had been claimed, the European Commission and the Council of Transport Ministers decided airports had to provide a special regulatory body that would seek a fair division of the remaining slots.[64] The establishment of such coordinating bodies, usually in the form of a private enterprise at least partially controlled by the airport authorities, was yet another indication that liberalization and rising air traffic volumes were making airport capacity into a scarce commodity. In April 1999 the director general of IATA, Pierre Jeanniot, complained that shortcomings in the infrastructure annulled the relaxing of regulatory controls. After 80 years of near continuous growth it appeared that air traffic in Europe might end in a lack of space.[65]

Yet scarcity also created new possibilities. These were explored vigorously by the upstart Irish carrier Ryanair. Founded in 1985, Ryanair seized the new opportunities offered by the European Commission's liberalization measures that took effect in 1997. As a low-cost carrier, Ryanair combined quick airport turnaround times—minimal onboard catering (for which the customer paid extra) and the absence of designated seating reduced the time spent on the ground—with the operation of a single type of aircraft. Overhead was kept small by outsourcing as many aspects of airline operation as possible. From the turn of the century direct ticket sales through the Internet—one-way tickets only, without guarantees for connecting flights at intermediary stops —improved revenue even further. The new type of marketing tied into the evolving new information society, where individuality of choice became the norm in every walk of life. Ryanair developed a point-to-point network of routes that connected secondary airports, rather than the big traffic hubs. Doing so, the carrier was able to profit from landing and handling charges that were substantially lower than those at the larger

established international airports. And as the airline rapidly got bigger, it was able to negotiate special deep discount rates at regional airports wishing to attract its business. Indeed, the Irish carrier operated only those routes that secured the highest profitability and managed to negotiate subsidies from regional authorities to operate specific routes. At the same time, European liberalization opened up new development possibilities for regional airports to attract the services of carriers like Ryanair in a situation where the larger airports were increasingly saturated with traffic, both in the air and on the road system around them. The effect of these new services was considerable. First of all on air transport as such: towards the end of the 1990s economic growth and the new markets explored by low-cost airlines provided the basis for a rapid growth of air services in Europe—at 5 to 6 percent per year double the community's general economic growth per annum. Within a few years low-cost airlines became important operators for the regional airports as such, contributing substantially to their development—and indirectly to the regional economy around them. This was particularly so in the cases where the regional airports served were situated in areas that suffered from an adverse economic conditions—such as Charleroi in Belgium, where in 1997 Ryanair was the only scheduled operator—or in areas where the arrival of cheap air transport provided a boost to the economy, such as in Cracow, Poland. In Charleroi Ryanair by itself became something of a motor for economic (re)development, whereas its Hungarian competitor Wizz Air fulfilled a similar role in redeveloping regional airports across the border in Poland, boosting their outreach into the economy after the enlargement of the European Union in 2004.[66]

The rapid growth of low-cost airlines put pressure on the traditional carriers to attune their services to the possibilities of the information age. One after the other airlines started adapting their computer reservations systems to enable so-called direct e-ticketing through the Internet, often in combination with home check-in facilities. Consumers welcomed such changes as they opened up the possibility to become their own travel agents and compare flight schedules and prices for each air trip in the comfort of their homes. The advent of online booking cut airline costs and also provided travelers with nearly full information about fare and service combinations. This significantly reduced the ability of airlines to manage their demand curves and extract maximum revenues from their customers.[67] Digital direct booking thus became yet another addition to the downward pressure on prices—and thus on service levels in economy class. Meanwhile the traditional paper airline ticket was on the way out—to be replaced by digital references in computer systems. The parsimonious customer for whom ticket price was the sole factor deciding the process of travel choice, rather than the airline, began to set the standard of travel—a decisive departure from previous practice. Through these developments flying had, at the start of the new century, even become cheaper than long-distance car, rail, or sea trips.

Such changes also held their repercussions for the holiday charter market. The same digitalization processes that governed the changes in scheduled air transport also had their effects in the charter and tourist business. Controlling costs became pivotal here too, while margins became smaller because of the increased options for price comparisons and on-line booking that the Internet held for consumers. Travel organizations began running their own air services, instead of contracting an external charter carrier. This vertical integration of the holiday travel business brought cost savings. Whether for leisure or for business purposes, travel arrangements could henceforth be made from home, by pressing a few computer keys.

Further new developments also announced themselves on the global market, particularly in Asia. An emerging shift in world industrial production to the newly industrializing countries of the Asian Pacific rim produced rapid economic growth in the region. This development had a notable effect on air transportation to and in Asia, which even grew faster than the world average. Despite a temporary slowdown resulting from a financial crisis in Asia in 1997–1998, the economy in this part of the world veered up in the new millennium.

China stood out. With over 1.2 billion potential new customers waiting to be served the Chinese government had gradually relaxed its stranglehold on the economy and steered the planet's most populous nation into the world market as a major producer, and consumer, of industrial goods. Since the start of the economic reforms in 1978, China witnessed a tenfold increase in its gross domestic product, with growth figures accelerating from the early 1990s. In October 2002 the Civil Aviation System Reform Program amalgamated the Chinese air transport industry. With its two state owned carriers—Air China and China Eastern—and the privately owned China Southern, China had captured some 7.5 percent of the world passenger total in 2004, a percentage rising by the year.[68] Predictions were that China would become the largest commercial aviation market outside the United States. By 2010 some 51 percent of all international scheduled passenger traffic would be in the Asia-Pacific region.[69] This rapid expansion was helped by a combination of economic growth and a relaxation of American and European controls on the export of advanced technology to China—and by the new rules on the international trade in civil aircraft. These were agreed to in the context of the GATT in Geneva in 1979, a far cry from the situation in earlier decades.[70] Nonetheless, such potential was not without its problems. China's airports and air traffic control systems had only limited capacity, while the airspace itself was divided between military and civilian authorities. In addition, the national flight reservation system was incompatible with the systems in use in the rest of the world. Foreign airlines also considered the controls over ticket pricing and revenue flows problematic.[71] In 2007 the Chinese government even had to issue a decree ordering a temporary *reduction* of flights to and from Beijing for reasons of safety and airport

space. Elsewhere in the country flight schedules also had to be reduced to relinquish pressure on the system.[72] Despite liberalization, the state was never far away.

Air Transport and Global Society

Pushed by economic growth the combined effects of détente, liberalization, and increasingly cost-effective airline operations that brought down ticket prices resulted in an unprecedented boom in air transport. By the turn of the millennium over 1.5 billion people were flying annually, and some 28 million worldwide made their living from air transportation.[73] Between 1977 and the start of the new century airline passenger numbers tripled. At the end of 2003, when aviation celebrated its centennial birthday, the world total for that year stood at 1,657 million. Since the dawn of aviation, over 35.6 billion people had flown on an airplane as passengers.[74] There was hardly an area in the world left untouched by commercial aviation. People from nations rich and poor were accumulating many more air miles than ever before. Surprisingly, the most rapid growth in passenger numbers had not occurred in the economic boom of the second half of the 1990s but between 1977 and 1987, when world airline embarkations doubled despite a stagnant economy.[75]

Such figures reflected ongoing processes of globalization, both in the sense of widening horizons for many individuals and also in the sense of globalization of the business and industrial environments. Sought-after professionals traveled the world constantly, on the move from one corporate or academic assignment to the next. In the 1990s outsourcing of production to lower wage economies became the norm in many areas of industrial production, giving an enormous boost to the movement of goods and people across the planet. Air cargo became an integral part of international trade through the development of global supply chains, just-in-time delivery schedules, and intermodal logistics. Improvements in education and transport technologies meant that high-value goods, like computers and electronic equipment generally—hitherto typically produced in the Western world—were outsourced to factories in low-wage developing countries like India, Thailand, China, and Vietnam. From there manufactured goods were airlifted to distribution centers in the industrialized world.[76] Smaller goods shipments received preferential treatment by a rapidly expanding new type of integrated air and surface couriers, like Federal Express, United Parcel Service, and Germany-based DHL (Dalsey, Hillblom and Lynn) that offered overnight deliveries anywhere in the world, operating their own fleets of aircraft and vehicles.

Yet industrial products and parcels were not the only goods to cover great distances across the globe to reach Western consumers: agriculture

too proved a booming market. From the 1980s flowers and an increasing array of vegetables were purpose grown in developing countries, profiting from warm climates, lots of sunlight, and continuous crop growth. The East African climate, for example, turned out to be especially suitable for flowers that had hitherto been produced in countries like Holland, under glass and with the aid of artificial light and heating. It proved to be cheaper to grow roses in Kenya and Ethiopia and fly them to markets in Europe and North America than to grow them locally—proof of enormous advances in air transport efficiency and of changing perceptions of the world as such. In 2006, the value of the Kenyan flower exports to Holland alone stood at some $300 million.[77]

Tourism represented another major factor in globalization. If, until the late 1970s, air tourism consisted of relatively short flights from the colder reaches of the Northern Hemisphere to the sunny beaches and tourist resorts one to three flying hours away in the South, the 1980s and beyond saw a gradual widening of tourist destinations served by air. After a slump in travel because of sharp rises in oil prices in 1979 and 1980, air tourism continued to grow throughout the 1980s and 1990s. Spending on holidays quadrupled in western European countries.[78] The numbers of flying tourists went up accordingly: In most Western countries airline embarkations doubled in the 1990s. In a good many Western countries spending on air travel received a deliberate further boost through consumer "savings" programs that issued "air miles" as travel incentives for every dollar or euro spent in shops. The "credits" thus saved could be redeemed for airplane tickets. The most discerning and affluent tourists began to opt for new "exotic" destinations. Figures of Europeans going on holidays to a different continent reflected this: in the final decade of the 20th century their figure almost tripled.[79] Long-distance holiday flights explored the tourist possibilities of places like Venezuela's Isla Margarita and Cuba. Each year growing numbers of holiday makers disembarked to take in the grasslands and wildlife of Kenya, the beaches of Gambia, Sri Lanka, and Thailand, or the exotic culture of the Indonesian island Bali. Hardly any area in the world was left untouched by this latest spread of tourism. On the remote Galapagos Islands (600 miles off the coast of Ecuador in the Pacific), to name one example, the arrival of tourism—40,000 visitors in 1990; 140,000 in 2006—even upset the age-old unique ecological balance and threatened vegetation and wildlife not found anywhere else on the planet.[80] Air tourism became a worldwide business, often stimulated by governments of the recipient countries, regarding tourism as a force for economic development.[81]

Apart from photos and memories, tourists brought back a taste for the local entourage in the form of decorative objects and culinary experiences. Restaurants specializing in exotic foods and foreign dishes first explored by tourists popped up throughout the Western world, drawing a clientele familiar with its specifics. Shops selling typical "indigenous" products

followed in their wake. At the turn of the century, tourism had come to belong to the major foreign currency earners of many destination countries, and the hospitality industry registered as one of the world's largest in terms of jobs and contribution to the national income and foreign exchange. In the case of Thailand, for example, the total economic impact from tourism and tourists—almost invariably arriving by air—contributed as much as 15 percent of the country's gross domestic product in 2007.[82] From the mid-1980s the tourism industry outstripped rice exports as Thailand's principal source of foreign exchange. But apart from having an impact on the economy, the social and cultural effects of the rapid influx of Western air tourists and their hard currency were considerable. Tourism contributed to debt reduction, capital accumulation, and a shift in the balance of trade. Yet the effects could be much more profound. In a country like Gambia as much as 30 per cent of the workforce came to depend directly or indirectly on tourism, all of which was dependent on air transport.[83] Such dependency made the destination countries vulnerable to the uncertainties of international events. Stimulated by the Gulf War of 1991 and Egypt's participation in the America-led coalition of Operation Desert Storm, anti-Western sentiments fueled a string of attacks on tourists in Egypt between 1992 and 1997 and again from 2004, after the Iraq War. Vulnerability was demonstrated in temporary drops in tourist arrivals after such attacks. Nonetheless tourism still remained a growing industry in Egypt, contributing over 15 percent of the gross domestic product. Approximately 80 percent of the total arrivals in Egypt were air travelers.[84] But violence or not, the social and environmental impacts and the clash between traditional and Western values was still considerable in the new tourist countries.[85] The saddest of such effects was the emergence of sex tourism—charter flights full of lustful males—reflecting the fact that sex had become a basic economic element wherever tourism was marketed. The phenomenon could be witnessed in the Caribbean and parts of southeast Asia and Africa.[86]

The combined effects of emerging globalization and tourism meant that no nation, no matter how small, could continue without its own international airport. In the late 1970s the affluent oil states of the Persian Gulf were quick to respond to this trend. On January 1, 1977, the sheikhdom of Sharjah opened its own airport, despite the fact that it was situated at no more than 12 minutes' drive from Dubai International Airport.[87]

Nations in the developing world, such as in sub-Saharan Africa, were considerably more cash-strapped and needed foreign assistance to improve their air infrastructure as their integration into the world economy continued. Improved connections were deemed of importance to international trade and economic development. Development programs of several donor countries specifically targeted air transport. In the early 1970s the Italians built a complete airport near Dar es Salaam, Tanzania. Ten years later France provided modern technical installations and a new terminal. In Malawi Japanese

money enabled the construction of an international airport at the nation's capital, Lilongwe, whereas the Soviet Union refurbished the national airport at Antananarivo, Madagascar. Yet the planning of such programs, financed from budgets for development aid and more often than not immersed in national politics of the recipient country, was sometimes far from clear. The construction of aircraft maintenance facilities at the airport near Mount Kilimanjaro in Tanzania provided a case in point. The idea was to build a maintenance base for Air Tanzania at Kilimanjaro International Airport—at the request of Tanzania, which hoped to use the airport for the development of tourism in the region. Yet Kilimanjaro was hardly serviced at all by Air Tanzania. Over the course of its construction the "white elephant" hangar that was built there with Dutch money got bigger and bigger and cost three times the amount originally estimated when it was finished in 1983. By that time the Tanzanians had reasoned that they preferred to upgrade the existing maintenance facilities at Dar es Salaam instead, where Air Tanzania had its main operating base. Even before the new hangar was completed, the work at Dar-es-Salaam entailed that the new facilities would not be used, as it would be uneconomical to separate maintenance from aircraft operations.[88] The case showed that internal dynamics could be important complicating factors in upgrading the air transport infrastructure in developing nations.

The reverse side of the continued growth and reach of air transport was, however, also becoming increasingly evident, especially in the sense of aggravated environmental problems. Although the issue was universal, the environmental consequences of commercial aviation were most acutely recognized in the industrialized nations. To begin with, the noise situation around major airports there had become worse as time went by. Despite continuous efforts in the aviation industry to develop engines and aircraft that would produce less noise—the 1980s produced new types of by-pass jet engines that had considerably lower noise emissions the public's susceptibility to noise increased ever further. Western countries put penalties on the continued use of noisy aircraft, eventually banning them from their airports. The noisiest jets, with engines from the 1960s, were banned from the European Union in 1988; slightly less noisy aircraft were grounded in 2002. Yet such gains as there were in reducing the noise imprints from individual aircraft were more than annulled by the ever-increasing density of traffic and the numbers of passenger aircraft in daily use. For people living in the often built-up vicinity of airports, the number of planes passing low overhead became a growing problem. In fact the airports contributed to the predicament because of the adaptation of new styles of airport management. Airports came to be surrounded by industrial estates, in turn requiring extra housing for employees. The ultimate example of this trend was provided by the new Charles-de-Gaulle Airport, north of Paris. Initially situated in a predominantly agricultural area that was but sparsely populated, the successful business exploitation of the new airport and its rapid growth resulted in a

building spree before the airport's first decade was out. The growing number of complaints about noise went hand in hand with residential expansion and the growth of traffic volume. In even more densely populated countries, considerable pressure was exercised on airport authorities to invest major funds into the geographic reorientation of those runways that lay at the basis of most complaints. In Zurich an extra runway was opened in the 1970s, while Holland saw the construction of a whole new remote satellite runway 3 miles away from the terminal facilities at Amsterdam's Schiphol Airport two decades later. It was specifically situated in such a position so as to produce least nuisance.[89]

Besides concern over noise, air transport also enticed growing anxiety over its long-term environmental consequences. The increasing traffic volume meant that by the turn of the millennium, air transport had produced about 3 percent of the world's annual carbon dioxide emissions, "visible" to anyone who cared to look up at the shape of long contrails of condensing exhaust fumes dragged across the sky by aircraft passing high overhead. Although jet fuel mainly produces water vapor as it burns, the vapors accelerate the formation of ice crystals around small particles present in aircraft exhaust gasses. Data collected after the 2001 attacks on New York and Washington, when federal authorities instituted a 3-day ban on all civil flights to and over the United States, suggested that the slow dissolving vapor trails might have an effect on the Earth's climate by trapping a portion of the outbound infrared radiation and thus contribute to global warming.[90] Such findings, and the easy identification of aviation as a contributor to global warming, made air transport into a focal point for mounting public concern over the polluting effects of internal combustion engines on the Earth's atmosphere. In the early years of the new century, apprehension over the contribution that commercial aviation made to the rise of carbon dioxide in the Earth's atmosphere even led to initiatives to entice travelers to pay for environmental compensations such as the *atmosfair* initiative to offset the greenhouse effects of their flight on the environment by planting new trees.[91]

Hydrocarbons, which had harmful effects on the Earth's ozone layer, and nitrogen oxides were also a concern. Although the level of unburnt hydrocarbons in the exhaust fumes was reduced by 90 percent over the 1980s and 1990s, there was no immediate solution to this problem. Despite efforts from engine manufacturers, progress in reducing nitrogen oxides, partial contributors to the newly recognized environmental problem of acid rain and another likely catalyst in ozone depletion, was considerably less spectacular. In this area no significant reductions were achieved. Nonetheless, latest types of aircraft engines were less taxing on the environment.[92]

Environmental concerns were, however, immediately pushed aside in the case of emergencies or disasters, when any and all aircraft available were needed for rapid transportation of relief goods to stricken victims. In general, humanitarian operations welcomed any aircraft they could lay their hands

on. With the increasing speed and visibility of the news, dramatic events unfolding anywhere in the world brought on more and quicker responses than ever before. Aircraft were crucial in this respect, whether it was to take food to famine victims in Ethiopia in 1984 or to Darfur, southern Sudan, in 2007.

After prolonged droughts, coinciding with bad agricultural policies that resulted in failed harvests in Ethiopia, the International Red Cross began relief flights on October 24, 1984. As the final link of what amounted to a major international air bridge, Western Hercules C-130 transports, aided by Russian cargo aircraft, carried over 1 million tons of food and medical supplies to the stricken areas where as many as 9 million people were threatened by starvation. Fearing that the drought might last several years, the Ethiopian government announced a policy of forced migration to move as many as 1½ million people out of the most affected areas and resettle them in more fertile parts of the country. On the return legs of their relief flights, aircraft carried many thousands of hunger-stricken people, delivering them bereft of their possessions on the tarmac at the airport of the capital Addis Ababa.[93] It was but a sad precursor of a number of such aerial relief operations that were to follow in the decades ahead. Time and again catastrophe, whether caused by natural causes, or by human action, had to be met by aerial relief operations, either under the flag of the International Red Cross or the United Nations. In cataclysms air transport was recognized as vital. The phenomenon was not limited to Third World countries and came to include operations in Europe as well. In July 1992 a French Hercules made the first flight in what would grow into the longest airlift in history. A United Nations' air bridge kept Sarajevo, the besieged capital of the Republic of Bosnia-Herzegovina in the war in former Yugoslavia, alive for 3½ years. The operations only ended with the return of peace in January 1996, after 12,895 sorties had been flown. Deliveries totaled more than 160,000 metric tons of food, medicine, and general relief supplies. During some months, 85 percent of the aid that reached the city came via the airlift operation.[94]

But if air transport was crucial to raise people's chances of survival after calamities, aviation also came to play a role in spreading catastrophe as such, particularly with respect to the spread of diseases. Like it was influenced by sea transport in the centuries before flight, world health was also influenced by air transport. If aircraft were used to spray insecticides in the first decade after the Second World War, their role changed since. Because of the constant, rapid movement of large numbers of people across the globe, microorganisms were carried and spread across the continents at an unprecedented rate. Defenses, such as the Australian practice of spraying aircraft cabins with disinfectants before landing, were shown to be only partially effective. In late November 2002 to June 2003, the outbreak in

Asia of the virus that caused the potentially deadly Severe Acute Respiratory Syndrome (SARS) sickened more than 8,000 people and killed nearly 800 as it spread rapidly from China to at least twenty other countries. This was modern air transport at its most dangerous and led to worldwide concern about the risks of air travel. Air traffic to and in the region was cut dramatically. At the height of the crisis major carriers grounded up to 40 percent of their flights. Leading hotels operated at but a fraction of their capacity. Because of the reduction of air services trade and manufacturing in the region were also severely implicated. Within 3 weeks after the recognition of the first official victim, the economies of China, Taiwan, and Singapore were suffering the consequences. It was found that SARS could spread rapidly on a global scale through international travel if quarantine control measures were not implemented immediately.[95] But while professionals at the World Health Organization put in overtime to develop a defense against the virus that caused SARS, airline embarkations on flights to China and other Asian countries showed a dramatic decline, although traffic soon picked up in the second half of 2003, when the crisis was declared over. While SARS was by no means the first disease to spread in this fashion—as the earlier spread of AIDS was suspected to have evolved along similar patterns—it provided evidence of how vulnerable the world had become to the unseen effects of the rapid movement of great numbers of people across the planet.[96] SARS heightened awareness of the dangers of mass air travel. In May 2005 all 250 passengers of a KLM flight from New Delhi to Amsterdam received a letter in the mail some days after their arrival, informing them that one of the passengers on the flight, a young boy, had been suffering from cholera. All were urgently advised to see their local physician for a checkup, just to be on the safe side.[97] Two years later, American health officials placed a man into quarantine suspected of infecting other passengers with a dangerous form of tuberculosis on transatlantic flights.[98]

But perhaps the most far-reaching effect in the long term of the spread and the growing use of air transport was the way in which it had come to influence global migration patterns around the turn of the millennium. The widening gap between rich and poor countries brought on a growing stream of migrants from the Third World towards the rich industrialized nations. Air travel played a substantial role in this movement. In the past distance and isolation, and the cost of transportation, had pushed migrants towards integration into the dominant residential culture. Now the need to integrate was reduced because of modern communications and rapid air travel. Such possibilities worked as forces against integration of migrants in their new society of residence. Culture and family took on a new, global dimension. At the same time it became increasingly difficult for migrants to enter countries in the rich northern half of the world, as regulations were sharpened and immigration procedures became more complicated.

It was peculiar that while the jumbo jet made the movement of people across the globe easier than ever before, borders became more difficult to cross, instead of less. Within the time frame of a decade or so air transport became the vehicle of a phenomenon that caused considerable anxiety: for the persecuted, the victims of war and violence, and for economic refugees from the Third World the airline became the ultimate lifeline to escape to the safety and riches of the Western nations. While political refugees were generally allowed to stay, economic refugees were forced to return. Under the UN Comprehensive Plan of Action for Vietnamese boat refugees, nearly half a million people from former South Vietnam were flown from camps in southeast Asia to be resettled in the United States, western Europe, and in Australia between 1978 and 1996.[99] Not all refugees ended up in Western countries. On April 5, 1980, some 10,000 Cubans stormed the Peruvian embassy in Havana, hoping they would somehow get a permit to leave the country. It was June before the last of them were granted leave to be flown out, many of them to Latin American destinations.[100] In August 1982 over 4,000 refugees from the war that followed the Soviet invasion of Afghanistan in 1979 were flown to resettle in Turkey.[101] And on January 17, 1983, Nigeria suddenly decided to expel some 2 million illegal foreign migrants from neighboring African countries before the month was out. Some 10,000 of them decided not to risk the hazards of the long overland journey to the border, and managed to find a seat on board of a series of chartered aircraft that flew people out.[102] Three years later, another such exodus started in Senegal, as hundreds of thousands small vendors and craftsmen from Mauritania were expelled after conflicts over arable land between different ethnic groups. Senegal retorted with a similar measure. In May 1989 an international air bridge had to be set up in haste to carry the 50,000 or so people who found themselves suddenly forced to leave their belongings behind and flee from escalating violence.[103] But crisis-related or not, migration took on hitherto unknown proportions, speeded up by air transport. By the mid-1990s some 40 to 50 million people were living outside their native country.[104]

In the early years of the 21st century, record numbers of people were on the move to find jobs or join their families, despite a temporary economic downturn. In some European countries immigration was up by as much as 15 percent, while Canada and New Zealand also saw sharp increases in their immigration flows. Only Japan, Korea, and northern Europe witnessed declining migration.[105] A substantial part of this traffic came by air. Go-betweens, whether bona fide or not, amassed fortunes "arranging" air tickets and passports for growing numbers of desperate people looking for asylum and a better existence. In Holland alone, several thousand people were smuggled into the country by airport workers earning "a bit on the side" between 2000 and 2005.[106]

In a way, air transport had come full circle. If conceived in its early days as a means to shorten journey time, thus tightening the bond between Europe and its dependent territories for the happy few who could afford to travel, air transport now drew the old European mother countries closer to the problems that a retreating colonialism had left behind in Asia and Africa, just as the United States did in Latin America. In several countries the "refugee problem" led to extended, wide-ranging debates in politics and in the media, which, if anything, showed that it was very difficult indeed to influence such patterns. Border restrictions in the rich industrialized nations were upgraded year after year in an effort to control immigration in an ever-shrinking world. In this new, interwoven world very different cultures were only a plane ride or even a narrow aircraft seat apart. Once outside the realm of air transportation, the mix of cultures that came into existence as a result of the proliferation of air travel provided human society with new challenges everywhere. Modern mass air transport emphasized the need to address and understand the cultures, conceptions, and beliefs outside one's own cultural field. In a world where borders were only lines on a map, the lines in the air contributed to the shaping of a new, global civilization. In more ways than one the toy of the rich had become the tool of the poor.

Nonetheless, aviation was not only a tool of an emerging new world order. It also continued to be the symbol of Western dominance that it had been from its early beginnings. It was against this background that the terrorist group of al-Qaeda decided to hijack airliners for their attack against what they saw as the material expressions of American imperialism on September 11, 2001.

It was inevitable that the dramatic events of that day would find their way into cinematographic representation, especially as they involved air transport—always at the high-water mark of media attention. In 2006 this resulted in the movie *United 93*, focusing on the fourth hijacked plane, in which passengers fought back against their captors. Directed by Paul Greengrass and filmed in real time—106 minutes, the actual duration of the fateful flight—and semidocumentary in style, *United 93* depicted the dramatic events of that morning.[107] In doing so the movie drama stayed away from what was crucial to understanding the 9-11 plot. By addressing cinema audiences from one single (American) perspective, movie audiences learned little about the mutually exclusive worlds of the perpetrators and their victims—the very thing the attacks hinged on. And yet the attacks in themselves, however gruesome and unjustified, provided food for thought about the way that air transport had contributed to the shaping of a new and global community of man, intertwined by technology but nonetheless separated culturally and mentally in spite of the things that brought us so close together. In a little over 100 years, that technology had evolved much

more rapidly than people and cultures. In such a closely knit world, the personal experience and perception of other cultures was revealed to hold just as many risks of rejection than of acceptance of different beliefs and ways of life. Aviation opened *and* closed the door on the emergence of a true global society—the very thing that visionaries of its glorious future such as Saint-Exupéry had held so high when flight was still about uniting all peoples in a new and better society.[108]

Appendix: Air Transport Statistics

Year	Number of passengers (millions)	Cargo ton/km transported (millions)	Airmail ton/km transported (millions)	Average number of passengers on board
1929	0.639			2
1930	0.290			2.4
1931	0.331			2.4
1932	0.404			2.9
1933	0.543			3.5
1934	0.652			4.0
1935	0.976			4.9
1936	1.3			5.5
1937	1.4			5.3
1938	1.7			5.6
1939	2			6.8
1940	2.5			8.5
1941	3.3			9.6
1942	3.5			11.1
1943	4.2			13.1
1944	5.5			13.3
1945	8.2	113	132	13.7
1946	15.5	120	98	16.5
1947	18.9	273	128	16.6
1948	20.9	417	166	16.5
1949	23.3	569	187	17.3

Year	Number of passengers (millions)	Cargo ton/km transported (millions)	Airmail ton/km transported (millions)	Average number of passengers on board
1950	27.3	757	209	19.1
1951	34.4	905	234	21.9
1952	39.5	975	256	23.2
1953	46	1026	274	24.7
1954	52.5	1118	323	26.1
1955	68	1317	371	27
1956	77	1497	402	28
1957	85	1643	432	29
1958	87	1681	469	56.2
1959	97	1939	524	59.0
1960	106	2040	610	59.2
1961	111	2360	720	55.2
1962	121	2770	810	53.4
1963	135	3110	860	53.8
1964	155	3770	910	55.9
1965	177	4800	1100	56.1
1966	200	5700	1530	57.6
1967	233	6530	1890	57
1968	262	7920	2350	53.4
1969	293	9770	2520	51.8
1970	311	10460	2750	52.2
1971	333	13230	2900	54
1972	368	15020	2780	57
1973	404	17530	2880	58
1974	424	19020	2880	59
1975	436	19370	2900	59
1976	475	21540	3030	60
1977	517	23630	3180	61
1978	581	25940	3270	65
1979	652	28010	3420	66
1980	645	29380	3680	63
1981	752	30880	3790	64
1982	766	31540	3870	64
1983	798	35110	4000	64
1984	848	39670	4310	65
1985	899	39840	4400	66
1986	960	43190	4550	65
1987	1027	48370	4680	67
1988	1082	53360	4830	67
1989	1119	57260	5050	68
1990	1165	58820	5330	68
1991	1134	58620	5100	66

Year	Number of passengers (millions)	Cargo ton/km transported (millions)	Airmail ton/km transported (millions)	Average number of passengers on board
1992	1161	62810	5120	66
1993	1171	67650	5260	66
1994	1233	77220	5410	66
1995	1304	83130	5630	67
1996	1391	89200	5800	68
1997	1457	102880	5990	69
1998	1471	101820	5760	68
1999	1562	108660	5720	69
2000	1672	118080	6050	71
2001	1640	110800	5310	69
2002	1639	119840	4570	71
2003	1657	125240	4620	71
2004	1888	139040	4580	71
2005	2022	142580	4660	72

Sources: ICAO figures.

Notes

Introduction

1. Opening adapted from South African director Jamie Uys' film *The Gods Must Be Crazy* (CAT Films, 1980). In a humorous way, the film mocks the contrast between a tribal community in the Kalahari Desert and modern, "civilized" society. After a coke bottle appears out of the sky, the traditional society of the Bushmen, who do not know the concept of personal possessions, comes under stress as all tribe members develop uses for this single *thing* they cannot share. The bottle becomes an *evil thing*, and a decision is taken to throw it off the end of the Earth, a task that brings Xi in contact with the outside world.

2. Jyrki Siukonen, *Uplifted Spirits, Earthbound Machines. Studies on Artists and the Dream of Flight, 1900–1935* (Helsinki: Suomalaisen Kirjallisuuden Seura, 2001), 13.

3. J. G. Ballard, "The Ultimate Departure Lounge," in *The Most Important New Buildings of the Twentieth Century: Airports* (London: The Photographers' Gallery, 1997), 118–121, taken from p. 120.

4. The collection presently covers four Dutch newspapers that appeared between 1910 and 1940, *Het Centrum* (1910–1930), *Nieuwe Rotterdamsche Courant* (1910–1930), *Het Vaderland* (1920–1940), and *Het Volk* (1910–1920). Available at http://kranten.kb.nl (2008).

5. For the present book the Dutch edition was used, which is available at http://www.kha.nl (2008). The American edition is also available online at http://www.keesings.com (2008).

Chapter 1: Heroics–Flying as an Icon of the Modern Age, 1919—1945

1. After Antoine de Saint-Exupéry, *Night Flight* (New York: Century, 1932), chapter XII. In 1933 the book formed the basis of a major Hollywood film production, *Night Flight*, directed by Clarence Brown and produced by David Selznick. It starred Clark Gable as Fabien (named Jules in the movie), Helen Hayes as his wife, and John Barrymore as his hard-driving boss Rivière (modeled on Aéropostale's manager Didier Daurat).

2. Antoine de Saint-Exupéry, *Terre des Hommes* (Paris: Gallimard, 1938), 40–41, 63–68. The book was translated into English and appeared in America under the strangely elusive titile of *Wind, Sand and Stars* (New York: Reynal & Hitchcock, 1939).

3. H. Zeise, *Die Aeronautik früher und jetzt, nebst theoretischen und practischen Vorschlägen zu einer vervollkommneteren Luftschifffahrtskunst und Benutzung des Luftballs für technische und industrielle Zwecke: Vorträge, gehalten im Altonaer Bürgerverein im Winter 1849/50* (Altona: Schlüter, 1850).

4. A. M. Lester, "The Sources and Nature of Statistical Information in Special Fields of Statistics: International Air Transport Statistics," *Journal of the Royal Statistical Society*, Series A (General), 116(4) (1953): 409–423, reference taken from p. 409.

5. Jules Verne, *Robur le Conquérant* (Paris: Bibliothèque d'Éducation et de Récréation Hetzel, 1886).

6. Robert Wohl, *A Passion for Wings. Aviation and the Western Imagination* (New Haven, CT: Yale University Press, 1994), 42.

7. Emmanuel Chadeau, *Le rêve et la Puissance. L'Avion et son Siècle* (Paris: Fayard, 1996), 19–44; A. Bowdoin Van Riper, *Imagining Flight: Aviation and Popular Culture* (College Station: Texas A&M University Press, 2004), 11–31.

8. Paul Hoffman, *Wings of Madness: Alberto Santos-Dumont and the Invention of Flight* (London: Fourth Estate, 2003), 2.

9. H. G. Wells, *The War in the Air* (Harmondsworth: Penguin Books, 1976), 15.

10. A. A. W. Hubrecht, "Een vluchtig bezoek aan de vliegvlakte te Reims," *De Gids* 27 (1909): 101–116.

11. Felix Ingold, *Literatur und Aviatik. Europäische Flugdichtung, 1909–1927* (Basel: Birkhäuser Verlag, 1978), 21.

12. David T. Courtwright, *Sky as Frontier. Adventure, Aviation, and Empire* (College Station: Texas A&M University Press, 2005), 30.

13. Scott W. Palmer, *Dictatorship of the Air. Aviation Culture and the Fate of Modern Russia* (New York: Cambridge University Press, 2006), 40.

14. Robert Wohl, *A Passion for Wings*, 56–65.

15. John H. Morrow Jr., *The Great War in the Air. Military Aviation from 1909 to 1921* (Washington, DC: Smithsonian Institution Press, 1993), 59–87.

16. John H. Morrow, *The Great War in the Air*, 25: Sven Lindqvist, *A History of Bombing* (New York: The New Press, 2001), 1–2.

17. Bowdoin Van Riper, *Imagining Flight*, 64–65.

18. Vera Brittain, *War Diary 1913–1917: Chronicle of Youth* (London: Victor Gollancz, 1981), 247, quoted in Ariela Freedman, "Zeppelin Fictions and the British Home Front," *Journal of Modern Literature*, 27(3) (Winter 2004), 47–62.

19. Hans van Lith, *Plotseling een vreselijke knal. Bommen en mijnen treffen neutraal Nederland, 1914–1918* (Zaltbommel: Europese Bibliotheek, 2001), 90–95.

20. Hans van Lith, *Plotseling een vreselijke knal*, 252–253.

21. David E. Omissi, *Air Power and Colonial Control. The Royal Air Force, 1919–1939* (Manchester: MUP, 1990), 52–59.

22. T. E. Lawrence, *The Mint. A Day-Book of the RAF Depot between August and December 1922, with Later Notes by 352087 A/c Ross* (London: Jonathan Cape, 1955), 78.

23. Antoine de Saint-Exupéry, *Vol de Nuit* (Paris: Gallimard, 1931).

24. See http://www.century-of-flight.freeola.com/Aviation%20history/daredevils/Atlantic%202.htm (2006).

25. Antoine de Saint-Exupéry, *Terre des Hommes*, 43–56; Emmanuel Chadeau, *Le Rêve et la Puissance*, 134.

26. Marc Dierikx, *Fokker. A Transatlantic Biography* (Washington, DC: Smithsonian Institution Press, 1997), 106.

27. Memorandum of conversation between KLM's director Albert Plesman and senior civil servants of the Dutch Aeronautics Branch, Jan. 27, 1921, at Netherlands National Archive, The Hague, 2.16.19.39, inv. nr. 14.

28. Official report by Iwan Smirnoff of the accident with the aircraft H-NAHB on the Goodwin Sands, October 19, 1923, at Archive of the Netherlands Ministry of Foreign Affairs, The Hague, DEZ 151 *Luchtvaart, bepalingen enz.* Smirnoff's more personalized account later appeared in his autobiographical *Smirnoff Vertelt* (Amsterdam: Andries Blitz, 1938), 187–193, and was recounted for an international audience in Anne Coupar, *The Smirnoff Story* (London: Jarrolds Publishers, 1960), 69–74.

29. Film images by Haghe Film of the celebrations of April 25, 1925, in possession of the author. *Programma Nationale Sport-Betooging 25 April 1925 op het Terrein Houtrust te 's-Gravenhage* (Leiden: Eduard IJdo, 1925).

30. Judy Lomax, *Women of the Air* (London: John Murray, 1986); Valerie Moolman, *Women Aloft* (New York: Time-Life books, 1981).

31. M. L. J. Dierikx, *Begrensde Horizonten. De internationale burgerlucht-vaartpolitiek van Nederland in het interbellum* (Zwolle: Tjeenk Willink, 1988), 44–49.

32. David Edgerton, *England and the Aeroplane. An Essay on a Militant and Technological Nation* (Basingstoke: Macmillan, 1991).

33. The Civil Aerial Transport Committee (Cd.9218, 1918) recommended government support. Churchill was Secretary of State for War and Air until 1921. Hansard, *House of Commons, Debates*, 5th Series, Vol. 126, March 11, 1920, column 1622.

34. Scott W. Palmer, *Dictatorship of the Air: Aviation Culture and the Fate of Modern Russia*, 1–8, 80–102, 283.

35. Scott W. Palmer, "Peasants into Pilots. Soviet Air-Mindedness as an Ideology of Dominance," *Technology & Culture* 41(1) (2000): 1–26.

36. Scott W. Palmer, *Dictatorship of the Air*, 158–159.

37. See http://www.marxists.org/history/ussr/government/1928/sufds/ch07.htm (2007).

38. Guy Vanthemsche, *La Sabena, 1923–2001. Des origines au crash* (Brussels: De Boeck, 2002), 23–25. An English "summary" of the early history of Belgian civil air transport appeared as "The Birth of Commercial Air Transport in Belgium, 1919–1923," in *Revue Belge de Philologie et d'Histoire* 78 (2000): 913–944.

39. Guy Vanthemsche, *La Sabena*, 70–79; Henri Mézière, Jean-Marie Sauvage, *Les Ailes françaises. L'Aviation marchande de 1919 à nos jours* (Paris: Éditions Rive Droite, 1999), 10–17.

40. Report of the Imperial Air Communications Special Sub-Committee, 17 November 1926, British National Archives, London, Air Ministry, AIR 5, nr. 907.

41. M. L. J. Dierikx, *Begrensde horizonten*, 54–63.

42. M. L. J. Dierikx, *Begrensde horizonten*, 85–99; Marc Dierikx, "Struggle for Prominence: Clashing Dutch and British Interests on the Colonial Air Routes, 1918–1942," *Journal of Contemporary History* 26 (1991): 333–351.

43. Confidential Foreign Office note by Alexander Leeper on the question of KLM services accross India (Leeper's underscore), 14 December 1929, British National Archives, London, ForeIgn Office Files, FO 371, nr. 14095.

44. De Marees van Swinderen to the Netherlands' minister for Foreign Affairs, 7 December 1928, Archive Netherlands Ministry of Foreign Affairs, The Hague, DEZ 151 Ned.Indië.

45. Plesman to the minister of Waterworks, H. van de Vegte, 21 September 1928, Archive Netherlands Ministry of Foreign Affairs, The Hague, DEZ 151, Ned.Indië.

46. Lyons to Dominions Office, 8 June 1932, British National Archives, London, Foregn Office Files, FO 371, 16413.

47. Peter Ewer, "A Gentlemen's Club in the Clouds. Reassessing the Empire Air Mail Scheme, 1933–1939," *Journal of Transport History* 28(1) (2007): 75–92; Peter Ewer, "Servants of the National Interest? Conservatives and Aviation Policy-Making in the 1930s," *Australian Historical Studies* 38(1) (April 2007): 52–70; Peter Lyth, "Failed Notions in Air Transport, 1920–1950. An Historical Model," in Hans-Liudger Dienel and Helmuth Trischler (eds.), *Geschichte der Zukunft des Verkehrs. Verkehskonzepte von der Frühen Neuzeit bis zum 21. Jahrhundert* (Frankfurt/Main: Campus, 1997), 177–180.

48. Gordon Pirie, "Passenger Traffic in the 1930s on British Imperial Air Routes: Refinement and Revision," *Journal of Transport History* 25(1) (2004): 63–83, taken from p. 69; Statistics for KLM from KLM annual reports, 1919–1940 (in possession of the author).

49. Eiichiro Sekigawa, "Japan's Commercial Air Transportation and Military Missions in World War II," in William F. Trimble (ed.), *From Airship to Airbus. The History of Civiland Commercial Aviation: Pioneers and Operations*, Vol. 2

(Washington, DC: Smithsonian Institution Press, 1995), 168–183; R.E.G. Davies, *Airlines of Asia since 1920* (McLean, VA: Paladwr Press, 1997), 426–445.

50. Chandra D. Bhimull, "Major Mayo Goes to the West Indies: Anglo-American Aviation and the Empire Question in the Early Twentieth Century," paper presented at the conference of the Society for the History of Technology, Amsterdam, October 2004.

51. R. E. G. Davies, *Airlines of Latin America since 1919* (London: Putnam, 1984), 216–220.

52. Peter Fritzsche, *A Nation of Fliers. German Aviation and the Polular Imagination* (Cambridge, MA: Harvard University Press, 1992), 173–184.

53. Wolfgang Wagner, *Hugo Junkers, Pionier der Luftfahrt—seine Flugzeuge* (Bonn: Bernard & Graefe Verlag, 1996), 186–207; Marc Dierikx, *Fokker. A Transatlantic Biography*, 75–77; Scott W. Palmer, *Dictatorship of the Air*, 92–93.

54. Hans-Liudger Dienel and Martin Schiefelbusch, "German Commercial Air Transport until 1945," *Revue Belge de Philologie et d'Histoire* 78 (2000): 945–967, taken from p. 956.

55. Klaus J. Bade, *Auswanderer—Wanderarbeiter—Gastarbeiter. Bevölkerung, Arbeitsmarkt und Wanderung in Deutschland seit der Mitte des 19. Jahrhunderts* (Ostfildern: Scripta Mercaturae Verlag, 1984), 270–271; Hermann Kellenbenz and Jürgen Schneider, "La emigracion Alemane para America Latine (1818–1929/31)," *La emigración europea a la América Latina: Fuentes y estado de investigación. Informes presentado a la IV. Reunión de Historiadores Latinoamericanistas Europeos* (Berlin: Colloquium Verlag, 1979), 179–193; Anne Saint Sauveur-Henn, *Un siècle d'emigration allemande vers l'Argentine, 1953–1945* (Köln: Böhlau Verlag, 1995), 783–785.

56. *10 Jahre Deutsche Lufthansa, 6. Januar 1926–6. Januar 1936* (Halle: War-necke, 1936), 23; R.E.G. Davies, *Airlines of Latin America since 1919*, 338–344, 347–350; Paper on the history of Iberia by Javier Vidal Olivares at the T2M Conference, Eindhoven, 2004.

57. *Erfolgsperspectieven in Fernost. 80 Jahre Lufthansa in China*, digital Lufthansa booklet, available at http://konzern.lufthansa.com/de/downloads/presse/downloads/publikationen/lh_china.pdf (2006); R.E.G. Davies, *Airlines of Asia*, 335–337.

58. Ulrich Albrecht, "Military Technology and National Socialist Ideology," in Monika Renneberg and Mark Walker (eds.), *Science, Technology, and National Socialism* (Cambridge, UK: Cambridge University Press, 1994), 88–126, taken from pp. 94–95.

59. Guillaume de Syon, *The Socio-Politics of Technology: The Zeppelin in Official and Popular Culture, 1900–1939*, dissertation (Boston: Boston University, 1994), 243–247.

60. Martin Staniland, *Government Birds. Air Transport and the State in Western Europe* (Lanham: Rowman & Littlefield, 2003), 22; Albert Fischer, *Luftverkehr*

zwischen Markt und Macht (1919–1937). *Lufthansa, Verkehrsflug und der Kampf ums Monopol* (Wiesbaden: Franz Steiner Verlag, 2003), 15–19.

61. Marc Dierikx, *Bevlogen Jaren*. *Nederlandse Burgerluchtvaart tussen de Wereldoorlogen* (Houten: Unieboek, 1986), 157–158; Albert Fischer, *Luftverkehr zwischen Markt und Macht*, 317.

62. Robert Wohl, *The Spectacle of Flight*. *Aviation and the Western Imagination, 1920–1950* (New Haven: Yale University Press, 2005), 49–106.

63. For the transcript of the screenplay and some viewing samples, see http://www.geocities.com/emruf4/triumph.html (2006).

64. Text of the speech at http://www.britannia.com/history/docs/peacetime.html (2006).

65. Donald C. Watt, *How War Came*. *The Immediate Origins of the Second World War*, 1938–1939 (London: Mandarin, 1989), 447–448.

66. Marc Dierikx, *Blauw in de Lucht*. *Koninklijke Luchtvaart Maatschappij 1919–1999* (Den Haag: Sdu, 1999), 87–88.

67. Air Ministry, *Resumé of commercial aviation* (London: HMSO, April 1938); Albert Fischer, *Luftverkehr zwischen Markt und Macht*, 258–260, 324–328.

68. Société des Nations, *Études sur la Situation Economique, Administrative en Juridique de la Navigation Aérienne Internationale* (Genève: Société des Nations, 1930), 59.

69. ICAO Circulars *The Economic Situation of Air Transport*. *Review and Outlook* (Montreal: ICAO—various years).

70. François Pernot, "Le role des aviateurs militaires français dans le défrichement des lignes aériennes dans les années vingt et le début des années trante," in *Actes du Colloque International 'l' Avioation Civile et Commerciale des Années 1920 à Nos Jours* (Paris: Service Historique de l'Armée de l'Air, 1994), 47–51.

71. Laurent Bonnaud, "Brésil, l'autre rive (1925–1935)," in *Actes du Colloque International 'l' Avioation Civile et Commerciale des Années 1920 à Nos Jours*, 73–110; R.E.G. Davies, *Rebels and Reformers of the Airways* (Shrewsbury, MA: Airlife, 1987), 283–298.

72. Antoine de Saint-Exupéry, *Vol de Nuit* (Paris: Gallimard, 1931), chapter IV.

73. Antoine de Saint-Exupéry, *Courier Sud* (Paris: Gallimard, 1930); *Vol de Nuit*; *Terre des Hommes*.

74. Alexandre Herlea, "The First Transcontinental Airline: Franco-Roumaine, 1920–1925," in William F. Trimble (ed.), *From Airships to Airbus. The History of Civil and Commercial Aviation, Pioneers and Operations*, Vol. 2 (Washington, DC: Smithsonian Institution Press, 1995), 53–64, taken from p. 57.

75. Alan Cobham, *Twenty Thousand Miles in a Flying Boat. My Flight Round Africa* (London: George Harrap & Co., 1930).

76. R. E. G. Davies, *A History of the World's Airlines* (London: Oxford University Press, 1964), 180–182; Peter Lyth, "The Empire's Airway: British Civil Aviation from 1919 to 1939," *Revue Belge de Philologie et d'Histoire* 78 (2000): 865–887.

77. Figures on the basis of traffic comparisons between Imperial Airways, KLM, and Air Orient on the colonial services to Asia.

78. Beryl Markham, *West with the Night* (Boston: Houghton Mifflin, 1942), 197.

79. Figures kindly provided by Professor Gordon Pirie, University of Western Cape, South Africa.

80. Gordon Pirie, "Passenger Traffic in the 1930s on British Imperial Air Routes: Refinement and Revision," *Journal of Transport History* 25(1) (2004): 63–83, taken from p. 75.

81. Martin Staniland, *Government Birds*, 15.

82. Marc Dierikx, *Blauw in de Lucht*, 30–31.

83. Povl Westphall, *Københavns Lufthavn, 1925–1975* (København: Københavns Lufthavnsvæsen, 1975), 14.

84. KLM report on Copenhagen aerodrome facilities, undated (1920), taken from Archive Amsterdam Airport Schiphol (unnumbered).

85. Letecké Zprávy Ministersva Verejných Prací, Rocník VII-1938, taken from Archive Amsterdam Airport Schiphol (unnumbered).

86. *Aéroport Le Bourget*, Brochure (Paris: Direction de l'Aéronautique du Ministère de l'Air, 1937). Translation by the author.

87. Helmut Conin, *Gelandet in Berlin. Zur Geschichte der Berliner Flughäfen* (Berlin: Berliner Flughafengesellschaft, 1974), 181–205; Hans-Joachim Braun, "The Airport as a Symbol: Air Transport and Politics at Berlin-Tempelhof, 1923–1948," in William M. Leary (ed.), *From Airship to Airbus: The History of Civil and Commercial Aviation. Infrastructure and Environment*, Vol. I (Washington, DC: Smithsonian Institution Press, 1995), 45–54.

88. Société des Nations, *Études sur la Situation Economique, Administrative en Juridique de la Navigation Aérienne Internationale*, 9. Exchange rate conversion based on Lawrence H. Officer, "Exchange Rate between the United States Dollar and Forty Other Countries, 1913–1999," Economic History Services, EH.Net, 2002, available at http://eh.net/hmit/exchangerates (2006).

89. Société des Nations, *Études sur la Situation Economique, Administrative en Juridique de la Navigation Aérienne Internationale*, 77–78.

90. Société des Nations, *Études sur la Situation Economique, Administrative en Juridique de la Navigation Aérienne Internationale*, 59.

91. "Statistic of Daily Money Wage Rates of Building Craftsmen and Labourers in Southern England," available at http://privatewww.essex.ac.uk/~alan/family/N-Money.html#1914 (2007).

92. Gordon Pirie, "Passenger Traffic in the 1930s on British imperial Air Routes."

93. The diary was published on the Internet in 2005, and it is available at http://home.wanadoo.nl/hardemanstamboom/vliegr.htm. It is physically kept at the amateur film museum in Utrecht, Holland (http://www.smalfilmmuseum.nl). Hardeman was an avid amateur filmmaker. The film of his journey can be seen online at http://www.vpro.nl/MediaController?media=23321011 (2006).

94. E. Rusman, *Wings across Continents. The KLM Amsterdam-Batavia Line* (Amsterdam: Andries Blitz, 1935).

95. Carl Pirath, *Konjunktur und Luftverkehr* (Berlin: Verkehrswissenschaftliche Lehrmittelgesellschaft, 1935), 42; Oliver J. Lissitzyn, *International Air Transport and National Policy* (New York: Council on Foreign Relations, 1942), 46. Figures corroborate with data provided to the author by Professor Gordon Pirie, University of Western Cape, South Africa.

96. Annual Reports KNILM, 1928–1941 (in possession of the author).

97. Marc Dierikx, *Blauw in de Lucht*, 73–78.

Chapter 2: Technology—Air Transport around the World, 1945–1961

1. After: Nevil Shute, *No Highway* (London: William Heinemann, 1948), end of chapter IV. In 1951 the book was made into the motion picture, *No Highway in the Sky*, by director Henry Koster, starring James Stewart as Theodore Honey and Marlène Dietrich as actress Monica Teasdale, the only person on board to believe Honey. The book was loosely based on the development of the eight-engine Bristol Brabazon, for which extensive fatigue stress tests on the tail configuration of the aircraft were undertaken at the Royal Aircraft Establishment at Farnborough. The Brabazon never made it into airline service.

2. *Report of the Public Inquiry into the Causes and Circumstances of the Accident Which Occurred on the 10th January, 1954, to the Comet Aircraft G-ALYP*, Appendix VI, Para. 4, February 1, 1955, available at http://aviation-safety.net/database/record.php?id=19540110-1&lang=en (2007).

3. Ad Vlot, *Glare. History of the Development of a New Aircraft Material* (Dordrecht/London/Boston: Kluwer Academic Publishers, 2001), 7–9.

4. Keesings Historical Archive (KHA), ICAO: vliegen over twintig jaar (July 9, 1956).

5. Uri Bialer, *The Shadow of the Bomber. The Fear of Air Attack and British Politics, 1932–1939* (London: Royal Historical Society, 1980).

6. For accounts from various angles on the Allied air offensive, see Denis Richards, *RAF Bomber Command in the Second World War. The Hardest Victory* (London: Penguin Books, 1994); Sven Lindqvist, *A History of Bombing* (New York: The New Press, 2001); Jörg Friedrich, *Der Brand. Deutschland im Bombenkrieg, 1940–1945* (München: Propyläen Verlag, 2002); Stephan Burgdorff and Christian Habbe (eds.), *Als Feuer vom Himmel viel. Der Bombenkrieg in Deutschland* (Darmstadt: Wissenschaftliche Buchgesellschaft, 2003); A.C. Grayling, *Among the Dead Cities: The History and Moral Legacy of the WWII Bombing of Civilians in Germany and Japan* (New York: Walker & Company, 2006).

7. KHA (World Air Fleet 1949), ICAO figures.

8. Jeffrey A. Engel, "The Surly Bonds: American Cold War Constraints on British Aviation," *Enterprise & Society* 6(1) (March 2005): 1–45, taken from p. 10.

9. ICAO figures.

10. United Nations Conference on Trade and Development (UNCTAD), Final Act, clause 17 (Geneva: 1964).

11. *The Economic Situation of Air Transport. Review and Outlook*, ICAO Circulars (various years).

12. Roger E. Bilstein, *The American Aerospace Industry. From Workshop to Golbal Enterprise* (New York: Twayne Publishers, 1996), 80–87.

13. Jeffrey A. Engel, "The Surly Bonds," 8–18; See also Virginia Dawson, "The American Turbojet Industry and British Competition. The Mediating Role of Government Research," in William M. Leary (ed.), *From Airship to Airbus. The History of Civil an Commercial Aviation, Infrastructure and Environment*, Vol. 1 (Washington DC: Smithsonian Institution Press, 1995), 127–150.

14. Jeffrey A. Engel, "The Surly Bonds," 26–30; For a more extensive coverage, see Jeffrey A. Engel, *Cold War at 30,000 feet. The Anglo-American Fight for Aviation Supremacy* (Cambridge, MA: Harvard University Press, 2007), 53–158.

15. See http://www.ksamc.com/eng/history/index.php?page=1946–1995.htm (2007).

16. State Department Dispatch on Anglo-American Aviation Differences, July 9, 1957: U.S. National Archives and Records Administration (NA), Washington, DC, State Department Decimal Files, Record Group 59, 611.4194/7-957.

17. See http://web.worldbank.org/wbsite/external/extaboutus/extarchives (2005).

18. Marc Dierikx, "Shaping World Aviation: Anglo-American Civil Aviation Relations, 1944–1946," *Journal of Air Law and Commerce* 57(4) (1992): 795–840; N.M. Matte, *Treatise on Air-Aeronautical law* (Toronto: Carswell, 1981), 125–130.

19. Alan P. Dobson, *Peaceful Air Warfare. The United States, Britain and the Politics of International Aviation* (Oxford: Oxford University Press, 1991), 188–191.

20. Dierikx, "Shaping world aviation," 803–808.

21. N. M. Matte, "Text of the Chicago Convention, Annexes and Agreements," in *Treatise on Air-Aeronautical Law*, 605–632, for interpretation and explanation, see 140–157.

22. Dierikx, "Shaping world aviation," 830–840; Alan P. Dobson, *Peaceful Air Warfare*, 173–210.

23. See H.A. Wassenbergh, *Post-War International Civil Aviation Policy and the Law of the Air* (The Hague: Martinus Nijhoff, 1962).

24. David T. Courtwright, *Sky as Frontier. Adventure, Aviation, and Empire* (College Station: Texas A&M University Press, 2005), 200.

25. Christopher Endy, *Cold War Holidays. American Tourism in France* (Chapel Hill: University of North Carolina Press, 2004), 40.

26. Ann Tusa and John Tusa, *The Berlin Airlift* (New York: Atheneum, 1988).

27. See http://aviation-safety.net/database (2007).

28. "Question of the Safety of Commercial Aircraft flying in the Vicinity of, or Inadvertently Crossing, International Frontiers," Resolution 927 (X) of United

Nations General Assembly, 554th Plenary Meeting, December 14, 1955. Available at http://www.un.org/documents/ga/res/10/ares10.htm (2007).

29. "Some Considerations Involved in U.S. Aviation Policy toward the Soviet Union and Its Satellites," Memorandum, May 28, 1948; U.S. National Archives, Record Group 59, State Department, Policy Planning Staff, Subject File Aviation, Box 7.

30. Stefan Albrecht, "Internationale Luftverkehrspolitik in der Zeit des Kalten Krieges von 1944–1965: das Beispiel Tschechoslowakei," in *Jahrbuch für Wirtschaftsgeschichte, 2007/1, Verkehrsgeschichte auf neuen Wegen* (Berlin: Akademie Verlag, 2007), 93–109, taken from pp. 100–101.

31. KHA, Protest Czecho-Slovakia at ICAO (January 20, 1956).

32. Joanna Filipczyk, "LOT: Connecting East and West in Poland," in Hans-Liudger Dienel and Peter Lyth (eds.), *Flying the Flag. European Commercial Air Transport since 1945* (London: Macmillan, 1998), 195–222.

33. KHA, Soviet News (1948).

34. Christian Henrich-Franke, "From a Supranational Air Authority to the Founding of the European Civil Aviation Conference (ECAC)," Paper before the TIE Conference, Eindhoven, The Netherlands, April 2006, 3.

35. Henrich-Franke, "From a Supranational Air Authority to the founding of the European Civil Aviation Conference," 5–11.

36. Air Research Bureau, *Report on Coordination of Intra-European Air Transport* (Brussels: ARB, 1953).

37. M. Zylicz, *International Air Transport Law* (Dordrecht: Martinus Nijhoff, 1992), 120.

38. Kenneth Hudson and Julian Pettifer, *Diamonds in the Sky. A Social History of Air Travel* (London: Bodley Head/BBC, 1979), 129.

39. Christopher Endy, *Cold War Holidays*, 40–41.

40. Duncan Cumming, "Aviation in Africa," in *African Affairs. Journal of the Royal African Society* 61(242) (1962): 29–39, taken from pp. 34–35.

41. See R. E. G. Davies, *Airlines of Latin America since 1919* (London: Putnam, 1984).

42. Kenneth Hudson and Julian Pettifer, *A Social History of Air Travel*, 171.

43. Ministry of Civil Aviation Memorandum on Civil Aviation Development in Europe as Related to Britain, June 25, 1945, British National Archives, Ministry of Civil Aviation, BT217, inv. nr. 126.

44. Peter Lyth, "Chosen Instruments: The Evolution of British Airways," in Hans-Liudger Dienel and Peter Lyth (eds.), *Flying the Flag. European Commercial Air Transport since 1945* (London: Macmillan, 1997), 51–52; Martin Staniland, *Government Birds. Air Transport and the State in Western Europe* (Lanham: Rowman & Littlefield, 2003), 74–75.

45. Nicolas Neiertz, "Air France: An Elephant in an Evening Suit?," in Hans-Liudger Dienel and Peter Lyth (eds.), *Flying the Flag*, 19.

46. Martin Staniland, *Government Birds*, 72–73; Nicolas Neiertz, "Air France," 19.

47. Marc Dierikx and Peter Lyth, "The Development of the European Scheduled Air Transport Network, 1920–1970: An Explanatory Model," in *Proceedings 11th World Economic History Congress, Milan 1994*, Vol. B8 (Milano: Università Bocconi, 1994), 73–91.

48. Marc Dierikx and Bram Bouwens, *Building Castles of the Air. Schiphol Amsterdam and the Development of Airport Infrastructure in Europe, 1916–1996* (The Hague: Sdu, 1997), 77–78.

49. Nederlands Instituut voor Oorlogsdocumentatie (Netherlands Institute for War Documentation) photo archive, Amsterdam, contemporary caption to photo number 11607.

50. Exchange of notes between the US and Switzerland, May 16, 1949, US National Archives, State Department Decimal Files, RG 59, 711.5427/5-1649.

51. Letter from the Swedish ambassador to the United States, Erik Boheman, to Secretary of State Dean Acheson, October 2, 1952, NA, STD, 59, 611.5894/10-252; Letter of Livie Merchant (State Dept.) to Norwegian and Swedish ambassadors, November 10, 1853, US National Archives, STD, RG59, 6115794/11-1053.

52. State Department Office memorandum, June 10, 1955, US National Archives, STD, RG59, 611.62A94/6-1055.

53. Alan Dobson, *Peaceful Air Warfare*, 226ff.

54. Letter of George Cribbett (Deputy Chairman of BOAC) to Lord Douglas (Chairman of BEA), March 26, 1957, British Airways Archive, London, BEA Board Papers, nr.114.

55. C. Douglas Dillon to U.S. Embassy in Paris, 29/5/59, U.S. National Archives, STD, RG.59, 611.5194/5-2959. The discussions were minuted by STD in a Memorandum of Conversation dd. 3/6/59: STD, 611.5194/6-359.

56. Marc Dierikx, "'Een spel zonder kaarten': KLM-landingsrechten als nationaal belang, 1945–1957," in D.A. Hellema, C. Wiebes, and B. Zeeman (eds.), *Jaarboek Buitenlandse Zaken: Derde Jaarboek voor de geschiedenis van de Nederlandse buitenlandse politiek* (Den Haag: Sdu, 1997), 11–25; Also see Marc Dierikx, *An Image of Freedom: The Netherlands and the United States, 1945 to the Present* (Den Haag: Sdu Publishers, 1997), 33–34.

57. KLM, Annual Reports, 1946, 1947, 1948, 1949, KLM Archive, Amstelveen, The Netherlands.

58. Alexander Freund, *Aufbrüche nach dem Zusammenbruch. Die deutsche Nordamerika-Auswanderung nach dem Zweiten Weltkrieg* (Göttingen: V&R Unipress, 2004), 170.

59. Javier Vidal Olivares, Paper on the History of Iberia, Eindhoven, T2M Conference, The Netherlands, 2004; Uki Goñi, *The Real Odessa. How Perón brought the Nazi War Criminals to Argentina* (London: Granta Books, 2002).

60. Louis Zweers, *De crash van de Franeker. Een Amerikaanse persreis naar Nederlands-Indië in 1949* (Amsterdam: Boom, 2001), 23–30.

61. Letter of Foreign Office (Edden) to Ratcliffe-Cousins (MCA), 7 August 1947, British National Archives, Foreign Office papers, FO371, inv. nr. 65478.

62. Note by the Dutch civil air attaché in London, Daniel Goedhuis, August 8, 1947, Netherlands National Archive, 2.16.18, Archief Luchtvaartattaché Londen, nr.5, Foreign Office minute, August 13, 1947, British National Archives, Foreign Office papers, FO371, inv. nr. 65478.

63. Arnold Lamping to Minister of Foreign Affairs Dirk U. Stikker and chief Directie Verre Oosten (Tom Elink Schuurman), 23 december 1948, published in P. J. Drooglever and M. B. Schouten (eds.), *Officiële bescheiden betreffende de Nederlands-Indonesisische betrekkingen, 1945–1950*, Vol. 16, nr. 232, December 1, 1948–January 12, 1949 (Den Haag: ING, 1991).

64. Leo van Maare, *De Mauritius Route: KLM Constellations in het kielzog van Abel Tasman* (Hilversum: All Media Productions, 2005), 26–27.

65. Ibid., 27–38, 111.

66. P. J. Drooglever and M.J.B. Schouten (eds.), *Officiële bescheiden betreffende de Nederlands-Indonesische betrekkingen 1945–1950*, Vol. 17, nr.266, January 13, 1949–February 28, 1949 (Den Haag: ING, 1992), note 6.

67. John Prados, *Presidents' Secret Wars. CIA and Pentagon Secret Operations since World War II* (New York: William Morrow, 1986), 61–64, 67–75, 113–114. For an extensive history of CAT, see William M. Leary, *Perilous Missions: Civil Air Transport and CIA Covert Operations in Asia* (Washington: Smithsonian Institution Press, 2002).

68. Annual Reports, Amsterdam Airport Schiphol, 1946–1955, Archive Amsterdam Airport Schiphol.

69. "TWA's Graceful New Terminal," in *Architectural Forum* (January 1958); John Zukowsky, *Building for Air Travel. Architecture and Design for Commercial Aviation* (Munich/New York: Prestel, 1996), 88, 137.

70. R. T. Appleyard, *British Emigration to Australia* (Canberra: Australian National University, 1964), 22–23; Alexander Freund, *Aufbrüche nach dem Zusammenbruch: die deutsche Nordamerika-Auswanderung nach dem Zweiten Weltkrieg* (Göttingen: V&R Unipress, 2004), 396.

71. See http://www.stats.govt.nz/analytical-reports/tourism-migration-2000/tourism-and-migration-part1.htm (2006).

72. See http://www.uscis.gov/graphics/aboutus/history (2006)

73. See http://www.archives.gov/research/microfilm/t715.pdf. (2006)

74. Shlomo Hillel, *Operation Babylon. Jewish clandestine activity in the Middle East, 1946–1951* (London: Collins, 1988). The reference is to the Dutch edition, Shlomo Hillel, *Operatie Babylon. Illegale emigratie van Joden uit Irak, 1947–1951* (Baarn: Ten Have, 1997), 193–317.

75. R. E. G. Davies, *Airlines of the United States since 1914* (London: Putnam, 1972), 336–339.

76. Telegram of U.S. Embassy in London to State Department, December 1, 1945, U.S. National Archives, RG 59, STD, 711.4127/12-145.

77. Roger Bilstein, "Air Travel and the Travelling Public: The American Experience, 1920–1970," in *From Airships to Airbus. The History of Civil and Commercial*

Aviation, Pioneers and Operations, Vol. 2, edited by William F. Trimble (Washington, DC: Smithsonian Institution Press, 1995), 91–111; David T. Courtwright, *Sky as frontier*, 130–131; Christopher Endy, *Cold War Holidays*, 125.

78. Christopher Endy, *Cold War Holidays*, 128.

79. Ibid., 54.

80. Ibid., 33–35, 42–50.

81. Ibid., 84–85, 100–103.

82. Ibid., 123.

83. Minutes of KLM Supervisory Board (RvC), October 31, 1957, KLM Archive, Amstelveen.

84. Report of 19th IATA Breaches Commission, case nr. 36, PAA and TWA versus Air France, KLM, SAS, Swissair, April 18–19, 1958, KLM Archive, Board papers (RvB).

85. KLM advertisement, reproduced in G. H. van Heusden, *Een eeuw adverteerkunde. De sociaal-economische en psychologische ontwikkeling van het adverteren in Nederlandse kranten* (Assen: Van Gorcum, 1962) 86.

86. Report 19[e] Breaches Commission van de IATA, case nr. 36, PAA and TWA versus Air France, KLM, SAS, Swissair, April 18–19, 1958, Archive KLM, Board Papers.

87. Roger Bray and Vladimir Raitz, *Flight to the Sun. The Story of the Holiday Revolution* (London: Continuum, 2001), 1–10.

88. See http://www.ltu.de/docs/de/internal/history/index.html (2006) Also see http://www12.condor.com/tcf-de/geschichte.jsp (2006).

89. Peter Lyth and Marc Dierikx, "From Privilege to Popularity. The Growth of Leisure Air travel since 1945," *Journal of Transport History* 15(2) (September 1994): 97–115; B. K. Humphreys, "Trooping and the Development of British Independent Airlines," in Peter Lyth (ed.), *Air Transport* (Aldershot: Scholar Press, 1996), 120–133.

90. Walter Borner, *Swissair—From Mittelholzer to Baltensweiler* (Zurich: AS Buchkonzept, 1992), 16.

91. United Nations, *UN Statistical Yearbook, 1968* (New York: UNO, 1969), 440–458 (Table 160: Civil Aviation—Total Scheduled Services).

92. United Nations, *UN Statistical Yearbook, 1960* (New York: UNO, 1960), 354–355 (Table 142: Civil Aviation—Total Scheduled Services). Statistics are provided for passenger-kilometers and (freight) ton-kilometers only.

93. United Nations, *UN Statistical Yearbook, 1968* (New York: UNO, 1969), 440–458 (Table 160: Civil Aviation—Total Scheduled Services).

94. Ibid.

95. KHA, Jetstreams (1954).

96. Adriaan Viruly, *De zee en de overkant: 30 jaar vliegen* (Den Haag: Bert Bakker, 1961), 176–213.

97. Phil Patton, *Made in USA. The Secret Histories of the Things that Made America* (London: Penguin, 1993), 211.

98. Philippe-Michel Thibault, *Inflight Mythologies* (Paris: Gallimard, 2005), 194.

99. Marc Dierikx, *Blauw in de Lucht*, 156.

100. See http://www.airfrance-lavieabord.com (2006).

101. KLM Show Card, 1953, in G. I. Smit, R. C. J. Wunderink, and I. Hoogland, *KLM in beeld. 75 jaar vormgeving en promotie* (Naarden: V+K Publishing, 1994), 87; Also see Kenneth Hudson and Julian Pettifer, *Diamonds in the Sky*, 130–152.

102. Robin Higham, "A Matter of the Utmost Urgency: The Search for a Third London Airport, 1918–1992," in William M. Leary (ed.), *From Airship to Airbus: the History of Civil and Commercial Aviation, Infrastructure and Environment*, Vol. 1 (Washington DC: Smithsonian Institution Press, 1995), 21.

103. Nicolas Neiertz, "Une évolution technologique: aéroports de Paris (1945–1992)," in *Actes du Colloque International 'l'Aviation civile et commerciale des années 1920 à nos jours'* (Paris: Ecole nationale supérieure de techniques avancées, 1994), 221–244 (quote on p. 244).

104. Gérard Maoui and Nicolas Neiertz, *Entre ciel et terre. Aéroports de Paris* (Paris: Le Cherche Midi, 1995), 36–45.

105. Gérard Maoui and Nicolas Neiertz, *Entre ciel et terre*, 60, 76–78.

106. See http://www.infraero.gov.br/link_gera.php?lgi=86&menuid=aero (2007).

107. Jan Dellaert, *Luchthaven Schiphol. Plan voor uitbreiding* (Amsterdam: Municipal Public Works, 1949), 119.

108. Nirmal Kishani, *Changi by Design* (Singapore: Page One Publishing, 2002), 19–20, 26.

109. See http://www.cairo-airport.com/airport_history.asp.

110. Hans Castendijk and Gilles Hondius, *50 jaar NACO, 1949–1999* (Den Haag: Netherlands Airport Consultants, 1999), 18–28.

111. Marc Dierikx and Bram Bouwens, *Building Castles of the Air*, 97 (Table 6: Cargo Transport in Tonnes, Schiphol and Its Main Competitors, 1946–1966).

112. Duncan Cumming, "Aviation in Africa," 32–33.

113. "De economische aspecten van de technische hulp voor Nederland, July 1953," a memorandum, in M. L. J. Dierikx (eds.), *Nederlandse Ontwikkelings-samenwerking*, Vol. 1 (The Hague: Instituut voor Nedrlandse Geschiedenis, 2002), 265–270.

114. Saurashtra Project file, Archive Netherlands Ministry of Foreign Affairs, The Hague, DTH, file number 241.

115. Duncan Cumming, "Aviation in Africa," 31–32.

Chapter 3: Usage—The Rise and Fall of the Jet Set, 1961–1977

1. Scenes from the film *Airport*, a Universal Pictures adaptation of Arthur Hailey's 1968 best-selling novel of the same title, directed by George Seaton in 1970. The film, with an all-star cast including Burt Lancaster, Dean Martin, Jean Seberg,

Jacqueline Bisset, and George Kennedy, became a classic and set the tone for a series of disaster movies in the 1970s. It presented the ingredients for an airline disaster in a grippingly dramatic mix: a snowstorm-swept airport, barely controllable technical difficulties, and big personal problems, all touched by a bomb exploding on board an airline flight.

2. Lewis Mumford, quoted in David Pascoe, *Airspaces* (London: Reaction Books, 2001), 139.

3. GATT, International Trade 1975/76, quoted in Preliminary memorandum (IRHP/BG/UNCTAD 78-5) for the Dutch negotiators in the European Community, Asian and Pacific Countries group, February 6, 1978, Archive Netherlands Ministry of Foreign Affairs, Code 996 (EEG), 1975–1984, inv. nr. 1236 (996.613. 211.430).

4. OECD, *Tourism in OECD Member Countries—1969* (Paris: OECD, 1970), 25; OECD, *Tourism Policy and International Tourism in OECD Member Countries—1980* (Paris: OECD, 1981), 55.

5. Marc Dierikx and Bram Bouwens, *Building Castles of the Air. Schiphol Amsterdam and the Development of Airport Infrastructure in Europe, 1916–1996* (The Hague: Sdu, 1997), 201.

6. David T. Courtwright, *Sky as frontier. Adventure, Aviation, and Empire* (College Station: Texas A&M University Press, 2005), 145.

7. S. Walmsley, "The noise problem," in J. T. Henshaw (ed), *Supersonic Engineering* (London: Heinemann, 1962), 39–59.

8. U. S. Airport Operators Council, *Supersonic Planning*, S.S.I.S. (document number 64–4) March 24, 1964, Archive Amsterdam Airport Schiphol, unnumbered.

9. James R. Hansen, "What Went Wrong? Some New Insights into the Cancellation of the American SST Program," in William M. Leary (ed.), *From Airship to Airbus: The History of Civil and Commercial Aviation* (Washington, DC: Smithsonian Institution Press, 1995), 168–189.

10. Alan Dobson, "Regulation or Competition? Negotiating the Anglo-American Air Service Agreement of 1977," *Journal of Transport History* 15(1994): 144–164; Kenneth Owen, *Concorde and the Americans. International Politics of the Supersonic Transport* (Washington, DC: Smithsonian Institution Press, 1997).

11. James R. Hansen, "Bigger. The Quest for Size," in John T. Greenwood, *Milestones of Aviation* (New York: Hugh Lauter Levin Inc., 1989), 214–221.

12. Roger Béteille, "Airbus; or the Reconstruction of European Civil Aeronautics," in William Leary (ed.), *From Airship to Airbus*, 1–14.

13. ICAO figures, 1970–1973.

14. Anthony Sampson, *Empires of the Sky. The Politics, Contests and Cartels of World Airlines* (London: Hodder and Stoughton, 1984), 211.

15. Crash reporting in *The New York Times*, September 25, 1975; *de Volkskrant* (The Netherlands), September 25, 1975.

16. Report by Vice President Johnson on his visit to Germany, August 19–20, 1961 (undated) *Foreign Relations of the United States* (FRUS), *Kennedy*

Administration, Volume XIV, *Berlin Crisis, 1961–1962* (Washington, DC: United States Government Printing Office, 1993), nr. 121.

17. Telegram from the Mission at Berlin to the Department of State, February 17, 1962, FRUS, Kennedy Administration, Volume XIV, nr. 297.

18. Telegram from the Department of State to the Embassy in the Soviet Union, March 1, 1962, FRUS, Kennedy Administration, Volume XIV, nr. 309; KHA (February 1962). Western recognition of the GDR was not effected before 1972.

19. Jeffrey A. Engel, *Cold War at 30,000 feet. The Anglo-American Fight for Aviation Supremacy* (Cambridge, MA: Harvard University Press, 2007), 187–251.

20. See http://www.answers.com/topic/egyptair (2007).

21. See http://home.iprimus.com.au/rob_rickards/viscounts/history.htm (2007).

22. Guy Vanthemsche, *La Sabena, 1923–2001. Des Origines au Crash* (Brussels: De Boeck, 2002), 162.

23. A summary of the investigations into the probable causes of the crash can be read at http://aviation-safety.net/database/record.php?id=19610917-1&lang=en. (2007).

24. Guy Vanthemsche, *La Sabena*, 165–169.

25. KHA (June 1967).

26. KHA (October 1966).

27. KHA (July-September 1967).

28. M. L. J. Dierikx (ed.), *Nederlandse Ontwikkelingssamenwerking. Bronnenuitgave*, Vol. 3 (The Hague: Instituut voor Nederlandse Geschiedenis, 2005), nos. 81, 104, 117.

29. KHA (July 1968).

30. Dick Morriën, *Vliegtuigkapingen en aanslagen op vliegvelden en andere luchtvaartgebonden objecten*, Extensive Report before the Board of Amsterdam Airport Schiphol, 1989.

31. See N. M. Matte, *Treatise on Air-Aeronautical Law* (Toronto: Carswell, 1981), 697–705; Convention for the Suppression of Unlawful Acts Against the Safety of Civil Aviation, Montreal, December 16, 1970; Convention for the Suppression of Unlawful Acts against the Safety of Civil Aviation, Montreal, September 23, 1971.

32. Dick Morriën, *Vliegtuigkapingen*; Walter Borner, *Swissair—From Mittelholzer to Baltensweiler* (Zurich: AS Buchkonzept, 1992), 21.

33. Dick Morriën, *Vliegtuigkapingen*; Also http://en.wikipedia.org/wiki/Munich_massacre (2007).

34. KHA (November 1972 and February 1973).

35. Dick Morriën, *Vliegtuigkapingen*.

36. Duco Hellema, Cees Wiebes, and Toby Witte, *Doelwit Rotterdam. Nederland en de oliecrisis, 1973–1974* (Den Haag: Sdu, 1998), 72–74.

37. Henry Kissinger, *Years of Upheaval* (London: Weidenfeld & Nicolson, 1982), 490–515, 525–526.

38. Duco Hellema, Cees Wiebes, and Toby Witte, *Doelwit Rotterdam*, 72–74.

39. Henry Kissinger, *Years of Upheaval*, 819.

40. Ibid., 818–821.

41. Marc Dierikx, *Blauw in de Lucht. Koninklijke Luchtvaart Maatschappij 1919–1999* (Den Haag: Sdu, 1999), 181.

42. ICAO figures, quoted in KHA (May 1961).

43. ICAO statistics.

44. OECD, *Tourism in OECD Member Countries, 1964* (Paris: OECD, 1965), 27.

45. KHA (May 1963).

46. U. S. State Department to Senator Lyndon B. Johnson, May 6, 1956, United States National Archives, Washington, DC, State Department, Record Group 59, 611.5694/5-2456.

47. R. E. G. Davies, *History of the World's Airlines* (London: Oxford University Press, 1964), 456–459; Also see http://www.keflavikairport.com/history (2007).

48. Marc Dierikx, *Blauw in de lucht*, 155–156.

49. H. A. Wassenbergh, *Aspects of Air Law and Civil Air Policy in the Seventies* (The Hague: Nijhoff, 1970), 28–32; R. L. M. Schreurs, "Positie van Nederland in de internationale luchtvaartpolitiek," in F.A. van Bakelen (ed.), *Teksten vervoerrecht: Luchtrecht* (Zwolle: Tjeenk Willink, 1983), 87–90.

50. Javier Vidal Olivares, "El fracaso de la expansión internacional de la aerolínea Iberia en América Latina: los casos de Panamá y República Dominicana, 1966–1973," in *Transportes, Servicios y Telecomunicaciones* (2003), no. 6, 23–39.

51. Martin Staniland, *Government Birds. Air Transport and the State in Western Europe* (Lanham: Rowman & Littlefield, 2003), 130–133.

52. Notes for Minister Douglas Jay's speech, February 16, 1966, British National Archives, Board of Trade papers, BT245, nr. 859; U.K./U.S.A. Air Services Agreement: Other Matters Arising, 1958–1967.

53. ICAO figures. On the growth of charter carriers' share, see H. A. Wassenbergh, *Public International Air Transportation Law in a New Era. Economic Regulation of International Air Carrier Operations* (Deventer: Kluwer, 1976), 51.

54. Martin Staniland, *Government Birds*, 69.

55. Netherlands Cabinet Minutes, June 23, 1967, Netherlands National Archive, 2.02.05.01, inv. nr. 844.

56. Memo to Alison Munro (Under Secretary, Ministry of Civil Aviation), November 6, 1961, British National Archives, Board of Trade papers, BT245, nr. 928.

57. Michael Peters, *International Tourism. The Economics and Development of the International Tourist Trade* (London: Hutchinson, 1969), 79.

58. Anthony Sampson, *Empires of the Sky. The Politics, Contests and Cartels of World Airlines* (London: Hodder and Stoughton, 1984), 112.

59. See also P. Lyth and M. Dierikx, "From Privilege to Popularity. The Growth of Leisure Air Travel since 1945," *Journal of Transport History* 15(3) (1994): nr. 3, 97–116.

60. KHA (July 1969).

61. H. A. Wassenbergh, *Public International Air Transportation Law in a New Era*, 75–81.

62. Rigas Doganis, *Flying Off Course. The Economics of International Airlines* (London: George Allen & Unwin, 1985), 18.

63. H. A. Wassenbergh, *Public International Air Transport Law in a New Era*, 12, 26–36.

64. Nicolas Neiertz, "Air France: An Elephant in an Evening Suit?" in Dienel en Lyth, *Flying the Flag* (London: Macmillan, 1998), 37–38; Amilcare Mantegazza, "Alitalia and Commercial Aviation in Italy," in Dienel en Lyth, *Flying the Flag*, 182–183.

65. Netherlands Parliamentary Reports (Handelingen der Staten-Generaal) 1975–1976, Verslag, Notes 2224–2227; Netherlands Parliamentary Reports 1976–1977, Supplements, Chapter XII number 2, 39–40; Netherlands Parliamentary Reports 1977–1978, 14.800, Chapter XII number 2, 44.

66. ICAO, Standard Bilateral Tariff Clause, approved by the Council and published by its decision, ICAO Doc. 9228-C/1036; Rigas Doganis, *Flying Off Course*, 45–51; Jacques Naveau, *International Air Transport in a Changing World* (Brussels: Bruylant, 1989), 126–130.

67. See Paul S. Dempsey, *Law and Foreign Policy in International Aviation* (Dobbs Ferry: Transnational Publishers, 1987).

68. See http://www.airfrance.fr/histoire (2007).

69. Alitalia, *Winging Our Way: Alitalia's First Fifty Years* (Rome: Alitalia, 1997), 89–108.

70. Philippe-Michel Thibault, *Inflight Mythologies* (Paris: Gallimard, 2005), 49–76; Keith Lovegrove, *Airline. Identity, Design and Culture* (London: Laurence King Publishing, 2000), 8–52.

71. David Pascoe, *Airspaces*, 54–55.

72. *The New York Times*, February 8, 1964; Hunter Davies, *The Beatles. The Only Authorized Biography* (London: Arrow Books, 1992), 272–273.

73. See www.wilsonsalmanac.com/book/jun11.html (2007).

74. C&A Fashion, advertisements in *de Volkskrant* (1968).

75. ICAO, *A Review of the Economic Situation of Air Transport, 1960–1970* (Montreal: ICAO, 1971), 3.

76. ICAO figures (excluding U.S.S.R.).

77. ICAO, *A Review of the Economic Situation of Air Transport, 1960–1970* 3–6; ICAO, *A Review of the Economic Situation of Air transport, 1969–1979* (Montreal: ICAO, 1980), 5.

78. Pan Am advertisement, *Telegraaf* (The Netherlands), July 1967.

79. David T. Courtwright, *Sky as Frontier*, 148.

80. United Nations Conference on Trade and Development, Geneva 1964, Final Act, clauses 333–338.

81. Christopher Endy, *Cold War Holidays American Tourism in France* (Chapel Hill: University of North Carolina Press, 2004), 11, 182–183, 191–192; Also see KHA (February 1968).

82. KHA (April 1965).

83. European figures, Annual Reports Amsterdam Airport Schiphol, 1962–1970.

84. ICAO, *A Review of the Economic Situation of Air Transport, 1960–1970*, ICAO Circular 105-AT/16, April 1971. For figures for 1984–1985, see Stephen Wheatcroft and Geoffrey Lipman, *Air Transport in a Competitive European Market. Problems, Prospects and Strategies*, Travel and Tourism Report number 3 (London: The Economist Intelligence Unit, 1986), 24–26.

85. Figures for 1965 and 1975 from Subsecretaria de Aviacion Civil, *Evolucion del trafico aéreo no regular entre España y el reste de Europa (1965–1975)* (Madrid: Subsecretaria de Aviacion Civil, 1976); Also see Javier Vidal Olivares, "Turismo, transporte aéreo e infraestructuras aeroportuarias en el arco mediterráneo español: el caso valenciano," in José Vicente Colomer (ed.), *El Arco Mediterráneo y las infraestructuras de transporte* (Valencia, Generalitat Valenciana/Universidad Politécnica de Valencia, 2006), 114–144.

86. Michael Peters, *International Tourism*, 50.

87. P. Lyth and M. Dierikx, "From Privilege to Popularity," 97–117.

88. Javier Vidal Olivares, "Turismo, transporte aéreo e infraestructuras aeroportuarias en el arco mediterráneo español: el caso valenciano," 114–144; Also see http://www.aena.es (2007).

89. Michael Peters, *International Tourism*, 23–24.

90. Javier Vidal Olivares, "Turismo, transporte aéreo e infraestructuras aeroportuarias en el arco mediterráneo español: el caso valenciano," 114–144.

91. Subsecretaria de Aviacion Civil, *Evolucion del trafico aéreo no regular entre Espana y el reste e Europa*.

92. Marc Dierikx and Bram Bouwens, *Building Castles of the Air*, 163–165.

93. Rigas Doganis, *The Airport Business* (London: Routledge, 1992), 36.

94. Marc Dierikx and Bram Bouwens, *Building Castles of the Air*, 168, 173.

95. Michael Donne, *Above Us the Skies. The Story of BAA* (Whitley: GB Publications Ltd., 1991), 28.

96. Ministry of Civil Aviation, Report of the London Airport Development Committee; Michal Donne, *Above Us the skies*, 34–40.

97. Marc Dierikx and Bram Bouwens, *Building Castles of the Air*, 93, 168.

98. Gerard Maoui and Nicolas Neiertz, *Entre Ciel et Terre Aéroports de Paris* (Paris: Le Cherche Midi, 1995), 64–66.

99. Marc Dierikx and Bram Bouwens, *Building Castles of the Air*, 181–185.

100. Zbigniew Landau and Vaclav Prucha, "The Rise, Operation and Decay of Centrally Planned Economies in Central-Eastern and South-Eastern Europe after World War II," in Vaclav Prucha (ed.), *The System of Centrally Planned Economies in Central-Eastern and South-Eastern Europe after World War II and the Causes of Its Decay* (Prague: Vysoka Skola Economika v Praze, 1994), 9–37.

101. Stefan Albrecht, "Internationale Luftverkehrspolitik in der Zeit des Kalten Krieges von 1944–1965: das Beispiel Tschechoslowakei," in *Jahrbuch*

für Wirtschaftsgeschichte, 2007/1, Verkehrsgeschichte auf neuen Wegen (Berlin: Akademie Verlag, 2007), 93–109 (taken from 96).

102. Ceska Správa Letišt, Chronologie Letište Praha (1996).

103. R. J. Crampton, *Eastern Europe in the Twentieth Century* (London: Routledge, 1994), 322.

104. Ceska Správa Letišt, Chronologie Letište Praha (1996).

105. Joanna Filipzcyk, "LOT: Connecting East and West in Poland, 1945–1995," in P. J. Lyth and H. L. Dienel, *Flying the Flag* (London: Macmillan, 1998), 195–222; "Przewozy w Centralnym Porcie Lotniczym Okecie w latach 1945–1978 (table)," in J. Osinski and H. Zwirko, *Raport informacyjny lotnictwa cywilnego. 50 lat PLL LOT. Wydanie Specjalne 20/80* (Warsaw: Branzowy Osrodek Informacji Technicznej Ekonomicznej Lotnictwa Cywilnego, 1980), 201.

106. J. L. Kneifel, *Fluggesellschaften und Luftverkehrssysteme der sozialistischen Staaten: UdSSR, Polen, CSSR, Ungarn, Bulgarien, Rumanien, Kuba, Jugoslawien unde der VR China* (Nördlingen: Verlag F. Steinmeier, 1980), 246–247.

107. Emmanuel Chadeau, *La Rêve et la Puissance. L'avion et son Siècle* (Paris: Fayard, 1996), 364.

108. See http://www.vnukovo.ru/media/for_specialist/articles_en/VKO_Intl._At_Your_Service.pdf (2007).

109. ICAO, *A Review of the Economic Situation of Air Transport, 1960–1970,* ICAO Circular 105-AT/16, April 1971, 3–4.

110. ICAO, *A Review of the Economic Situation of Air Transport, 1969–1979,* 37.

111. Ibid., 47 (table V-6).

112. ICAO, *A Review of the Economic Situation of Air Transport, 1960–1970,* ICAO Circular 105-AT/16, April 1971, 9–14.

113. Ibid., 37; United Nations, *UN Statistical Yearbook 1968* (New York: UNO, 1969), 440. The Air Afrique nations were Cameroon, Central African Republic, Chad, Congo (Brazzaville), Dahomey (Benin), Gabon, Ivory Coast, Mauretania, Niger, Senegal, Togo, and Upper Volta (Burkina Faso).

114. United Nations, *UN Statistical Yearbook 1982* (New York: UNO, 1985), 991.

115. Alan B. Mountjoy and David Hilling, *Africa. Geography and Development* (London: Hutchinson, 1988), 79.

116. Paul Johnson, *Modern Times. The World from the Twenties to the Eighties* (New York: Harper & Row, 1983), 534.

117. ICAO, *A Review of the Economic Situation of Air Transport, 1960–1970,* ICAO Circular 105-AT/16, April 1971, 37.

118. ICAO, *A Review of the Economic Situation of Air Transport, 1969–1979,* 18. United Nations, *UN Statistical Yearbook 1982* (New York: UNO, 1985), 1001.

119. ICAO, *A Review of the Economic Situation of Air Transport, 1960–1970,* ICAO Circular 105-AT/16, April 1971, 37.

120. United Nations, *UN Statistical Yearbook 1982* (New York: UNO, 1985), 999.

121. See http://www.unhcr.org/publ/PUBL/3b811f6e4.html (2007).

122. ICAO, *A Review of the Economic Situation of Air Transport, 1969–1979*, ICAO Circular 158-AT/57, 1980, 49.

123. H. G. de Maar, *De uitbreiding van Schiphol. Hoe de komst van het straalverkeersvliegtuig invloed heeft gehad op het bestuur* (Deventer: Kluwer, 1976) 32–33.

124. Bolt, Beranek and Newman Inc., *Comparison of the Take-Off Noise Characteristics of the Comet Jet Airliner and of Conventional Propeller-Driven Airliners* (Cambridge, MA: Bolt, Beranek, and Newman, 1958).

125. Aéroports de Paris, Laboratoire, *Boeing 707–120: Experimentation du 12 Septembre 1958* (Paris: ADP, 1958).

126. Air France, Airports and Buildings Department, Airport Division, *Report on the Problems of Deodorising Kerosene Fumes inside Buildings as well as on Airport Areas*, February 6, 1959, Archive Amsterdam Airport Schiphol, vB, 3/1, Werkgroep.

127. Adresses to President Dwight D. Eisenhower at the White House by the mayors of Woodsburgh, Hewlett Neck, Hewlett Bay Park, and Hewlett Harbor, October 9, 1958, Archive Amsterdam Airport Schiphol, doss. 94, Straalvliegtuigen.

128. Bolt, Beranek and Newman Inc., *Studies of Noise Characteristics of the Boeing 707-120*, 1–11.

129. *Informations aéroports de Paris*, April 4, 1958. Archive Amsterdam Airport Schiphol, doss. 94, Straalvliegtuigen.

130. Pierre Cot (director of ADP) to Jan Dellaert (director of Amsterdam Airport Schiphol), June 27, 1958, Archive Amsterdam Airport Schiphol, doss. 94: straalvliegtuigen.

131. "Quieting the Jets," *The Times* (London), August 26, 1958.

132. Robin Higham, "A Matter of Utmost Urgency," in William M. Leary (ed.), *From Airships to Airbus*, Vol. I, 19–44.

133. Flughafen Frankfurt-Main, *Geschäftsbericht 1965*, 9.

134. Dieter Rucht, *Flughafenprojekte als Politikum. Die Konflikte in Stuttgart, München und Frankfurt* (Frankfurt/Main: Campus Verlag, 1984).

135. See http://en.wikipedia.org/wiki/Narita_International_Airport#History; (2007). Also see http://asiacable.blogspot.com/2005/07/end-to-39-year-war.html (2007) and http://search.japantimes.co.jp/cgi-bin/nn20051030a2.html; "Narita Activists to Pay Old Debt. Raising Funds to Cover Civil Damages from '78 Tower Siege," *Japan Times* (October 30, 2005); "Narita Fiasco: Never Again" [Editorial], *Japan Times* (July 26, 2005), available at http://search.japantimes.co.jp/print/opinion/ed2005/ed20050726a1.htm (2007). David Pascoe, *Airspaces*, 104–108.

136. *Airplane!* was a Howard W. Koch production for Paramount Pictures and was actually labelled in 2000 as one of the ten funniest movies ever made by the American Film Institute. Details given are based on the spoken commentary by the makers on the DVD release in 2003.

Chapter 4: Effects—present Global Travel for All, 1977—present

1. *The Terminal—Life Is Waiting* (2004) was a Steven Spielberg film that told the story of Viktor Navorski (played by actor Tom Hanks), from the imaginary former Soviet republic of Krakozhia who arrives in New York to find his passport revoked while in the air. Denied entrance into the United States, he is told to wait at the airport until his status can be cleared up. Stuck in the transit lounge for months, he manages to adapt to life in the airport terminal and even gathers a small circle of friends, including a romantically inclined flight attendant Amelia Warren (Catherine Zeta-Jones) whom he meets from time to time as she passes through the airport.

2. Mark Gottdiener, *Life in the Air. Surviving the New Culture of Air Travel* (Lanham: Rowman & Littlefield, 2001), 27–28; Also see http://en.wikipedia.org/wiki/Merhan_Karimi_Nasseri (2007).

3. David T. Courtwright, *Sky as frontier. Adventure, Aviation, and Empire* (College Station: Texas A&M University Press, 2005), 161–163.

4. Figures based on various European newspaper advertisements, 1977 and 2000.

5. Mark Gottdiener, *Life in the Air*, 2–4.

6. Marc Dierikx, "Airports and the Railways since 1945: Amsterdam, Paris, Frankfurt, London," in Hans-Liudger Dienel (ed.), *Unconnected Transport Networks. European Intermodal Traffic Junctions, 1800–2000* (Frankfurt: Campus Verlag, 2004), 183–198.

7. Thomas Sauter-Servaes and Stephan Rammler, *Delaytainment an Flughäfen. Die Notwendigkeit eines Verspätungsservices und erste Gestaltungsideen* (Berlin: Wissenschaftszentrum Berlin für Sozialforschung, 2002), 12, 55–69. Available at http://bibliothek.wz-berlin.de/pdf/2002/ii02-112.pdf (2007).

8. OECD, *Tourism Policy and International Tourism in OECD Member Countries* (Paris: OECD, 1981), 49.

9. Reporting in: *De Volkskrant*, February 15 and March 14, 2005.

10. Deborah G. Douglas, *United States Women in Aviation 1940–1985* (Washington, DC: Smithsonian Institution Press, 1991), 93–114; Gertrud Blauwhof, *Women in Aviation: Life-Stories and the Interface between (Oral) History and Sociology* (Amsterdam: Belle van Zuylen Institute, 1996); For a more in-depth account, see Gertrud Blauwhof, *Van passie tot professie. Vrouwelijke vliegers in de Nederlandse luchtvaart* (Amsterdam: SUN, 1998), 118–201; Also see Drew Whitelegg, "Cabin Pressure. The Dialectics of Emotional Labour in the Airline Industry," *Journal of Transport History* 23(1) (2002): 73–86, taken from p. 80.

11. ICAO figures.

12. KHA (Dec. 1985).

13. Richard K. Smith, "Better: The Quest for Excellence," in John T. Greenwood (ed), *Milestones of Aviation* (New York: Hugh Lauter Levin Associates, 1989), 222–295, taken from pp. 280–281.

14. Final report (nr. f-sc000725a) of the Bureau d'Enquêtes et d'Analyses pour la Sécurité de l'Aviation Civile on the accident involving the Concorde registered

F-BTSC, operated by Air France on July 25, 2000 at Gonesse (France). Available at http://www.bea-fr.org/docspa/2000/f-sc000725a/htm/f-sc000725a.html (2007).

15. KHA (March 1971, July 1976).

16. R.W. Johnson, *Shootdown. The Verdict on KAL 007* (London: Chatto & Windus, 1986), 256–276.

17. Statement on the Soviet Attack on a Korean Civilian Airliner, September 1, 1983, in *Public Papers of the Presidents of the United States. Ronald Reagan, 1983, Book II, July to December 1983* (Washington, DC: US Government Printing Office, 1985), 1221.

18. Address to the Nation on the Soviet Attack on a Korean Civilian Airliner, September 5, 1983, in *Public Papers of the Presidents of the United States. Ronald Reagan, 1983, Book II,* 1227–1230, taken from p. 1228.

19. R.W. Johnson, *Shootdown,* 130–132.

20. R.W. Johnson, *Shootdown,* 286–287; Various reporting in KHA (1983–1986).

21. See http://www.icao.int/cgi/goto_m.pl?icao/en/trivia/kal_flight_007.htm (2007).

22. Statement by Deputy Press Secretary Larry M. Speakes on the Soviet Attack on a Korean Civilian Airliner, September 16, 1983, in *Public Papers of the Presidents of the United States. Ronald Reagan, 1983, Book II,* 1294–1295. Available at http://usinfo.state.gov/xarchives/display.html?p=washfile-english&y=2006&m=February&x=20060203125928lcnirellep0.5061609 (2007).

23. KHA (Nov. 1977); *Dokumentation zu den Ereignissen und Entscheidungen im Zusammenhang mit der Entführung von Hanns Martin Schleyer und der Lufthansa-Maschine 'Landshut'* (Bonn: Presse- und Informationsamt der Bundesregierung, 1977).

24. Reporting in *NRC Handelsblad,* January 31 and February 1, 2001; John Ashton and Ian Ferguson, *Cover Up of Convenience. The Hidden Scandal of Lockerbie* (Edinburgh: Mainstream Publishing, 2001).

25. Lawrence Wright, *The Looming Tower. Al-Quaeda and the Road to 9/11* (New York: Alfred A. Knopf, 2006), 31–55, 76–81.

26. National Commission on Terrorist Attacks upon the United States, "Outline of the 9/11 Plot (pdf)" (Washington, DC: June 2004), see: www.9-11commission. gov/staff_statements/staff_statement_16.pdf (2008).

27. National Commission on Terrorist Attacks upon the United States, "The Four Flights (pdf)" (Washington, DC: June 2004). See: www.9-11commission.gov/ staff_statements/staff_statement_4.pdf (2008).

28. "Final Report of the National Commission on Terrorist Attacks Upon the United States [pdf]" (Washington, DC: 2004). Available at http://www.gpoaccess. gov/911/pdf/fullreport.pdf (2008).

29. NOS Nieuws Web site April 8 and 17, 2005. Available at http://www.nos. nl/nosjournaal/artikelen/2005/4/08 (2005).

30. See http://news.bbc.co.uk/2/hi/help/3681938.stm (accessed August 10, 2006).

31. R. L. M. Schreurs, "Positie van Nederland in de internationale luchtvaart-politiek," in F. A. van Bakelen (ed.), *Teksten vervoerrecht: Luchtrecht* (Zwolle: Tjeenk Willink, 1983), 91–94; Rigas Doganis, *Flying Off Course. The Economics of International Airlines* (London: George Allen & Unwin, 1985), 57–60. In 1992 the Open Skies Agreement with the United States was much enlarged. The airliners of both countries got almost total freedom to serve the market. See Netherlands Parliamentary Reports (Handelingen der Staten-Generaal), Second Chamber, 1992–1993, 23.069, nr. 1.

32. Jacques Naveau, *International Air Transport in a Changing World* (Brussels: Bruylant, 1989), 142–151.

33. Memorandum of the European Commission "Contributions of the European Communities to the Development of Aviation," Document COM (79) 311, 4 July 1979.

34. Economic and Social Committee of the European Comminities, "EEC Air Transport Policy," Civil Aviation Memorandum nr. 2, in *Progress towards the Development of a Community Air Transport Policy* (Brussel: EG, 1985).

35. F. A. van Bakelen, *"Nouvelles frontières"—European Court of Decision 30 April 1986* (Groningen: Faculteit Rechtsgeleerdheid, 1986); E. Giemulla, R. Schmid, and W. Mölls (eds), *European Air Law; Band 1.* (Deventer: Kluwer, 1994), 19–30; S. A. Williams, "Internal Market and Common Market—The Single European Act versus the Treaty of Rome: Protectionism or Competitiveness in European Civil Aviation?" in Peter P. C. Haanappel, George Petsikas, Rex Rosales, and Jitendra Thaker (eds), *EEC Air Transport Policy and Regulation, and Their Implications for North America* (Deventer: Kluwer, 1990), 3–32; C. O. Lenz, "The Decisions of the European Court of Justice on the Applicability of the Rules of the Treaty of Rome to Air Transport," in *EEC Air Transport Policy and Regulation*, 33–48.

36. See P. J. Slot and P. D. Dagtoglou, *Toward a Community Air Transport Policy. The legal Dimension* (Deventer: Kluwer, 1989); Peter P. C. Haanappel, George Petsikas, Rex Rosales, Jitendra Thaker (eds.), *EEC Air Transport Policy.*

37. Martin Staniland, *Government Birds. Air Transport and the State in Western Europe* (Lanham: Rowman & Littlefield, 2003), 185.

38. Ibid., 170–172.

39. P. P. C. Haanappel, "External Aviation Relations of the European Economic Community and of EEC Member States into the Twenty-First Century," *Air Law* 14(2) (1989): 69–87; 14(3) (1989): 122–146.

40. Henri A. Wassenbergh, External Aviation Relations of the European Community [Includes the Proceedings of Two Mock Negotiations by the "European Commission" with Respectively the "USA" and "Czechoslovakia" (Deventer: Kluwer, 1992); See also Chapter 1.

41. EEC Council Regulation 2408/92 on access for Community air carriers to intra-Community air routes, 23 juli 1992. EEC Council Regulation 2409/92 on fares and rates for air services, July 23, 1992; EEC Council Regulation 2410/92 amending

Regulation (EEC) No. 3975/87 laying down the procedure for the application of the rules on competition to undertakings in the air transport sector, July 23, 1992; EEC Council Regulation 2411/92 amending Regulation (EEC) No. 3976/87 on the application of Article 85(3) of the Treaty to certain categories pf agreements and concerted parties in the air transport sector, July 23, 1992.

42. "European Experience of Air Transport Liberalization" (ICAO paper, February 2003). Available at http://www.icao.int/icao/en/atb/ecp/CaseStudies/EuropeLiberalization_En.pdf (2007).

43. Belgische Kamer van Volksvertegenwoordigers, *Parlementair Onderzoek van de omstandigheden die hebben geleid tot het faillissment van Sabena en de bepaling van de eventuele verantwoordelijkheden en de formulering van aanbevelingen voor de toekomst* (Brussels: Parliamentary Printing Office, 2003).

44. Siobhán Creaton, *Ryanair. How a Small Irish Airline Conquered Europe* (London: Aurum Press, 2005), 179–180.

45. Traffic data Frankfurt-Hahn Airport. Available at http://www.hahn-airport.de/default.aspx?menu=traffic_data&cc=en (2007).

46. European Commission press release IP/03/806, June 5, 2003. Available at http://europa.eu/rapid/pressReleasesAction.do?reference=IP/03/806&format=HTML&aged=0&language=EN;&guiLanguage=en (2007).

47. Press Release by the European Commission, April 30, 2007. Available at http://ec.europa.eu/transport/air_portal/international/pillars/global_partners/doc/us/press_release_signature_30_04_07.pdf (2007).

48. World Travel & Tourism Council, *Aviation in Egypt: The Impact on Travel & Tourism, Jobs and the Economy* (London: World Travel & Tourism Council, 2005), 10. Available at http://www.wttc.travel/bin/pdf/original_pdf_file/aviationinegypt2005.pdf (2007).

49. ICAO, "The Economic Situation of Air Transport. Review and Outlook, 1986," ICAO Circular 200-AT/78, 22.

50. Martin Staniland, *Government Birds*, 169–170.

51. Anthony Sampson, *Empires of the Sky. The Politics, Contests and Cartels of World Airlines* (London: Hodder and Stoughton, 1984), 145–162; R.E.G. Davies, *Rebels and Reformers of the Airways* (Shrewsbury: Airlife, 1987), 241–259; Kenneth Hudson and Julian Pettifer, *Diamonds in the Sky. A Social History of Air Travel* (London: Bodley Head/BBC, 1979), 196–207.

52. "The North Atlantic 'APEX' Traveler," a joint study conducted in 1975/76 by the European Travel Commission and the International Air Transport Association, Geneva, IATA, 1976.

53. Roger Bilstein, "The American Experience," in Hans-Liudger Dienel and Peter Lyth (eds.), *Flying the Flag. European Commercial Air Transport since 1945* (London: Macmillan, 1998), 223–252, taken from p. 246.

54. Pter Lyth, "Chosen Instruments," in *Flying the Flag*, 52–53.

55. Adam Thomson, *High Risk. The Politics of the Air* (London: Sidgwick & Jackson, 1990), 485–572.

56. Nicolas Neiertz, "Air France," in *Flying the Flag*, 21, 39–43; Pascal Perri, *Sauver Air France* (Paris: l'Harmattan, 1994), 91–94; Philippe-Michel Thibault, *Le Roman d'Air France* (Paris: Gallimard, 2003), 183–193.

57. Martin Staniland, *Government Birds*, 189.

58. KLM, Annual Report 1991/92, 36; KLM Annual Report 1995/96, 25–26.

59. KLM Annual Report, 1992/93, 31.

60. Thomas Petzinger, *Hard Landing. The Epic Contest for Power and Profits that Plunged the Airlines into Chaos* (New York: Three Rivers Press, 1996), 446–451.

61. Annex on Air Transport Services of the General Agreement on Trade in Services, April 15, 1994. Available at http://www.wto.org/english/res_e/booksp_e/analytic_index_e/gats_03_e.htm#supplB (2007).

62. James Ott and Raymond E. Neidl, *Airline Odyssey: The Airline Industry's Turbulent Flight into the Future* (New York: McGraw-Hill, 1995), 23.

63. See http://www.easyjet.com/EN/About/Information/infopack_keyevents.html (2007).

64. EEC Commission Regulation 2671/88 on the application of Article 85(3) of the Treaty to certain categories of agreements between undertakings, decisions of associations of undertakings and concerted practices concerning joint planning and coordination of capacity, sharing of revenue and consultations on tariffs on scheduled air services and slot allocation at airports, July 26, 1988; EEC Commission Regulation 84/91 on the application of Article 85(3) of the Treaty to certain categories of agreements, decisions and concerted practices concerning joint planning and coordination of capacity, consultations on passenger and cargo tariffs rates on scheduled air services and slot allocation at airports, December 5, 1990; EEC Council Regulation 95/93 on common rules for the allocation of slots of Community airports, January 18, 1993; See also: Rigas Doganis, *The Airport Business* (London: Routledge, 1992), 99–111.

65. Pierre J. Jeanniot at the Airports Council International "Greenport" Conference on Airport Development in the 21st Century, Amsterdam April 22, 1999. Internet information at www.iata.org. (2005).

66. Siobhán Creaton, *Ryanair*, 198–201; Also see http://wizzair.com/about_us/company_information (2007).

67. Kenneth Button, "The Failings of the Scheduled Airline Market," in *Aerlines Magazine* e-zine edition, Issue 29 (2005).

68. See http://www.airchina.com.cn/AboutAirChina/Introduction/default.shtml (2007).

69. Tae Hoon Oum and Chunyan Yu, *Winning Airlines. Productivity and Cost Competitiveness of the World's Major Airlines* (Boston/Dordrecht: Kluwer Academic Publishers, 1998), 199.

70. GATT, "Agreement on Trade in Civil Aircraft," April 12, 1979. Available at: http://www.austlii.edu.au/au/other/dfat/seldoc/1979/2716.html (2006).

71. World Travel and Tourism Council, "The Impact of Travel &Tourism on Jobs and the Economy. China and China Hong Kong SAR" (London: World

Travel & Tourism Council, 2003). Available at http://www.wttc.travel/bin/pdf/ original_pdf_file/chksar2003eng.pdf (2007).

72. Reporting on aviation developments in China, in: *De Volkskrant*, August 17, 2007.

73. Martin Courtwright, *Sky as Frontier*, 201.

74. ICAO figures.

75. ICAO figures.

76. Thomas Friedman, *The World is Flat. A Brief History of the Twenty-First Century* (New York: Farrar, Straus and Giroux, 2005), 103–130.

77. Ilona Eveleen, "De groene oorlog rond bloemen uit Kenia," *Nederlands Dagblad*, March 9, 2007.

78. Netherlands Central Bureau of Statistics (CBS), "Historische reeks van de lange vakanties van Nederlanders." Available at http://statline.cbs.nl/StatWeb/table. asp?STB=G1&LA=nl&DM=SLNL&PA=03770&D1=0-3,57,66-68&D2=0-1,6, 11,16,21,26,31,l&HDR=T (2007).

79. Ibid.

80. Reporting in *de Volkskrant*, September 29, 2007.

81. Colin Michael Hall, *Tourism and Politics. Policy, Power and Place* (Chichester, UK: John Wiley & Sons, 1994), 119–147.

82. World Travel and Tourism Council, "The 2007 Travel & Tourism Economic Research – Thailand." Available at http://www.wttc.travel/bin/pdf/original_pdf_file/ 1thailand.pdf (2007).

83. See http://www.uneptie.org/pc/tourism/sust-tourism/economic.htm (2007).

84. World Travel & Tourism Council, *Aviation in Egypt: The Impact on Travel & Tourism, Jobs and the Economy* (London: World Travel & Tourism Council, 2005). Available at http://www.wttc.travel/bin/pdf/original_pdf_file/ aviationinegypt2005.pdf (2007).

85. See, for such issues, *Annals of Tourism Research: A Social Sciences Journal* (Vol. I, 1973–).

86. Lillian S. Robinson, "Sex Tourism," in Roland Robertson and Jan Aart Scholte (eds.), *Ecyclopedia of Globalization*, Vol. 3 (New York: Routledge, 2007).

87. KHA.

88. Paul Hoebink, *Geven is Nemen. De Nederlandse Ontwikkelingshulp aan Tanzania en Sri Lanka* (Nijmegen: Stichting Derde Wereld Publicaties, 1988), 110–118, 277–278.

89. Marc Dierikx, Bram Bouwens, *Building Castles of the Air. Schiphol Amsterdam and the Development of Airport Infrastructure in Europe, 1916–1996* (The Hague: Sdu, 1997), 273–279.

90. American Meteorological Society. Available at http://ams.confex.com/ams/ 13ac10av/10ARAM/abstracts/39764.htm (2005).

91. See http://www.atmosfair.de (2007).

92. Robert V. Garvin, "Aircraft Engines and the Environment: Cleaner and Quieter Is the Promise of the Nineties," in Pablo Mendez de Leon (ed.), *Air Transport*

Law and policy in the 1990s. Controlling the Boom (Dordrecht: Nijhoff, 1991), 53–60.

93. KHA (Oct.– Nov. 1984).

94. See http://www.af.mil/history/decade.asp?dec=1990 (2008) and www.rand.org/pubs/monograph_reports/MR1187/MR1187.appd.pdf (2008), 238–239.

95. U.S. Department of Health and Human Services, Center for Disease Control and Prevention. Available at http://www.cdc.gov/NCIDOD/SARS (2007).

96. Martin Courtwright, *Sky as Frontier*, 203–206.

97. NOS News. Available at http://www.nos.nl/nosjournaal/artikelen/2005/5/231 (2005).

98. Tiscali News. Available at http://www.tiscali.nl/home/home_center.asp (accessed May 30, 2005).

99. UNHCR, *Refugees* Magazine, issue 113 (1999). Available at http://www.unhcr.org/publ/PUBL/3b811f6e4.html (2007).

100. KHA, 1980.

101. KHA, Aug. 1982.

102. KHA, Jan. 1983.

103. KHA, Apr. 1989.

104. See http://www.let.leidenuniv.nl/history/migration/chapter10.html (2007).

105. OECD Observer No. 242, March 2004.

106. "Personeel Schiphol smokkelt illegalen land in," in *Elsevier*, January 20, 2005.

107. *United 93* was released by Universal Pictures in April 2006.

108. Antoine de Saint-Exupéry, *Terre des Hommes* (Paris: Gallimard, 1938).

Bibliography

Actes du Colloque International l' Aviation Civile et Commerciale des Années 1920 à Nos Jours (Paris: Service Historique de l'Armée de l'Air, 1994).

Aéroports de Paris, Laboratoire. *Boeing 707-120: Experimentation du 12 Septembre 1958* (Paris: ADP, 1958).

Air Ministry. *Resumé of commercial aviation* (London: HMSO, April 1938).

Air Research Bureau. *Report on Coordination of Intra-European Air Transport* (Brussels: ARB, 1953).

Alitalia. *Winging Our Way: Alitalia's First Fifty Years* (Rome: Alitalia, 1997).

Appleyard, R. T. *British Emigration to Australia* (Canberra: Australian National University, 1964).

Ashton, John, and Ian Ferguson. *Cover Up of Convenience. The Hidden Scandal of Lockerbie* (Edinburgh: Mainstream Publishing, 2001).

Bade, Klaus J. *Auswanderer–Wanderarbeiter–Gastarbeiter. Bevölkerung, Arbeits- markt und Wanderung in Deutschland seit der Mitte des 19. Jahrhunderts* (Ostfildern: Scripta Mercaturae Verlag, 1984).

Bakelen, F. A. van (ed.). *Teksten vervoerrecht: Luchtrecht* (Zwolle: Tjeenk Willink, 1983).

———. *'Nouvelles frontières' European Court of Decision 30 April 1986* (Gronin- gen: Faculteit Rechtsgeleerdheid, 1986).

Belgische Kamer van Volksvertegenwoordigers. *Parlementair Onderzoek van de om- standigheden die hebben geleid tot het faillissment van Sabena en de bepaling van de eventuele verantwoordelijkheden en de formulering van aanbevelingen voor de toekomst* (Brussels: Parliamentary Printing Office, 2003).

Bialer, Uri. *The Shadow of the Bomber: The Fear of Air Attack and British Politics, 1932–1939* (London: Royal Historical Society, 1980).

Bilstein, Roger E. *The American Aerospace Industry. From Workshop to Global Enterprise* (New York: Twayne Publishers, 1996).

Blauwhof, Gertrud. *Van passie tot professie. Vrouwelijke vliegers in de Nederlandse luchtvaart* (Amsterdam: SUN, 1998).

———. *Women in Aviation: Life-Stories and the Interface between (Oral) History and Sociology* (Amsterdam: Belle van Zuylen Institute, 1996).

Bode, Steven, and Jeremy Millar (eds.). *The Most Important New Buildings of the Twentieth Century: Airport* (London: The Photographers' Gallery, 1997).

Bolt, Beranek, and Newman Inc. *Studies of Noise Characteristics of the Boeing 707—120 Jet Airliner and of Large Conventional Propeller-Driven Airliners* (Cambridge, MA: Bolt, Beranek, and Newman, 1958).

Borner, Walter. *Swissair—From Mittelholzer to Baltensweiler* (Zurich: AS Buchkonzept, 1992).

Bray, Roger, and Vladimir Raitz. *Flight to the Sun. The Story of the Holiday Revolution* (London: Continuum, 2001).

Burgdorff, Stephan, and Christian Habbe (eds.). *Als Feuer vom Himmel viel. Der Bombenkrieg in Deutschland* (Darmstadt: Wissenschaftliche Buchgesellschaft, 2003).

Castendijk, Hans, and Gilles Hondius, *50 jaar NACO, 1949–1999* (Den Haag: Netherlands Airport Consultants, 1999).

Chadeau, Emmanuel. *Le rêve et la Puissance. L'Avion et son Siècle* (Paris: Fayard, 1996).

Cobham, Alan. *Twenty Thousand Miles in a Flying Boat. My Flight Round Africa* (London: George Harrap & Co., 1930).

Colomer, José Vicente (ed.). *El Arco Mediterráneo y las infraestructuras de transporte* (Valencia: Generalitat Valenciana/Universidad Politécnica de Valencia, 2006).

Conin, Helmut. *Gelandet in Berlin. Zur Geschichte der Berliner Flughäfen* (Berlin: Berliner Flughafengesellschaft, 1974).

Coupar, Anne. *The Smirnoff Story* (London: Jarrolds Publishers, 1960).

Courtwright, David T. *Sky as Frontier. Adventure, Aviation, and Empire* (College Station: Texas A&M University Press, 2005).

Crampton, R. J. *Eastern Europe in the Twentieth Century* (London: Routledge, 1994).

Creaton, Siobhán. *Ryanair. How a Small Irish Airline Conquered Europe* (London: Aurum Press, 2005).

Davies, Hunter. *The Beatles. The Only Authorized Biography* (London: Arrow Books, 1992).

Davies, R.E.G. *Airlines of Asia since 1920* (McLean, VA: Paladwr Press, 1997).

———. *Airlines of Latin America since 1919* (London: Putnam, 1984).

———. *Airlines of the United States since 1914* (London: Putnam, 1972).

———. *A History of the World's Airlines* (London: Oxford University Press, 1964).

———. *Rebels and Reformers of the Airways* (Shrewsbury, MA: Airlife, 1987).

Dellaert, Jan. *Luchthaven Schiphol. Plan voor uitbreiding* (Amsterdam: Municipal Public Works, 1949).

Dempsey, Paul S. *Law and Foreign Policy in International Aviation* (Dobbs Ferry, NY: Transnational Publishers, 1987).

Dienel, Hans-Liudger (ed.). *Unconnected Transport Networks. European Intermodal Traffic Junctions, 1800–2000* (Frankfurt: Campus Verlag, 2004).

Dienel, Hans-Liudger, and Helmuth Trischler. *Geschichte der Zukunft des Verkehrs. Verkehrskonzepte von der Frühen Neuzeit bis zum 21. Jahrhundert* (Frankfurt/Main: Campus, 1997).

Dienel, Hans-Liudger, and Peter Lyth (eds.). *Flying the Flag. European Commercial Air Transport since 1945* (London: Macmillan, 1998).

Dierikx, Marc. *Begrensde Horizonten. De internationale burgerluchtvaartpolitiek van Nederland in het interbellum* (Zwolle: Tjeenk Willink, 1988).

———. *Bevlogen Jaren. Nederlandse Burgerluchtvaart tussen de Wereldoorlogen* (Houten: Unieboek, 1986).

———. *Blauw in de Lucht. Koninklijke Luchtvaart Maatschappij 1919–1999* (Den Haag: Sdu, 1999).

———. *Fokker. A Transatlantic Biography* (Washington DC: Smithsonian Institution Press, 1997).

———. *An Image of Freedom: The Netherlands and the United States, 1945 to the Present* (Den Haag: Sdu, 1997).

Dierikx, Marc, and Bram Bouwens. *Building Castles of the Air. Schiphol Amsterdam and the Development of Airport Infrastructure in Europe, 1916–1996* (The Hague: Sdu, 1997).

Dierikx, M. L. J., a. o. (ed.). *Nederlandse Ontwikkelingssamenwerking, Bronnenuitgave*, Vol. 1 (The Hague: Instituut voor Nederlandse Geschiedenis, 2002).

———. *Nederlandse Ontwikkelingssamenwerking. Bronnenuitgave*, Vol. 3 (The Hague: Instituut voor Nederlandse Geschiedenis, 2005).

Dobson, Alan P. *Peaceful Air Warfare. The United States, Britain and the Politics of International Aviation* (Oxford: Oxford University Press, 1991).

Doganis, Rigas. *The Airport Business* (London: Routledge, 1992).

———. *Flying Off Course. The Economics of International Airlines* (London: George Allen & Unwin, 1985).

Dokumentation zu den Ereignissen und Entscheidungen im Zusammenhang mit der Entführung von Hanns Martin Schleyer und der Lufthansa-Maschine "Landshut" (Bonn : Presse- und Informationsamt der Bundesregierung, 1977).

Donne, Michael. *Above Us the Skies. The Story of BAA* (Whitley: GB Publications Ltd., 1991).

Douglas, Deborah G. *United States Women in Aviation 1940–1985* (Washington, DC: Smithsonian Institution Press, 1991).

Drooglever, P. J., and M. J. B. Schouten (eds.). *Officiële bescheiden betreffende de Nederlands-Indonesisische betrekkingen, 1945–1950*, Vol. 16: 1 December 1948—12 January 1949 (Den Haag: Instituut voor Nederlandse Geschiedenis, 1991).

———. *Officiële bescheiden betreffende de Nederlands-Indonesische betrekkingen 1945–1950*, Vol. 17: 13 January 1949—28 February 1949 (Den Haag: Instituut voor Nederlandse Geschiedenis, 1992).

Edgerton, David. *England and the Aeroplane. An Essay on a Militant and Technological Nation* (Basingstoke: MacMillan, 1991).

Ehmer, Josef, Rainer Fremdling, and Hartmut Kaelble (eds.). *Jahrbuch für Wirtschaftsgeschichte, 2007/1, Verkehrsgeschichte auf neuen Wegen* (Berlin: Akademie Verlag, 2007).

La emigración europea a la América Latina: Fuentes y estado de investigación. Informes presentado a la IV. Reunión de Historiadores Latinoamericanistas Europeos (Berlin: Colloquium Verlag, 1979).

Endy, Christopher. *Cold War Holidays. American Tourism in France* (Chapel Hill: University of North Carolina Press, 2004).

Engel, Jeffrey A. *Cold War at 30000 feet. The Anglo-American Fight for Aviation Supremacy* (Cambridge, MA: Harvard University Press, 2007).

Fischer, Albert. *Luftverkehr zwischen Markt und Macht (1919–1937). Lufthansa, Verkehrsflug und der Kampf ums Monopol* (Wiesbaden: Franz Steiner Verlag, 2003).

Foreign Relations of the United States. *Kennedy Administration, Vol. XIV: Berlin Crisis, 1961–1962* (Washington, DC: United States Government Printing Office, 1993).

Freund, Alexander. *Aufbrüche nach dem Zusammenbruch. Die deutsche Nordamerika-Auswanderung nach dem Zweiten Weltkrieg* (Göttingen: V&R Unipress, 2004).

Friedman, Thomas. *The World Is Flat. A Brief History of the Twenty-First Century* (New York: Farrar, Straus and Giroux, 2005).

Friedrich, Jörg. *Der Brand. Deutschland im Bombenkrieg, 1940–1945* (München: Propyläen Verlag, 2002).

Fritzsche, Peter. *A Nation of Fliers. German Aviation and the Polular Imagination* (Cambridge, UK: Harvard University Press, 1992).

Giemulla, E., R. Schmid, and W. Mölls (eds). *European Air Law; Band 1* (Deventer: Kluwer, 1994).

Goñi, Uki. *The Real Odessa. How Perón brought the Nazi War Criminals to Argentina* (London: Granta Books, 2002).

Gottdiener, Mark. *Life in the Air. Surviving the New Culture of Air Travel* (Lanham: Rowman & Littlefield, 2001).

Grayling, A. C. *Among the Dead Cities: The History and Moral Legacy of the WWII Bombing of Civilians in Germany and Japan* (New York: Walker & Company, 2006).

Gunston, Bill (ed.). *Chronicle of Aviation* (Liberty, MO: JL International Publishing, 1992).

Haanappel, Peter P. C., George Petsikas, Rex Rosales, and Jitendra Thaker (eds). *EEC Air Transport Policy and Regulation, and Their Implications for North America* (Deventer: Kluwer, 1990).

Hailey, Arthur. *Airport* (London: Michael Joseph Ltd, 1968).

Hall, Colin Michael. *Tourism and Politics. Policy, Power and Place* (Chichester: John Wiley & Sons, 1994).

Hawlena, Joanna. *Determinanty Kształtowania cen Usług Transportowych* (Katowice: Wydawnictwo Akademii Ekonomicznej, 2004).

Hellema, D. A., C. Wiebes, and B. Zeeman (eds.). *Jaarboek Buitenlandse Zaken: Derde Jaarboek voor de geschiedenis van de Nederlandse buitenlandse politiek* (Den Haag: Sdu, 1997).

Hellema, Duco, Cees Wiebes, and Toby Witte. *Doelwit Rotterdam. Nederland en de oliecrisis, 1973–1974* (Den Haag: Sdu, 1998).

Henshaw, J. T (ed). *Supersonic Engineering* (London: Heinemann, 1962).

Heusden, G. H. van. *Een eeuw adverteerkunde. De sociaal-economische en psychologische ontwikkeling van het adverteren in Nederlandse kranten* (Assen, 1962).

Hillel, Shlomo. *Operation Babylon. Jewish Clandestine Activity in the Middle East, 1946–1951* (London: Collins, 1988).

Hoebink, Paul. *Geven is Nemen. De Nederlandse Ontwikkelingshulp aan Tanzania en Sri Lanka* (Nijmegen: Stichting Derde Wereld Publicaties, 1988).

Hoffman, Paul. *Wings of Madness: Alberto Santos-Dumont and the Invention of Flight* (London: Fourth Estate, 2003).

Hudson, Kenneth and Julian Pettifer. *Diamonds in the Sky. A Social History of Air Travel* (London: Bodley Head/BBC, 1979).

ICAO Circulars. *The Economic Situation of Air Transport. Review and Outlook* (Montreal: ICAO—various years).

Ingold, Felix. *Literatur und Aviatik. Europäische Flugdichtung, 1909–1927* (Basel: Birkhäuser Verlag, 1978).

Johnson, Paul. *Modern Times. The World from the Twenties to the Eighties* (New York: Harper & Row, 1983).

Johnson, R. W. *Shootdown. The Verdict on KAL 007* (London: Chatto & Windus, 1986).

Kishani, Nirmal. *Changi by Design* (Singapore: Page One Publishing, 2002).

Kissinger, Henry. *Years of Upheaval* (London: Weidenfeld & Nicolson, 1982).

Kneifel, J. L. *Fluggesellschaften und Luftverkehrssysteme der sozialistischen Staaten: UdSSR, Polen, CSSR, Ungarn, Bulgarien, Rumanien, Kuba, Jugoslawien unde der VR China* (Nördlingen: Verlag F. Steinmeier, 1980).

Lawrence, T. E. *The Mint. A Day-Book of the RAF Depot between August and December 1922, with Later Notes by 352087 A/c Ross* (London: Jonathan Cape, 1955).

Leary, William M. (ed.). *From Airship to Airbus*, Vol. I (Washington, DC: Smithsonian Institution Press, 1995).

———. *Perilous Missions: Civil Air Transport and CIA Covert Operations in Asia* (Washington, DC: Smithsonian Institution Press, 2002).

Lindqvist, Sven. *A History of Bombing* (New York: The New Press, 2001).

Lissitzyn, Oliver J. *International Air Transport and National Policy* (New York: Council on Foreign Relations, 1942).

Lith, Hans van. *Plotseling een vreselijke knal. Bommen en mijnen treffen neutraal Nederland, 1914–1918* (Zaltbommel: Europese Bibliotheek, 2001)

Lomax, Judy. *Women of the Air* (London: John Murray, 1986).

Lovegrove, Keith. *Airline. Identity, Design and Culture* (London: Laurence King Publishing Ltd, 2000).

Lyth, Peter (ed.). *Air Transport* (Aldershot: Scholar Press, 1996).

Maar, H. G. de. *De uitbreiding van Schiphol. Hoe de komst van het straalver-keersvliegtuig invloed heeft gehad op het bestuur* (Deventer: Kluwer, 1976)

Maare, Leo van. *De Mauritius Route: KLM Constellations in het kielzog van Abel Tasman* (Hilversum: All Media Productions, 2005)

Maoui, Gérard, and Nicolas Neiertz. *Entre ciel et terre. Aéroports de Paris* (Paris: Le Cherche Midi, 1995).

Markham, Beryl. *West with the Night* (Boston: Houghton Mifflin, 1942).

Matte, N. M. *Treatise on Air-Aeronautical Law* (Toronto: Carswell, 1981).

Mendez de Leon, Pablo (ed.). *Air Transport Law and Policy in the 1990's. Controlling the Boom* (Dordrecht: Nijhoff, 1991).

Mézière, Henri, and Jean-Marie Sauvage. *Les Ailes françaises. L'Aviation marchande de 1919 à nos jours* (Paris: Éditions Rive Droite, 1999).

Moolman, Valerie. *Women Aloft* (New York: Time-Life Books, 1981).

Morrow, John H., Jr. *The Great War in the Air. Military Aviation from 1909 to 1921* (Washington, DC: Smithsonian Institution Press, 1993).

Mountjoy, Alan B., and David Hilling. *Africa. Geography and Development* (London: Hutchinson, 1988).

Naveau, Jacques. *International Air Transport in a Changing World* (Brussels: Bruylant, 1989).

OECD. *Tourism in OECD Member Countries, 1964* (Paris: OECD, 1965).

OECD. *Tourism in OECD Member Countries, 1969* (Paris: OECD, 1970).

OECD. *Tourism Policy and International Tourism in OECD Member Countries, 1980* (Paris: OECD, 1981).

Omissi, David E. *Air Power and Colonial Control. The Royal Air Force, 1919–1939* (Manchester: MUP, 1990).

Osinski, J., and H. Zwirko. *Raport informacyjny lotnictwa cywilnego. 50 lat PLL LOT. Wydanie Specjalne 20/80* (Warsaw: Branzowy Osrodek Informacji Technicznej Ekonomicznej Lotnictwa Cywilnego, 1980).

Ott, James, and Raymond E. Neidl. *Airline Odyssey: The airline Industry's Turbulent Flight into the Future* (New York: McGraw-Hill, 1995).

Oum, Tae Hoon, and Chunyan Yu. *Winning Airlines. Productivity and Cost Competitiveness of the World's Major Airlines* (Boston/Dordrecht: Kluwer, 1998).

Owen, Kenneth. *Concorde and the Americans. International Politics of the Supersonic Transport* (Washington, DC: Smithsonian Institution Press, 1997).

Palmer, Scott W. *Dictatorship of the Air. Aviation Culture and the Fate of Modern Russia* (New York: Cambridge University Press, 2006).

Pascoe, David. *Airspaces* (London: Reaction Books, 2001).

Patton, Phil. *Made in USA. The Secret Histories of the Things that Made America* (London: Penguin, 1993).

Perri, Pascal. *Sauver Air France* (Paris: l'Harmattan, 1994).

Peters, Michael. *International Tourism. The Economics and Development of the International Tourist Trade* (London: Hutchinson, 1969).

Petzinger, Thomas. *Hard Landing. The Epic Contest for Power and Profits That Plunged the Airlines into Chaos* (New York: Three Rivers Press, 1996).

Pirath, Carl. *Konjunktur und Luftverkehr* (Berlin: Verkehrswissenschaftliche Lehrmittelgesellschaft, 1935).

Prados, John. *Presidents' Secret Wars. CIA and Pentagon Secret Operations since World War II* (New York: William Morrow, 1986).

Programma Nationale Sport-Betooging 25 April 1925 op het Terrein Houtrust te 's-Gravenhage (Leiden: Eduard IJdo, 1925).

Prucha, Vaclav (ed). *The System of Centrally Planned Economies in Central-Eastern and South-Eastern Europe after World War II and the Causes of Its Decay* (Prague: Vysoka Skola Economika v Praze, 1994).

Public Papers of the Presidents of the United States. *Ronald Reagan, 1983, Book II, July to December 1983* (Washington, DC: US Government Printing Office, 1985).

Renneberg, Monika, and Mark Walker (eds.). *Science, Technology, and National Socialism* (Cambridge, UK: Cambridge University Press, 1994).

Richards, Denis. *RAF Bomber Command in the Second World War. The Hardest Victory* (London: Penguin Books, 1994).

Riper, A. Bowdoin van. *Imagining flight. Aviation and Popular Culture* (College Station: Texas A&M University Press, 2004).

Roland Robertson, Roland, and Jan Aart Scholte (eds.). *Encyclopedia of Globalization* (New York: Routledge, 2007).

Rucht, Dieter. *Flughafenprojekte als Politikum. Die Konflikte in Stuttgart, München und Frankfurt* (Frankfurt/Main: Campus Verlag, 1984).

Rusman, E. *Wings across Continents. The KLM Amsterdam–Batavia Line* (Amsterdam: Andries Blitz, 1935).

Saint-Exupéry, Antoine de. *Courier Sud* (Paris: Gallimard, 1930).

———. *Terre des Hommes* (Paris: Gallimard, 1938).

———. *Vol de Nuit* (Paris: Gallimard, 1931).

Saint Sauveur-Henn, Anne. *Un siècle d'emigration allemande vers l'Argentine, 1953– 1945* (Köln: Böhlau Verlag, 1995).

Sampson, Anthony. *Empires of the Sky. The Politics, Contests and Cartels of World Airlines* (London: Hodder and Stoughton, 1984).

Sauter-Servaes, Thomas, and Stephan Rammler. *Delaytainment an Flughäfen. Die Notwendigkeit eines Verspätungsservices und erste Gestaltungsideen* (Berlin: Wissenschaftszentrum Berlin für Sozialforschung, 2002).

Shute, Nevil. *No Highway* (London: William Heinemann, 1948).

Siukonen, Jyrki. *Uplifted Spirits, Earthbound Machines. Studies on Artists and the Dream of Flight, 1900–1935* (Helsinki: Suomalaisen Kirjallisuuden Seura, 2001).

Slot, P. J., and P.D. Dagtoglou. *Toward a Community Air Transport Policy. The Legal Dimension* (Deventer: Kluwer, 1989).

Smirnoff, Iwan. *Smirnoff Vertelt* (Amsterdam: Andries Blitz, 1938).

Smit, G. I., and R. C. J. Wunderink, I. Hoogland. *KLM in beeld. 75 jaar vormgeving en promotie* (Naarden: V+K Publishing, 1994).

Société des Nations. *Études sur la Situation Economique, Administrative en Juridique de la Navigation Aérienne Internationale* (Genève: Société des Nations, 1930).

Staniland, Martin. *Government Birds. Air Transport and the State in Western Europe* (Lanham: Rowman & Littlefield, 2003).

Subsecretaria de Aviacion Civil. *Evolucion del trafico aéreo no regular entre España y el reste de Europa (1965–1975).* (Madrid: Subsecretaria de Aviacion Civil, 1976).

Syon, Guillaume de. *The Socio-Politics of Technology: The Zeppelin in Official and Popular Culture, 1900–1939.* Dissertation (Boston: Boston University, 1994).

10 Jahre Deutsche Lufthansa, 6. Januar 1926—6. Januar 1936 (Halle: Warnecke, 1936).

Thibault, Philippe-Michel. *Inflight Mythologies* (Paris: Gallimard, 2005).

———. *Le Roman d'Air France* (Paris: Gallimard, 2003).

Thomson, Adam. *High risk. The Politics of the Air* (London: Sidgwick & Jackson, 1990).

Trimble, William F. (ed.). *From Airship to Airbus. The History of Civil and Commercial Aviation, Vol. 2: Pioneers and Operations* (Washington, DC: Smithsonian Institution Press, 1995).

Tusa, Ann, and John Tusa. *The Berlin Airlift* (New York: Atheneum, 1988).

United Nations. *UN Statistical Yearbook* (New York: UNO, various years).

Vanthemsche, Guy. *La Sabena, 1923–2001. Des origines au crash* (Brussels: De Boeck, 2002).

Verne, Jules. *Robur le Conquérant* (Paris: Bibliothèque d'Éducation et de Récréation Hetzel, 1886).

Viruly, Adriaan. *De zee en de overkant: 30 jaar vliegen* (Den Haag: Bert Bakker, 1961)

Vlot, Ad. *Glare. History of the Development of a New Aircraft Material* (Dordrecht/London/Boston: Kluwer, 2001).

Wagner, Wolfgang. *Hugo Junkers, Pionier der Luftfahrt—seine Flugzeuge* (Bonn: Bernard & Graefe Verlag, 1996).

Wassenbergh, H. A. *Aspects of Air Law and Civil Air Policy in the Seventies* (The Hague: Nijhoff, 1970).

———. *External Aviation Relations of the European Community—Includes the Proceedings of Two Mock Negotiations by the "European Commision" with Respectively the "USA" and "Czechoslovakia"* (Deventer: Kluwer, 1992).

———. *Post-War International Civil Aviation Policy and the Law of the Air* (The Hague: Martinus Nijhoff, 1962).

———. *Public International Air Transportation Law in a New Era. Economic Regulation of International Air Carrier Operations* (Deventer: Kluwer, 1976).

Watt, Donald C. *How War Came. The Immediate Origins of the Second World War, 1938–1939* (London: Mandarin, 1989).

Wells, H. G. *The War in the Air* (Harmondsworth: Penguin Books, 1976).

Westphall, Povl. *Københavns Lufthavn, 1925–1975* (København: Københavns Lufthavnsvæsen, 1975).

Wheatcroft, Stephen, and Geoffrey Lipman. *Air Transport in a Competitive European Market. Problems, Prospects and Strategies* (London: The Economist Intelligence Unit, 1986).

Wohl, Robert. *A Passion for Wings. Aviation and the Western Imagination* (New Haven: Yale University Press, 1994).

———. *The Spectacle of Flight. Aviation and the Western Imagination, 1920–1950* (New Haven: Yale University Press, 2005).

Wright, Lawrence. *The Looming Tower. Al-Quaeda and the Road to 9/11* (New York: Alfred A. Knopf, 2006).

Zeise, H. *Die Aeronautik früher und jetzt, nebst theoretischen und practischen Vorschlägen zu einer vervollkommneteren Luftschifffahrtskunst und Benutzung des Luftballs für technische und industrielle Zwecke: Vorträge, gehalten im Altonaer Bürgerverein im Winter 1849/50* (Altona: Schlüter, 1850).

Zukowsky, John. *Building for Air Travel. Architecture and Design for Commercial Aviation* (Munich/New York: Prestel, 1996).

Zweers, Louis. *De crash van de Franeker. Een Amerikaanse persreis naar Nederlands-Indië in 1949* (Amsterdam: Boom, 2001).

Zylicz, M. *International Air Transport Law* (Dordrecht: Martinus Nijhoff, 1992).

Index

Nazi: political party, regime, in Germany, 17–19, 33; use of aviation by, 19–20, 29

NATO (North Atlantic Treaty Organization), 51–52, 59, 116–17

N'Djili Airport (Kinshasa), 81

Near East Air Transport, 58

Negombo Air Base (Ceylon), 54

Netherlands, viii, ix, 2, 4–5, 8, 12, 16, 27, 29, 37–38, 47–48, 52–56, 60, 74, 82, 90, 92, 94, 119, 123, 128, 136, 139, 142

Netherlands East Indies (Indonesia), 8, 14–15, 29, 32–33, 53–55

Newark Airport (New Jersey), 104, 120

New York, gateway function of, 51, 57, 65–66, 75, 117; New York Stock Exchange (Wall Street), 90; attack on World Trade Center in, 114, 119–20

New York Times, The, 95

New Zealand, 9, 57, 125, 142

NGAT (Netherlands Government Air Transport) service, 53

Nicaragua, 125

Nigeria, 48, 63, 82–83, 142

Nigerian Airways, 48

Night Flight, 1, 9

Nkruma, Kwame, 82

NKYKK (Nihon Koku Yuso Kabushiki Kaisha), 16

No Highway in the Sky, 35

Noise nuisance, caused by jet aircraft, issues of, 72–73, 75–76, 104–7, 138; protests against, 105–7

Non-Aligned states, movement of, 47

Norddeutsche Lloyd shipping line, 61

North American P-51 Mustang, 54

North Pole, air services across, 51, 53, 65

Northcliffe, Lord. See Harmsworth, Alfred

Northern Rhodesia (Zambia), 80–81

Northwest Airlines, 58, 128

Norway, 51, 65, 94

Norway, Neville Shute, 35

Nouvelle Frontières: travel agency, 122

Nuclear-powered aircraft, possible development of, 36

Nungesser, Charles, 7

Nuremberg, political rally by Nazis in, 19–20

O'Hare Airport (Chicago), 68, 78

Oil Crisis (1973), effects of, 73, 77, 93, 96, 121

Okęcie Airport (Warsaw), 101

Olympic Games: Berlin (1936), 20; Munich (1972), 86

Open Skies agreement: between European Union and United States of America, 125; other such agreements, 125–26

Organization of African Unity, 81

Orly Airport (Paris), 66–67, 95, 99

Oxfam (Oxford Committee for Famine Relief), 83

Ozone depletion, risk of, caused by aircraft, 76, 139

Pacific Ocean, air services across, 51, 53, 56

Pacific Overseas Airways, 54

Package holiday. See Tourism

Pakistan, 53–55, 103, 115; relationship between government and air transport in, 47, 62, 115

Palacio, Loyola de, 124

Palestine, issue of Palestinian cause, in air transport, 84–86, 117–19

Pan African Movement, 82

Pan Am (Pan American Airways, Pan American World Airways), 16, 42–44, 49, 56, 71, 78, 95, 97, 131; attacks on and hijacks of aircraft of, 81–82, 86, 118–19; chosen instrument in U.S. foreign policy, 16, 42–43, 90, 94; clipper flying boat service of, 33; introduction of Boeing

About the Author

MARC DIERIKX is Program Director of Development Cooperation Studies at the Institute of Netherlands History, Netherlands Organization for Scientific Research, The Hague, Netherlands. He has written numerous books and articles on air travel, airlines, and airports, including: *Fokker: A Transatlantic Biography,* and *An Image of Freedom: The Netherlands and the United States, 1945 to the Present.*